THE USURPER KING

Book Three of
The Plantagenet Legacy

BOOKS BY MERCEDES ROCHELLE

Heir to a Prophecy

The Last Great Saxon Earls Series
Godwine Kingmaker
The Sons of Godwine
Fatal Rivalry

The Plantagenet Legacy Series
A King Under Siege
The King's Retribution
The Usurper King

THE USURPER KING

Book Three of
The Plantagenet Legacy

by Mercedes Rochelle

Cover art: from Chroniques de France ou de St Denis, BL Royal 20 C VII f.29v.
Reproduced by courtesy of © The British Library Board

Contents

Acknowledgements

I'd like to give a big thanks for the beta readers who have offered invaluable advice and helped me keep me on the "straight and narrow": the awesome Kelly Evans, who has been working with me for years, the talented Brook Allen who missed her calling as an editor, and the exquisite Shirley Nomakeo, who has the most amazing memory. I feel much richer for your considered reflections.

CAST OF CHARACTERS

APPELLANTS: see Lords Appellant

ARUNDEL, THOMAS FITZALAN, 4th EARL OF: One of the original Lords Appellant. Condemned for treason at the 1397 Parliament.

ARUNDEL, THOMAS FITZALAN, 5th EARL OF, 10th Earl of Surrey, son of Richard Arundel

ARUNDEL, THOMAS, Archbishop of Canterbury and Lord Chancellor of England, Uncle of Thomas Arundel 5th Earl

AUMALE, EDWARD DUKE OF: See Rutland, Edward

BAGOT, SIR WILLIAM: One of King Richard's councilors who was tasked with the king's "dirty work" and acquired an infamous reputation.

BEAUFORT, HENRY, second son of John of Gaunt and Katherine Swynford, Bishop of Lincoln, Bishop of Winchester, later Cardinal

BEAUFORT, JOHN, EARL OF SOMERSET, Eldest son of John of Gaunt and Katherine Swynford, one of the Counter-Appellants of 1397, created Marquis of Dorset in 1397* (reverts to earl 1399)

BOLINGBROKE, HENRY, DUKE OF HEREFORD, Earl of Derby, Duke of Lancaster, and future King of England (Henry IV). Son of John of Gaunt, Duke of Lancaster

BURGUNDY, PHILIP THE BOLD, DUKE of: Uncle of King Charles VI and Louis Duke of Orleans, Regent of France during the king's illness

COUNTER-APPELLANTS: Eight members of King Richard's close circle who accused the Appellants of treason during the Revenge Parliament of 1397: John Holland, Tom Holland, Edward of Rutland, John Earl of Salisbury, Thomas Despenser, Thomas Mowbray, John Beaufort, William LeScrope.

DESPENSER, THOMAS, one of the Counter-Appellants of 1397, earl of Gloucester 1397* (deprived 1399)

EDMUND OF LANGLEY: See York, Duke of

EDWARD of RUTLAND: See Rutland

ERPINGHAM, SIR THOMAS, Served John of Gaunt then Henry IV; accompanied Henry into exile and back. Also served Henry V and fought at Agincourt.

FITZALAN: See Arundel

GAUNT, JOHN OF: Duke of Lancaster, Henry Bolingbroke's father

GLOUCESTER, DUKE OF: Thomas of Woodstock, youngest son of Edward III and uncle of King Richard. One of the original Lords Appellant. Condemned for treason in absentia at the 1397 Parliament and died in confinement at Calais.

HENRY IV, KING OF ENGLAND: also see Bolingbroke

HENRY OF MONMOUTH (Hal), Oldest son of Henry IV, Prince of Wales, Duke of Cornwall and Earl of Chester

HOLLAND, JOHN, EARL OF HUNTINGDON, half-brother of King Richard II through his mother Joan of Kent, one of the Counter-Appellants of 1397, Duke of Exeter 1397* (reverts to earl, 1399), Chamberlain of England 1389

HOLLAND, THOMAS (Tom) the YOUNGER, 3rd EARL OF KENT, nephew of King Richard, one of the Counter-Appellants of 1397, 1st Duke of Surrey 1397* (reverts to earl, 1399), 4th Baron Holand

HOTSPUR: See Percy, Sir Henry

HUMPHREY, later Duke of Gloucester, 4th son of Henry Bolingbroke, b.1390

HUMPHREY, 2nd EARL OF BUCKINGHAM, son of Thomas of Woodstock Duke of Gloucester

HUNTINGDON: See Holland, John

ISABELLA OF VALOIS, Queen of England (married 1396 aged 7), daughter of Charles VI of France

JOANNA OF NAVARRE, QUEEN OF ENGLAND, 2nd wife of Henry IV, originally Duchess of Brittany

JOHN, later Duke of Bedford, 3rd son of Henry Bolingbroke, b.1389

KENT, EARL OF: See Holland, Thomas

LeSCROPE, WILLIAM, one of the Counter-Appellants of 1397, Earl of Wiltshire 1397*, Lord High Treasurer 1398

LORDS APPELLANT: The men responsible for King Richard's humiliation and near deposition during the Merciless Parliament of 1387-88. The senior three were the targets of Richard's retribution during the Revenge Parliament of 1397: Richard Fitzalan, Earl of Arundel; Thomas Beauchamp, Earl of Warwick; Thomas of Woodstock, Duke of Gloucester. The two junior Appellants were Henry Bolingbroke (future Henry IV) and Thomas Mowbray, Earl of Norfolk

MARCH, EARL OF, see Mortimer, Roger

MAUDELEYN, RICHARD, cleric. Probable half-brother to King Richard who he resembled perfectly.

MONTAGUE, JOHN, one of the Counter-Appellants of 1397, 3rd Earl of Salisbury 1397*

MORTIMER, EDMUND, 5th Earl of March and 7th Earl of Ulster, (born 1391) thought by many to be the heir presumptive to the throne after Richard.

MOWBRAY, THOMAS DE, 1st DUKE OF NORFOLK, 1st Earl of Nottingham, 3rd Earl of Norfolk, 6th Baron Mowbray, 7th Baron Segrave, Earl Marshal, One of the Counter-Appellants in 1387-88, exiled in 1398

ORLEANS, LOUIS I DUKE of: younger brother of King Charles VI of France, nephew of the Duke of Burgundy

PERCY, HENRY, 1st EARL OF NORTHUMBERLAND: 4th Baron Percy, father of Hotspur

PERCY, SIR HARRY a.k.a. HOTSPUR: Son of the Earl of Northumberland

PERCY, THOMAS, 1st EARL OF WORCESTER, younger brother of the Earl of Northumberland. Uncle to Hotspur.

RICHARD II, KING OF ENGLAND, son of Edward Plantagenet the Black Prince and Joan of Kent

ROBERT III, KING OF SCOTLAND, born John Stewart, also Earl of Carrick before ascending the throne

RUTLAND, EDWARD, Earl of, eldest son of Edmund Langley, Duke of York. One of the Counter-Appellants of 1397, Duke of Aumale (or Aumerle or Albemarle) in 1397* (reverts to earl, 1399), later Earl of Cambridge 1402, 2nd Duke of York 1402

SALISBURY, JOHN DE MONTACUTE or MONTAGU, 3rd Earl, one of the Counter-Appellants of 1397, accompanied Richard to Ireland in 1395

SCROPE, WILLIAM, see LeScrope, William

SOMERSET: see Beaufort, John

THOMAS OF LANCASTER, 1st Duke of Clarence, second son of Henry IV, b.1387

WARWICK, THOMAS DE BEAUCHAMP, 12TH EARL OF, One of the Appellants in 1387-88. Condemned for treason in the 1397 Parliament and imprisoned.

WESTMORLAND, RALPH NEVILLE, 1st EARL OF, created earl in 1397, rival northern magnate to the Percies, brother in-law to Henry IV

WORCESTER, EARL OF: See Percy, Thomas

YORK, EDMUND OF LANGLEY, 1st DUKE OF, Fourth surviving son of Edward III and uncle of King Richard and Henry Bolingbroke, father of Edward of Rutland

*To save the reader the confusion I experienced trying to keep these dukes and earls created in 1397 (then deprived in 1399) straight, I have decided to refer to them throughout by their original titles, with rare exceptions.

Map of England

Map by Gregg Sollisch

CHAPTER 1

There was never any doubt. As his father had predicted, Henry Bolingbroke's reputation guaranteed his welcome at the French court. He was known far and wide as a gallant knight, a champion in the lists, witty and clever. And wealthy. He was also the most handsome Englishman ever to grace the royal palace, with lush brown hair, kindly eyes, high cheekbones, and perfect teeth. The ladies thought he filled out his thigh-length houppelande in a most robust fashion, with wide shoulders and a thin waist, muscular legs and rounded calves. Having been widowed for five years now, he was conspicuously eligible and many of the women regarded him with flirtatious glances.

It had been over three months since Henry set foot in Paris and he still wasn't sure of his standing. He was welcomed pleasantly enough by King Charles and given the use of the famous Hôtel de Clisson, a short walk from the royal residence at L'Hôtel de Saint-Pol. Clisson was built by Charles V just the other side of the Seine from l'île de la Cité. Grateful though Henry was for such opulent lodgings, he found it difficult to hold up his head and ignore the fact that things were not quite right. He missed his home. He missed his children. He missed his honor.

Everyone knew he had been outlawed from England. No one mentioned his exile in polite conversation, but he imagined people talking behind their hands, assessing him discreetly, trying to figure out just what he had done to warrant such treatment. It was bitterly ironic that he didn't entirely know, himself. The covert hostility between Lancaster and King Richard had been growing for years although it was well hidden beneath a façade of courtly etiquette. But ever since the last parliament, when the king wreaked terrible revenge on his old enemies, no one felt safe. In all likelihood, for Henry and Thomas Mowbray—whose offenses were not yet called to account—it was only a matter of time before the king turned his attention to them.

Although, to be fair, if Mowbray hadn't stirred things up, maybe Richard would have left them alone.

Perhaps Henry should have felt lucky that he suffered only exile, though it gave him no comfort to know that Mowbray was outlawed for life compared to his own six year sentence. At least his old friendships on the continent would sustain him. In his younger, more carefree days he was very free with his father's money. You never knew when you would need to rely on someone's good will.

Since this was the last winter of the fourteenth century, the French king delighted in having an excuse to throw yet another interminable fête to while away the January evenings. Fortunately, Henry was happily distracted by the charming Marie de Berry, first cousin to King Charles VI and daughter of the famous Duke de Berry. Marie was a twenty-three year old countess, already twice-widowed; she brought great riches and powerful alliances with her name. Henry found her most suitable and they had already discussed the possibility of marriage, though negotiations hadn't proceeded any farther. Naturally, because they were seen frequently in each other's company, rumors ran rampant.

While Henry and Marie sat at the banqueting table with Marshal Boucicaut, the ladies of the French court flitted around them, commanding attention with their tight-fitting bodices and voluminous skirts. Wide v-shaped collars exposed a little panel of fabric barely covering their cleavage. Their hair was hidden beneath elaborate contraptions extending high above their heads—sometimes pointed, sometimes winged, always draped in the finest gauze. All-in-all, the French fashions were way ahead of those in England.

But tonight, Henry was too engrossed in his conversation to notice the disappointed coquettes. He and Boucicaut entertained Marie with exploits from the famous Tournament at St. Inglevert, held eight years before.

"Just three French knights took on the whole world," Henry said to Marie. "Jean, I mean Boucicaut, here, Reginald de Roye and the lord of Saimpy challenged one and all. It was the most glorious, the most dangerous tournament of the century. It went on for a month! And when it was finished, our French hosts

2

emerged absolutely unbeatable. It was not at all unusual for each of them to take on five or six courses in a day. What stamina you had," he added, turning to Boucicaut.

"Fortunately, we got to rest on Sundays and a handful of holidays in between—not counting the few days I was abed, recovering from wounds."

Henry laughed. "We won't talk about what your opponents looked like. You see, Marie, each knight was permitted six courses, not usually all at once. Your champions hung two shields under a hawthorn tree—one, a shield of war for sharp lances, and the other a shield of peace, for blunted lances. The first challenger, my brother in-law John Holland, immediately chose the war shield, and after that no one would dare pick the peace target for fear of being called cowardly."

Boucicaut shook his head. "It's amazing no one was killed."

"Of course, that's the fun of it." Henry poured some wine for Marie. "You should have seen the tournament field. Big, tall pavilions lined both sides of the course, with dormers in each roof. It was beautiful. The largest pavilions were joined together and they hosted banquets, which were served to the guests every night. And the lists...a wooden tilt ran down the center of each list, which was sixty paces long and forty paces wide. The knights—oh, they were like peacocks. Each one had to outshine the other."

"If I remember correctly, you outstripped them all," laughed the marshal. "With your ducal arms and the Bohun swan atop your helm."

"It was so hard to keep that from breaking!"

"I remember our first course," Boucicaut mused to Marie. "Henry showed up about a week after the tournament started, with young Harry Percy—Hotspur, they call him—Thomas Mowbray, and Sir Thomas Erpingham, of course. There were so many I can't recall them all. Anyway, after Henry and I took our distances we spurred our mounts and met with such force I pierced his shield. The point of my lance slipped down his arm but he wasn't wounded. We rode to the end of the list and turned around for our second course. This time, we hit each other's helmet so hard sparks of fire flew from them. Luckily, neither of us was unhorsed. We decided to go for a third run, and I broke my lance on Henry's shield. At the same time he struck off my helmet, though thankfully I held my seat. I ran no more courses that day!" He laughed. "Each knight was supposed to run six lances total. But I had received a letter from John of Gaunt, who told me he sent his son to learn from me, and he begged me to joust ten strokes with him! In the end, I don't know who learned more from whom!"

Chuckling, Henry put his elbow on the table. "Those were the days." He was about to take a sip of wine then paused, staring across the room. John de Montacute, the Earl of Salisbury was speaking with King Charles, and both men had turned to stare at him.

"What in God's name is he doing here?" Henry growled. "Up to no good, I am certain." There was no love lost between Salisbury and Lancaster. Montacute was a favorite of King Richard, and he served on the parliamentary committee that voted to outlaw Henry and Mowbray after the tournament at Coventry. "He's stirring up trouble against me."

The day was ruined. Both Henry's companions shifted uncomfortably.

"Well, Henry, perhaps I can help," Boucicaut said, breaking the silence. "One of the reasons I came here was to invite you to join my expedition against the Turks. We must avenge the disastrous defeat at Nicopolis."

For a moment, Henry's face glowed with expectation. "Let me write to my father for advice," he said. "If I do go, I'll need him to help defray my expenses." Turning to Marie, he picked up her hand, kissing it. "Though I would miss this fair lady."

Marie smiled, a rosy blush enhancing her pretty round face. "We women spend most of our time waiting. I think the missing is more on our side."

About to reply, Henry glanced back at the king and froze again. The Duke of Burgundy had joined him and was conversing earnestly with Salisbury. Ever since the king's repeated bouts with insanity, Burgundy had acted as the unofficial head of the regency council. Known as Philip the Bold, the king's uncle aptly deserved his sobriquet; he was fierce, battle-hardened, and a ruthless politician. He towered over Charles, whose illness had left him permanently stooped, and whose natural kindness usually gave way to Burgundy's assertiveness.

Henry's unease was soon confirmed. The following day, the king requested his presence. Donning his best robes, he presented himself, to be immediately ushered into the king's chamber where he faced both Charles and Burgundy. His heart sank; there was only one reason he was summoned. Bending his knee, Henry kissed the king's ring.

"Duke Henry," Charles said, raising him up, "we spoke to the Countess of Berry last night, and we understand you are considering marriage."

Henry closed his eyes for a moment, gathering his thoughts. "We have spoken about it, though I haven't approached her father."

"You must understand," Burgundy said, a little more forcefully. "We cannot give our cousin to a traitor."

Damn the man for his bluntness! "My Lord Duke, I never was, nor ever thought of being a traitor—and I defy anyone who should call me thus!" Taking a deep breath, Henry tried to control his indignation.

Distressed, Charles put out a hand. "Cousin, cousin," he said gently, "the words of my uncle came from England, not ourselves. No one here in France doubts your honor."

"You are referring to the Earl of Salisbury, are you not?"

Charles nodded briefly in agreement. "Be appeased, my friend. This matter will end well. But as to this marriage, let us speak of it another time. Before you can consider taking such a step, you must obtain your inheritance. After all, it will be necessary for you to make provision for your wife."

This was not totally unreasonable, and Henry was obliged to concede. Who knew what Salisbury really said to the king? Coming from Richard, it couldn't have been beneficial.

Salisbury pointedly avoided him and left Paris as quickly as possible. Henry vowed he would regret his insolence.

Perhaps a new crusade would be exactly the diversion Henry needed. However, the answer he received from his father was not what he expected. The day after his letter came, when sitting in a place of honor next to King Charles, he looked up—belatedly recognizing that he had just been asked a question.

"I beg forgiveness, your majesty," Henry said. "My thoughts were elsewhere."

The king gestured for a servant to refill his goblet. "Something is troubling you."

Henry sighed. "I just received a letter from my father. He advises me not to go on crusade. He said if I felt the urge to travel, I should visit my sisters in Portugal or Castile. This is unlike him. Sire, I fear he is not well."

"Ah, my poor cousin. This is unfortunate. When you write back to your father, send my regards."

Henry did write back at once, and when the response came he learned that his father had fallen seriously ill, just like he thought. He was frantic, knowing he could not return to England under any circumstances. Although he was surrounded by his supporters at the Hôtel de Clisson, he would not be comforted. It was just so unfair! He had done nothing to deserve this treatment.

For weeks Henry heard nothing further. Then suddenly, in February, the dreaded news came. John of Gaunt was dead. He was gone. Forever. Henry would never see his father again. The entire French royal family attended a mass with him to pray for the soul of the Duke of Lancaster, which he appreciated. He could let his grief show, but he must keep everything else inside—anger, hurt, and hatred against the king who ruined his life. Even if Richard let him return to England, Henry would never forgive being forced into exile when Gaunt's health was so fragile. Nonetheless, he knew better than to complain. Charles's sympathies lay with Richard; after all, he was the king's father in-law. So Henry had to keep his recriminations to himself. How long could he dissemble?

Gaunt left funeral instructions that he was not to be embalmed for forty days and that he would be buried in St. Paul's next to his first wife, Blanche. Under normal circumstances, Henry would have had enough time to return to England; perhaps this is what his father had intended. But no, he didn't dare go back, not even for a funeral. Richard's edict was explicit, and the punishment would be fatal.

It was so much more difficult to mourn a loss away from home! Throwing a cloak over his shoulders, Henry went looking for his son, thinking to gain comfort from what little family remained to him. He found the boy practicing his sword play with Erpingham in the courtyard. He leaned against a pillar, watching the pair. An exile at only eleven years of age, Thomas was obliged to grow up very quickly in his father's household. In the nursery he had been a headstrong child, always ready to start a fight with his brother Hal who was only a year older than him. But now, in this new environment, Thomas had lost much of his assertiveness. Was it because he had no one his own age to interact with? Or was he simply lost, much as his father was?

Watching his son reminded Henry about his relationship with his own father. Once again he felt his eyes fill with tears. There were so many things left unsaid—so many words of comfort unspoken. He didn't realize how fortunate he was—how much he had taken for granted. Henry was the only son and got all the attention he needed. The older he grew, the more his father doted on him; everything Gaunt did was with Henry's future in mind. And now that the time had come, it looked like all might be for naught.

For the next month, Henry found the suspense almost unbearable. His inheritance was at stake. There was nothing he could do but wait. Would Richard honor his promise and allow Henry's attorneys to sue for his endowment, or would he find a way to renege? His envoys were already on their way to London, though it was impossible not to expect the worst. Richard had broken his word many times before. Now that Gaunt was safely out of the way, would the king show his true colors? Who was there to protect the hapless exile?

So when an unexpected message was hand-delivered from William Bagot, his heart sank. It was too soon. Bagot's squire knelt before him while Henry opened the letter. The warning was brief: *He is your sworn enemy and you should help yourself with manhood.*

Frowning, Henry looked at the messenger. "Did he say anything else?"

The man nodded briefly. "He said to prepare for the worst." That was all. But it was enough. Bagot was one of the king's most trusted advisors; before Richard he had served John of Gaunt. The man honored his old loyalties to Lancaster, yet he had to be careful not to betray the king's confidence. Hence his cryptic message.

What was Henry to do now?

He had two choices: do nothing and wait for the official notifications to confirm the bad tidings. Or start preparing to defy his outlawry and fight for his rights. Of course, as a declared traitor his life would be forfeit if he returned home—unless he could command such a following that he could defy the king.

Calling for his friend Sir Thomas Erpingham, Henry laid out the latest batch of letters he had received from England. Most of them bemoaned the state of affairs in the kingdom. Richard was extorting money wherever he could. There were the usual complaints against the Cheshire archers, raping and pillaging as they traveled with the royal party. What interested Henry most, however, were the preparations for Richard's second expedition to Ireland. Apparently, Richard felt the need to punish the Irish for the recent slaying of Roger Mortimer, the Earl of March, who was serving as Lieutenant there. Or maybe he merely felt the need to re-establish royal authority.

Mortimer's death had been quite a shock. Many saw him as Richard's heir since he was descended from Edward III's second son Lionel—through the daughter. However, Roger left behind a seven year-old boy. No one needed another child king. That made Lancaster the obvious choice as heir presumptive seeing that Richard's second queen was only nine years old. There would many years before a royal heir could even become a possibility. If the king's first marriage was any indication, it might never happen.

Henry pursed his lips, banishing the notion. Richard was a young man yet. There was plenty of time for him to have children.

Interrupting his thoughts, Erpingham came into the room, accompanied by Henry's son Thomas. Seeing the boy brought a smile to Henry's face, though it slowly faded as his melancholy took over.

"Sit, son," he said, patting the bench next to him. "This concerns all of us."

"What news?" asked Erpingham as he sat across the table.

Henry handed over Bagot's letter. "The messenger said I should prepare for the worst," he added.

The knight placed the paper on the table and smoothed it out carefully. "The king means to keep your inheritance," he said thoughtfully, looking up. "What else can it be?"

"It will be something like that, most certainly. Whatever he can get away with."

"Will we be poor, father?" Thomas bit his lip, trying to understand.

"No, not exactly, son. I was made Duke of Hereford on my own accord. I haven't lost that. No, it's the dukedom and Palatinate of Lancaster at risk; those I would inherit from my father. Without them, I lose much of my endowment. And influence. The Palatinate is a territory with its own government. The duke has sovereign rights there, which cannot be touched by the king. That's why Richard wants it for himself. He wants to control it, and he needs the revenue." He sighed, wiping a tear from his eye. "Nothing will happen until after the funeral. Oh dear God, I wish I were there."

Henry soon learned that his worst fears were realized. With indecent haste, the Parliamentary Committee repealed the letters patent given to him after the Coventry tournament—the trial by combat that led to his exile. Not only was Henry denied permission to claim his inheritance, Richard immediately partitioned out his estates, giving them in trust to his favorites. Henry could only groan and mumble as he read letter after letter from outraged stewards, forced to bend to the will of their new masters. Some were even imprisoned over "local quarrels", whatever they were. There was nothing he could do about it.

Torn with indecision, Henry spent many hours with Erpingham, trying to decide what to do. Going through another pile of letters, he held one up from the London merchants. "Listen to this. They are encouraging me to return and claim my inheritance. They are even willing to send me money to hire mercenaries. What do they expect me to do? How could I be sure anyone would support me in face of the king's wrath? They would deny everything if threatened with violence."

Erpingham shook his head. "I would not rely on them. In the North, on the other hand—"

"Oh, I trust my own retainers. If I do decide to go back—"

"We'll instruct them to hold your castles for you. Nothing easier."

Somewhat encouraged, Henry poured himself some wine. "I won't be able to ask the French for help. They are under Richard's influence." He grimaced, knowing he was already negligent, having made many excuses about his long absence from court. He could only put it off for so long. Undoubtedly, they would be fully informed about his difficulties; it might take more courage than he could summon, to stand firm and pretend nothing was amiss. The king and his courtiers would look at him with pity while sneering behind his back. It would be unbearable. And yet, how else to uphold his dignity?

"On the other hand, there is the Duke of Orleans," Erpingham mused. "Since he hates Burgundy so much, he might help us, just to spite his uncle."

"That's possible. He has been friendly so far. We'll have to see how receptive he is..." Henry looked at the door. One of his squires had opened it and he could see a tall man in the shadows, dressed as a friar.

"My Lord, the Archbishop of Canterbury," the squire said.

Blinking, Henry stood. This was most unexpected. Thomas Arundel had been outlawed during the same parliament that condemned his elder brother Richard for treason—with Henry's cooperation. The only thing saving Arundel's life was his clerical status; Richard could not send an archbishop to the scaffold. But the king knew how dangerous Arundel was. When Henry was outlawed, Richard demanded that he never communicate with the archbishop. Upon pain of death. And yet, here was the man on Henry's doorstep.

Thomas Arundel strode quickly into the room, followed by a youth Henry didn't know. The archbishop dropped to one knee.

"I don't know whether to greet you or banish you," Henry said, nonplussed.

"Because we are forbidden to meet?" Arundel said, more sardonic than inquiringly. "We are already outlawed. How much worse can it get?"

Henry shrugged, encouraging the archbishop to stand. "Well, you are here. How far have you traveled to see me?" He led the newcomers back to the table. Erpingham nodded his greeting.

"Most recently I was at Utrecht, where I communicated with many Londoners who told me they were prepared to receive you as a deliverer from the tyrant. Oh, this is my nephew Thomas FitzAlan, son of the late earl." He gestured to the youth. "He escaped from the custody of Sir John Holland and made his way to the continent."

Henry studied his visitors. The young heir of Arundel was short and stocky like his father, with the same pale blue eyes that fortunately did not bulge from his face. That was an improvement, though his expression was just as dour. At least he seemed content to keep his feelings to himself. Good. Henry had enough of his own problems.

He wasn't particularly fond of the archbishop—a man of political leanings who, nonetheless, had already shown his competence during many years as chancellor. His only mistake was siding with the Lords Appellant during the Merciless Parliament, which Richard never forgave. Sitting there studying his fingernails, Arundel exuded confidence. He didn't seem to have suffered from his exile; if anything, he had put on a couple of pounds which he was able to carry because of his height. He had meticulously shaved his tonsure, so there was no mistaking his vocation.

At first, Henry didn't know what to say. Luckily, Arundel had already thought things through.

"My Lord," he said, gesturing for his nephew to pour some wine. "Our families were not on the best of terms when we were at liberty. But now that we are in exile, everything has changed. Furthermore, something happened to me I need to tell you about."

Henry raised his eyebrows, intrigued.

"While I was in Utrecht, your father appeared to me in a dream. He begged my forgiveness for all the wrongs he had inflicted on myself and my brother. He was barefoot and penitent. I called on God to forgive him, and promised to pray for his soul." Arundel crossed himself then paused, his eyes fixed on Henry. "Only later did I discover this was the night he died."

A shiver ran down Henry's back. Could this be true? Or did the wily archbishop concoct this unprovable story to gloss over their differences? Since Arundel was the wronged man, who was Henry to object? He forced himself to relax.

The archbishop cleared his throat. "As I was saying, there have been calls for your return. Many calls. I already heard that King Richard has disinherited you." He paused.

Despite himself, Henry clenched his fists. "It's bad enough they call me traitor," he growled. "Now I am bereft of my patrimony. The king even arrested my attorney and declared it would be treason for me to press my suit. I don't even know if I'll receive my annuity."

"Then you have much to gain if you return and put things to right."

"Put things to right," muttered Henry. He got up and walked over to the window, looking down at the beautiful garden. The tulips reared their heads to the sun, glowing red and orange and yellow—unmindful of the cataclysms that could shatter an empire. The archbishop's words were full of meaning. Of course he had thought of it himself; what duke in exile wouldn't?

He turned, leaning against the window sill. "What could a defenseless wanderer achieve against a king so powerful he can deny a man's heritage with the strike of a pen? I don't know who I can depend on in England. Once a supporter is threatened, what's to stop him from giving in?"

"This is what I am saying," countered Arundel. "They will *all* feel threatened. A king whose oaths are worthless has already forfeited his divine right. After what he has done to you, do you think any noble in the land feels safe?"

Henry shrank at the possible consequences. "If I fail, my life will be forfeit. I will die a traitor's death."

"There are ways to ensure your safety. We can send letters ahead with instructions to your retainers. They can prepare your castles for your return." Arundel didn't know Erpingham had already made the same suggestion. "We can touch the coast at various spots to determine whether there is resistance. Once you disembark in Yorkshire, our safety is almost assured."

Too distracted to notice that Arundel included himself in a possible return, Henry started pacing the room. "I have no ships, no army, no funds to launch an offensive." He stopped, admitting to his only hope. "It is rumored Richard plans to campaign in Ireland."

"Yes!" That came out too quickly, and Arundel took a deep breath, controlling his excitement. "I understand he is taking a large army with him, including almost all his nobles. He will leave the Duke of York as regent."

"My uncle." Henry looked at the archbishop appraisingly. "I could win him over to my side."

"Yes." *That was more measured.* "I heard York already voiced his objections to your disinheritance. He will be torn between his two nephews—you can count on that."

Henry stroked his beard. "With Richard out of the country, my uncle York will have his hands full already. Before he realizes what has happened, we could be gathering our forces."

"If we move quickly, we can secure our position before the king even learns of our intentions. Think of it this way: Richard needs to be brought to heel, just as he was during the Merciless Parliament. Only this time, it will be permanent. We won't give him the chance to wreak revenge on us. He will have to answer to a council for the rest of his reign."

Still dubious, Henry grimaced. "That is ambitious. How do we make it stick? Besides, I would need the support of the people."

Arundel spread his hands apart. "You already have plenty of support, I assure you." He stood. "No need to be hasty. You have much to think about. I suggest you discuss this with your household council. Young Thomas and I are traveling in secrecy, so we are staying at a local inn. I will come back in a couple of days." Pulling his hood over his head, Arundel gestured for his nephew to follow.

Henry accompanied them to the door. Closing it, he turned to Erpingham.

The knight shrugged. "It's worth thinking about," he said. "We only lack the means. At least we have many friends."

The same evening, Henry called his household together. He always leaned heavily on the advice of his old comrades-in-arms, Thomas Erpingham, Thomas Rempston, and John Norbury. Many other knights in the room had accompanied him as well—without question—and their voices also needed to be heard. The duke stood, looking around the room.

"As many of you already know," he said, "Archbishop Arundel was here. He has been in contact with many Londoners who clamor for my return. I cannot take this lightly. We all know it could be my death if I misjudge the temper of our countrymen." He paused as the men grumbled. "On the other hand, if I do nothing I lose my patrimony for six years or possibly forever." The grumbling turned into shouts of outrage.

"Curse the king!" one man shouted. "He should never have outlawed you!"

"He wanted your lands for the crown," Rempston grumbled. "To fill his coffers."

"Who knows what will happen to your estates in your absence," growled a third. "It's not right."

Henry was gratified by the response. He crossed his arms, walking back and forth.

Erpingham stood. "The way I see it, my lord, you have been robbed and wronged. As a result, we also are robbed and wronged, for you are deprived the means of rewarding us for our service." He grinned as whoops of agreement met with his statement. "You have every right to drive those robbers from your dukedom."

With tears in his eyes, Henry listened as his men cheered. Finally, he threw out his arms. "Very well, my friends. This is a sentiment I can agree with. Let us return to England with a clear conscience." He received a goblet of wine and held it up. Everyone joined him in a toast. "Now we just have to figure out when and how."

The details could wait. Everyone went on with their daily tasks as the disguised Archbishop of Arundel came and went, planning Henry's next move. All knew who Arundel was and were enjoined to keep his secret. For if King Richard discovered that the archbishop and Henry were plotting, he would surely complain to the King of France—with dire consequences. King Charles may be fond of Henry, but as Richard's father in-law he had his priorities.

Following Arundel's suggestions, they sent letters to important leaders they assumed would be sympathetic: the earls of Northumberland and Westmorland, John Beaufort—Henry's half-brother—the Bishop of Winchester, and many lesser magnates. The castellans of his castles and sheriffs of his towns were next on the list.

Meanwhile, Henry continued to visit the Hôtel de Saint-Pol. He was relieved to find himself welcome there—for the most part. Lately, there were reports of plague in the outskirts of Paris, and people were beginning to disappear. The Duke of Burgundy had already left for his estates, leaving Louis, Duke of Orleans in control of the city. That was all right with Louis; as brother to the king, Orleans had long ago initiated a power struggle against his uncle. Anything Burgundy disliked, he was sure to do the opposite. He was willing to take the risk to stay in power.

Surprisingly, Louis and Henry discovered they had much in common, and they spent more and more time together. Finally, Henry decided to confide in the duke. Inviting him to the Hôtel de Clisson, he entertained Louis with an extravagant dinner before offering the finest wine from his cellars. Orleans had exquisite table manners; he was fastidious, patting his mouth frequently with a napkin. His straight brown hair hung just below his ears, he was clean-shaven with a long narrow face and eyes just a little too close together. However, any suggestion of plainness was erased by an engaging smile.

Henry poured more wine into Louis' chalice. "How is your wife?"

"Ah, Valentia. She is more beautiful than ever. She is visiting her father Gian Galeazzo right now."

"I love Milan," Henry mused. "You know, the duke sent me this dagger just a few months before I left." He fumbled at his belt, drawing the blade from an intricately wrought sheath and handing it over. "He has such exquisite taste."

"I knew you were still writing to each other." He sighed, admiring the dagger. "I was looking forward to bringing you into the Visconti family. My wife's cousin Lucia was heartbroken when marriage negotiations between the two of you were broken off." He handed back the dagger.

Henry's face clouded. "Another casualty of my outlawry. That was the worst misfortune on top of all the other adversities."

Louis took a sip of wine. "She so desperately wanted to marry you. Valentia heard her say she was willing to wait to the very end of her life, even if she knew that she would die three days after the marriage."

Henry put a hand on his chest. "Oh, poor girl. That breaks my heart. She is so sweet."

The other shook his head. "She was a great prize. Just last month, her father married her to the Elector of Saxony, though she went most unwillingly."

Saddened, Henry had nothing to say. For a few minutes, they listened to the minstrels playing quietly in the corner of the room. Finally, Henry leaned toward his companion.

"They came with me from England." He gestured to the musicians.

Orleans nodded. "You have very loyal followers."

"Yes, I do. Alas, in due time they will be forced to pursue their own interests."

"Unless their interests continue to align with yours." The duke smiled around the rim of his goblet.

Henry slowly spun his cup in his hands. "Sitting here will not do me any good."

"None."

"I wonder how King Charles would feel if I went back."

"To reclaim your inheritance?" Orleans suddenly looked serious. "Kings have a way of seeing things differently. Nobles, on the other hand, would understand completely."

"Like yourself?"

"Undoubtedly. If I was threatened, I would hope my peers would support my efforts."

Henry looked sideways at him. He knew about the friction between Orleans and Burgundy. "As you would support me?" he asked.

"Most certainly. Now that Burgundy has left the city, your movements will be much less restricted. He was King Richard's watchdog, you know." Orleans put a hand on Henry's arm. "But I am here for you, as much as I can be. In fact, I suggest we compose a treaty. A treaty of alliance."

"Let us take an oath to support each other's friends, oppose each other's enemies, uphold each other's honor, and come to each other's help in times of war or unrest."

"Magnificent," said Louis. "I can think of nothing better."

Henry frowned, momentarily irresolute. "We should make some exceptions. The kings of France and England. And the Duke of York. This treaty is not directed against them."

Louis shrugged. "As you wish. Let us finish this on the morrow when I have my seal."

"That gives us time to draw it up. I shall have my secretary make two copies."

Satisfied, the dukes drank more wine and decided to indulge themselves in a game of chess. Or two. Henry could finally relax; all was as it should be. He knew he had at least one friend in the French court.

The next day, after affixing his seal to the Treaty of Alliance with the Duke of Orleans, Henry sought out Marie de Berry at the king's court. He had been avoiding her ever since his uncomfortable interview with Burgundy, though it wasn't her fault. He just could not tolerate yet another humiliation.

He needn't have worried. After two marriages, Marie was experienced beyond her years and she greeted him evenly, smiling as he moved up beside her. "There you are, my lord. I've missed your company."

Bowing slightly, Henry kissed her hand. "For a man in exile, I have been surprisingly busy."

"I see. And what are your plans?"

Looking around, Henry pointed toward the gardens. "May we walk?"

"Gladly." She put her hand on his arm and they moved slowly through the courtiers who bowed as Henry passed. Once outside, they found a bench beneath a rose trellis.

"I'm sure you know I cannot discuss marriage until I have achieved my inheritance."

"Yes. The king told me about it. I understand the Duke of Burgundy spoke rudely to you."

Henry had to suppress a shudder. "My position is most unfortunate. I stand accused of treason and no matter what I say, the disgrace won't go away. I fear I would make an undesirable bridegroom."

She looked at him appraisingly. "I'm sure there are plenty of ladies who would be honored to consider your suit," she said flatly.

Henry was taken aback by her indifference. Her lack of enthusiasm was not helping. "If I were to return to England and reclaim my patrimony..." His voice fell to a whisper; perhaps he shouldn't be telling her.

"Dear Henry. Your life is full of uncertainties. Would you want me to wait for you? I fear that would not be possible."

Sitting straight up, he was momentarily insulted. "What?"

"The Duke of Bourbon has already approached the king for his son John. The king is highly in favor of this match."

"Bourbon," Henry grumbled. "I don't remember him."

"He's in the royal family. I have no objections."

Standing, Henry plucked a rose and handed it to her. "I wish you well, Marie. You are right; I am too much of a risk. It was just a momentary whim." He tried to keep the bitterness from his voice. He knew he had been fortunate with his beloved Mary de Bohun; there were few arranged marriages as happy as his first. How could he possibly flourish against such an icicle as Marie? But it hurt to be treated so coldly. He wasn't used to it. He didn't like being a man with no prospects.

Without realizing it, Henry had taken another step closer to leaving this life of exile. This was not for him. He must find a way to reclaim his heritage—or die in the process.

CHAPTER 2

Henry looked up from his writing table as the archbishop entered the room, face flushed with excitement. He had never seen the man like this; Arundel prided himself on his composure and one rarely knew what he was thinking. He pulled up a chair and sat at the table.

"Momentous news," Arundel said, holding out his letter. "King Richard has left the country."

His eyes widening, Henry reached for the missive. "To Ireland?"

As he read the letter, the archbishop rubbed his hands together. "We couldn't ask for a better opportunity. He is taking his great officers with him, his barons, even his Cheshire archers. He's appropriated all the shipping, wagons, horses, arms and armor. Your poor uncle York will be hard put to raise a defensive army."

Henry crossed his arms. "I find this so hard to believe. I never thought he'd go through with his expedition." He narrowed his eyes. "What are we missing?"

Taking the letter back, Arundel tucked it into his sleeve. "From what I can tell, our king thinks he has taken care of everything. He sees you as no threat."

"After taking away my inheritance?" Henry threw his quill to the side.

"Perhaps he thinks he has removed your sting."

"Perhaps he thinks I have no resolution." He stood, walking to the window. "Or that I fear the consequences. I do, you know." He turned to Arundel. "He would put me to death without hesitation. Gladly." He rubbed his forehead, closing his eyes. "He has my son Hal. As hostage."

The archbishop gestured his dismissal. "Richard is many things but he is no child killer. As for putting you to death...who would enforce his punishment? Think about this: right now, all his commanders are in Ireland with him. He has scoured the country for the most experienced soldiers and taken them along. York has been left with an insignificant force. You, on the other hand, will gather supporters everywhere you go. You will have an army at your back so formidable that King Richard will be forced to negotiate with you."

"Ha! Listen to you talk."

"You *should* listen. You have everything to gain. If you stay here and let this opportunity pass, you will languish in disgrace. What's to stop King Richard from extending your outlawry for life?"

"Nothing." Henry returned to the window. "He's already broken his word."

"Many times. Too many to count."

Sitting down again, Henry picked up his quill. Arundel waited for a response—not that he had asked a question that needed answering. Frowning, Henry stared at him, annoyed at the smug expression on his face. Or was he annoyed with himself? *Why was he hesitating? He had already made his decision.*

"All right. When shall we start?"

It was hard to say who was happier to see Henry leave Paris—himself or King Charles. Although the French continued to extend every welcome, after Salisbury's visit Henry felt that he was a continual embarrassment to Richard's father in-law. After discussing his options with his household, he decided to take his chances with the Duke of Brittany, who had married his father's sister. Admittedly, that was many years ago—in fact, she died five years before he was born. Nonetheless, Duke John—called the Valiant—had always been on good terms with the English and especially Gaunt.

Henry announced plans to visit his sisters. It was safer to pretend he was making an innocuous journey south; if King Charles knew he intended to invade England he might have felt compelled to interfere. So far, so good. Henry hosted a great feast at the Hôtel de Clisson where he gave handsome gifts to the king's officers, as well as knights and ladies who attended. The following morning, he and his immediate retinue took leave of King Charles, then they all left Paris by the gate of St. James, taking the road to Blois. By now there were about sixty men left, including Thomas Arundel, still in disguise, and young FitzAlan, his nephew.

They stayed at Orleans' castle of Blois for eight days, though the duke was not in residence. Just beyond the borders of Brittany, Blois was a safe place to wait while Henry sent one of his knights to Duke John, asking permission to visit. The answer was most emphatic.

"Listen to this," Henry laughed as he read John's letter. "He says he is piqued at my mistrust. *'I have always loved the Duke of Lancaster better than the other sons of Edward III.'* Ha! I wonder if that's true. And here, he also says, *'Why have you stopped on the road? It is foolish; for there is no knight I would rather see in Bretagne than my fair nephew the Earl of Derby. Come to Nantes and find a hearty welcome.'*"

Henry handed the letter to Erpingham. "I can think of no better invitation. Let us leave on the morrow."

An old Roman city, Nantes was located on the Loire River, with easy access to the sea. The dukes of Brittany resided in a castle near the cathedral. Henry's entourage crossed the drawbridge over the moat which brought them between two huge, round turrets. The duke had been alerted to their arrival and waited in the great hall. Henry was announced by the herald and approached eagerly, wearing a surcoat decorated with the Lancaster coat of arms. He knelt at the duke's feet and kissed his hand.

"Come, come, nephew," John said, lifting him up. "That's no way to greet family." He hugged Henry and stepped back, holding him at arm's length. "Your father must have been proud. From everything I have heard, you are England's most chivalrous knight."

Henry was relieved. The duke's reputation was that of a boar rather than an ermine—the emblem of Brittany. He was well known for his unscrupulous behavior toward rivals, so Lancaster was happy to be counted among his friends.

A woman appeared in the doorway across the hall. Tall and slim, she wore a blue cotehardie with a low-cut neck laying slightly below the shoulder, tight in the bodice and full in the skirt. A simple coronet adorned her hair. Judging from her age, which looked to be the same as his own, Henry initially thought she might be the duke's daughter. But he was soon undeceived.

"Ah, there you are, my dear," Duke John said, holding out his hand. "We've been honored with a visit from the new Duke of Lancaster. Henry Bolingbroke, meet my wife, Joanna of Navarre."

Coming forward, Joanna extended her hand. As Henry bent to kiss it, he was momentarily struck by her half-smile. Up close, she wasn't what one would call beautiful yet her face was pleasant to look at. Her serenity reminded him of good Queen Anne, whose tranquility had never failed to calm King Richard. Joanna's violet eyes gave her a certain radiance, and he was filled with a sense of comfort. All this happened in a moment.

Straightening, Henry put his hand on his son's shoulder. "And this is Thomas, my second boy." The lad bowed self-consciously.

"Welcome to Brittany." Joanna smiled at the youth. "Come sit beside me, Thomas," she said, holding out her hand. "We would offer you some refreshments. Have you ever had marchpane?"

Thomas shook his head.

"It's sweet. It's my favorite. Comes from almond paste and sugar."

"Oh, I love sweets," Thomas said enthusiastically, taking her hand.

With a smile, Henry followed the duke and duchess into an adjoining chamber, where servants laid out comfits and wine for the tired travelers. Henry's immediate retinue was invited, while the rest of his traveling companions were taken to lodgings in the city. It was understood they would be visiting for a while.

Once they were settled, Duke John asked politely about King Charles and the situation at court, though it was clear he didn't pay much attention to the answers. After giving Henry enough time to finish, John leaned forward.

"I'm really interested in what brings you here," he said.

Henry glanced at Joanna before answering. "I'm sure you heard about my outlawry," he said uncomfortably.

"I heard something about a tournament that was interrupted and the decision to outlaw both you and the Duke of Norfolk. By the time the story reached us, it was all very confused."

"I'm not surprised," Henry grunted. "Even after all these months, I still don't understand, myself. What started as a disagreement somehow turned into treason. Norfolk and I...well, we were involved with the Lords Appellant during that unpleasant situation ten years ago..." He looked at John and concluded the whole event was unclear to him. "During the Parliament of 1388, King Richard was brought under the control of the barons." He didn't need to go into details; he wasn't proud of what happened— especially the execution of Richard's closest advisors. Duke John was frowning.

"King Richard was still in his minority," Henry added in his own defense. "He was ruling badly and needed the help of counsel. My role, and that of Norfolk, was minor. The Duke of Gloucester, on the other hand, directed the opposition, having gained the cooperation of the Commons. The other two Appellants were the Earls of Arundel and Warwick." He paused, feeling himself sweating. "Two years ago, King Richard convicted the Lords Appellant of treason, in Parliament. Norfolk and I were given pardons. But Norfolk believed we would be next to suffer the king's retribution, and that's when my trouble started." He paused again, sighing. It was painful to bring this up. "He made certain...accusations too dangerous to ignore."

"My lord duke, you must have been under a lot of stress," said Joanna, taking a fig from a bowl and handing it to Thomas. "It must have been difficult to remain neutral."

"My feelings exactly," Henry said, gratified. "My father decided to bring Norfolk's concerns to the king, and before we knew it the controversy had grown into a confrontation between the two of us. Once the court of chivalry addressed our dispute, it became a matter of trial by combat. By then, we had gone too far to retreat."

"We had heard about the tournament," said John. "The Count of St. Pol told us. He said you had just started forward when the king threw in his baton."

"Oh," sighed Henry, "that was the most difficult moment of my life. I was committed to victory or death. My whole essence was focused on the point of my lance. I could barely stop in time."

"Then Richard declared you both outlaw, I assume," said Joanna.

"To preserve our lives," Henry said bitterly. "He said we were too close to the throne. What nonsense."

"Why do you really think he did it?" she pursued.

Looking at Erpingham, who sat with pursed lips, Henry sighed again. "I wish I knew. Perhaps he just wanted to be rid of the both of us—not just one. I don't think he acted from affection, that's for certes. Richard and I were never close."

"From affection toward your father?" wondered John.

"Perhaps. Though I was never to see him again." He cleared his throat and swallowed. "The king's subsequent behavior proved what I never dared to presume."

"What was that?" John asked.

"You don't know? When he declared my outlawry, Richard swore if my father died I could sue for my inheritance. Then, when it happened—" he crossed himself—"may my father rest in peace, King Richard forbade my attorneys to petition for me under penalty of treason. He broke his promise," he added bitterly. "He seized my inheritance. The Dukedom and Palatinate of Lancaster."

The duke of Brittany was speechless. Joanna put a hand on her chest, her eyes wide.

"What was his justification?" she asked.

"His counselors stated that a man convicted of treason is not in a position to claim any benefits. Now tell me, where is the conviction of treason?"

The others stared at him, unable to answer.

"I am permitted to sue for my patrimony only after I return and do homage to him—after my exile! Unless he finds a way to keep me from returning." Henry sighed. "I understand he has partitioned my lands and given them out to his favorites. To hold until I can claim them back. They have replaced my officers with their own retainers. I have no say in the matter. My own estates!" Catching himself, he lowered his voice. "I am sorry. This upsets me. My good uncle, I would ask your advice."

John shifted in his seat. "I can see why you are upset. You know that as Earl of Richmond I have a good relationship with King Richard. But what you're talking about threatens every noble and his God-given rights. Even a king must respect his magnates." He leaned toward his steward, whispering in his ear. "I must give this some thought. Please, for now, consider this as your home. What is mine, is yours."

This was so much more than Henry dared hope. Blinking back tears of gratitude, he asked one more favor. "Do I have your leave to communicate with my supporters back in England?"

"By all means, by all means. The straightest road is the surest and the best. In due time, God's will shall reveal itself."

Henry and his son were given lodgings in one of the great towers of the castle. They wanted for nothing. The first night, Henry slept better than he remembered since he came to France. Naturally, considering his nature, the next day he was restless. Time was of the essence; he needed to organize his return. Taking his son with him, he met up with Erpingham and Arundel.

The archbishop, still disguised as a clerk, was already busy at work. Henry sat beside him. "Have you heard from Beaufort yet?"

"John?" Arundel pulled a letter from the top of a pile. "These dispatches followed us from Paris. They came yesterday evening. Here." He handed over the letter. "He is concerned about his own safety, not that I blame him. As constable of Dover Castle and Warden of the Cinque Ports, he is deep in the king's confidence. He can't give himself away too soon."

Henry read the letter. "I see he still retains a handful of ships under his command." He glanced up at Arundel. "I'm sure he will let us borrow three of them. But he can't send them here. That would be too much."

"I agree. We must find our own way across the Channel."

"I think so, too." Henry put his chin in his hand. "Perhaps Duke John will let us hire some ships to cross over."

"A very good idea. Once we have his answer, we will write to your brother. I'm thinking we can put in at Pevensey where your knight, John Pelham, is constable if I'm not mistaken. Sir John can have supplies waiting for us at the castle."

Henry was amazed at Arundel's organization. He shouldn't have been; the archbishop had years of administrative skills behind him. The planning went on for a couple of hours until his son asked if they could have some food. Henry decided it was a good time to take a break and rose from the table. Arundel waved them on, barely pausing in his letter-writing.

Hoping to find the duke, Henry made his way to the great hall, his arm around his son's shoulders. Duke John was nowhere to be seen, and Henry was surprised to find the duchess sitting in a high chair, playing a lute. Her ladies gathered behind her, sewing. Father and son stood for a few minutes, listening until Joanna looked up. She smiled as they approached.

"That was beautiful," Henry said.

"You are very kind. I've been playing since I was a child."

"May I join you? I brought along a portable harp."

Astonished, she turned to her ladies. "Did you hear? A duet!"

"If you go to our room and bring my harp," Henry said to Thomas, "perhaps I can persuade Duchess Joanna to arrange for some food."

"Gladly," she said, turning to the other side. A boy, about ten years old, got up from the floor where he had been playing with tin soldiers. She waved him closer. "You haven't met my son Johnny, yet." Holding out an arm, Joanna gave the boy a hug. "Johnny, this is Thomas of Lancaster and Duke Henry, his father. Could you show Thomas the way to his room? By the time you get back, I'll have had our steward set out your dinner."

The two boys observed each other for a moment before deciding they could get along. "This way," Johnny said. "I'll show you." They went off together and Joanna patted the chair next to her.

"Sit, Duke Henry. My husband has to finish some business in town and won't be back until later. I'll return in a moment." She put down the lute and waved to her steward, who happened to be passing by.

Watching her conversation, Henry caught himself admiring her slim waist and her tight bodice. *What was he thinking?* He hadn't looked at a woman like that since Mary died. Right then Joanna glanced at him and he was glad she was far enough away not to see a slight flush on his face. He bit his lip. *This would not do.*

Fortunately, the moment passed. She came back and seated herself comfortably. "I'm not at all familiar with English music," she said, "but perhaps you can play something for me and I'll try to follow you."

He laughed. "That's fair enough. Then you can play a Breton tune and I'll try to follow you. We'll see who has the most skill at making it up as we go along."

"Or perhaps a nursery rhyme would be a good start."

"A much better idea! Oh, here they come now."

Thomas and Johnny were chatting happily, and Henry took his harp while the boys made their way across the room to where a small feast was being laid out, just for them. "That should keep them occupied," he said. He plucked a couple of strings while Joanna tuned her lute to match. Then they looked at each other, two musicians enthused at the possibilities.

Thinking for a moment, Henry picked out a rhyme, sprightly and simple. After a few notes, Joanna nodded. "I know that one," she said happily and bent over her lute, summoning a harmony perfectly matched to his tune. He tried a variation on the theme and she followed him, humming along until he helped her with the words:

> *When to the flowers*
> *so beautiful the Father gave a name,*
> *Back came a little blue-eyed one*
> *All timidly it came;*
> *And standing at its Father's feet*
> *and gazing in His face,*
> *It said, in low and trembling tone*
> *and with a modest grace,*
> *"Dear God, the name Thou gavest me,*
> *Alas I have forgot!"*
> *Kindly the Father looked him down*
> *and said: "Forget-me-not."*

"Ah," she laughed. "I haven't heard that one since I was a child." Henry warmed at the sound; he hadn't heard genuine laughter for a long time.

Then it was her turn; she tried something quieter, more melodic, and though it was new to Henry he did his best to accompany her. This went on until Duke John returned, smiling broadly at the happy musicians, surrounded by ladies and courtiers who were always attracted to something different.

Joanna looked up. "Welcome back, my dear." She handed her lute to one of her ladies and got up, smoothing her skirt. "If I'm not mistaken, you are just in time for supper." She nodded at the steward, who waited behind the duke.

Henry put his harp under his arm, almost sorry to stop. He hadn't had a partner for a long time. "What a marvelous way to spend the afternoon. Can we try again tomorrow?"

Smiling, Joanna nodded. Henry wasn't the only one who appreciated the diversion.

Duke John's conversation at supper was enough to make Henry forget about entertaining himself. "I've been considering your situation," he said, pouring himself some wine. "And although I love and respect King Richard, I feel you have been treated unjustly. I am prepared to assist you in your efforts to recover your inheritance."

Henry dropped his head back and looked at the heavens. "Your Grace, I am overwhelmed by your kindness."

"Nonsense. The king owes a duty to his vassals just as they owe their loyalty to him. It is a sacred trust. I will assist you with vessels, men-at-arms, and cross-bows. You shall be conveyed to the shores of England, and my men will defend you from any perils you might encounter along the way."

"I can ask for no more. I am prepared to pay their wages and reimburse your expenses."

"No, that won't be necessary. Speak no more of this."

Duke John was as good as his word. The following day, he took Henry with him to prepare his purveyances. Already, provisions were being stockpiled to be loaded onto the ships, weapons were counted and repaired, soldiers reported for duty. All would be ready within a few days.

Henry checked on his own companions, making sure they would be ready to embark. The archbishop was still busy sending out messages, and he reassured Henry that his Lancastrian retainers were already preparing for his arrival. Castles were being fortified, troops were gathering for his expected landing in Yorkshire.

The next two days proceeded in pretty much the same manner. In the afternoons, Henry kept company with the duke. In the evenings, he and Joanna amused both themselves and their immediate circle with music.

The third evening, once again Henry brought out his harp and the duchess arranged chairs in her favorite solar. Duke John joined them, along with the boys and a couple of Henry's knights. The gathering was very intimate and light conversation continued in the background as Henry experimented with new melodies and Joanna switched to other stringed instruments. Eventually, the old duke tired and excused himself for the night, encouraging the others to continue. One by one their companions slipped away as the evening wore on. Finally, only the two of them were left, aside from her ladies who sat quietly in the back of the room.

Henry put his harp aside, reaching for his wine. He had long since tired of playing, but he didn't want to give up Joanna's company. She continued picking quietly on her lute. He admired her long fingers and the way she hung her head over the instrument. Finally, she stopped, looking at him.

"I think I know what you are thinking," she said, softly so her women couldn't hear. "I understand. There is a bond between us that cannot be defined. Of the spirit. I feel it too."

Henry glanced at the lady maids, relieved that their faces remained neutral. "I was afraid to say anything," he said. "But, yes. I can't explain it."

"That is all we can say for now. My duke has been nothing but kind to me. You've only met my eldest son. John has given me nine children, though only seven survived."

"Nine?" Henry looked at her slim form. "One would never know to look at you."

"I've been very fortunate." She smiled briefly. "I think little Blanche will be the last one. She's two years old. Alas, Duke John has been ailing. Fortunately you have caught him at a good time." She sighed. "I have a great responsibility toward my children."

Henry accepted her words with equanimity. He could see she was a loyal wife—kind, compassionate. He smiled at her warmly and she blinked, flushing.

"And what about you?" Joanna said, covering her awkwardness. "How many children do you have?"

"Four boys and two girls. My first born, Hal, is just a year older than Thomas." His face clouded for a moment. "He's a difficult boy—very restrained, at least in my company. With Thomas on the other hand—" He rolled his eyes. "They are constantly fighting. I don't know whether they are just being competitive, or if they seriously dislike each other."

"It's not unusual with boys," Joanna said. "Perhaps when they get older…"

"I hope so. I admit I don't understand Hal very well. He won't open up to me."

"Are you away a lot?"

He chuckled. "You could say that! I spent two years on crusade and traveled all over Europe. Then at home, the dukedom required constant attention." He looked hard at her. "You think he felt neglected?"

She shrugged. "Every child is different. What about the others?"

"Well, John came two years after Thomas, then Humphrey. That makes Humphrey nine this year. After them, finally we had two girls, Blanche and Philippa. My dear wife died in childbirth with the last one five years ago." His voice trailed off. "The girls live with their grandmother, Mary's mother."

"Oh, I am so sorry. You must have loved her very much."

"I did. She was beautiful and had such a generous spirit. Much like you."

There he went again. He couldn't hide his admiration for Joanna. She had all the qualities he would have wanted in a duchess. But she was right; there was nothing else to say. He was a lonely man and easily susceptible. This, too, would pass.

But it didn't. The next day at dinner, sitting on the other side of Duke John, he found himself surreptitiously glancing at her. He admired the way she sipped her soup, the way she directed the servants, her self-assurance when she spoke to her husband; John obviously doted on her even after all those years. Afterward, when all three walked together in the garden, he was distracted by the desire to brush up against her. Of course, he did nothing of the sort. She did catch him looking at her and responded with a smile.

This evening, the duke showed signs of fatigue. "I need to go inside, my dear," he said, and Joanna willingly took his arm and led the way. Once they were settled, John fell asleep in his chair. Joanna called for a light blanket.

"He gets cold, even in the summer," she said sadly. "Sometimes his feet tingle and I have to rub them."

Henry looked at the duke's pale face. "He looks drawn, like he's in pain."

"I think he is, though he never complains. I fear for my boys; the Constable, Olivier de Clisson—the same who built the Hôtel you stayed at in Paris—has been a rival of my husband for as long as I can remember. Although lately, they have made peace between them, I fear for my son if John dies while he is a boy..." She looked up, tears in her eyes. "I would be called upon to act as peacemaker, as I have done many times before."

"I'm sure you excel at the task," Henry said, taking her hands in his. After a moment, he let go. "I will be leaving tomorrow, and once I reestablish myself—"

"You will. I have no doubt."

He smiled sadly. "I had better, for the consequences would be dire, otherwise."

"I can't imagine such a chivalrous knight failing to win his course."

"I appreciate your faith in me. It gives me courage." He hesitated. "When I reestablish myself, I will write. Rest assured. If you have need of my arm, I will be there."

Nodding, she busied herself by adjusting the blanket. "Henry?"

"Yes?"

"How will you convince King Richard to accept you back?"

He took a deep breath. "All my retainers, from the top ranks to the servants, rise and fall with me. When Richard gave my estates to his favorites, they undoubtedly replaced my officers with their own men. Some of my vassals will have lost their homes and wages; many will suffer displacement. When I return, I am depending on them to gather around my banner. Together we can force the king to recognize his error."

"You will wage war on the king."

"I hope it doesn't come to that. With disaffected magnates supporting me, the king will have to back down. After all, what he did to me he can just as easily do to them. Richard couldn't have thought of a better way to alienate his nobles."

"I hope you are right."

"It's happened before. The barons are a powerful force."

"Edward II."

"Yes." Henry got up and walked to the sideboard. He poured them both some wine. "It was ugly. My ancestor the Earl of Lancaster was beheaded for treason. But in the end, the king's tyranny was overturned." He brought the wine back and handed her the goblet. "The most powerful barons were divided in their loyalty. I don't think we will be, this time. Richard has very little to offer my fellow magnates. His new creations have no teeth. They are mostly with him in Ireland, anyway." He sat, taking a drink. "I will know within a couple of weeks if the reality matches my ambitions. Who knows? I might be back?" He gave her a half-smile.

"For your sake, I hope not."

"If I am to prove worthy, I must succeed."

Worthy of what? she wondered. Best to leave it unspoken.

CHAPTER 3

Duke John and Duchess Joanna accompanied Henry and his companions to the wharf. It took three ships to accommodate his men and supplies, and Henry was well satisfied with all the preparations. As the last of his followers ascended the ramp, Henry took his leave. Duke John held out a hand and he grasped it with both his own.

"My gratitude knows no bounds," he said. "I hope to repay you someday."

"Stay safe, nephew. Your father would have been proud of you."

Bowing his head, Henry turned to Joanna. He fumbled with his belt and pulled out a little velvet pouch, handing it to her. Surprised, she drew it open and lifted out a precious brooch: tiny flowers set with jeweled petals and pearl centers.

"Look, dear," she said, showing it to her husband. "*Myosotis arvensis*. Forget-me-nots!" Her eyes filled with tears. "Duke Henry, I shall cherish this." She stepped forward, kissing him on the cheek. It was the first kiss she gave him.

"Farewell, my dear friends," Henry swept off his hat with a flourish then turned to the ship; he was the last one aboard. Just before mounting the ramp he turned with one more backward look. John held up a hand in farewell.

Archbishop Arundel was waiting for Henry. They both leaned on the gunwale and watched the Bretons as the shipmaster prepared to leave. "They were very gracious," said Arundel. "We were fortunate. Now, all we have to worry about is the Channel."

That bit of levity shook Henry from his melancholy. He gave the other a wry smile. "Now you can get out of your ugly black robe. No more need for disguises."

"Actually, I never felt more freedom in my life. Of course, I'd probably get tired of being ignored."

Henry laughed. "There won't be much of that where we are going. So what are our immediate plans?"

"Our first stop will be Pevensey. Sir John Pelham will have provisions all ready for us, and three new vessels borrowed from Sir John Beaufort. We will disembark quickly and send the duke's ships back to Brittany. Then we will proceed north. If all goes as planned, Pelham will create a diversion there after we leave. Maybe we can draw your uncle York south in an attempt to intercept us.

"My brother won't be at Pevensey, I assume."

"No. It's better for all of us if he remains neutral. But I do have a letter from him, declaring his loyalty to your cause."

"My dear brother. I never doubted."

It took two days to cross the Channel, and once they came in sight of Pevensey the sea had calmed. Everything went as Arundel had predicted, and they were soon on their way north along the coast. They made landfall at Cromer in Norfolk—north of Norwich—one of the Lancastrian estates Henry was certain had already declared for him. There, they loaded more provisions and continued on their way. Touching down at the mouth of the Humber where the old settlement of Ravenspur used to be, they took heart that no organized resistance lay in wait for them. So far.

"I think it's safe to make our landing at Bridlington," Henry said to Arundel. He put his hand on his son's back as they surveyed the estuary. "It's only about thirty miles north of us. Bridlington has a good-sized port with a quay and a large harbor. It's on the Roman road, so we'll be able to get messengers out quickly. Most importantly, it doesn't have a castle so there won't be a garrison trying to stop us."

"Will there be plenty of food, father?" Thomas asked.

Henry chuckled indulgently. "Don't worry. It's a big town. We'll be there for a few days while we make sure we are safe."

Bridlington was due east of York and sixty miles from Pontefract, Henry's most powerful castle in the north. It was famous for its local holy man Prior John, considered far and wide as a prophet who had died early in Richard II's reign. By now the priory had grown into one of the largest monastic houses of the Augustinian order. It had recently received a license to crenellate, though the construction was more for decoration than defense. From a distance, it certainly looked like a castle.

Lancaster had been a donor for years and Henry's little company was welcomed to stay in its precincts. The monks also recognized Archbishop Arundel, who had finally chosen to relinquish his friar's robes.

The first thing Henry did was purchase horses locally and send messengers to his supporters in East Yorkshire. At the moment they were at their most vulnerable; there was no way of knowing whether the local sheriffs were gathering forces to attack. Henry's tiny force would be helpless against a concerted strike. Even Arundel was uncomfortable, for he knew his own life would be forfeit if he was caught.

There was nothing to do but wait for Lancaster's retainers to answer Henry's messages. No one slept well the first night. Henry was up early the next morning, checking the ships to make sure they were prepared for a quick departure—just in case. He turned at the sound of pounding feet, stiffening as one of his knights ran toward him.

"My lord, a small band of warriors are approaching bearing Percy arms."

"Percy?" Henry whirled around, touching Erpingham who was distracted by the ship's captain. "Thomas, why would Percy be here?"

"Which Percy?" Erpingham asked.

"The younger, I believe," said the knight.

"Hotspur," Henry said to himself. "He's Warden of the East March of Scotland if I'm not mistaken." He glanced at the knight. "You say he has only a small group?"

"I counted six men."

"Not enough to attack us, unless more are in hiding."

"Let us greet him," Erpingham said. "Best to deal with him directly."

Both Henry and Thomas knew Harry Hotspur well, so-named by the Scots because he was always ready to dash into battle. Just a few years older than Henry, he had also distinguished himself at the St. Inglevert tournament. They had spent many long evenings drinking and feasting together in those heady days, but once the festivities were over they had not crossed paths again. Hotspur and his father, Henry Percy, Earl of Northumberland had their hands full keeping peace in the Marches.

Henry was well aware that the Percies were pivotal in his upcoming struggle. They were the most powerful force in the North by far, and their experience with the restive Scots was invaluable. Their only rival was Ralph Neville, the Earl of Westmorland—a new earl, one of King Richard's derisively named *duketti*. He was given his new title after the Revenge Parliament that condemned the Appellants. Bolingbroke was counting on Westmorland as a potential ally because Ralph had recently married his half-sister Joan Beaufort. At the same time, Henry knew the Percies weren't going to let Neville get ahead of them when there was a chance to grab more power.

But he wasn't prepared to face them so soon! At least he only had to confront the son; the father would ride roughshod over any perceived threat. Still, Henry wasn't sure how to manage Harry yet. By law, Percy could use his office to arrest him as a declared outlaw. *Or at least he could try.*

As Hotspur and his followers entered through the gates of the priory, Henry, Arundel, and Erpingham waited for them in the courtyard. "My lord, what a surprise to see you here," said Henry, holding the reins of Hotspur's horse.

Dismounting, Harry brushed his hands across his legs. "Dusty out there," he said amiably. "One of your messengers rode across my land and naturally I questioned him. I was at my manor of Seamer, which is only about twelve miles away."

"What brings you so far south?" Henry asked, pretending not to be concerned. As Warden of the East March of Scotland, Hotspur spent most of his time in Northumberland—not here, in Yorkshire. Putting on his most amiable expression, Henry led the others into the priory where the good friars laid out food and drink for them.

"I came to collect payment from the exchequer for my services as warden." Hotspur accepted a mug of ale from a servant. "I think it would be more appropriate to ask what *you* are doing here?" He softened the remark with a smile.

It was hard to resist his grin. Harry had a certain openness about him that invited trust. Tall, bearded, brown-haired, sincere, and intense, Percy's son was well-known for his honesty and chivalry. He was the opposite of his brusque father.

Even Henry was not immune to Hotspur's charm. "I have come back to reclaim my patrimony, which was unjustly taken from me," he answered softly. For a moment there was silence around the table.

"I think my father received a letter from you last month."

Henry grunted. He had sent letters to both of them. "What happened to me concerns us all," he said in earnest.

Young FitzAlan walked into the room. Henry pointed to him. "Harry, this is Thomas, son of the late Earl Arundel. Like me, he comes to reclaim his earldom. Thomas, meet Sir Harry Percy, son of the Earl of Northumberland." The lad came forward and bowed.

"And this is his uncle Thomas Arundel, the Archbishop of Canterbury," Henry continued, nodding to his side. "I don't believe you ever met."

Arundel nodded. Hotspur gave him a long look; he knew the archbishop had also been outlawed. "I don't think we have," he said finally. "Well met, your Grace. I see you all have the same purpose in returning to England."

"There are injustices that need to be put to right," Henry said. "I hope to gather enough support to convince King Richard he must reverse his unlawful decisions."

"I see." Harry looked around the room. "It appears you have made a modest start."

Despite himself, Henry blushed. "I came with my closest companions, who accompanied me to France. I have faith my Lancastrian affinity will swell my ranks."

Percy nodded. Again his smile rescued an uncomfortable situation. "I have no doubt. King Richard's policies have even disturbed our stability in the North."

Was that an invitation? "You must know I have great respect for your family. Between your lordship and Lancaster—and the Nevilles, secondarily—the North is a force to be reckoned with."

Hotspur nodded, uncommitted.

"I would have you with me, Harry."

Taking a sip of his ale, Hotspur looked at the table. "You're asking for much, my lord."

"Duke Henry speaks for all the nobles in the land," interjected the archbishop. "If Richard could take away the great Lancastrian patrimony with a strike of his quill, what's to stop him from doing the same to everyone else?"

"Or declaring a loyal subject a traitor?" added Henry, unable to suppress his bitterness. "We are all at the mercy of his impulses." He sensed Hotspur's resistance was half-hearted, and his heart pounded in response.

"We've considered that, ourselves," Harry said. He turned his whole body, facing Henry. "What are your real intentions?"

Blinking, Henry drew himself up. "I have stated them. I came here to reclaim my own."

"Nothing more?"

Henry didn't know whether to be surprised or offended. But, he admitted to himself, this question was going to be asked again and again. *There was no easy way to put this.* "Are you wondering if I covet the throne?"

There. It was said. For the first time.

"It crossed my mind." Hotspur stared at him, trying to measure his honesty. Henry shook his head.

"I have no interest in Richard's crown. The Lancastrian inheritance is more than enough."

"How do you intend to convince the king, as you say?"

Henry pursed his lips. It was a fair question. "It won't be easy. I think, as in the past, a group of magnates," he said slowly, "if united by a common goal, can force an obstinate king to rule more wisely, with their help."

"We don't have to look any farther back than 1387," Arundel asserted. "The parliamentary Continual Council was only established for one year. It would need to be permanent this time."

"There were other examples," Percy mused. "The Council of Fifteen under Simon de Montfort. Or more lately, the Lords Ordainers against Edward II. Both ended badly for the barons if I'm not mistaken. We don't even need to talk about the Lords Appellant."

Henry squirmed uncomfortably. Percy was right. But he had to try again. "This time around, the king has no powerful supporters. Richard's new appointees have no teeth. Besides, they are with him in Ireland."

"Perhaps." Hotspur turned his cup in his hand.

"Between the Lancastrian affinity and the North, I trust, we will prove an irresistible force." Henry leaned forward. "I am prepared to pay the wages of any men who choose to follow me."

"Ah, that will be a great benefit." Percy cocked his head. "You have no intention of usurping the king?"

"None."

"Are you prepared to swear an oath?"

Without hesitation, Henry put a hand on Percy's arm. "My lord, I will do so at once."

Getting up and gesturing for everyone in the room to follow, Henry called for a monk to meet them in the chapel. They approached the altar and waited while the brother reverently unlocked a casket and produced a bible. Henry knelt, putting his hand on the precious volume.

"I swear, before this room full of witnesses and God himself, my only intent in returning to England is to reclaim my inheritance. By the grace of God, I will recover my patrimony and serve the king as a loyal subject."

He held his hand on the bible as every man crossed himself. Then he stood, a reverential glow on his face. "Are you with me, Harry?"

Percy was suitably impressed by his sincerity. Only hesitating for a moment, he extended his hand. "You may count on me. I will go at once to my father so we can gather our resources."

After some discussion, Henry decided he would use Doncaster as a gathering point for his collective forces before proceeding south. They would aim at two weeks hence. Since Doncaster was just south of Pontefract, he knew that by then he would be able to rely on many thousands of retainers from his own estates.

The day after Percy left, the first of Henry's anxiously expected troops arrived. Sir Robert Waterton brought 200 foresters with him from Pontefract—and, even more welcome, a large sum of cash from the Lancastrian exchequer. Encouraged,

Henry decided to leave the safety of Bridlington and venture forth to see if he met any resistance.

His first destination was his father's castle at Pickering, about thirty-five miles away and due north of York. It was too soon to take his chances with York itself; there was every expectation Richard's regent would fortify it with funds and possibly troops. Instead, Henry decided to flank it, establishing bases first at Pickering, then Knaresborough, just west of the city.

Already the ranks of Henry's army were beginning to swell. The more men he welcomed, the bolder he got. They purchased horses and supplies from willing locals; no one put up the least resistance to his presence.

After a few days, Henry's force amounted to several hundred. They reached the great stronghold at Pontefract, built on a large hill with an expansive view of the countryside. The curtain walls enclosed a huge outer bailey leading to the inner bailey through a second fortified barbican. They waited a few days, gathering more supporters. Henry wasn't disappointed; new arrivals came from as far away as Lancashire, Staffordshire, Derbyshire, and Lincolnshire.

The evening before they were to leave for their next destination, Henry went to pray before the altar in the priory chapel, built especially for his ancestor Thomas, Earl of Lancaster. Thomas was beheaded on this very spot following the failed rebellion against Edward II. He was locally venerated as a martyr and a saint; nobody really cared that the pope refused to approve his canonization.

Henry left the door slightly ajar, listening as the dry leaves rustled across the stone floor. He felt a hush in the chapel, as though the spirit of his ancestor filled the little space. Moving to the altar, he picked up a withered rose and turned with it, studying the painted coat of arms in the dirty window. "Dust," he murmured, putting the rose back. "That's all we are. Countries go to war, dynasties are overturned, and in the end, we all end up in a silent vault, alone and irrelevant." Kneeling before the tomb, he closed his eyes. "I understand, now, how you must have felt," Henry whispered over his folded hands. "Leading a revolt against the king. As soon as the wheel of fortune turned, your downfall was precipitous. No matter how noble your intentions, the king's will prevailed. I remember what my father told me. They gave you no opportunity to defend yourself. Oh, how I fear to be in the same position." His lips moving silently, he said a prayer to the saint.

Looking up, hoping for some kind of relief, Henry took little comfort from the stern expression on the effigy. He stood, crossing himself. Enough of this self-pity.

Leaving the chapel, Henry closed the door firmly behind him. Turning, he saw his son and FitzAlan throwing a ball back and forth. The lad was six years older than Thomas, and Henry figured he was probably just humoring his son because he had no one his own age around. He watched them for a few minutes before they stopped and ran up to him.

"Father, where are we going next?"

"Doncaster, son. Then Nottingham. Many great lords will join us at Doncaster if all goes well."

"Isn't Doncaster one of the Duke of York's estates?" asked Arundel.

Henry was surprised he was so well informed. "Yes, it is."

"Aren't you worried he will stop you?"

"Very good question. I am counting on the goodwill between my uncle York and my family. He and my father were very close. If he does try to stop me..." He ran a hand over his hair. "Well, already I have so many supporters he'll have to think twice before attacking us. As you have seen, so far he has kept quiet."

"Maybe he doesn't know we are here."

"It's possible." Henry put an arm around both boys' shoulders. "I have heard that he supports my cause, even though he is regent. Come, I'm famished. Let's get something to eat."

Always hungry, the boys cheered. They went into the old hall where Henry ordered the servants to bring a late supper. They were soon joined by Erpingham and the archbishop.

"Good news," said Erpingham. "I just learned that Lord Greystoke and Lord Willoughby are on their way to Doncaster."

"Ah, their support is so encouraging," Henry said, passing a piece of cheese to his son. "Have you heard from Percy?"

Erpingham shook his head. "Not yet. They had farther to come, as you know. I trust they won't want to miss any opportunity to advance themselves."

"Ha! I hope that's how they see it. They could make the difference between our success and failure," he said, more to his son than anyone else. "Henry Percy is the power in the North. He commands a great many men."

"And what about Hotspur?" Thomas asked.

"Oh, whatever his father decides, he will go along."

"I reckon they will catch up with us at Doncaster," Erpingham said, taking a drink of ale.

"We will wait for them."

CHAPTER 4

The Percies didn't disappoint. When they showed up at Doncaster, they brought Ralph Neville, the Earl of Westmorland with them. This was more than Henry dared hope for. He knew the two families were rivals in the North; the fact that they rode together was a good sign. And here they were, entering the Carmelite friary while Henry was occupied flattering the lords Roos, Greystoke, and Willoughby and listening to their complaints about King Richard. The three of them—Percy, Hotspur, and Westmorland—walked through the great hall while the other attendees parted before them like a wave before a ship.

Relieved, Henry raised his arm. "Well come, Earl Percy! I've been waiting for you."

"My lord," bellowed Percy. "We have brought a vast host to represent the North in your worthy cause."

Henry hoped his relief wasn't too obvious. The earl was a force to be reckoned with, and Henry wasn't quite sure how to behave toward him. Percy and Gaunt had not been on the best of terms. Although they were once close friends, all this changed eighteen years ago when Lancaster was appointed Lieutenant in Scotland. Percy felt that Gaunt was usurping his position as Warden of the East Marches. During the Peasants' Revolt, Gaunt was denied entrance to any of Percy's castles on his way back from Scotland. This put him in grave danger while inflicting one of the worst humiliations of his life. John saw this as Percy's revenge—which it probably was—and he bitterly complained to the king after all was over. The uproar nearly started a civil war. They never patched up the argument, and Henry had heard his father's side of the story most of his life.

And now, Gaunt's son needed Percy as his ally. Henry eyed the earl curiously as the three newcomers approached. Percy was the same age as his father, though he was in much better condition; in fact, he glowed with good health. His pointed beard was white even though his closely-cropped hair was still mostly brown. Strong and broad in the chest, he had a slight squint to the eye that could be quite daunting. This probably helped him in his negotiations, as his reputation preceded him.

Taking courage at Percy's greeting, Henry welcomed them cheerfully. "Henry, Harry, Ralph," he said, clasping each of their hands in turn. "There is much for us to discuss. Please, dine with me."

He had already arranged for the archbishop to take charge of the other attendees, freeing him up to speak privately with key supporters. Always a gracious host, Thomas Arundel encouraged the men to follow him into the refectory, where a large feast had been prepared. The Whitefriars had long been beneficiaries of Gaunt, and they were anxious to please the new duke. Henry brought his northern lords into a private chamber, where the friars were busy setting out a generous meal.

They all ate heartily—or at least, his guests did. Henry picked at his food, trying to prepare himself for the inevitable ordeal. It wasn't long in coming.

"My son told me about your meeting at Bridlington," Percy started, cutting at a piece of chicken while holding it down with a spoon. "It is good for all of us that the king is busy in Ireland."

"Indeed," said Henry.

Percy waited a moment but nothing further was said. "He told me you have come to claim your inheritance."

"Which was taken from me illegally," Henry insisted.

"Yes, yes. This is why we are here. The king is not above the law, no matter what he thinks."

"I'm glad you are with me."

"But surely you understand we are taking a great risk in supporting an exile." Percy narrowed his eyes at Henry, trying to gauge his resolution. Up until now, Bolingbroke had been a nondescript son of a powerful noble. He had yet to prove himself.

Shifting in his seat, Henry wasn't sure what to say.

Losing patience, Percy put down his knife. "Come now, Henry. This is not the time for equivocation. If we are to risk our lives supporting you, we must know what your intentions are."

Although he and Arundel had previously discussed what he should say, Henry hadn't decided what kind of official

44

announcement he was prepared to make. He could see it was time to commit himself. He had an army now, and his supporters would be expecting him to act with purpose.

He had already made his first declaration to Hotspur, and that worked out all right. Now was his real test—against the father.

Taking a deep breath, Henry finally faced Percy. "All right. I appreciate you are my major support. You know this. I understand you're not about to risk everything you own—including your lives—just to help me get back my patrimony." He glanced at Harry and Ralph then back to Percy. "What I am going to tell the world is that I have come to reclaim my duchy as rightful heir. I have no designs on the crown. However, if I get the support I need, I intend to put the king under our control and reform his household. This is no more than we did ten years ago."

Percy took a slice of mincemeat pie, putting it on his trencher. "This is all you intend to do. To make the king a figurehead, answerable to a council."

"And why not? He has demonstrated poor judgment in running the country."

"I'll grant you that. What happens in five or ten years, when he regains power?"

This was the very question that kept Henry awake at night. He looked fixedly at the earl. "We'll have to ensure he never regains power, won't we?" Once he said the words, Henry conceded to himself what he had been unwilling to confront; there were to be no half measures. He didn't want to be Richard's next victim.

Meanwhile, Hotspur was already fidgeting. "You have no intention of usurping him, then?"

"None." *There must be a way to make this work.*

Harry frowned. "Will you swear an oath?"

An oath. Another oath. Of course, he knew this was coming. He had even asked the monks to borrow the relics of St. Bridlington for this eventuality. Considering for a moment, Bolingbroke nodded. "You are right, Harry. I need to come out into the open. I will swear an oath publicly—right here—before everyone who has gathered at Doncaster. Will that satisfy you?"

The other nodded. "Yes. Very well."

45

Percy cleared his throat. "Where will you go from here?"

"South. Toward Bristol. Unless I learn otherwise, I'm assuming King Richard has heard about my landing by now. He'll have to come back and confront us. It makes sense for him to return the way he left. Through Wales, with an army. And quickly. Our own movements depend on when and where we encounter my uncle York."

"As regent, he is bound to summon a large army." Percy glanced at Westmorland. "Ours needs to be larger."

"And so, much of my itinerary will be through my Lancastrian estates," Henry said in agreement. "My retainers have every reason to ensure I don't lose control of my patrimony." He paused. "As I already have, at least on paper. Though if I am correct, the reality is very different." He stood, pushing back his chair. "And now, my friends, I have much to do before tomorrow."

He was exhausted. This was all he could take for the moment. These three were his most difficult allies, and he hoped they were satisfied. After Percy, at least, everyone else would be easy.

The following day, Henry waited for them in the great hall at Whitefriars. Many of the leaders camped with their armies and they slowly trickled in, consulting each other while looking up at him. Bolingbroke stood on a raised platform with the two Arundels and his closest knights under the banner of Lancaster. Finally the Percies came in with Westmorland, acting like they were in charge—and, considering the size of their army, that wasn't far from the truth.

Clearing his throat, Henry got right to the point. As the talking diminished in the hall, he held up a jeweled box. "Here are the relics of Bridlington, lent to us by the good friars so I may swear a holy oath before all of you. My intentions are clear. I seek only the inheritance of my father, John of Gaunt, Duke of Lancaster. But that is not enough!" His voice boomed through the room. "I am your champion of justice and liberties! I am here to ensure good government. Here is the seal of the Lord High Steward of England which I inherited from my father." He held it up. "And I intend to use it." Henry paused, heartened by the applause. "All Cheshiremen will be removed from King Richard's household." The cheering increased; the Cheshire archers had gotten away with terrorizing the public too long.

As the noise continued, Henry was encouraged. So far, everything was going as planned. Holding up his hands, he was about to say more when a sharp voice cut through the din.

"Will you take the crown?"

It was Hotspur. *Will that man ever be satisfied?* Clearly, he was still suspicious. Henry knew that Hotspur's wife was aunt to the young Mortimer, considered by many to be heir presumptive. But the boy was only eight years old! Surely they didn't expect to put another child on the throne. *Or did they?*

"No, that is not my intention," Henry said clearly, hiding his annoyance. "I intend to put the king in good governance under the direction of lords spiritual and temporal. I will reform his household. I swear to this on the relics of Bridlington!" He turned to the bishop who took the box and held it firmly while Bolingbroke placed a gloved hand on the lid. "I swear before God I seek only to reclaim my inheritance. I do not seek the crown. Nonetheless, I will ensure you are governed well, as is your right. And if anyone more worthy of the crown could be found, I will willingly withdraw."

There was jostling among the crowd and Henry saw Hotspur force his way outside. Maybe he misspoke himself at the last. Well, let him go. He would deal with Harry later.

By the time they left Doncaster, Henry's forces numbered 30,000. The vast majority of them were Percy's men. Already it was becoming a problem feeding all these mouths, but fortunately he could supply them from his own Lancastrian estates—at least for a while. By 20 July, he was at Leicester, and his men were already helping themselves to local food and supplies. Three days later they moved to Coventry, and the next day, Warwick. His scouts had informed him that the former retainers of Thomas Beauchamp had already subjugated the castle in Henry's name. That made life a little easier.

Sitting astride his horse in front of the tall gatehouse, Henry raised an arm in greeting as the drawbridge was lowered. A score of knights, armored and dressed in Beauchamp's arms, ceremoniously crossed the moat and lined up before the duke, raising their swords in respect.

"Isn't this a beautiful sight?" Henry said to Arundel. "At this rate, I won't have to do any fighting at all." Nodding his acknowledgment, he nudged his mount forward as the knights parted, preparing to follow him back over the drawbridge.

"We can only hope so," said the archbishop. "Wait. Look. What is that atop the gateway?" He pointed toward the stone arch.

Henry pulled rein. "I don't believe it," he said, craning his neck. Mounted to the left above the gate, the king's white hart had been carved onto a stone block. On the right, Tom Holland's white hind was similarly displayed. Exercising his right as one of Richard's new dukes, the Earl of Kent had already imposed his livery on the castle.

Henry turned to the leading knight. "Tear them down," he ordered, pointing at the offending crests. "Both of them."

Beauchamp's retainers were more than willing to oblige. Shouting commands, the knights immediately went about their work as the duke and his party entered the castle bailey. Bolingbroke felt a strange elation. Though it was a small gesture, this was his first real act against the king. It felt good! And as he was Warwick's guest, it would be appropriate to carry out a second affront. It was time to bring the old earl back from exile; he had been languishing on the Isle of Man since the Revenge Parliament of 1398. Before the hour was out, one of the Beauchamp retainers was on his way to his master's prison, release in hand.

The castle was well stocked and a large dinner was being prepared. While they waited, Henry and Thomas Arundel sat down to address more of their incessant letter-writing to local sheriffs.

"I know you are invigorated by all this work," Henry laughed. "I can't keep up with you! Where's your nephew, by the way?"

"He'll be with us shortly," said the archbishop, picking up the papers and tapping them against the table. "He has been busy enlisting a large group of followers from among his father's retainers. Oh, there he is."

Buoyed by his success; young Arundel carried himself proudly as he came into the room. Henry empathized with the lad's need to fill his father's shoes; he had spent most of his own life in John of Gaunt's shadow.

As they moved into the feasting hall, the Percies joined them, keeping their distance from Westmorland. Already the northerners chafed at their uneasy alliance; unfortunately, their rivalry was a fact of life. For now, they would remain civil, but everyone knew it wouldn't last. The Lords Greystoke, Willoughby, and Roos came in, as well as Henry's knights.

Henry looked around the table. "Now that you are all here," he said, "I wanted you to know the Duke of York has sent a messenger." He unfolded a parchment. "Here is what he said: *As the King's Regent, I am very distressed that you have marched across the country with an army, illegally assembled. I demand to know why you are here in violation of your outlawry, and what is your intent?"*

Henry put the message down. "I answered that I will not send a response by messenger. I will go to him and answer his questions directly."

The others mumbled their assent. This was as good an approach as any.

"My scouts tell me the Duke of York tarries at Berkeley," said the Earl of Northumberland. "Perhaps he waits for you there. His army shrinks by the day."

"Thank you, my lord. That is indeed good news. I do not want to fight him."

"Do you think we can bring him over to our side?"

"I hope to appeal to his sense of family. He is my favorite uncle." Henry smiled briefly. York was the next brother after Gaunt, and the two had been so close in age they were nearly inseparable in life—as were their followers. "There might be a conflict of interest within his ranks," Henry added. "Many of my father's retainers also served York and it went both ways. Never had they been forced to choose sides."

"We shall see whether his sense of duty is stronger than his personal inclinations," added Arundel. "I suspect King Richard's behavior has tried his patience."

"Do we have tidings about the king's whereabouts?" asked Westmorland.

"Not yet. Our plans must be flexible until we learn where he chooses to land."

"If York is at Berkeley, the king must be expected at Bristol," Percy said.

"You're probably right. Let us leave tomorrow. There is no time to waste."

They had to pass through Gloucester on the way to Berkeley, and here another messenger searched them out, sent by John Beaufort, Henry's half-brother—the same who lent them the ships at Pevensey. John had joined York's forces and extended the duke's invitation to meet them. They spent the night in town before moving the last thirty miles to their destination.

Edmund Langley, the Duke of York was waiting for them at the Church of St. Mary's. It was an old edifice hosting many generations of the Berkeley family within its humble vaulted nave. Accompanied by his nobles, Henry pushed open the door and slowly entered, looking over the silent effigies lining both sides of the church. His uncle stood before the altar, waiting in the gloom. At his side hovered John Beaufort and a handful of knights like so many ghosts.

Henry could just imagine that the Duke of York wanted nothing more than to sit down; he knew his uncle suffered from severe arthritis, and this audience was undoubtedly a strain for him.

The newcomers moved closer. York's face, usually so affable, was drawn and frowning. Despite himself, Henry felt a pang of guilt.

Putting his hands on his hips, the duke stuck out his chin. "You have much to answer for, Henry Bolingbroke. How dare you drag your horde of bandits across England, pillaging the good people who have done nothing to deserve this outrage?"

Henry extended his hands. "Uncle, uncle. Give me a chance to explain."

"Don't uncle me! You have been forbidden to return these six years, and here you are, just as soon as the king conveniently leaves the country. Surely you must know I speak for him."

"I do, your grace. And I trust your good judgment."

50

"My good judgment!" York sputtered. "My good judgment! I judge that you are outlawed." He threw up his hands, turning around. Fists went back onto his hips.

Despite York's words, Henry felt his uncle spoke out of obligation rather than conviction. He took a step forward. "It was Bolingbroke who was outlawed. I speak for Lancaster."

Temporarily at a loss, York opened and closed his mouth. The trembling of his thin white beard betrayed his inner conflict. Henry took advantage of his discomfiture.

"Uncle, listen to me. My poor father, whom I was not allowed to see even at the last, would have trusted you to look after my entitlements—just as he would have looked after your son's claims had they been challenged. I ask no less of you. You know I have been wronged..." He paused, waiting for an answer. None was forthcoming.

Percy stepped up next to Henry. "This issue touches all of us," he said in his gruff voice. "We stand united behind Lancaster. If such a great inheritance can be thus taken away, then none of us are safe."

Unresolved, York lowered his head.

"And what have I done to deserve this treatment?" Henry pleaded. "What treason have I committed? I only ask to be given what I was promised: the ability to sue for my inheritance. I have come to claim my own." He dropped to one knee. "I am prepared to swear to this, before the altar."

Throwing up his hands, York turned toward the sepulcher. "Then do so, nephew." He crossed his arms, waiting.

Exchanging glances with Percy, Henry moved forward, kneeling under the great crucifix. "I swear, as God is my witness, I have come to claim my inheritance. That is all." He crossed himself.

"Hmm." York was unconvinced. "Why do you need such a large army to merely claim your inheritance?"

Considering his oath discharged, Henry stood. "I am well aware that if I fell into the king's hands, my life would be forfeit."

"So you will confront the king as well?"

"If I must, uncle. I believe he seeks to enrich himself with Lancaster's patrimony. Many would call King Richard a tyrant. Many feel he needs the guidance of wiser heads."

51

"Like yours, I suppose?" York's voice was shrill.

"And yours, uncle. We have had ruling councils before."

Snorting in disgust, the duke turned away.

"Surely you have heard the cries of the people," Henry pleaded. "The king is not satisfied with one pardon. He requires many. He demands surety from every side. No man knows whether he is safe from arrest. No one knows whether their possessions will fall prey to the king's cupidity. As Lord High Steward of England, I have sworn to right these wrongs." He paused; whether he should be acting High Steward was anyone's guess. So far, no one debated his right to it—even York, it seemed.

Turning again, the duke balanced on legs spread wide. "You have sworn to right these wrongs? By deposing the king?"

"That is not my intent." Henry gestured to the others. "Ask them. They would not follow a usurper."

Setting his mouth, York glared at Henry's companions. They stared back at him, not giving an inch. The silence stretched uncomfortably.

Finally, the duke gave in, shaking his head. "All right. So be it. I no longer have the means to oppose you." Pausing, he raised a finger threateningly. "But do not assume I give you a free hand in this. You are bound by your word."

Allowing himself a sigh of relief, Henry put on his gloves. "I hope to convince you we mean to do the best for England's sake."

Grunting again, York sat heavily on the nearest pew. It was the dismissal Henry was waiting for. He knew that in time, he would be able to cozen his uncle. For the moment, however, it would probably be better to let him get used to his failure as regent. It wasn't York's fault. He had done the best he could, considering that the king had left him with very few resources. Luckily for Henry. Luckily for Lancaster. So far, things had gone amazingly well. Henry almost couldn't believe it.

As soon as they were outside, Percy grabbed him by the arm, reminding Henry of his obligations to his supporters. "John Beaufort is a traitor. He needs to be arrested."

Henry turned a frown on the earl. "You are mistaken, Earl Percy. He has been quietly working with us ever since Paris."

"He is a royalist! Don't let a viper into your bed!"

"No, Henry. This is not so. Listen, I have a letter from him. When we get back to our quarters, I will show it to you. He had to cover his tracks so as not to raise suspicion."

Percy was clearly unconvinced. "We shall see."

This should have been the end of their little misunderstanding, but Percy wasn't finished yet. They were camped outside of Berkeley, and when Bolingbroke showed the two Percies into his tent and pulled out the letter, the earl quickly dismissed it and sat on a stool. Henry offered him and Hotspur some wine, resigned that things were not going to be as easy as he thought.

"It's been almost two weeks since Doncaster," Percy said, stretching out his legs. "My army is expensive to maintain in the field."

Henry had wondered how long it would take before the earl talked about money. "I am most certainly aware of that," he said. "My stewards have orders to bring me what available funds they can gather, and once I reestablish myself..." He hesitated for a moment. "Once I have recovered my dukedom, you will be amply reimbursed."

"I daresay," said Percy in his most conciliating voice. "But there is something closer to our hearts I would mention to you." He nodded at his son. "One of the main reasons we are unhappy with the king is his efforts to undermine our authority in the Marches."

Henry suspected as much. Over the last couple of years, in an attempt to counteract the Percies' ambitions, Richard had removed both of them from the wardenship. In their place, he substituted a dizzying number of royal appointees who only served to destabilize the whole region. Desperate, in the last year, the king appointed Edward, the Earl of Rutland—son of the Duke of York—to the wardenship. Yet he, too, was inadequate without help. He begged the king to make Percy Warden of the Middle Marches, and still, Richard had refused.

"At the moment, there is no oversight in the North," Percy continued. "Even Rutland, ineffectual though he was, has gone to Ireland."

Pouring more wine, Henry looked askance at Percy. Of course he wouldn't take the rebel path simply to support Henry's ambitions. The earl had ambitions of his own—and big ones.

As if he was reading Bolingbroke's mind, Percy cocked his head. "I would venture to say you could use the great seal of the Duchy of Lancaster to appoint a new warden."

Ah. And so it starts. The wardenship was the gift of the king. Everyone knew that. On the other hand... "It's worth considering," Henry said finally. "Let me consult some of my attorneys."

"Fine idea." Percy stood, putting down his cup. "In the morning, then, we head to Bristol?"

Henry nodded, suddenly exhausted. He was holding the tiger by the tail. Someday, this fierce creature was bound to break loose. *Who was in control here?* Percy had decades of experience in negotiating, and Henry had almost none. He was painfully aware of his inadequacies.

When Archbishop Arundel slipped through the tent flap, acknowledging father and son on their way out, Henry felt a surge of relief. There, at least, stood a bulwark against the formidable northerners. Arundel was a complication in his own way, but Henry felt their interests were closely aligned. The archbishop needed him as much as he needed the archbishop. He couldn't say the same for the Percies, who were an entity all to themselves.

After verifying Percy was out of earshot, Arundel turned around until he found a bench to sit on. "Better," he said with a sigh. "So, what was that all about?"

"Our friend Henry Percy has enlightened me as to why he is here," Bolingbroke said wryly, "as if I didn't know already."

"Money, undoubtedly."

Grunting, Henry sat on the stool. "Naturally. And power. He suggested I use my duchy seal to appoint him Warden of the March toward Scotland."

Arundel rubbed his chin with his hand. "That man will always land on his feet. Not a bad idea, though."

Henry raised his eyebrows. "Can I do this thing?"

"It's unprecedented. On the other hand, there's no one to stop you."

"The king..."

"Unlikely, wouldn't you say? Once he is in our power."

"My uncle..."

"I just spoke at length with him," said the archbishop. "He's exhausted. At the same time, I think he's relieved. He had no interest in fighting you."

"And he's giving up the regency, just like that."

"He had little stomach for it. He kept mentioning his duty."

Henry leaned over for his wine cup. "Perhaps we can send him to Wallingford, where Queen Isabella resides. I understand he moved the important government offices there as well, for their protection."

"And he can oversee the routine tasks. I think that will suit him well."

"I don't want to try his conscience overmuch," Henry sighed. "But there's something we need to do first. We must take Bristol." They gazed at each other, considering the implications. Bristol had a large port and a well-defended castle. It was the key to South Wales. "We'll need my uncle's help."

"I think York will oblige," said the archbishop. "Now that the decision-making is out of his hands, he need only offer his countenance. As far as the castellan at Bristol is concerned, York is still regent. We can keep up the fiction a while longer."

"If I can only get there before the king," Henry added. "I wish I knew where he was."

CHAPTER 5

As they marched toward Bristol, Henry frequently looked back at his army which extended for miles; he couldn't see the end of the column. York's standard fluttered next to his own, as well as Northumberland's and Westmorland's. A band of minstrels led the way, blaring horns and pounding drums—making such a racket he almost wanted to cover his ears. But no—surely this was the best way to announce himself.

The city center of Bristol nestled in a loop created by the River Avon and its tributary, the River Frome; the narrow land entry was guarded by the castle. Having long ago outgrown its watery boundary, the city was surrounded by sprawling communities, also protected by a sturdy defensive wall. A stone bridge crossed the river, lined on both sides with tall buildings, just like back in London.

The rebel force spread out before the gates to the city. Although he had no siege equipment, Henry hoped the constable would respect the Duke of York's standard. If he chose to hold out for King Richard, things would get difficult very quickly. Henry could take the city by escalade but it would be time-consuming and a waste of resources.

York sent a herald while the leaders nudged their mounts forward. They could see some heads looking at them from the walls.

"Oyea, Oyea," the herald announced, his voice booming. "The honorable Richard, Duke of York, Henry, Duke of Lancaster, and the earls of Somerset, Northumberland, and Westmorland require entry into this city of Bristol."

Silence greeted their request, though not for long. Without any wrangling, the city gates opened. While the bulk of the army stayed outside the walls, several hundred men-at-arms accompanied the commanders. Riding in the first rank side-by-side with his uncle, Henry proceeded down the main road. The citizens paused in what they were doing to watch the cavalcade. There were no welcoming faces; at least they weren't hostile.

The castle was in the middle of the city. A moat surrounded the citadel's outer wall and the drawbridge had not been raised; they crossed it and continued down Castle Street toward the fortification. This time they weren't so fortunate; the barbican gates were firmly shut.

The Duke of York turned to Henry. "William LeScrope, Sir John Bushy, and Sir Henry Green will most certainly be inside," he said. "They rode here to meet the king. And to ensure their own safety," he added contemptuously. "Peter Courtenay is the castellan here. He has been very loyal to King Richard."

"Let's hope he has a change of heart," said Percy. "That will make it easier on everyone."

"Perhaps he's persuaded already, since the citizens haven't refused us entry," Henry ventured.

"We shall see about that." Taking matters into his own hands, Percy moved forward, gesturing for the herald to back away.

"Edmund Langley Duke of York, and Henry Bolingbroke, Duke of Lancaster and Lord High Steward of England, order you to surrender this castle." His voice echoed off the walls.

A soldier appeared atop the barbican gate. "My master Peter Courtenay, holds this castle for King Richard."

"Tell your master that Duke Henry commands an army of fifty thousand and requires the use of this castle."

The soldier disappeared. Percy sat on his horse for five minutes before running out of patience. He pulled on the reins and walked his mount back and forth in front of the wall. "I give you fair warning," he bellowed, "anyone who wishes to surrender now will be allowed to go free. Anyone who does not will be beheaded. It is your decision!" Turning, he rode back to Henry.

It didn't take long to get a response. Ropes flew from the top of the ramparts and men began climbing down, hand over hand. Hitting the ground, they dashed away. Soon, others jumped from the lower window of the castle and ran to the wall, making use of the ropes. It was too much. More men emerged, dashing across the bailey and finding escape wherever they could. The barbican gates eventually gave way and soldiers poured out, hands over their heads. Finally, Peter Courtenay came out of the castle, walking slowly as his men ran past him. He stopped before Bolingbroke and handed him the keys.

"My lord, we are ill prepared for a siege," he said. "The castle is yours." He glared at the Duke of York though refrained from saying anything more.

Nodding to the castellan, Henry rode through the gatehouse. There were no guards left to greet them, but a handful of grooms rushed forward to take their mounts. Trying to retain his sense of command, Courtenay ushered the nobles into the great hall.

"My staff is preparing a dinner for you," he said, gesturing to the tables. "I will order some wine."

Approaching the high table, Henry put a hand on his uncle's arm. "I am glad they gave us no trouble," he said. "It is not my intention to fight anyone if I can help it."

York was still disgruntled. "You may not have done any fighting, but tell that to the locals who have been plundered of all their possessions."

"What? You must tell me who they are so I can recompense them." Henry was truly concerned. This was not what he wanted.

The duke scrutinized him, seeing nothing to indicate his nephew was playing false. Somewhat mollified, he grunted. "I will do what I can. Most of my men stayed with us, at least. They believe your cause is honorable." He narrowed his eyes. "At least, if you stay the course."

"Rest assured, uncle." Henry gave him the place of honor at the table, sitting beside him. He turned as Henry Percy approached.

"Where did you go?"

"We captured LeScrope, Bushy, and Green. They were trying to flee but they didn't get far. My son is locking them into the dungeon."

Uneasily, Henry watched as a servant put a platter of mixed meats before them.

"They must be executed," Percy growled, sitting at his other side.

Henry blinked, surprised. "What's this? What have they done to warrant death by my order?"

58

"Can't you see?" The earl pulled out a knife and thrust the point into a roasted pigeon. "Those men are corrupt. They encouraged King Richard's tyranny. They were his enforcers. The people despise them. You will see; they will acclaim you for executing them!"

Despite himself, Henry grimaced. "Execution is not my aim."

Percy exchanged glances with Westmorland before taking a bite. "There are times when severity is required. These men deserve death. If you want our continued support, you must go through with this."

Sipping his wine, Henry observed Percy over the rim. *Is this how it was going to be? Was Percy going to threaten me every time he didn't get his way?* He didn't come this far to serve as Northumberland's puppet.

York was silent, and Henry could tell he was restraining himself. Those three prisoners had served him under his regency. In all likelihood, if they were put to death he would hold himself responsible. Henry looked back and forth from one man to the other. He empathized with his uncle's position. He didn't like Percy's stance, either. On the other hand, he needed the earl; it was impossible to forget that the bulk of the army came from the North.

"Listen," Percy pursued, pointing his knife, "your future hangs in the balance. As Steward of England, you have the responsibility and power to act for the security of the realm. Show the world you are strong. You must demonstrate your resolve. Let these men live, and you set a feeble precedent."

Do Percy's bidding and he will own me, Henry thought. He was about to respond when his uncle choked on his food. He thumped him on the back.

"I'm all right. I'm all right." The duke coughed into his hand.

Henry watched him for a moment, sharing his distress. *That was no accident.* York covered his embarrassment by taking a drink of wine. He put the cup down and sighed deeply. But he didn't object.

Henry reached for a loaf of bread, tearing off a piece. Perhaps Percy was right. He had to show a firmness of purpose. In the end, what really mattered was the message the king would receive. He could save a confrontation with the earl until much less was at stake.

"Very well," he sighed. "Our prisoners will serve as an example."

Satisfied, Percy made space on the bench for Hotspur. "All secure?"

The other nodded while he sat, then looked up as Courtney approached the table.

"I just heard tidings this afternoon," the castellan said, stopping before Bolingbroke. "King Richard has landed in Wales."

Henry stopped before taking a bite. "When?"

"My messenger tells me he landed at Milford Haven four days ago with a small fleet."

"I was supposed to meet him here, at Bristol," York said, shaking his head regretfully.

"It was fortunate for us he changed his mind," mused Henry. "I wonder why he stopped there."

"Perhaps he thought to gather support from Wales." The duke grimaced, still uncomfortable about changing sides. "He may still try to sail here."

"He could." Henry was relieved to hear the tidings—any tidings. Now he could finally start making plans. "Depends on how well informed he keeps himself. I think he will find he has limited choices. His approach to Bristol by land will be challenged. I have many estates along the southern coast of Wales and I have already sent them messages. My castles up and down the Wye valley are well-armed and will resist any loyalist approach. Now that Bristol is under my flag, he will have no reason to come here."

"What, then?" asked York.

Suddenly the bread tasted better. Henry chewed for a minute before answering. "Chester. That's what I would do. We'll just have to get there first."

It was time for the tribunal. Henry knew he was exceeding his authority in declaring anyone traitor. Although Bushy and Green were mere knights—no matter how close to the king—William

LeScrope was Earl of Wiltshire and treasurer of England. Only the king had the authority to execute him. But who was going to stop him now?

Henry sat at a table with the two Percies, Archbishop Arundel and the Duke of York. The three prisoners were led into the room then pushed onto their knees. They were tied together, their clothes in disarray, hair hanging lankly about their faces. Their eyes were dull, their expressions hopeless.

Bolingbroke looked hard at the captives. "For decades you have served the House of Lancaster," he said accusingly, "and yet now you are accomplices to the seizure of my inheritance. You, William LeScrope. What gave you the right to take over my castle and Honour of Pickering?"

"And you," interrupted Percy, not giving LeScrope a chance to answer. He leaned forward over the table, pointing a finger at Bushy and Green. "Did you think I would just stand by and watch you steal my estates on the Scottish Marches? First, you mishandled the truce we worked so hard to establish, then you seized lands in the king's name."

Archbishop Arundel put a hand on Percy's shoulder, wanting his turn. "I haven't forgotten your vicious attacks on my brother Richard at the Parliament of 1397. Then you turned your attention to me and accused me of treason. I was given no chance to defend myself. For that alone, Sir John Bushy, you deserve death!"

Bushy's mouth worked, yet he restrained himself. The only thing he had left was his dignity; he wouldn't diminish it with useless objections. Outside the window, the crowd was roaring— and they weren't begging for the prisoners to be set free.

Bolingbroke stood. "As Lord High Steward of England I condemn you to death," he said, gesturing his dismissal. "Take these men and remove their heads." He frowned as the prisoners were dragged away. When they reached the castle bailey, the crowd's frenzy redoubled.

"See what I mean?" said Percy, well-pleased with himself. "This will only increase your popularity. I recommend you send their heads to London, where they are most hated."

Henry glared at the earl, disliking what Percy had made him do. What was he becoming? Where once he was the dutiful son, the carefree traveler, the champion jouster, now he was a murderer who ordered a man's execution with the wave of his hand.

However, Percy's judgment concerning London was sound. With the archbishop's help, Henry composed a letter: "*I, Henry of Lancaster, Duke of Hereford and Earl of Derby, commend myself to all the people of London, high and low. My good friends, I send you my salutations and I am letting you know I have come over to take my rightful inheritance. I beg you, let me know whether you are on my side or not. I don't care which, because I have enough men to fight all the world for one day, thank God!*" His eyes unfathomable, Henry looked up at Percy. Then he wrote a last sentence: "*Either way, accept this gift I am sending you.*"

The executioner entered the room with the three heads in a basket, covered by a cloth. Henry refused to look at them. He handed the letter to Percy. "See that it is sent, my lord."

At that moment, Henry felt a little part of himself—the merciful part—dry up and fade away. There was no turning back. These executions had his name attached to them; no one else would be held accountable. Henceforth, all decisions needed be his—no more bending his will to Henry Percy. Or anyone else, for that matter. He alone would be responsible for judgments affecting the whole of England. From now on, Lancaster was a man to be reckoned with.

"What shall be our next step?" Henry asked the room, in general, to get the discussion started. He was anxious to put the unpleasant tribunal behind him.

As chancellor, the archbishop had long ago proven himself a master of strategy. He stood, taking charge. "Until we know what the king is going to do, we cannot act decisively. Once he learns we have taken Bristol, I wouldn't be surprised if he boarded a ship back to Ireland. Or to France, to get help from his father in-law." He started pacing. "If he decides to stay in England and march to Chester, like Duke Henry suggested, he will want to stay as far away from us as possible. And so...it makes sense he might travel north along the west coast of Wales and take shelter in one or more of the castles that have access to the sea."

"That would put the Cambrian mountains between him and us," said Henry.

"Exactly. We would have to send many scouts to find him."

"On the other hand, it would not be easy for him to drag an army across the wilds of Wales. Not with those roads."

"If you could even call them that. More like animal tracks." Arundel smiled. There was a smattering of laughter.

"How much of his army could he have brought back from Ireland, on short notice?" Henry wondered.

The Duke of York leaned forward. "I was able to collect about fifty ships in July. His own fleet would have been dismissed as soon as he disembarked—or at least most of it. What's left to him would have to make multiple voyages back and forth. I'd say each trip would take a couple of days, weather permitting. It won't be easy for him to hold his army together."

"We can't just sit here and wait for him to grow his forces. King Richard is very resourceful and we dare not underestimate him."

"Granted," Arundel said. "We won't make that mistake again." Just the thought of his unexpected exile made him cringe. "I say we move north into regions friendly both to Lancaster and Arundel. We have many allies who will offer us sustenance."

"And perhaps it would serve us best to take the city of Chester," Henry concluded. "The center of Richard's influence. I can't think of a better way to forestall him."

It didn't take long for them to get moving. York went east, agreeing to stop at Wallingford to visit Queen Isabella on his way to London. The army moved north along the Welsh Marches, back to Gloucester where they crossed the Severn, then northwest to Hereford. Everywhere he stopped Henry was approached by anxious locals—Lancastrian and Ricardian—more than pleased to accept annuities from him out of his ducal revenues. Loyalties were easily purchased when the alternative was to be plundered.

When they reached Hereford on 2 August, Bolingbroke was welcomed by the bishop and offered hospitality for the night. He and his noble followers were well-fed while the army encamped outside the city walls. Only Percy's surly face marred an otherwise relaxing evening. After exchanging a few pleasantries with Hotspur, Henry finally moved over to the earl, pulling him aside.

63

"What is it?" he asked.

Percy grimaced. "I can't help but notice the excessive annuities you are distributing, while our troops have to forage for their meals."

Henry suppressed a frown. "Their loyalty is critical to our cause."

"Do you realize how much money you are spending?"

Gesturing his dismissal, Henry changed the subject. "I've made a decision. Tomorrow I will grant you the Wardenship of the West Marches toward Scotland. The archbishop agreed I could do so under my ducal seal. My secretary is drafting the warrant as we speak."

As expected, Percy's objections evaporated. It was fortunate this appointment was as necessary as it was rewarding. The Northerners had customs all their own that outsiders just couldn't understand. Percy's family had been major landowners since shortly after the Conquest; their sway over local politics couldn't be doubted. There must be a way to temper their ambitions while benefitting from Percy's influence.

As the earl turned to his son, Henry looked across the room at Westmorland, deep in conversation with the archbishop. Ralph Neville was a new earl with considerably less authority than Percy. Still, his family had lived in the North for generations, as well. He could be the very man to offset Percy's pretensions. Having Neville as a brother in-law didn't hurt; that should secure his loyalty—and he was biddable. Walking over to the pair, Henry pulled up a chair and joined their theological discussion. No point in worrying about future conflicts. He had enough problems to keep him busy right now.

CHAPTER 6

The army spent three nights in Hereford, waiting to hear from Henry's scouts. Finally, they moved forward to Shrewsbury, on the way to Chester. This city held troubled memories for Henry. It was here during the king's infamous Revenge Parliament that Bolingbroke and Thomas Mowbray accused each other of treason. Henry still didn't understand how their dispute got so far out of control. It was the beginning of the end for both of them, precipitating the famous trial by combat that never happened and sending them into exile instead.

Henry was relieved to find one of his scouts waiting for him. Anxious for information, the others gathered quickly. Henry was already pacing. "We've finally discovered his whereabouts," he said, relief in his voice. "Apparently the king has left his army in south Wales, for our scout saw him traveling secretly with only fifteen companions. He was discovered just above Aberystwyth, traveling up the coast. You were right, Thomas."

"Only fifteen?" Arundel was astonished.

"And disguised as a friar. Our scout verified it was him with some locals."

"Imagine that!" The archbishop shook his head. "He is either frantic or desperate."

"Since he didn't leave the country while in Milford Haven, we can assume he intends to stay," said Percy.

"And do what?" Henry scratched his cheek. "What could he possibly have in mind?"

"At least we can put together some kind of plan," Arundel said. "It seems we are both heading in the same direction."

Further speculation brought them nowhere. It wasn't until later in the evening that Bolingbroke had his real answer. Having eaten a light meal, he and Percy were concentrating on a game of chess when the door opened the earl looked up, casually interested. Suddenly, he jumped to his feet, knocking over his chair.

"Thomas!"

Henry whirled around. There at the door stood Thomas Percy, Earl of Worcester, and Edward, Earl of Rutland, looking harried and hungry. They had both gone to Ireland with the king and no one knew where they ended up at this confused juncture. Percy dashed forward and embraced his brother.

"Look at you, man! Where have you come from?"

Trying to smile—and failing—Worcester grasped his brother's hand. He was two years younger than the earl and had proven himself the ablest if least flamboyant member of his family. He had chosen a military career followed by a diplomatic one, which ultimately put him at the king's right hand. Worcester had been steward of the royal household for the last six years and had been created earl after the king's last parliament. Throughout he maintained a becoming modesty which had made him many friends.

"It's been a long way," he said. "We rode from Carmarthen."

"Carmarthen? South Wales?" Percy glanced at Henry. "I'm relieved to see you, but I don't understand. What has happened?"

Rutland went over to the table, sitting heavily. He reached for an apple and took a big bite. "My God, where do we start? Is my father here?" He was the eldest son of the Duke of York and one of Richard's closest companions—as well as cousin to both Henry and the king.

Henry poured him an ale. "Your father is on his way to Wallingford, then on to London."

Rutland nodded, disappointed.

Worcester joined them as others came into the room. Arundel sat next to him. "This is a surprise. Did Richard send you?"

The other grimaced. "No, no. We have come to join you."

"Then you are even more welcome," said Henry, pouring another ale. "How many men did you bring?"

"Just a handful," said Rutland. "You see, Richard's army fell apart shortly after we landed in Milford Haven." He hesitated, then took a sip.

"The men had no heart for a fight," Worcester finished for him.

"And the king?" asked Henry.

"Before he left Ireland he sent the Earl of Salisbury to Conwy to raise an army. Richard had planned to link up with the Duke of York and march north. We were trying to raise additional troops from South Wales. But when word reached us you had taken Bristol...once we learned that the Duke of York—" Worcester glanced at Rutland. He took a deep breath. "When we learned he had joined your, uh, campaign, the king decided his best choice was to unite with Salisbury. He chose to make the journey overland with a small following so they would lose no time."

"Ah, that explains it," said Percy. His brother looked questioningly at him.

"Just today we learned of the king's whereabouts. We couldn't understand what he was doing."

Henry put his elbow on the table, his cheek on his hand. He was deep in thought. "How could it have happened?"

Clearing his throat, Worcester hung his head. He was ashamed at his own part in abandoning the king. "Things did not go well. His ships were scattered. Everything was disorganized. The king was confounded." He didn't dare go into detail; Richard was distraught at the execution of his closest officials. Though it wouldn't help to accuse Bolingbroke now.

"He left secretly, in the night," Rutland said, taking up the narrative. "Those in his army who had not deserted took it very badly the next morning when they found out he was missing. I don't need to tell you they felt abandoned." He hesitated. "I had received a letter from my father, telling me the king's cause was hopeless." Again, he and Worcester exchanged glances. "Neither one of us wanted to fight against our own family..."

"There was nothing more we could do," said the other. "I broke the staff of office across my knee and disbanded the king's household. What was left of it."

Percy moved over to him, sitting at his side. "I was worried about you. I'm right glad you made that decision. King Richard didn't deserve your loyalty."

Henry noted the pain in Worcester's eyes. He could see the answer wasn't so simple. "I will arrange lodging for you in the castle. You'll be needing a bath!" Standing, he put a hand on the earl's shoulder. "I will call on you later."

As Bolingbroke went in search of the steward, Arundel leaned over. "So Salisbury is raising an army near Conwy, you say?"

Rutland nodded. "That was the plan. The king is relying on his loyal supporters in North Wales, and in the Palatinate of Chester."

"Why didn't the king go there himself?"

Clearing his throat, Rutland poured more ale. Actually, the king had wanted to go with Salisbury and he's the one who talked Richard out of it. "We were in the middle of a campaign. His forces were scattered. He needed time to gather what resources we could before returning, instead of just running off. Besides, he thought my father was waiting for him at Bristol. It made sense to meet up with him there and march to Chester with a second army. So Salisbury went ahead." He frowned, looking at his hands. They were clenched around his mug.

Fortunately, Arundel accepted his explanation. He wouldn't have to defend himself further.

"Things progressed very quickly," the archbishop said. "Henry met few obstacles. Even your father's army deserted in great numbers. He had nothing to stop us with."

"So it all depends on Salisbury, then," Rutland mused. "Perhaps the king was right in hurrying north."

"We shall see. It's in God's hands."

Later that evening, as Worcester was getting ready to retire, a knock on his door was followed by Henry himself—alone. He stood but the duke gestured for him to sit.

"I wanted to thank you for joining us," Henry said quietly. "Yours was not an easy decision."

Surprised at Henry's understanding, Worcester had to fight back tears. "King Richard has treated me very well," he sighed. "I feel no animosity toward him. Still, these last couple of years, he seems to have lost his way."

Henry couldn't agree more. But he knew better than to interrupt.

"He was afraid it would all happen again." Thomas spoke so softly Henry had to step forward to hear him. "Destroying the Lords Appellant wasn't enough. He saw enemies at every turn. No amount of oath-taking and forced pardons could make him feel safe from his subjects." He glanced up. "And now look what happened. Everything he feared came true, and he brought it about, himself." Startled at his own words, he blinked. "I don't fault you, my lord. You did what any wronged nobleman would do. Once I heard my brother and nephew had joined you, I couldn't in good conscience fight against them."

"I do understand. And I value your trust in me. I know you served with my father in Spain and Gascony."

"Yes." Reminiscing, Worcester couldn't help a smile. "He was a good man, your father, and a good friend."

"I hope to be a good friend to you as well." Henry moved to leave.

The other put out a hand, stopping him. "I trust you will treat Richard fairly."

Henry nodded. "I have come back to reclaim my own. The archbishop as well. We seek justice, nothing more."

Dropping his hand, Worcester nodded, watching the duke open the door. He leaned back, suppressing a sigh. He knew he wasn't the only one with conflicting loyalties. Though it would have been so much easier if Richard hadn't taken him into his confidence. How does one excuse a breach of trust?

Could he ever forgive himself?

Throughout the night, other refugees from Richard's army trickled in, some with only the clothes on their backs, stripped of their weapons, supplies, and the rumored plunder from the king's own wagons. The Welsh had been thorough in taking advantage of the disintegration of Richard's army. As far as they were concerned, England's problems had nothing to do with them.

69

This was only a distraction to Henry; the stragglers would be absorbed into his own forces.

The next morning provided him with a real surprise. Sir Robert Leigh, sheriff of Chester, showed up at Shrewsbury with a small party of aldermen. Quickly donning his best garments and his ducal coronet, Henry met the newcomers in the great hall of the castle, accompanied by his supporters. The Cheshiremen bowed deeply.

"My lord," said Leigh, stepping forward, "we are here because the Earl of Salisbury has succeeded in raising a large force of men loyal to the king. Once he moved his army to Conwy Castle, we felt that Cheshire might find itself with no defense between warring factions. Hence, the members of our city have voted to submit ourselves willingly to you, under certain conditions."

"How many men has Salisbury raised?" asked Henry, starting to pace.

The sheriff looked at his companions. "We're not sure, my Lord."

"That would help both of us if you know. But go on. I welcome your frankness."

Leigh cleared his throat. "Because we are submitting by mediation rather than force," he continued, "our condition is that you proclaim to your army that the people and the county will be spared."

Such a Godsend! It was much better to enter the city as a welcome guest than an occupying army. Pretending to consult his advisors, Henry took his time in answering. Finally, he drew himself up. "Very well. Tomorrow I will put out a proclamation to leave Chester and your county at peace. Prepare the city. In two days we will make our entrance."

The following morning Bolingbroke sent out heralds to every segment of his army, forbidding them to break the peace. No killing, burning, or plundering was to be permitted. Nothing was to be taken except victuals for men and horses in return for payment.

Hotspur was the one who returned with the news. "I've just come from the field," he told Henry. "It seems some of our men have gone home. They were disgruntled that there was no plunder to be had. Rascals!"

Henry looked up from a pile of petitions. "Can't be helped. Too bad we don't know the size of Salisbury's force. We may regret losing them." He nodded, apparently coming to a decision. "Harry, I would like to put you in charge of all the forces. I dare say they will prove a challenge."

The other brightened. "You may rely on me. They have already shown signs of unruliness."

Pursing his lips, Henry shrugged. "Do what you can. I know many of our men hold grudges against Richard's Cheshire archers. They may take matters into their own hands."

Bolingbroke's army moved on to Chester 8 August. They proceeded directly to the castle, where Sheriff Leigh was waiting for them, anxious to share his news.

"My lord," he said, barely sketching a bow. "We've had a great turn of events." He threw back his shoulders, much more confident than the previous day.

"Oh?" Henry pulled off his livery tabard, handing it to a page. "What happened?"

"We sent scouts to investigate the size of Salisbury's army. Your grace, they have dispersed!"

"What?" All talking stopped as men turned toward the sheriff.

"The wait was too long. Fearing the approach of your army and believing rumors that the king was dead, the new recruits disbanded. Salisbury couldn't hold his forces together and they slipped away, though he begged them to stay. Just two days later, King Richard showed up at Conwy Castle with a handful of followers, only to see an empty field."

Henry stared in disbelief. "You are telling me the king is holed up at Conwy Castle without an army? God is surely with us." He crossed himself before turning to Henry Percy. "We must get him into our hands before he flees the country."

The possibilities were staggering. King Richard had just turned from a threat to a fugitive.

"Harry," he said, grasping Hotspur's arm. "Do you know what this means? The king deposited part of his treasury at Holt Castle. We need to secure it before it falls into the wrong hands."

71

Hotspur nodded in agreement; Holt was ten miles south of Chester, an easy distance for a mounted force. "There is no time to waste. I'll take a small detachment and demand entrance."

"If they refuse, we can reinforce you," said Henry.

Eager for action, Hotspur bowed and left.

"I don't think he will have any trouble," Henry said, turning to Percy. He was about to say more when he noticed the earl was looking over his shoulder. Whirling around, Henry gasped in amazement. Surrounded by guards, John and Tom Holland were escorted into the room.

"What a day full of surprises!" Henry exclaimed. These were the last people he expected to see, for they, too, had gone to Ireland with the king. He strode up to them, grasping John's hand. *Could it be they were joining him, like Rutland and Worcester?* After all, John had married his sister. It was possible.

Looking sheepish for a moment, Holland gave him a half-smile. "We just arrived today, like yourself it appears. We come from the king."

Oh, so that's how it is. With great effort, Henry hid his disappointment. He smiled, knowing it must have looked forced. "Welcome, both of you. Come, sit. We just discovered the sheriff has left us a cellar full of his best wine."

Silently, the Hollands followed Henry to the table, glancing at his companions. The archbishop eyed them suspiciously and Percy was equally dubious. Rutland and Worcester sat at the foot of the table; their guilty expressions gave them away.

Looking at the sour faces, Henry dropped his friendly pretense. "My son?" he asked. He hadn't heard from Hal since his exile.

After glaring at Rutland, John Holland brought his attention back to Bolingbroke. "Hal? Richard left him at Trim Castle with Humphrey, Gloucester's boy. For their protection."

"Was he all right?"

"The king was very fond of him. You know, your son promises to be a great warrior one day. In fact, Richard knighted him."

"In Ireland?" Henry felt a pang of jealousy. *He* should have been involved in his son's knighting, not his enemy.

Archbishop Arundel had no patience for this small talk. He leaned forward. "Tell us, I pray you, what news do you bring?"

John lowered his eyes. "None, that is very good for my lord. It leaves me most sorrowful and distressed."

Henry exchanged glances with Arundel. "Go on, John."

"The king has been confounded at every turn. We left him at Conwy with a small retinue of loyal men—" he glanced at Rutland— "but he sent us with a message. He hopes you bear in mind your fidelity to your king. If you go through with this rebellion you will bring great shame to yourself and scandal to your lineage forever. You will be hated by all who love honor and loyalty. On the other hand, if you do your duty and refrain from this disobedience, the king will heartily and freely pardon you and return your land and substance."

Henry let out a sigh. "That was well-rehearsed. You have spoken much to the purpose."

Taking heart, John continued. "I beseech you, brother in-law, give us your answer, for the king is anxiously expecting us."

He was taken aback when Henry abruptly stood.

"By God, you shall go neither today nor next week. It was not right for the king to send you here. What was he thinking? Couldn't he find anyone else but you two?"

"I offered to come," said John, shaken. "Richard knew you would not harm us."

"And he was right."

"So you must let us return. The king will think we are betraying him. He will never forgive us."

"That can't be helped," interjected Percy.

"Please, my lord. This isn't right." John couldn't believe this was happening. "I entreat you, for honor's sake, let us be gone."

"Speak no more of this. Norbury," he said with a gesture. "Take these men and put them in comfortable confinement. After that, arrange for a ship to sail at once. We need to bring back my son from Ireland." He put a hand on Holland's arm. "John, you must be patient for now."

The room was filled with anticipation. As the prisoners were led away, Henry put his hands on his hips. "This is truly a delicate situation. At any moment Richard could take ship and be gone. How shall we proceed?"

The archbishop was the first to speak. "We don't want to be seen bearing arms against the king. However, I see nothing wrong with sending a deputation to negotiate with him. I believe there is no other way to bring him forth. We shall make fair promises and gain his confidence."

Nodding, Henry raised his eyebrows at Worcester. The other cleared his throat. "I suspect King Richard will rely on his regality to carry the day."

Accepting this, Henry glanced at Rutland. "The archbishop has given us good counsel," the other said.

One by one the others concurred. Satisfied, Bolingbroke sat next to Henry Percy. "I agree this is a good plan. I propose that my cousin, the Earl of Northumberland, set out tomorrow early in the morning."

Percy was more than willing. "By reason or by craft I will bring him," he said.

"Good. Take four hundred lances and a thousand archers; make sure they are very diligent. I shall stay at Chester until you return, or until I hear from you. Sir Thomas Erpingham, will you go with him?"

"Gladly, my lord."

"Then it is settled. We all know Richard has been in difficult situations before and has managed to wriggle out of them. We must not underestimate him."

Henry Percy took a sip of his wine, thinking. "We must not let him know I have seen the Hollands."

Henry agreed. "The less he knows the better."

While making plans for his departure in the morning, Percy was troubled by Bolingbroke's attitude. It's not that he had done anything blatantly unacceptable; but there was a new edge to his demeanor—as though he felt himself above his fellow nobles. They weren't partners anymore; they were his subordinates. Did he think himself king already?

All this talk about reclaiming Henry's patrimony: it was nothing more than pretense. Lancaster using them all for his own personal gain. That was painfully obvious. On the other hand, if Bolingbroke wanted to go for the crown, Percy was well-positioned to benefit. Why else would he support a rebel? Let Henry take on the stigma of usurpation, if that's what he wanted. Northumberland would keep his hands clean.

Tying his traveling pack, Percy stopped for a moment to study his signet ring. He had won and lost the wardenship too often in the last ten years. Perhaps this time around he could achieve his goals, if he gave Lancaster proper guidance. As what? Advisor to King Henry? He grimaced, not liking the sound of that. Couldn't they achieve the same end by bringing King Richard under their complete control—like the last time? Wouldn't that be better?

He couldn't help the nagging impression that Henry didn't really appreciate his efforts. He would have to ensure his position was unassailable. He would have to make himself indispensable. Henry must be made to understand he could be taken down as easily as he was raised up. After all, he was setting his own precedent.

With these thoughts in mind, Percy sought out the duke. It was time to solidify their plans.

Henry was waiting for him in his solar. He was writing a letter and put down his quill, gesturing to a chair. "Sit, my friend. Who would have thought, a mere month ago, we would be so close?"

Grunting, Percy obliged, reaching for a pitcher of ale. He poured the golden liquid into an empty cup and took a deep draught, wiping his mouth with his sleeve. "The worst is yet to come. How are we going to convince the king to give himself up?"

"Once you assure him I have no designs on the crown, that pledge should remove his most serious doubts."

"Can I assure him of this in good faith?"

Henry looked shocked at the question though Percy doubted his sincerity. "Nothing has changed," said the duke.

"Do you give me your word?"

"Of course I do!" Fighting his annoyance, Henry pushed his papers aside and leaned over the table. "You will tell the king I desire we be friends for all time. I seek nothing more than to regain my inheritance." He paused, thinking. "To give him a semblance of control, you might also petition him to restore the

Stewardship of England to me." He laughed shortly. "Though by God I will never give it up. It's been in my family for generations."

Percy leaned back in his chair. "I think we need to go farther than that. I see no reason for him to comply."

"You could be right." Henry scratched his forehead. "We must give him something to negotiate with."

They both sat in silence for a moment until Henry slapped the table. "I've got it. Tell him I will humbly bend my knee before him and sue for mercy. He'll like that." Now that his mind was on the subject, Bolingbroke's face clouded. "But he cannot escape unscathed. Tell him he must arrest all those who counseled him to put my uncle Gloucester to death. If these men deny their guilt, they can await the judgment of parliament, which we shall call in his name. In fact, I intend to call parliament for the end of next month. I shall act as chief judge there, as my father had done, and those who have been found guilty of treason shall be punished without partiality."

"Who is to be arrested?"

"You decide. It matters not. Maudeleyn, perhaps, or the Hollands. Not Rutland!" He smiled awkwardly. "He's redeeming himself. Regardless, Richard will find a way to evade the issue. It's all pretense, anyway. We just need to get him into our hands."

Grimacing, Percy shrugged. "Won't that put him on the defensive?"

"If we make it too easy for him, he'll be suspicious. Best to give him a distraction. Let him think he can find his own way to London after he meets me in Chester, and all he'll be thinking about is escape. And of course, you won't let that happen."

"Hmm."

"We certainly don't want to scare him off. He must be convinced he will still retain his crown."

"Will he?"

"Didn't we discuss that already?" A note of exasperation slipped through. "At length?" He pursed his lips, letting his breath out through his nose. "When you bring him back, I'll deal with him directly."

"All right." Percy stood. "By hook or by crook, I'll persuade him to come."

"I will wait here at Chester. I suggest you detain him at Flint Castle, and when I hear from you I will come. With a cavalcade."

Bowing briefly, Percy turned to leave.

"Erpingham is waiting to accompany you," Henry added. The other gestured his acknowledgment, already halfway out the door.

Bolingbroke grimaced, knowing he could have handled things better. "Godspeed," he said to the earl's back. This was the most important part of their whole plan, and he was leaving it in the hands of an unscrupulous emissary. Of course, perhaps that's just what the situation demanded. Percy was clever and resourceful. The man's job was straightforward—unlike his own.

What was he going to do next?

CHAPTER 7

Left alone, Henry retrieved his parchment and dipped his quill into the inkwell. He had almost finished a letter to the duke and duchess of Brittany when Percy interrupted him. It was just as well; he had so much to say to Joanna his heart was bursting. But it was only appropriate to write to the both of them, and as a result he had much less to say. He would have to be satisfied she knew she was in his thoughts.

"*My enterprise proceeds well*," he wrote. "*King Richard has been abandoned by two armies and awaits his fate at Conwy Castle. The whole country is behind me and cries out for remedy. The Earl of Northumberland is on his way from Chester to reason with the king and persuade him to surrender himself into our hands. I pray to God that all will be achieved without turmoil.*"

Folding the parchment, he dripped a dollop of wax and applied his signet. *This could be one of my last moments of peace,* he thought. Once the king was in his hands, he would have to decide how to proceed—and how to justify himself. He was under no illusions. Richard had to be confined. How else could he be persuaded to give up his prerogative? And once he was confined, what to do next? Could they really control him for the rest of his life?

More importantly, how could they stop the king from wreaking revenge in the future? Richard had proven all too clearly there was no limit to his vindictiveness. He was a patient man. And an unforgiving one, as the Lords Appellant had learned long after they thought they were pardoned. Two dead, one imprisoned, and two exiled.

Fortunately, Henry's disturbing thoughts were interrupted by the entrance of Hotspur, just back from Holt Castle. Sweeping into the room, Harry dramatically dropped a sack onto the table with a thump. A handful of gold coins fell out, rolling across the wooden surface.

"What a treasure!" Harry exclaimed. "We have recovered 100,000 marks, as well as a horde of jewels and plate. Not to mention piles of arms and armor."

"Ah!" Henry leaned back, not even trying to hide his relief. "Now I can pay your men and quit begging favors from every lord I meet. Welcome news indeed!"

Reaching for the half-empty pitcher of ale, Hotspur sat across from Bolingbroke, using the same cup his father left behind. "We brought it back in wagons. Although Holt Castle was well built for defense, the garrison had no stomach for it. They opened the gates without a fight as soon as I announced we came in your name."

"Well, even better tidings! Our cause gets stronger every day." Henry hesitated. "Did you see your father?"

"No. I came directly to you." Harry took a sip.

"He is going to persuade the king to join us."

"Oh? That will take some persuading." He narrowed his eyes. "By force?"

"No, no. He will negotiate."

Considering this for a moment, Hotspur put down the cup. "I should find him before he's gone. Shall I accompany him?"

"No, my friend. I need you here. We have so many new recruits I don't know what to do with them all."

Hotspur was full of energy, regardless of his long ride. He got up to leave.

Henry admired his stamina. "Stay for a moment. When your father brings back the king, he will tarry at Flint and send for us. It should only take a few days. I plan to ride there in force to meet the king on my terms. I'll need you to put together a contingent for us."

"As you wish. We will be ready."

Then he was gone, as quickly as he came.

Henry sighed. Of all his allies, the Percies promised to be the most difficult—and the most necessary. What would he do without them?

On the morning of the fifth day, Erpingham arrived with Percy's summons. All was in readiness, and before long Henry was on the road to Flint Castle with a large retinue. Leaving the Hollands in comfortable confinement, he took Rutland and Worcester with him. They followed the coastal road fourteen miles to their destination. As they got close to Flint, Henry ordered his minstrels to play as loud as they could. Trumpets blared, cymbals clashed, and bagpipes out-blew them all. Henry wanted to make sure Richard knew they were coming.

Flint Castle stood just on the Welsh side of the Dee's tidal estuary. Unique in its construction, Flint's fourth massive corner tower served as a keep—a fortified residence and last refuge in case of attack. Henry's party was very close when Percy rode across the drawbridge to meet them with a handful of knights. Bolingbroke raised his arm and the earl stopped to wait for him. Henry could see he was tired but triumphant.

"How goes the king?" asked Henry.

Percy looked back. They could see heads watching from the battlements.

"He bemoans his fate," said Percy, unsympathetically, "but he is easy to manage. All the fight has gone out of him."

"For now," Henry muttered.

"You will see. He has few supporters, and nowhere to turn."

Henry nodded, considering. Then he beckoned Archbishop Arundel forward. "Thomas, I think you should prepare him for me. Go on ahead and speak with him. Don't be too hard on the poor man," he said wryly. "He has a lot to answer for, though we don't want to frighten him too much!"

Arundel had been storing up recriminations for two years. He shook his shoulders to rid himself of unworthy impulses. "He's lucky I am a man of God. You are right, of course. I'm not the only one he has wronged."

"Take Worcester and Rutland with you," Henry added, gesturing to them. "I want the king to understand without a doubt that he has lost their support, as well."

Already fidgeting under Henry's livery, the two earls exchanged glances. The last thing they needed was to confront Richard. However, there was no helping it; they had committed themselves.

As the little party crossed the drawbridge again, Henry and Percy moved aside to speak alone.

"We have him. What next?" Percy said.

Henry frowned. The earl had just repeated the very words he had said to himself. "We will take him back to Chester with us. There is still much to do. I assume you mentioned parliament to Richard?"

"Oh, yes. And he made me swear an oath that you will not take the crown."

"An oath?" Henry's frown turned into a grimace. "How very like him. We could paper the great hall at Westminster with all the oaths we have sworn." He shrugged one shoulder, trying to release the tension in his neck. "How badly did he resist you?"

"He wanted to bargain with me. After I told him you only wanted your titles and inheritance back, of course he insisted you disband your army. I countered with your demand that he arrest the men who counseled him to put Gloucester to death. I accused John and Tom Holland, the Earl of Salisbury, the Bishop of Carlisle, and Maudeleyn."

"Ha! At least three of those men were with him, weren't they?"

"It certainly gave him pause. That's when I mentioned calling a parliament to try the scoundrels. He still hesitated, so I offered to swear an oath to the truth of your statement." His lip curled. "He made me wait a day and a half before answering."

Henry's horse made a restless sidestep and he patted its neck. "Then he agreed to come?"

"I only had a few men with me and he didn't feel threatened. It wasn't until we reached Colwyn Bay that Sir Thomas Erpingham revealed himself with the rest of my troops. By then, we had surrounded the king and he was in no position to get away. He lost all will to fight and has been submissive ever since."

The two fell silent for a moment. Henry looked out over the estuary—an expanse of mud, sand, water channels, and marsh grasses. A pair of herons picked their way through the shallow water, looking for fish. Low grey clouds threatened rain. The air was heavy with the smell of salt and rotting plants.

He scratched his nose. "You did very well, cousin. I don't think anyone could have managed better. I'm sure he won't agree to arrest his supporters." He waved his dismissal. "It's no matter. We have more important issues to address. As soon as we get back to Chester, we'll send out summonses for parliament to be held the end of next month. After we finish our business, we'll need to escort the king to London."

Percy looked askance at him. "As king or prisoner?"

There was no longer any opportunity to avoid the issue. Looking pained, Henry gripped his Steward's baton. "Until we have sorted things out, he must be kept under lock and key."

"No letting him find his own way to London."

Henry shrugged. "A necessary inducement. By the time he leaves Chester, he'll already know that option never existed." He took a deep breath, coming to a decision. "I think we should dispense with the show of homage. He is our prisoner; let us treat him so."

For once, Percy was shocked. "What, do you want us to bind him?"

"No. Nothing so extreme. I would take his magnificent horse and give him a palfrey instead."

"I don't know. That sounds too spiteful."

"Does it? It would establish our position perfectly."

"Do you really think that's necessary?"

Henry gave Percy a probing look. "Why pretend otherwise? But look. Here's what I propose: let us consider this a trial. If King Richard protests, we'll know he hasn't accepted his situation and we'll have to deal with him accordingly. If he doesn't object, we'll know we've got him."

Percy looked down at his hands. "I don't like it."

"Why not?"

"It strips him of all his dignity. He will never forget."

"Then we'll have to make sure he's never in a position to take his revenge."

They stared at each other, further words unspoken. Neither one was entirely sure how far he could push the other.

When Arundel returned, Henry observed him curiously. The archbishop wasn't exactly satisfied, yet he seemed more at peace with himself. He stopped his mount, facing the others.

"The king wants to partake of his dinner before meeting you."

Henry nodded. "Is that all?"

The other sneered. "I did all the talking. Yes, I restrained myself but I couldn't resist an accusation or two. He was at his most vulnerable. It was like beating a dead horse."

"It sounds like I won't have much trouble with him."

"I don't think so. At least until he regains his composure."

"If he ever does," said Percy. "He couldn't imagine that the whole country would turn against him. You could almost feel sorry for him." He shook his head. "Almost."

While waiting for his prisoners to finish their meal, Bolingbroke ordered his whole army forward to surround the castle. Finally, he rode over the drawbridge with the archbishop and nobles—eleven in all. "This shouldn't take long," Henry said to Percy.

The Lancastrian herald rode first into the bailey. On his approach, two men rushed forward, dropping to their knees. "My lord," said one of them in a French accent, "my companion and I have been visiting from King Charles's court, and we are caught in the middle of this situation. For the love of our Lord, would you help save our lives and bring us to Duke Henry your master?"

Taking pity on the distressed Frenchmen, the herald leaned forward, raising them up. "What is your name?"

"Jean Creton, if it pleases you, and my companion is Etienne Dubois."

"Well, monsieur Creton. Stay with me and I will do so right willingly."

They turned as Henry and the others came through the archway. Henry was dressed in full armor without his helmet, wearing a bonnet instead. The herald immediately led the two forward and once again they knelt. Henry looked at them inquiringly.

"These two men are from France," the herald said, "and their king had sent them to King Richard for recreation and to see the country. They sincerely request you to spare their lives."

Smiling, Henry answered them in French. "Fear not, my friends. Don't be dismayed by aught that you see, and keep close to me. I will answer for your lives."

Relieved, Jean gave one last glance backward as Richard and his little group of supporters came down the stairs. The Frenchmen slipped into the crowd behind Bolingbroke. Although he felt guilty for being a coward, Creton swore to himself that he would tell the world what really happened—after he was safely back in France.

King Richard was dressed in a friar's robe, looking even more humble than his followers. His face was shadowed by his hood. As he stopped across the bailey from the newcomers, he watched Henry bow deeply. Then they slowly approached each other, while Henry removed his bonnet and bowed a second time. In response, the king pulled off his own hood.

"Fair cousin of Lancaster," Richard said, "you are right welcome." His long face indicated the opposite.

Henry didn't care. Bowing a third time, he kept up pretenses. "My lord, I have come before you sent for me and I will tell you why. The people say you have governed them badly these last several years, and they are greatly discontented. But if it pleases our Lord, with the consent of the Commons I will help you govern them better than in times past."

Knowing he was at a disadvantage, Richard bit back his bile. "Fair cousin," he answered, almost choking on his words, "since it pleases you, it pleases us well."

Henry nodded to Bishop Merks and the two knights who stood beside the king. He pointedly avoided the Earl of Salisbury—standing behind the others—who was beyond his forgiveness. Leaning toward Erpingham, Henry said in a low voice, "Tell the Earl of Salisbury to rest assured that as he neglected to speak to me in Paris last year, I have nothing to say to him." *That should give him something to think about.*

There was no point in dragging this out. Turning to his followers, Henry called, "Bring the king's horses."

This was the moment. As agreed, the grooms led in six pitiful mounts not worth thirty shillings between them; Richard's beautiful horse was nowhere to be seen. The look of distress on the king's face was fleeting. He said nothing and climbed into the saddle; his companions mounted the other five.

Henry exchanged glances with Percy. The earl was frowning, but there was no more to be said. They had indeed captured their prey. It was an almost bloodless revolution—if you discount Richard's murdered advisors—and Lancaster had prevailed.

For now.

Bringing the unhappy king and his companions back to Chester, Henry barely paid attention to him as they entered the city to great acclaim. Richard was exposed to the jeers and taunting of the crowd, and Henry had to suppress an unworthy surge of satisfaction at the king's distress. On entering the castle bailey, another shock was in store for the king. Henry summoned young Thomas FitzAlan and Humphrey, Gloucester's son, to be his keepers. "My cousins," he said harshly, deference gone, "take the king and convey him to the corner tower. Bring as many people as you need, and guard him closely." Turning on his heel, he strode away without another word.

It was done. The king was in his hands. It was all so easy. Even the people of Chester had tired of Richard's misgovernment—and they were his favorites. Climbing the stairs to the wall walk, Henry slowed his pace, looking through the gaps in the battlements. Below him, the townspeople bustled about their business, calling out to each other. A pair of boys ran past an old man, practically knocking him over. Pigs snuffled in a ditch next to a house while a woman pushed them away with her broom.

Henry stopped, leaning on the embrasure. *Look at them all, so genial and relaxed.* It was instructive to see how they had turned vicious toward a king in disgrace—when just a few months ago they would have fallen all over themselves trying to please him. Would the same thing happen to him? He didn't want to think about it.

For now, Henry knew he was in the ascendancy; he would have to exploit it for all it was worth. After all, how would it be possible to restore the king to even a semblance of power if his own countrymen abandoned their fealty so easily? Did it make sense to throw away his own advantage? Of course not. He would ride this swell of popularity, all the way to the throne, if that was his destiny.

The feasting that evening was heady and unrestrained—by most, anyway. Many of Richard's adherents were present, such as John and Tom Holland, as well as Rutland and Worcester. Though they did their best to appear innocuous, they certainly didn't join in the merrymaking. Neither did Bolingbroke, who drank sparingly and spoke little, deep in thought. The archbishop frequently spoke into his ear and he nodded time and again, looking over at Percy who pointedly avoided him.

The next day, Henry and the archbishop were busy writing summons to parliament when a delegation from London was announced. This was good news; Henry had been sending letters to the mayor ever since Doncaster. Exchanging glances with Arundel, Henry gestured for them to enter. He stood while three aldermen and six wealthy burgesses came into the room and bowed, showing deference.

"You are welcome, one and all. What is it I can do for you?"

They looked at their spokesman who removed his hat. "My lord Duke, we have come as representatives of the City of London. We have been assigned to tell you the people have renounced their allegiance to King Richard and we pledge our loyalty to yourself. We have brought fifty citizens with us who wait to give you their oath. Here is our common seal to confirm our covenant."

Henry couldn't resist a glance of triumph at Arundel. London was the last great hurdle, and here they were, coming to him! Clearing his throat, he said, "I am deeply grateful for your trust."

Looking pleased, the spokesman briefly consulted with the others before turning back to Henry. "Dear sire," he continued, "the Commons of London, and all the Commons of the realm humbly beseech you to put King Richard to death, without bringing him any further."

What was this? Henry suppressed a shudder. A thousand accusations crowded into his brain. He would be decried as a regicide, a murderer. However, this was no time to insult his advocates.

"My friends," he said slowly, "I will certainly do nothing of the sort, for it would be great injustice to put the king to death without a trial. I *will* bring him to London for parliament to decide what shall be done with him." After a moment, the men bowed their acceptance, and Henry was relieved to see they hadn't really expected him to acquiesce. Perhaps it was their way of convincing him they were in earnest.

Striding toward them, Bolingbroke shook their hands then moved into the great room where the fifty citizens awaited. As one, the men dropped to their knees and uttered an acclaim, obviously rehearsed ahead of time. This was more than acceptable to the duke and he quickly bid them to stand. He called for refreshments, hoping to dispense with long and tedious oath-taking. That could wait.

The archbishop came forward and gave his blessing, and the tension in the room relaxed as Henry moved among the crowd, trying to exchange greetings with every one of them. He patted a stout merchant on the shoulder and turned around, almost bumping into his son Thomas.

"What are you doing here?"

The boy could see he was displeased. "I, I heard some noise and came to see what it was."

"Well, now you've come I need for you to go back to your chamber. This is not for you."

"Yes, father." Thomas bowed and sprinted from the room, bumping into a few men on his way out. Henry watched until he was satisfied his son had truly left. He wondered how much he heard.

It was a long evening but well spent, and Henry managed his most engaging smile until every Londoner had left the castle, buoyed up by the charisma of their chosen leader.

When it was all over, Henry and the archbishop sat in his solar, sipping some of Chester's choicest wine and idly paging through the summons they had been working on.

"Well, I hope you are convinced," Arundel said finally. "There is no surer sign that the crown is yours for the taking."

A chill went down Henry's back. "I have been fretting over this for so long. I made an oath."

The other nodded. "I am prepared to give you absolution. Much has changed since then; your candidacy is affirmed by divine mandate. Richard has lost the hearts of his people. They want *you*." He looked sideways at Henry. "Besides, there will be no peace in this country as long as he reigns."

"Peace," Bolingbroke scoffed. "Can a usurper expect peace?"

"As God wills." They both crossed themselves. "As long as we go about this correctly, the way should be smoothed for you. I've been giving this much thought." He gestured to the summonses. "We have between now and parliament to search for precedents; we need to establish your claim to the throne. I suggest we send messengers throughout the land with orders to bring all the old chronicles to Westminster. Obviously we have Edward II. Still, I think we need to investigate further. Edward abdicated in favor of his son, the direct successor. You're not quite so lucky."

Henry nodded, happy to put the matters into the archbishop's capable hands. All his life he had avoided politics whenever possible. He had always thought himself above subterfuge, but now he was beginning to understand. John of Gaunt's lessons were finally making sense. "I remember my father always asserted that our ancestor Edmund Crouchback was really the firstborn son of Henry III. He was passed over because of his...deformity." Those last words came out slowly because Arundel was already shaking his head.

"We can try. I sincerely doubt that old legend."

"Oh." Henry shrugged. "By right of conquest, then."

The archbishop shook his head again. "And leave yourself open to the same fate? Not only that, a claim based on conquest would threaten the liberties and property of all Englishmen. No, this will not do."

Pursing his lips, Henry bit back his annoyance. "Well then, we'll have to stress my double ancestry. I am descended from Henry III on both sides, whereas Richard's descent is only through the male line."

"That may well be what we use, unless we discover something better."

Henry pulled the papers across the table. "For now, then, I shall begin dating my documents by the calendar year rather than Richard's regnal year. That should send a subtle message."

Arundel nodded in encouragement. "Very good. Meanwhile, I shall investigate the procedure we should take. King Edward II was deposed, then he abdicated. I tend to think we need to do the opposite with Richard. We need to get him to sign a deed of resignation, then we present a set of deposition charges to parliament. This should make our undertaking unassailable."

Henry blinked. "Does it matter?"

"Edward II was not deposed by parliament; he was deposed by his powerful magnates with the acclaim of the people. That's why they needed his abdication, to make it more legitimate. It was all very confused, and if the magnates hadn't been united in their purpose, the…irregular procedure might have gone against them."

"It wasn't done by parliament?"

"No. Think of it this way. If the king does not preside—and Edward refused—then it is not a true parliament. It is only an assembly of the three estates: the lords, the commons, and the clergy. The parliament and king are one; without the king, there is no parliament." He leaned back in his chair, stretching. Henry could see he was clearly enjoying this intellectual exercise. "Even that is not the point. A king certainly can't be judged and deposed by his own parliament; that is not its function. The purpose of parliament is to advise him, petition him, and offer consent. They are never above the king.

"And so," Arundel went on, "we will be faced with the same dilemma. We will call parliament for the end of September, but since the king will not preside—because he will have just abdicated—we will merely proceed as an assembly of the estates. If we have Richard's resignation in hand, it will be a *fait accompli*. No need for argument. But that's not enough. If we do not go through the motion of deposing him, he could renounce his abdication later, saying he acted under duress. That cannot be allowed to happen. It must be final."

"Thomas, I see I am in good hands." Henry smiled ruefully. "Under your firm direction, we cannot go wrong."

CHAPTER 8

"Welcome home, son! You made good time." Henry stood, throwing out his arms in welcome. "I am so glad to see you."

Hal moved forward slowly, not quite sure how he felt. He hadn't seen his father since the previous October, when Henry left the country on his way to exile. That was nine months ago! He embraced his father briefly then stared at him as Henry held him at arm's length.

"By God, you've grown. You were a boy when I left, and now you are a man." Hal didn't respond and Henry suddenly felt uncomfortable. "You look tired. Please sit down."

Pulling up a chair, Hal obliged, perching on the edge. Henry leaned forward.

"Did the king treat you all right?"

The boy's eyes took on a faraway look. "He treated me like a son."

That didn't help. Henry's relationship with his children was typical of his class. He was away most of the time, leaving them in the charge of governesses. When Henry's beloved wife, Mary Bohun died in 1394, he had even less reason to return home. Hal would have been about eight years old then, and already he had three younger brothers and two sisters. At least his education was taken seriously; he was even sent to study at Oxford with his uncle, Henry Beaufort.

It was his next child, Thomas, that Henry had grown to love, especially as the boy had accompanied him into exile. Never before had he spent so much time with any of his children, and Thomas had thrived under the attention. Hal, his heir, never had that opportunity. Frankly, he and his eldest were practically strangers. How was he going to find the opportunity to bring him closer?

Hal reached across the desk and pulled over a bowl of figs. As Henry watched his son nibble on one then another, he thought back to the last time they saw each other, just before his exile. He so wanted to hug him close but there was something about Hal's demeanor that put him off—an invisible barrier between them. Where had he gone wrong? Why was it that he never seemed to know how to say the right thing?

He cleared his throat. "What happened on campaign?"

"The Irish wouldn't engage." On more familiar ground, Hal sat back in his chair. "We chased them into the most impassible forests imaginable and they picked us off like unwary stragglers. We nearly starved before making it back to the coast, where King Richard arranged for supply ships to meet us. We made it to Dublin and were planning the next course of action when the news came of your…return." He looked down, embarrassed. "King Richard sent me to Trim Castle for my own safety."

"So he allowed you to campaign with him."

"Father, he knighted me." The rebuff was almost tangible.

Henry looked down at his hands; they were tearing at the corner of a warrant. He pushed the papers aside. "That—that was an honor," he sputtered.

"It was." Hal hesitated before putting words to his thoughts. "I understand you took the king prisoner."

This was getting worse by the minute. How much honesty should I give him? Henry swallowed, wishing he had some wine. "Much has happened in the last five weeks. The king has lost all support. His policies have been a disaster."

"I see." Hal looked up again, his eyes shuttered. "What do you intend to do with him?"

Sighing, Henry shook his head. "It's up to parliament to settle," he lied, hating himself for dissembling. But it was just too soon to admit his plans; after all, he had hardly decided what to do. "For now, we must keep him under our control."

Henry knew his son wouldn't be satisfied and he was relieved when the boy stood.

"Thank you, father. I am very tired."

"I have a room prepared for you."

"I'll find my way." Bowing, Hal started to leave then paused at the door. "I'm glad to see you so well," he said shortly. Then he was gone.

Unbeknownst to his father, Hal didn't search out his sleeping quarters. He immediately went to discover where the king was confined. He had to see him. Ever since the day he went to Richard's court as a hostage, the king had treated him like family. He cared. He asked questions and listened to the answers. He took Hal into his confidence and explained what they were doing on campaign. When Richard left Ireland, the last thing he said to Hal was "There are times I think of you as the son I never had."

And now Richard was a prisoner. It broke his heart.

Questioning the guards, Hal finally located Richard's room in the largest tower of the castle. The door was flanked by two soldiers. Nodding at them, he went into the room.

The king was in a most pitiful state. He was wearing a ragged black friar's robe; his red hair hung about his face, unbrushed. Alone, abandoned, he was kneeling in front of the fireplace trying to strike a flint. It was obvious he didn't know how to do such a simple task; the servants had always taken care of these things. Striking the iron again and again, Richard finally gave up and threw the flint to the floor, breaking into tears.

Hal was heartbroken. He slipped over to the king and knelt beside him. Whirling around, Richard cast his arms around the lad's neck.

"Oh, my boy," he cried. "I've never been so glad to see anyone in my life!"

Hugging him back, Hal helped Richard to his feet. "This will not do. Let me go fetch a servant. Sit, Your Majesty."

Richard sat on the bed while Hal went to summon help. He was soon back with two pages in tow. "I will make sure someone is here to attend to your needs," he growled. "It is shameful they abandoned you so." He sat beside the king.

"How did you get to be here?" Richard asked.

"When my father reached Chester he sent for me. And Humphrey. We just got here today."

"You came by a shorter route than I did," Richard said bitterly. "I was ill-advised."

Hal frowned. "So much has happened. I'm not privy to most of it. It seems my father has taken on much."

"I'm afraid he means to do me harm."

92

Hal would have liked to have reassured the king. Unfortunately, he was worried, too.

"What of my brother?" Richard went on. "And my nephew? Do you know what happened to them?"

"I am told your brother spoke eloquently to my father, trying to persuade him against breaking his fidelity to you. Apparently, he only succeeded in making things worse. And when he insisted he be allowed to return to you, my father forbid him to go and detained him. He also imprisoned your nephew, though I know not why."

Richard sighed. "I feared my brother had gone over to Lancaster, like Rutland and Percy."

"No, I assure you. That was not the case."

Richard forced a smile, trying to lighten his tone. "Well, I have you, now, to keep me company."

That was some comfort to the both of them. Hal came and went for the next couple of days, keeping his movements as discreet as he could. It was not fated to last. On the third day, he had come in with an armful of books when the door crashed open behind him. Humphrey of Buckingham stepped into the room, his hand grasping and ungrasping his dagger. He shot a look of anger at Hal.

"I thought you were here. I forbid you to visit the king!"

Hal stood to his full height, putting the books on the table. "You have no authority over me."

"I have been given full authority over King Richard, and I say he is to have no visitors!"

"I answer only to my father."

"It matters not. I shall put extra guards on this door and you shall not enter."

"I warn you, Humphrey. Do not cross me."

Richard sadly watched the little altercation. This was only one additional humiliation that was bound to be inflicted upon him. Moving up beside Hal, he put a hand on his arm. "I would not be the cause of dissension between you and your father," he said quietly. "We both know what his answer would be. Thanks to you, I have recovered my equanimity. Go, my friend. I'll be all right."

Hal knelt before the king, kissing his ring. Then he got up and strode from the room without looking at Humphrey. Buckingham glared at Richard before closing the door.

It was not long afterward that Duke Henry announced they were leaving for London. He dismissed more than half his army; they were no longer needed and it was next to impossible to feed them all. Ignoring his proclamation, the rowdy adventurers had fallen into the practice of taking what they wanted from the hapless Cheshire population. It was rumored that Henry didn't even try to discourage them—not good for his reputation. Enough was enough. It was time to stop their depredations.

Richard was placed under heavy guard, and the cavalcade took a slow and majestic ride toward Leicester, their first destination. Henry rode in the front rank with both Percies, the Archbishop of Canterbury and the Earl of Westmorland. Following them, Hal and his brother Thomas were flanked by Rutland and Worcester. The king was several rows behind them, and Hal kept turning around to look at him.

He and Thomas hadn't had much opportunity to speak since Hal came back from Ireland. It wasn't an accident; although they were only one year apart in age, they were ages apart in temperament. They rode for a while in silence until finally, Thomas spoke up in annoyance.

"What are you looking at?"

Hal faced front, embarrassed. "I am concerned about the king. No one even gave him a change of clothing."

"The king?" Thomas's voice rang with sarcasm. "Your precious king? It's your king that got us into this mess. If he hadn't outlawed our father—"

"What are you complaining about? You don't seem to have suffered in Paris, having our father all to yourself."

"While you searched for glory in Ireland."

Hal snorted. "Glory? I nearly starved."

"I heard you were knighted. *Sir* Henry. By your precious king."

"*Our* king. Don't forget."

"Not if father has anything to do with it."

That was an uncomfortable subject. The Earl of Worcester put a hand on Thomas's arm. "I advise you to stop before you get into trouble," he said.

Thomas looked at the earl sheepishly. Once again, he had let his dislike for his brother get the better of him.

Hal caught what he said. "What did you mean, Thomas?"

"Nothing." Sullenly, Thomas looked straight ahead.

Hal glanced to his other side. Rutland looked back at him. "Your father has been greeted enthusiastically everywhere he goes," he said, almost apologetically. "You'll see. His popularity grows by the day."

Nodding to himself, Hal stared at his father's back. "I noticed an increase of people paying homage to him in Chester. New retainers."

"Many once belonged to Richard," Rutland said. "This has been going on for weeks."

"Oh." For a few minutes they rode in silence. "That doesn't necessarily mean he seeks to be king." His eyes narrowing, Hal turned back to Thomas. "Father confides in you now?"

Thomas shook his head, refusing to look at him.

"If he does, you had better learn some discretion. If that's possible."

His mouth curling into a sneer, Thomas ignored him.

But the damage was done. Hal could no longer pretend nothing was amiss. What other plans could his father have, treating the king so shamefully? And what did that mean for *him*? How could he contemplate his own destiny if it meant trampling over the liberties of the man who was like a second father? Or worse. It was all too terrible to contemplate, and he felt his heart harden toward the man who was going to make it all happen.

Since there was nothing Hal could do to help King Richard, he withdrew into himself, rarely speaking during the long rides through Nantwich, then Newcastle-under-Lyne. There they were joined by the Earl of Warwick, recently released from his exile to Isle of Man. The earl pointedly avoided the king, though Hal caught him looking at Richard with triumph.

Their travel was interrupted by an attack. Thousands of Welshmen poured out of the forest shrieking at the top of their lungs. It made the hair stand up on Hal's neck. He drew his sword but couldn't use it; several of the guards surrounded him and his brother, keeping them out of the action. The attackers split into two, some riding directly for Richard, others trying to outflank the rearmost riders. Initially caught off guard, Henry's knights recovered quickly and spurred to meet them—some couching spears under their arms, others drawing their swords. As they made contact with the charging Welshmen, there was a brief clash of arms, then a sudden reversal. Richard's erstwhile rescuers disappeared as quickly as they came. No one was fooled; they would be back.

For the next two days, the Welsh harassed the moving column, attacking here and there but never coming close to the king. When they reached Lichfield, Richard attempted to escape, lowering himself from the window of the old palace by sheets tied together. Hal supposed he was hoping to take refuge with the Welsh who assuredly were in the area; he was sorry the king was easily apprehended and returned to even stricter confinement.

They continued on to Coventry, then to Daventry, Northampton, Dunstable, and St. Albans before they rode the last stretch to London. As they progressed down Watling Street, Bolingbroke was pleased to see that a great procession was coming out to greet him. The blaring of horns and bagpipes announced the approaching delegation. Elated, Henry's own musicians took up the challenge.

As the Londoners came closer they made a pretty sight. Rank upon rank they marched, with each trade wearing its own liveries and carrying spears. The mayor walked in front, a sword held up before him. As the two parties faced each other, the foremost men saluted the duke.

"Long live Henry the noble Duke of Lancaster," they cried, "who has conquered all England in less than a month! Such a lord deserves to be king!"

Despite himself, Henry smiled. It was a heady combination, seeing the difficult Londoners bow at his feet and knowing the rejected king rode behind him, ragged and humiliated. He turned to the young Earl of Arundel. "Bring King Richard forward."

The king was only a few ranks behind him, and Arundel led the palfrey by the reins. Richard's face was covered with tears, which didn't help his dignity any. All the better for Henry; he dismounted and removed his own bonnet.

"My lord, alight," he said to Richard. "Here are your good friends of London who are come to see you!"

Giving the duke a nasty look, Richard obliged. Henry moved over to the king's left and gestured at him as he spoke to the gathering. "My lords and friends, I deliver King Richard into your custody, and beg you to do with him what you wish." Stepping back, he ignored Richard's look of surprise and panic. The lord mayor brought up a spare horse. Giving Henry one last despairing look, the king remounted, allowing himself to be led as before. Crossing his arms, Henry watched as the Londoners moved away with their prize.

"I'm well rid of him," he muttered to no one in particular. "Finally. Whatever happens to him tonight will not be my concern."

The archbishop stepped up beside him. "They will not harm him, though I daresay they won't give him much respect."

"It'll be more than he deserves. They will eventually take him to the Tower, and then we'll have to deal with him again. For now, I'm finally free to see my father's tomb. I've wanted to do this ever since we arrived in England."

They watched the retreating Londoners who parted for the king's horse then closed ranks behind him. "Let us rest here," Henry said. "We'll let them get ahead of us before we follow."

There was plenty of daylight left. After a short delay, the ducal entourage moved on. They had not gone more than a half-mile when they noticed the Londoners had veered off to the left. The mayor was taking the king by a less-traveled route, leaving the main road open. This allowed Henry to pick up his pace. As they passed over the Fleet River and through Ludgate on the west side of the city, the crowds had already gathered to greet him. More trumpets were blaring, people were waving and shouting "Long Live the Duke of Lancaster!"

"Thank the Lord for a Miracle!" Henry heard. "He's like Alexander the Great!" Church bells started ringing, women were singing and handing up flowers as he passed. Even Henry was surprised at the enthusiasm.

It was a short distance to St. Paul's. Henry dismounted at the gate to the churchyard, turning one last time to wave before he entered through the double doors. The silence of the cavernous cathedral surrounded him, subduing the noise from outside. The few people walking up and down the nave moved aside as he passed, conspicuous in his tabard bearing the Lancaster coat of arms. The archbishop and the Percies followed at a distance, giving him privacy. Henry walked up to the altar and made his devotions before paying his respects to his father.

John of Gaunt's chapel was located near the apse. The great man lay beneath his alabaster effigy, holding hands with the lifelike form of Blanche, his first wife and Henry's mother. Henry knelt beside the tomb; before he knew it he was weeping profusely. It all came out at once—the fury, the frustration—all those months in Paris, feigning indifference before King Charles. He had swallowed his anger, provoked beyond measure at Richard's refusal to allow him to attend his dying father. It was so unfair! And now that he had come to reclaim his patrimony, he knew Gaunt would have disapproved of his leading a rebellion.

Dashing tears from his face, Henry covered his eyes with his hands. "How can I make you understand?" he said to the stern effigy. "I know you protected the throne your whole life. You would never have considered taking it for yourself, though God knows you would have made a better king than my cousin. But what would you advise me? If Richard came back to power, he would give me a traitor's death." He crossed himself, struggling to suppress his sobs. "I know what I must do. I have to take the crown; I have no other choice."

It was a confession and there was to be no absolution. His father would not have granted it, anyway, if he were alive.

Henry continued to pray while his companions looked on sympathetically. Finally, he wiped his eyes and rose to his feet, sighing heavily.

"Friends," he said, joining the others, "let us move on to the Bishop's Palace. It is not appropriate for me to utilize any of the royal residences in London. We can make that our meeting place for now."

There was much to be done; everything had to be resolved by the upcoming parliament less than a month away. Under the supervision of Archbishop Arundel, Henry summoned the most trustworthy lawyers, prelates, and barons in the Lancastrian affinity. They needed to implement an unassailable strategy to replace the king. Archives were searched for a precedent; debates among the wisest men would continue for weeks. Henry was adamant; there must be no question about the legitimacy of Richard's deposition. This was not easily done and their meetings raised more problems than answers. Arundel did his best to minimize the objections, but this was uncharted territory and everyone knew it.

Needless to say, Richard knew nothing about all this. After one night at Westminster, the mayor moved him to the safety of the Tower. Richard's immediate concern was to recover from his trauma. Suddenly a bath and a change of clothing took on a whole new meaning. Sleep and solitude were his most welcome companions—which was fortunate because he was left totally alone. At least at first.

After three days had passed, Henry decided it was time to determine the king's frame of mind. He knew that Duke of York, was suffering pangs of guilt; perhaps this would be a good chance to reconcile him with the king. Reluctantly, York agreed, insisting Rutland come with him.

Henry sent young Arundel to bring Richard down to where they could comfortably meet. He was surprised when the lad came back alone, unsettled and embarrassed.

"He will not come," Arundel said. "He said you must go to him."

Grumbling, Henry rose and beckoned for the others to follow. "We will grant him this last demand," he said. "Perhaps it will make him less quarrelsome." They went to the royal apartments on the second floor of the White Tower. Richard was standing next to the fireplace.

One look at the king's face and Henry knew things were not going to be so easy. Showing respect he didn't feel, he removed his hat and bowed. The other two hung back uncomfortably. "My lord," he said, "our cousin and uncle wish to speak with you."

Paling in anger, Richard barely kept his voice civil. "Cousin, they are not worthy to speak to me."

"But have the goodness to hear them," Henry insisted, gesturing to his side.

The look of hate Richard turned on York would have made a greater man quail. The duke stepped back a pace.

"Thou villain! What could you possibly say to me? And you, traitor of Rutland! You are not worthy to bear the name of duke, earl, or even knight. You, and the villain your father, you have both foully betrayed me! Alas, that I should ever have been so fond of so false a traitor!" He stamped his foot. "For by thee the kingdom of England will be destroyed, I am convinced!"

Rather than show any remorse, the Earl of Rutland curled his lip. "You lie," he declared and threw his hat on the floor.

Furious, Richard kicked it away. "Traitor! I am king and thy lord, and will still continue king and will reach greater heights than ever before, despite all my enemies. And you are not fit to speak to me!"

Henry stepped in and put out a restraining hand. "Enough of this," he said to Rutland.

Richard whirled around, turning his anger on Henry. "And you! Why do you keep me so closely guarded by your men-at-arms? I wish to know if you acknowledge me as your lord and king, or what do you mean to do with me?"

Henry was surprised at his fervor. How many times could this man bounce back? He said carefully, "It is true you are my king and lord, but the council of the realm has ordered that you should be kept in confinement until the day parliament meets."

Seething, Richard railed at his helplessness. "Then at least bring the queen my wife to me so I may speak with her!"

Again, Henry pretended to be concerned. "Excuse me, my lord. It is forbidden by the council."

Richard couldn't contain himself. He strode back and forth. "You have acknowledged me as your king these twenty-two years! How dare you use me so cruelly?"

"My lord, we cannot do otherwise until parliament meets."

"Pretense! What nonsense! Such drivel!" As the others watched uneasily, Richard continued his pacing. "Oh God of Paradise!" He raised his hands, looking at the ceiling. "How can

You suffer the wrongs these people commit against me?" Then he pointed at Henry. "I declare that you are false traitors to God as well as me. And this I will prove against any four of the best of you with my body, like the loyal knight that I am. I never forfeited my knighthood! And here is my pledge!" This time it was Richard who threw his hat on the floor.

Regretting this scene, Henry dropped to his knees. "Please, my lord, restrain yourself until parliament meets. And then everyone can present his arguments."

Having spent his anger, Richard stood breathing heavily. "At least, for God's sake, let me be brought to trial so I can defend myself, and give answer to their complaints."

This had to end. Standing, Henry bowed his head. "My lord, be not afraid. Nothing unreasonable shall be done to you." Without waiting for an answer, he left the room. York and Rutland followed him.

Once they were out of earshot, Henry slowed his pace. "That certainly didn't go well," he said wryly. "How can we possibly convince him to abdicate?"

"Poor Richard," York said. "He doesn't even understand what brought him to this point."

"You are very generous, uncle," Henry said, putting an arm around his shoulder. "Perhaps, given more time alone, he will reconcile himself to his situation."

CHAPTER 9

Richard wasn't the only one who needed to be placated. Young Hal had decidedly distanced himself from his father, and Henry was at a loss where to start. Finally, he chose the direct approach. Later in the day, as he was writing a letter to Brittany, he looked up at a knock on the open door.

"You wanted to see me?" Hal walked into the room and seated himself across the table. Once again, Henry marveled at how stiff he looked.

"Yes." He cleared his throat. "It's time you were involved in our proceedings."

Hal looked pained. "Is this about King Richard?"

"Yes, son. We can no longer avoid this. We are about to begin deposition charges against him."

Looking aside, Hal gathered his thoughts. "Is there no other way?" he asked finally.

"I would that there was. But look at the king's tyranny. Again and again, he has broken his word, forced innocent men to sue for pardons or sign blank charters, condemned men to outlawry—actually, we don't have to look any farther than my own case. If the king had his way, I may have been an exile for life, penniless and powerless."

"But—"

"That would have extended to you, as well. Do you really think his fondness for you would have overcome his hostility toward our house?"

Closing his mouth, Hal studied his father. "Do you sincerely believe this?"

"My father feared for his very life on more than one occasion. At the king's hands. Yes, I believe this."

Hal grunted and Henry could see he wasn't convinced. "I need you beside me," he said. "Don't you see where we are headed?"

Hal refused to answer. He studied his hands.

"According to King Edward III's entail, I am next in line." Henry leaned forward, willing his son to understand. "And then you."

The boy's silence was maddening. He didn't look happy at the prospect of being king. Then he suddenly glanced up with a question. "Where is this entail?"

Leaning back, Henry let out a sigh. "It's possible Richard destroyed it."

"Then you don't even know if it exists."

"My father saw it. All the sons of Edward saw it. I'm sure your uncle York would verify its existence."

"If it exists no longer, what force does it have?"

Fighting his impatience, Henry pursed his lips. *Why did Hal fight him at every turn?* "There might be a copy at the Chancery. But that's not really the point, is it? I think the people of England have amply demonstrated they have chosen *me* for the kingship."

The truth of that statement was undeniable. Hal nodded reluctantly.

"You don't need to get involved in the politics, or the deliberations," Henry went on. "Archbishop Arundel has matters well under control. When the time comes..." He hesitated. This was such a delicate matter even he was uncomfortable speaking about it. "As soon as my coronation is over, I intend to declare you Prince of Wales."

There. It was out. No more prevarication. Hal's face was expressionless.

They looked at each other. "As I see it, this is your destiny," Henry urged. "I know your mettle. You will make a good king. It's up to me to ensure the stability of our new dynasty."

Hal was about to deny everything but he stopped. There was no point in pretending he hadn't thought about it. Of course, he had. He didn't want it this way; it only helped a little that he had nothing to do with the situation. He decided to try again. "Father, it doesn't feel right."

Henry understood. His son was so young. He hadn't been disillusioned yet. "There are many things in life that don't feel right. In the end, survival is what matters. I didn't cause this situation. He did. I'm fighting back the only way I know how." It wasn't a very satisfactory answer. At least it was honest.

He leaned forward, putting a hand on Hal's arm. "Please understand. I'm fighting for our family, as well."

Hal did understand. That's what was making all this so hard to accept. "But you swore an oath to let him keep his crown while you governed in his name. Everyone talks about it."

Henry sighed. This was his greatest regret—a mistake that was going to be the hardest to remedy. "I gave that oath in good faith. But I came to realize we could never make it work. Situations change. What if he regains power, like the last time? It took ten years, but Richard never forgot the wrongs done to him by the Lords Appellant. His revenge was merciless. Look what he did to my uncle the Duke of Gloucester. *I* only survived because of my father. I truly believe that." Henry wanted so much for Hal to understand that he squeezed his arm a little too hard.

Hal grimaced and his father caught himself, letting go and leaning back in his chair. "Think about it, son. This time around, his vindictiveness could be even worse. I can't take that chance. And if I fall—if he wreaked revenge on me—countless others would fall as well."

"I see." Hal stood, anxious to be alone with his thoughts. "Is there anything else?"

Henry didn't want him to go—not until he showed some acceptance. Nonetheless, he knew his son; the lad was sensible though he couldn't be pushed. "Can I depend on you?"

Nodding, Hal didn't trust himself to speak. He bowed and backed from the room. The only person he wanted to communicate with was Richard, and that was denied to him. How was he going to live with himself?

Henry was aware that the Earl of Northumberland was also unsatisfied; he had never completely come to terms with the evolving situation. None of this would have happened without Percy's aid, and Henry wondered whether the man was beginning to regret his support. More and more, the earl was testy—argumentative, even—when he was not avoiding Henry altogether. Perhaps he expected to wield more dominance; could he be disappointed that Bolingbroke had a mind of his own?

Unbeknownst to him, Henry Percy watched from the back of the room while he accepted submission from six more of Richard's retainers; they had just ridden in from Gloucester. Kneeling, the last man put his hands into Henry's outstretched palms. "I promise on my soul I will be faithful to you, my lord. I will never cause you harm and I will observe my homage to you against all persons in good faith and without deceit." Nodding graciously, the duke thanked him and instructed his steward to bestow his new livery, a collar of linked greyhounds.

At that, Percy had had enough. Striding forward, he approached the seated duke who looked up inquiringly.

"What is it?" Bolingbroke asked.

"Can't you guess? This has gone way beyond where we started."

"Yes?"

Tightening his lips, Percy sat next to Henry, not waiting for an invitation. "Is that all you have to say? After swearing an oath that you did not seek the crown? Then you affirmed it again before I went to fetch the king from Conwy—an oath I perpetuated by swearing on the host? Now both of us are forsworn!"

Sighing, Bolingbroke leaned back in his chair. "Can't you see, Henry? The people want it. Look how they flock to my standard. You know I had to send thousands back home because I couldn't afford to feed them all. How can I resist the crown when it is thrust upon me?"

"How can you repudiate your oath so easily?"

Henry sighed. "I will promise to go on Crusade. I will take it up personally with the Archbishop of Canterbury."

"Ha! That's no good. Archbishop Arundel has driven you to it."

Suddenly tired, Henry looked pleadingly at Percy, all pretense gone. "You know I must do this. I have no choice. You saw what happened to my uncle Gloucester. That could be me."

He watched the other's anger melt away. Although he didn't know it, this was the very thing Percy had said to his son before they marched to Doncaster.

"It was much easier at the beginning," Bolingbroke mused. "The people's champion, come from an unjust exile to right the wrongs inflicted by a vengeful king. It was so straightforward, Henry. That's all I wanted."

"Was it?" Percy scowled. "Do you expect me to believe that?"

Giving him a sideways glance, Henry shrugged. "I no longer know, myself. It doesn't really matter anymore, does it? We are set on our path and cannot diverge. Right or wrong, I am fated to be king."

During the month of September, Henry's committee worked on a document named the *Record and Process.* This would be used to accuse Richard of all his crimes, thus removing any objections. It would be brought into play during the deposition phase after the king's abdication had been accepted.

Unfortunately, no one had come up with a good suggestion as to how they should persuade Richard to abdicate in the first place. For lack of a better idea, a stream of carefully chosen emissaries were sent to visit the captive king. Some were instructed to gauge his mood; others dropped suggestions hinting at more drastic incarceration. Arundel sent a man to covertly threaten Richard's life, though Henry didn't approve. He didn't stop the man, either; one way or the other, the king needed to understand he had no choice but to resign. As the date for parliament approached, Henry sent one of Richard's more intimate followers, Thomas Despenser, who broke the news that he would be presented with a writ of abdication.

Bolingbroke waited impatiently for Despenser to return. When he finally did, the man looked faint.

"Here, take some wine," Henry said, pointing for Despenser to sit. Grimacing, the other moved very slowly, picking up the goblet and holding it with both hands. He was clearly uncomfortable. "What did Richard say?" Henry asked finally.

Pursing his lips, Despenser put the wine down. "He thinks you mean to kill him," he said finally.

Rolling his eyes in impatience, Henry stood and paced the room. "Why does everyone speak of killing?" he barked. "I am not a violent man."

The other lowered his head, not daring to speak.

"What else did he say?"

"He reminded me that if he fell, we all fall with him."

Frowning, Henry stopped pacing. "Will he accept the abdication papers?"

"I know not. He is a very complicated man."

"That he is. I thank you for your assistance."

Despenser didn't need any further encouragement to leave. Henry barely paid attention; he called for a servant to summon Richard LeScrope, the Archbishop of York. His job was to present the Act of Abdication the next day. Forcing a smile when the Archbishop entered, Henry waved at the newly vacated chair.

"Is everything ready, your Grace?"

LeScrope sat, nodding. "The writ has been finished. I will present myself to the king along with the minimum number of persons to represent the estates—spiritual and temporal. We shall have myself and the Bishop of Hereford for the clergy, Northumberland and Westmorland for the earls, two barons, two knights, plus two doctors and two notaries. All will be perfectly in order."

"Good. I do not know how the king will react. The man is unpredictable."

"If he does not show dignity, then that is one more reason he is unfit for his office."

Henry smiled, letting out a grunt. "One more reason. As if we need it."

The following morning, the deputation found Richard in his high-backed chair, dressed in the finest clothing they allowed him. His face was haggard and he watched them through narrowed eyes.

"Since I have no one to speak for me," the king said, looking directly at Henry Percy, "I shall speak for myself. What brings you here this day?"

The Archbishop of York stepped forward and unrolled a scroll. "On behalf of the Great Council of England, we have come to ascertain whether you are willing to resign the right you have to the crown of England with its appurtenances. That is to say, in the kingdoms of England, France, Ireland, and Scotland, the duchies of Guyenne and Normandy, the county of Ponthieu, and the town of Calais, and in all the other castles, fortresses and towns. This resignation stands for yourself and your heirs into perpetuity."

Although Richard accepted the scroll, he insisted they give him time to read it. He regally dismissed them and they filed out of the room, not knowing what else to do. Henry wasn't particularly surprised to hear about Richard's reaction. It was reasonable, and he was prepared to wait a little longer. But only a little. Time was running out. In two days the estates were scheduled to show up for parliament, little realizing the king would not be present to officiate. That part was already planned. However, Richard could throw everything else into turmoil if he refused to cooperate.

Henry slept badly that night. His stomach was upset and his back hurt. One disaster after another intruded itself on his mind, refusing to let him rest. Finally, he gave up and walked through the palace, envying the servants and soldiers who slumbered on their pallets, lined up against the wall. A few of them were sleeping on tables. They had so little to worry about! Yawning, he slipped outside, stopping to admire the pre-dawn clouds that were just beginning to turn pink. Was Richard looking at the same clouds from his gloomy chamber in the Tower? Henry suspected the king was as restless as he was. Once again his mind envisioned his cousin's lonely figure in prison, and the image wasn't as gratifying as he expected. Surely Richard deserved everything that was going to happen to him! So why couldn't Henry fight off a feeling of foreboding?

The morning passed slowly, though Henry had plenty to do. He still had one important speech to write—the one he intended to give when he claimed the crown. He had to reassure the nobles he would respect their property rights. After all, this was the very issue that prompted him to return from exile. He dipped his quill into the inkwell and began writing. Then he sat back, read his words again, crossed out a phrase, added another, and picked up the paper, reading aloud: *It is not my will for my countrymen to think that by way of conquest I would disinherit any man from his heritage, nor would I take away from him that which he has received by the good laws and customs of this country—except for those persons who have acted against the common profit of the realm.* He nodded to himself, satisfied.

Once again, his eyes took on a far-away look as he wondered how his delegation's second mission to Richard was progressing. By now they would be at the Tower. He was relieved when Thomas Arundel showed up; the archbishop provided the perfect distraction. Henry read his passage out loud and they made a few adjustments. A private dinner was served to the two of them, and Henry felt a little more at ease until the Archbishop of York was announced. One look at the man's face was enough to stiffen his shoulders. He cracked his neck to relieve the tension.

"What has happened now?" Henry asked, barely restraining his anxiety.

"Well, my lord, the king refused to sign."

"What!" Arundel exclaimed. "What are his reasons?"

LeScrope looked wistfully at a chair, then sighed. "King Richard asks how he could possibly resign the crown, and to whom?"

Cocking his head, Henry waited for more.

"He said he cannot renounce his holy anointing." LeScrope coughed while Henry grimaced.

"There is no end to his obstructions," the duke growled.

"Take heart, my lord. He may yet sign, but he insists you come in person so he can give you certain conditions."

"Conditions..." Henry looked at him. "Oh, sit down, your grace."

Obviously relieved, the archbishop complied.

"Tell us everything," said Arundel, leaning forward.

"Well, when we asked him if he had considered the writ, he said he would not sign it under any circumstances."

"That was a bad start," Henry muttered.

"Indeed. He insisted, in these words, 'You may force me to abdicate from governing, but you cannot expect me to abandon my kingship!'"

Arundel stroked his chin. "We can work with this." Henry glanced worriedly at him, only a little comforted.

Clearing his throat, LeScrope went on. "All the members present explained, one by one, why and how it was possible to resign the crown. The king listened closely then said he might be willing, under certain conditions, to abdicate. He would only resign to yourself. We assured him you would come in the afternoon. I hope I did not err in that, my lord."

"No, not at all." Henry felt his shoulders relax again. "Perhaps he has seen reason."

"I doubt it," said Arundel. "He has some deception planned, I suspect. Fortunately, we have a copy of the writ, just in case he has damaged the original."

Once they had finished eating, all three mounted and rode across the city to the Tower of London. The other members were waiting for them in the council chamber, and all proceeded to the king's quarters, dutifully filing in and facing the seated monarch. Henry and Arundel drew into a corner outside of everyone else's hearing. Appreciating the privacy, Richard got up and joined them, adjusting his sleeves.

Frustrated by this impasse, Henry stood with crossed arms, all pretense gone. Although Richard waited for him to bow, he waited in vain.

"What's this I hear about conditions?" Henry asked.

Richard pursed his lips in anger, then thought better of it. "I will agree to sign this document under three conditions."

"No. You must sign this abdication unconditionally."

Richard turned away, about to tear up the writ.

"No, wait," argued the archbishop. He whispered in Henry's ear, "At least hear what he has to say."

Exhaling in annoyance, Henry nodded. "What is it you want?"

Richard paced in front of him. "I will agree to resign the rule of the kingdom to you. But you must understand, I cannot change my essence as God's anointed and true king." He paused, waiting for a response.

Henry stared at him, thinking. If Richard wanted to go on calling himself king, what did it matter? He would spend the rest of his life under lock and key, anyway. He gave a slight nod.

"I also request that I may retain the lands I acquired in order to endow an anniversary for my soul at Westminster Abbey." He waited for an answer but Henry did not oblige. Richard sighed. "Cousin, if you agree to this I will sign the abdication papers in your favor—and only you; that is my third condition."

Henry exchanged glances with Arundel. "Very well," he said finally. "I agree to allow your obituary lands. Please now, sire, put your hand to this writ."

Straightening, Richard went back to the waiting committee and stood before them, holding up the parchment. He read it out loud, his voice firm and unwavering.

"I, Richard, by the grace of God, King of England and France and Lord of Ireland, resign my Crown. I understand that my government had not been acceptable to the people, and I relinquish the ruling to others."

"That's not how it's worded," Henry exclaimed to Arundel in a loud whisper.

The archbishop put a finger to his mouth. "Remember," he spoke into Henry's ear, "I have a copy of the original which we shall read before parliament tomorrow. Let the people in this room witness his signing. No one need know about his trifling alterations."

"And I swear on the holy gospels I shall never take exception to this resignation, so help me God." The king crossed himself. "I Richard, king aforesaid, with my own hand have written me underneath here."

He dipped a quill in the inkwell and signed with a flourish. Then the others moved up, one by one, and countersigned the document. Henry was last. He placed his own initials then stepped back in expectation. Richard knew what to do. Picking up his crown from the pillow, he studied it one last time before placing it on the floor at Henry's feet. Then he pulled off his signet ring and put it in the center of the circlet.

"I surrender this crown—not to you, but to God," he said.

Henry didn't particularly care. It was done. He would never need to see Richard again.

CHAPTER 10

On the last day of September, the Duke of Lancaster came to Westminster. A high mass was heard, and afterward the attendees lined up behind Sir Thomas Erpingham so they could leave the church in procession. He held aloft Duke Henry's bejeweled sword and led them to the great palace, which was just steps away. Directly behind the knight, dressed in a black houppelande and wearing a tall black chaperon, Henry walked slowly, greeting people to the right and left as they clamored for attention. Already a large crowd had gathered in the courtyard, for there was not enough space inside the building to accommodate them all. Finally, Henry and his retinue entered the Painted Chamber and progressed through the midst of the packed assembly. On the dais stood an empty throne, draped in cloth of gold. Bypassing it, Henry took the seat formerly assigned to his father.

Having been summoned to parliament, all the important men in the kingdom were present. There was a bit of confusion among the attendees; by now everyone knew King Richard was confined to the Tower. No king, no parliament. So what kind of meeting was this, anyway? Was parliament delayed—or was it canceled? Even Richard's favorites were present in their usual seats, for although the king had fallen, they still retained their titles. Admittedly they looked uncomfortable and no one spoke to them; even their friends knew their day of reckoning would follow soon.

Once all the preliminaries were over, the Archbishop of York nodded at the empty throne. "Yesterday, the king signed the Act of Abdication, which is why we are all gathered here." He paused while the members spoke amongst themselves; not everyone was aware that things had progressed so far. "Since this is not an official parliament," the archbishop continued, "we are here to represent the three estates: the Commons, the Lords, and the Clergy. A committee met the king yesterday of which I was a part. We witnessed the signing, and I have the writ here which I shall read to you." He cleared his throat. "I resign all my Kingly Majesty, Dignity and Crown with deed and word. For I know myself to be, and have been in the past, insufficient, unable, and unsuited, and I deem myself not unworthy to be brought down."

At that, Henry looked across to Arundel, who nodded sagely. This was the original copy, not the one altered by the king. "I swear on the holy gospels that I shall never take exception to this resignation, so help me God," continued the archbishop. "I Richard, with my own hand have written me underneath here." He held up the parchment for all to see.

Standing, Archbishop Arundel raised his arms. No need for discussion; best to get this over with quickly. "My lords, and members of all three estates, I ask you for your own welfare and for the good of the realm, do you agree with this abdication?"

There was little hesitation. "Yes, yes, yes," they all cried, to the extreme satisfaction of Henry Bolingbroke.

"Then I say to you, in order to remove any scruple or malevolent suspicion, we have set down in writing the many wrongs and shortcomings committed by the king that have rendered him worthy of deposition. I shall read you these thirty-three articles that demonstrate his incapacity to rule." Then Arundel proceeded to recite the *Record and Process*. The king was accused of perjuries, cruelties, wickedness, and faithlessness. Richard was vainglorious, deceitful, overbearing, crafty, and evil. He violated his coronation oath, undermined the liberties of the church, and forced his subjects to sign blank charters giving him unnatural control over their goods and property. He imposed unreasonable financial burdens and tried to fill parliament with his own chosen minions. The accusations went on and on until everyone was convinced the king indeed deserved to be deposed, and a further cry of "Yes, yes, yes," confirmed their assent.

Following this recitation, the next step would be to make a formal deposition of King Richard II. Certain proctors were assigned to meet the king the following day; they would represent the three estates and officially renounce their homage and fealty. Justice William Thirning was to lead the delegation.

Once this had all been arranged, Archbishop Arundel gestured to Henry Bolingbroke. "Not only has King Richard abdicated his throne, he has already appointed the Duke of Lancaster as his successor."

This was Henry's moment. Standing tall in front of his father's seat, he made the sign of the cross on his forehead and breast. He spoke loudly and clearly, in English rather than the usual French. "In the name of the Father, Son, and Holy Ghost, I, Henry of Lancaster challenge this Realm of England and the crown, inasmuch as I am descended by right line of blood from the good lord King Henry the third. God has sent me, with the help of my kin and friends, to recover this realm which was on the point of being undone by default of governance."

This was all a mere formality as far as Henry was concerned. Although he would rather have claimed the throne by right of arms, Justice Thirning had joined Arundel in warning him against it. Their arguments were difficult to dispute and he allowed himself to be persuaded.

Resuming his seat, Henry waited as the lords and bishops were questioned one by one to determine whether they objected to his claim. To a man they stated that Henry Bolingbroke was their choice to reign over them—all but one. At this moment, Bishop Merks stood and demanded to be heard. He had accompanied Richard all the way to the end until Henry Bolingbroke imprisoned the king at Chester.

Henry scowled at the Bishop of Carlisle yet nodded his permission.

"My lords," said Merks, turning to the assembly and holding out his arms, "consider well before you give judgment. For I maintain that no one present is competent and fit to judge the sovereign, whom we have acknowledged as our liege Lord these last twenty years. My lords, you have heard the accusations against King Richard. It appears to me you are about to condemn our king without hearing what he has to answer, or even his being present. Even the falsest traitor or the wickedest murderer has the right to be brought before the judge to hear his sentence. I declare that you ought to bring King Richard into your presence to hear what he has to say, and see whether he is truly willing to relinquish his crown to the duke or not."

When the bishop finished speaking, murmuring was heard in the room; no one dared support him. His was the sole voice raised in Richard's defense.

"Take the Bishop of Carlisle and detain him at St. Albans," Henry said simply. Even now no one objected. But something needed to be said to gloss over this unwelcome interruption. Pulling off Richard's signet ring, Henry held it up for all to see. "Behold," he cried, his voice ringing, "the king's signet, which he gave me willingly and declared me his successor."

The members mumbled again, which prompted Henry to utter spontaneously, "My lords spiritual and temporal, we beg you not to consent only with your mouths. It must come from your hearts as well. Nevertheless, should it happen that some of you do not in your hearts assent to this...it would be no great surprise to me."

It didn't take long for these earnest words to have their effect. The assembled shouted again "Yes, yes, yes".

Henry looked back and forth over the heads of his supporters. "I swear to you as king and Duke of Lancaster, I will live on my own resources and not resort to taxes except in case of emergency. And even then I will consult Parliament first." Finally, he finished with the passage he had written the day before, promising to respect their property rights.

This prompted an even more enthusiastic response. Seeking to take advantage of this propitious moment, both archbishops took him by the hand and conducted him to the vacant throne. First, he knelt with a prayer, then Henry rose, made the sign of the cross, and sat upon the cloth of gold draped over the seat. The acclaim took away the last of his doubts. The great officers approached and surrendered their seals and batons originally received from King Richard. Immediately Henry returned them, conferring their office under his new reign.

No one wanted to be on the deposition commission. But it had to be done. Most of the same people who had been present during the closed-door abdication attended this session as well, with the addition of a few more witnesses. Justice Thirning was appointed to head the committee, even though he was one of the newcomers.

It was decided that his presence would confer more gravity on the proceedings. He was not happy with this assignment; he knew his gravitas would be marred by his obvious discomfort.

On the following morning, as they filtered into the room, Richard did his best to appear regal, sitting on his chair and staring over their heads. The delegation suspected he knew nothing about what had occurred the day before, which made them even more uncomfortable. If they weren't so determined, they would have felt sorry for him.

Thirning stepped forward, bowing. "Sire, it is well known to you that there was a parliament summoned, and everything I shall say is on its behalf. We remind you that in this very room you resigned your lordship of your own free will, and discharged all your lieges of their obedience. Hence, we the commissioners as proctors of all three estates now retract their homage and fealty from yourself."

"No, I did not!" cried Richard, leaping to his feet. "I did not renounce my lordship! I am an anointed king. I am unable to renounce my sacramental unction. Ever."

Taken aback, the Justice glanced at the others. No one was bold enough to meet his eye. He pointed at the document he was holding. "But wait. In your own Renunciation, you said you were insufficient, unable, and unsuited to govern."

"This is not true! I merely said that my government had not been acceptable to the people."

"The words are clearly stated in the confession. It says so right here!" He held out the parchment for the king.

Richard snatched the document, reading it to himself while the others stood in silence. No one was aware of the Archbishop of Canterbury's ploy, substituting the document Richard had altered with the original. Too much had happened between that day and this, and they could be forgiven for not remembering the exact wording. There was even a signature, though again, who would have known if it was the king's hand or not?

But Richard knew. A succession of expressions crossed his face: anger, incredulity, and then—surprisingly—resignation. No one but the king knew that a similar substitution had occurred at Richard's behest when reading aloud the dead Duke of

Gloucester's confession. The king was a superstitious man. He sensed God's hand in judgment.

Smiling sadly, Richard passed the document back to Thirning. "I hope my cousin will be a good lord to me," he said sadly. Everyone heaved a sigh of relief. The way was open for Henry's coronation.

On Sunday, 12 October, Henry proceeded from the Tower of London to Westminster. As usual, it was customary for the new monarch to process across the city before the coronation, accompanied by a grand entourage.

As Henry nudged his gallant white charger out of the Tower grounds, the gloomy clouds burst into rain with a clap of thunder. He sighed in disappointment, looking down at his cloth-of-gold doublet. "Ruined," he said to no one in particular, looking back at the Mayor who led the aldermen of London, all in their scarlet liveries trimmed with fur. Already the robes dribbled a trail of red as the newly-dyed garments bled onto the ground.

"At least the crowd doesn't seem to mind," Erpingham said, pointing ahead. Lining the road and hanging out of every available window, the Londoners happily cheered their new hero. Already, wine ran from fountains in Cheapside and people lined up to take advantage of the bounty. The initial burst of rain slowed to a shower and Henry shook the water from his eyes; he wished he could have worn a hat.

Henry spent the night in Westminster Palace, rising early on Coronation day for confession and three masses. It was the Feast of St. Edward the Confessor, exactly one year since he left for France to begin his exile. Could there be a better affront to Richard, who considered the Confessor his own patron saint?

The monks of Westminster conducted Henry from the palace to the abbey. He walked beneath a canopy of blue silk, carried by four citizens of the Cinque Ports. On his left side, Hal bore the Sword of Justice— known as the Curtana—unsheathed and without a point, to represent the execution of justice without rancor. On his right, the Earl of Northumberland carried the sword Henry had worn when he landed at Ravenspur—henceforth to be called the Lancaster sword. On entering the church, they approached a raised platform on top of which sat the throne.

Placing himself behind his father with the other earls, Hal watched the monks strip Henry to the waist as he knelt on a cloth of gold. If anyone had bothered to look at him they would have seen a face deep in despondency. His father's usurpation had nothing to do with him—and everything to do with him. If it was God's will that Lancaster should take the throne, who was he to turn down the opportunity to reign after his father? And yet, he felt a pain in the pit of his stomach.

The Archbishop of Canterbury held up a figurine shaped like a golden eagle, garnished with pearls and precious stones. He opened it and pulled out a vial of sacred oil with which he anointed Henry in six places. Even this was an affront to Richard; the oil had been given to St. Thomas Becket by the Virgin Mary. It had been lost after the reign of Edward II and was recently discovered by Richard who had asked to be re-anointed with it. But no; Arundel had refused to sanctify him a second time. The sacred oil was later taken from the king during his imprisonment so it could be used on the usurper.

After draping the coronation robes around Henry's shoulders, the archbishop slipped red velvet slippers on his feet and spurs around his heel. Percy drew the Lancaster sword and held it up to be blessed. He handed it to Henry who resheathed it, and Arundel girt the sword around the king's waist. Then he took the crown of St. Edward and placed it upon the new king's head. Lastly, the archbishop slipped the signet ring onto Henry's finger—the one given him by Richard in the Tower.

Despite himself, Hal felt a chill go down his spine. Perhaps he was being too hard on his father. Perhaps it was God's will for Henry to raise Lancaster to its highest destiny. After all, they boasted royal blood, too. Much would have been different if his grandfather had worn the crown after the death of Edward III, instead of the ten year-old Richard. Gaunt had the stuff of kings. Hal hoped the same spark of greatness resided within his breast, as well.

Immediately after the ceremony, the attendees moved back to the palace for the banquet, which was held in the Great Hall under the new hammer-beam roof. The new king sat at the head table, alongside both archbishops and seventeen bishops. Hal stood behind him with his ceremonial sword, along with Percy; Henry's other sons sat at the lower end of the table. All the great magnates carried out their honorable duties: Arundel acted as butler; Lord Grey of Ruthin as naperer; Erpingham as chamberlain; the earl of Oxford as ewerer. The list went on and on.

The feast was served in three courses which included sturgeon, heron, boar's head, rabbit, partridge, eagle, along with spiced delicacies and sweetmeats. When the banquet was half over a great disturbance was heard at the north door and two knights on horseback clattered into the hall, fully armed. One carried a drawn sword and the other a lance. Behind them, Sir Thomas Dymock could be seen astride one of Henry's best war horses. He rode up to the king's herald and handed him a scroll.

"Oyez, oyez," the herald announced. "The king's champion proclaims he is ready to offer combat to any knight or gentleman who dared maintain that his liege lord here and present was not their lawful sovereign! He is ready to prove the contrary with his body here and now, or when and wheresoever it might please the king." Dymock nudged his stallion across the floor while the guests watched in silence.

Of course, this was standard practice at a king's coronation. Today it held special significance. "Thank you, Sir Thomas," Henry said. Anyone close by could see he was blushing. "If need be, I will ease thee of this office in mine own person."

Henry's skill as a jouster was legendary. It was true; he didn't really need a champion.

The day after coronation, parliament was called back into session. There were so many things to tend to, it was difficult to decide where to start.

First and foremost, Lancaster needed to secure his fledgling dynasty. With the approbation of the Commons, King Henry declared his son the Prince of Wales and heir apparent to the kingdom of England. Along with that, Hal automatically became Duke of Cornwall, Earl of Chester, and Duke of Aquitaine. Henry also declared Hal to be the Duke of Lancaster, which was to be kept separate from the crown. The dukedom had its own revenue and expenditures; it would be unwise to comingle them with the kingdom.

Hal knelt before his enthroned father, his face expressionless. Very few words had passed between them since the coronation. Hal was still fighting with his own conscience, and Henry struggled with the knowledge that he would have preferred his second son in Hal's place. Thomas would receive his own distinctions, but any title will pale in comparison with Hal's. Henry knew his sons didn't get along; how was he to keep peace in England if he couldn't even control his own household?

Never mind. Worry about that later. Best move onto the next order of business, which Henry knew would boost his popularity. At his signal, Archbishop Arundel stood to make the announcement: "The king declares that the acts of the 1397-98 Parliament are all to be repealed."

The hall burst into spontaneous exclamations. What a start! This was monumental. Richard had demanded so many oaths and fines to secure ratification that few of those present had been spared.

Arundel waited patiently until the noise died down. "The falsely accused victims or their heirs are be restored to their lands and titles," he continued. Most of the men who benefitted from the confiscations were Richard's favorites; it was almost a foregone conclusion that they were going to lose their positions. "Furthermore, the decisions of the Parliament of 1388, the eleventh year of King Richard, are henceforth to be reaffirmed."

And so, the last twelve years of Richard's reign were effectively nullified. Of course, this was easier said than done. Lives had been lost; fortunes had been snuffed out. Some disputes went back to Edward II's time. It would take years to sort it all out. But at least a start had been made. It was time to call certain malefactors to account.

The following day, the Commons declared it was time for justice to be served. Right away, they insisted King Richard should be arrested and put to death. This, Henry would absolutely not consider. They had no choice but to move on.

John Doreward, the speaker stepped forward. "We of the Commons declare that five major injustices were inflicted in the accursed Parliament of 1397. The first was that you yourself was ready to do wager by battle with the Duke of Norfolk. Instead you were exiled for ten years without cause. The second injustice was that the Archbishop of Canterbury was outlawed without being given the opportunity to defend himself. The third was that the Duke of Gloucester was murdered and judged a traitor after his death. The fourth was that the Earl of Arundel was not allowed his pardon and was adjudged a traitor. And the fifth injustice was that all the power of this evil parliament was placed in one person." The speaker turned to the Commons, holding out his arm for affirmation. He was not disappointed.

"I ask you, sire, how could all these injustices have been committed without the advice of the former king's counselors? We understand there were certain bills drawn up bearing their names, and we request that these records be read out in parliament."

Henry nodded. "I grant this request, provided you name the counselors so the bills can be read in their presence."

"We thank you, your majesty. To begin with, we declare the former king's advisors Bushy, Bagot, and Green, to be enemies of the people. They have practiced deceit, treachery, and embezzlement while executing the king's warrants."

Although Bushy and Greene had been dragged to the scaffold and beheaded in Bristol— along with LeScrope—Bagot had so far escaped punishment. He had gone to Ireland to warn Richard about Henry's landing but was subsequently arrested and hauled back to London in chains. At this juncture, he was brought into parliament to answer for his crimes.

Henry spoke first. "I read the bills you submitted in your defense. Do you still stand by them?"

"Yes I do." Bagot drew himself up, though it was difficult as he was still manacled. "I accuse Edward of Rutland, Duke of Aumale. He was King Richard's principal evil counselor." He glared at the duke. "It was you," he shouted, "who said that the Duke of Gloucester and the earls of Warwick and Arundel had to be killed. You claimed that if left alive, the king would never be able to exercise his regal power to the full." He turned to the assembly. "I know for a fact the king ordered Rutland to send two yeomen to Calais. They were to assist the Duke of Norfolk and assure that Gloucester was put to death."

Enraged, Rutland leaped to his feet. "You lie! You are a despicable scoundrel and a false liar and I shall prove it with my body!"

Henry pursed his lips. He could not afford to let this get out of hand. Bagot had been loyal to his house for decades. It was he who had sent a warning for Henry to be on his guard while still an exile in France. Rutland could not be spared either; he was the heir to the dukedom of York and his father was in poor health. "Cousin," Henry said sternly, "sit down."

Rutland gave him an angry glance but obeyed. However, Bagot was not to get off so easily.

"Tell me, Sir William Bagot," the Speaker pursued, "why did you countenance the bad advice given to the king, when you knew in all honesty you should have resisted?"

The prisoner's face turned red in anger. "Listen to you! Is there anyone in this room who would have dared to refuse, if King Richard demanded anything? I see many who should be asked the same question." He stared at the Hollands.

As two of the Counter-Appellants, John and Tom Holland were uncomfortably aware that Bagot told the truth. It was time to take the offensive or be accused along with Rutland. "How dare you try to shift the blame from yourself by denouncing others?" John shouted, leaping to his feet. His nephew stood, adding his voice to the hubbub. "We had nothing to do with the death of Gloucester! Anyone who says otherwise must answer to me!"

This time King Henry stood up. "My lords, this is unseemly. Take your seats."

Bowing in uneasy acquiescence, the Hollands cooperated.

Gathering his wits, Bagot saw an opportunity. "The responsibility must be shared by all those who gave their consent in parliament—both lords temporal and spiritual!" He continued to stare at Aumale. "If you really want to know what happened to the Duke of Gloucester, I suggest you ask Norfolk's valet John Hall. You can find him in Newgate prison."

CHAPTER 11

To almost everyone, the name John Hall meant absolutely nothing. But Henry assumed Bagot wouldn't bring him up unless he knew something meaningful. He leaned over to Archbishop Arundel, instructing him to recess parliament until the next day. In the interim, they could recover Hall from Newgate and question him.

The prisoner was easily found and brought into parliament, manacled at the ankles and shackled at the wrists. Looking about in trepidation at the glowering faces, he tripped as he was led up to the bar. The guard grabbed him and turned him around to face the members.

James Billingford, one of the king's clerks, was instructed to interrogate the prisoner. He walked up to Hall, jutting out his chin.

"John Hall, valet to the Duke of Norfolk, were you present at the death of the Duke of Gloucester?"

Taking a deep breath, Hall nodded. "Yes, I was there unwillingly. I was asleep when the Duke of Norfolk ordered my presence. It was around midnight. I went to his solar. He looked terrible, like he hadn't slept for days. 'What do you know about the Duke of Gloucester?' he asked. I was confused, for I thought the duke was dead and I told him so. Then he said no, the duke was not dead but that the king and the Duke of Aumale, who was then Earl of Rutland, sent men to Calais to kill him. He ordered me to accompany five of his own men, two valets of Rutland's, and William Serle, who was King Richard's chamber valet, to the Duke of Gloucester's cell. I knew what was going to happen." He looked imploringly at Billingford. "I'm not an assassin. I told Norfolk no, I did not want to do this thing, even if I had to be dismissed and suffer the loss of all my goods. Suddenly, he leaped to his feet and gave me such a blow to the side of the head he almost knocked me to the floor. 'You will go,' he said, 'or else you will hang tomorrow. For it is the king and the Earl of Rutland who have ordered his death and it must be accomplished'. What could I do? I was in fear for my life." He stopped talking while the members grumbled amongst themselves. Rutland was squirming in his seat but his father restrained him.

Refusing to look at the Duke of Aumale, Hall continued. "We were all taken to the Church of Our Lady of Calais and made to swear on the body of Christ that we would tell no one about what was to happen. Then we were taken to the castle where the duke was imprisoned. I guarded the door of his room while Serle and one of Rutland's valets strangled him with his own scarf then covered him with his mattress to make sure he was dead." He stopped abruptly as the hall burst into pandemonium. Although many suspected Gloucester had been murdered, this was the first time it came out into the open.

Aumale was frantic. He stood and tried to outshout his neighbors, punching his fist in the air. "The man lies," he cried, aware that nobody listened to him. "I sent no one to Calais!"

Hall grimaced, knowing it was his word against the duke's. However, it seemed Aumale had little support. No one could understand anyone else in all the ruckus; at least the fingers pointed at the duke rather than the hapless prisoner. Finally, the archbishop pounded his staff on the floor until the noise died down.

"I demand to be heard," shouted Lord Fitzwalter, who had an especial dispute with Aumale. After more pounding, he was given leave. "It was you who accused Gloucester of treason," he snarled at the duke. "And it was you who made the king hate him. For all these reasons, you were midwife to his murder, which I shall prove in battle." Tearing off his hood, he hurled it to the floor.

"And here is my hood!" cried Aumale, throwing his own in response.

The tumult began again. The old Earl of Warwick flung his hood on the floor, then Lord Morley, then Lord William of Beauchamp. Following their lead, every single earl and baron threw their hoods down while the Commons roared their outrage, threatening to charge across the room. The guards struggled to hold them back with halberds.

"My God, Thomas," Henry stood, grabbing the archbishop's wrist, "they are going to kill him right in front of me!" He held out his arms. "My lords, my lords, restrain yourselves. Please, for the love of God, stop this clamor!" He waved at the turmoil, and even took Arundel's staff, banging it on the floor. Nobody heard him.

"I command you to stop this uproar," he warned, still shouting. "You disregard my demands at your own risk!" Still, the men were so intent on their own anger that nobody heeded.

The king turned to Worcester, standing behind the throne. "Have the heralds sound the trumpets. We need to stop this now."

Horns blasted through the hall, drawing everyone's attention. Pausing in the middle of their scuffling, men finally noticed that the king was shaking with fury.

"I order you not to do anything which is against the law," Henry roared. "Where is your sense of decorum? Restrain yourselves until we can discuss this rationally."

Fortunately, Henry's speech had an effect and the hall quieted down. Men took their seats again. Hall looked around, hoping he was forgotten in all the excitement. No such luck. James Billingford, the king's clerk, was standing before him, watching the king. Henry nodded toward him.

"My lords, what is your judgment against this man?" He pointed at Hall.

"Death," someone shouted. "A traitor's death," shouted another. The room threatened to break out in an uproar again, when the king held out his hands. He was still standing.

"We need order," he called out. "One at a time, my lords, give me your judgment." As he waited, the earls and barons stood one by one and called out "death" in a determined voice.

The prisoner had visibly slumped; he needed help to stay on his feet. Wanting to get this ordeal over with, King Henry immediately gave his verdict. "John Hall, I condemn you to be drawn, disemboweled, then hanged, beheaded, and quartered. Lord Marshal, take him to Tyburn at once and perform your duty."

At first, Hall was dumbfounded; he had done nothing to deserve a traitor's death. Then he realized he was to be sacrificed to avenge Gloucester's murder. "No, no," he screamed. "I am innocent. I swear to you that I did not kill the Duke of Gloucester!" Two guards grasped his arms and dragged him from the room, for by then he had lost the use of his legs. "No! Spare me! I am innocent of wrongdoing!" As he was hauled out the door, his voice took a long time to fade away until finally he was gone, leaving the assembly with a sickening sense of relief.

But the Duke of Gloucester mystery hadn't been cleared up yet. The following day, William Rickhill was brought before parliament, having been arrested for his part in acquiring the duke's final confession. From the very beginning he had expected this day to come, and he had scrupulously documented every step of his unfortunate commission.

As Walter Clopton, chief justice, stood before him, Rickhill drew himself up, refusing to be intimidated. After all, he was once a justice of the common bench himself, which was why King Richard chose him to do this unwelcome task.

Clopton cleared his throat. "The circumstances surrounding the Duke of Gloucester's confession are unclear," he said in introduction. "We would like to hear from your lips exactly what happened."

Rickhill was ready. "Sire, my lords and gentlemen of the Commons. I will tell you the incidents as they happened. The night of the 6 September 1397 I was awoken from my bed and given a letter from the king, instructing me to accompany the Duke of Norfolk to Calais. Immediately. Under pain of forfeiture. I had no idea what this was all about but of course I obeyed." He paused, though no one had a question. "When I reached Calais, the Duke of Norfolk made me swear an oath not to reveal my commission to anyone, then he gave me a writ from the king. Both this writ and the original summons were dated three weeks previously." That elicited a bit of grumbling, but it didn't last long.

Taking a deep breath, Rickhill went on. "The writ commanded me to interview the Duke of Gloucester concerning the events of the Parliaments of 1386-88. I was astonished, because I believed the duke was already dead." He looked at Clopton. "It had been announced to all the people both in Calais and in England. However, Norfolk assured me the duke was very much alive. I was concerned about my participation in this irregular assignment and I demanded witnesses, which were permitted me. I respectfully ask you to call John Lovetot and John Lancaster, esquires, to corroborate my testimony." He paused as the clerk took note of their names. "I was taken to the duke who was imprisoned in Calais Castle. After determining he suffered no physical abuse, I showed him the king's writ, then left him alone for the rest of the afternoon to compose his statement. I told him to make a copy for his own records, which he did. Then I returned the same evening and he gave me his confession, asking that I come back in the morning in case there was something he needed to add. Unfortunately, the following day, I was refused entry and did not see the duke again."

After having heard Hall's testimony, it was evident to everyone the duke must have been murdered after turning over his confession to Rickhill. The witness was almost forgotten in the pandemonium that broke out once again, shattering the uneasy calm that had been enforced on the assembly. More pounding and shouting brought order back into the hall.

Clopton wiped the sweat from his forehead. "Please go on. What happened next?"

"I brought the confession back to the king; it happened to be the day before parliament started. Before I handed it over, I requested an official registered copy, sealed by the chancellor. Here it is." He pulled a document from under his arm. "This is the exact copy of the Duke of Gloucester's confession. You may compare it word for word with the duke's copy, which is in the possession of Sir Peter Courtenay, Captain of Calais." He held it out to the chief justice. "I am very fortunate to have done so, because when the confession was delivered to the Parliament of 1397, the statements which pleased the king were read, and the parts he didn't want known were not read."

Rickhill neglected to mention that he was the one who read the altered document, but he was in enough trouble as it was without incriminating himself. Fortunately, nobody noticed. There were too many more important issues to absorb.

"Let me get this straight," Clompton said. "When the confession was read out to parliament, no one knew it had been written just a week before?"

Rickhill lowered his head. "That is correct."

"It was undated?"

"The king removed the date."

"And you said nothing?"

127

"I had been sworn to secrecy. I was in fear for my life."

Everyone who had been there remembered the trepidation pervading Richard's parliament. The Earl of Arundel had just been executed after bravely and recklessly defending himself. His pardon had been revoked and he was declared traitor and his children disinherited. And now, to everyone's horror, it was more than ever apparent that the king was responsible for Gloucester's death and went to great lengths to cover his tracks. It was no wonder Rickhill feared for his life.

"Let me go on record," he said, "that I did nothing except what I was ordered to do. I passed on the Duke of Gloucester's confession exactly as it was given to me, and I feel I did everything that was legal."

The chief justice turned to the Lords, holding up the confession. "I move that Justice Rickhill has acted honorably in this matter and he should be fully acquitted. What say you?"

A chorus of ayes followed his suggestion. William Rickhill, King Richard's unwilling instrument, was exonerated.

The Speaker of the Commons stood forward. "We move that the former King Richard should be brought into the presence of parliament to answer for the crimes of which he is accused."

"Hear, hear," came the answers from all over the hall. "King Richard should be executed!" someone else shouted. "Kill King Richard!" "Execute the tyrant!"

Henry sat for a few minutes, listening to the furor. Then he stood. "My lords, my lords. This is not how we must proceed! I will not order Sir Richard's execution!"

Reminded that Richard was no longer king and Henry was no tyrant, the assembly quieted down.

"There is something of import that I shall do right now." Henry's voice was conciliatory. He turned to Arundel. "Have them bring in the chest."

The chest? What was this? He had gotten everyone's attention. As they waited, two guards carried in a large wooden box wrapped in straps. The archbishop made theatrical gestures as he untied the straps and threw them off. Henry opened the lid and pulled out two parchments, holding them up.

"Behold. Here are the blank charters the former king extorted from the lords and commons of the realm!" There was a collective intake of breath. Many in the room had been targeted by these very same writs. Their function was to hold the named person hostage for any actions the king found offensive. They served as Richard's *carte blanche* to impose any sized fine or confiscate a man's property at the king's will. "I hereby order these charters canceled. Sergeant, take these out and burn them immediately."

Henry's gesture couldn't fail to elicit a cheer. One of the most onerous aspects of Richard's rule had just been nullified. Henry's ploy worked; demands for the former king's execution were forgotten. At least for the moment.

But the king wasn't finished. "Consider this, my lords and members of parliament. Since my predecessor has redefined treason, this has opened up a whole new opportunity to pursue victims at the king's discretion! That was never the intent of good King Edward III. I put this to you: the first step in restoring justice is to reaffirm the Statute of Treasons of 1351. It should take more than disagreeing with the king to be declared a traitor. According to the original statute, a man is guilty if he plans the death of a king or his family, levies war against him or adheres to his enemies. Not simply because he speaks out against him."

Everyone agreed to the validity of this proposal. King Henry had gone far in restoring composure to the room. This was a promising start. The Statute was duly voted upon then the session was called to an end. That was enough business for one day.

The following morning, Archbishop Arundel gave a preliminary address. "My lords," he said. "It is time for you to decide how the former king should be dealt with, saving his life which King Henry wishes to be preserved."

This question was for the Lords to decide—all fifty-eight of them. Not the Commons. Among the Lords sat two archbishops, thirteen bishops, seven abbots, Prince Henry, the Duke of York, six earls, twenty-four lords, and four knights. For three days they discussed their options before they came to an agreement. Richard was to be kept in total isolation in perpetuity. He was to be moved to a secret place, and with no delay.

That very night, Richard had been asleep for a couple of hours when he was awakened by a knock on his door, immediately followed by the entry of two guards carrying candles.

"Awake, sire," one of them said in a gruff voice.

Richard sat on his bed. "What is the meaning of this?"

"You are to come with us," the other demanded, pushing forward a young page carrying a black garment. "Put on those clothes."

Irritation was turning into alarm. "By whose orders?"

"By order of the king."

"I was not told!"

"Sire, our orders were very clear. We are to take you by boat to your next destination."

"In the middle of the night?" Richard stood, ignoring the servant who was proffering the tunic. "I shall not go."

"You shall, sire, or we are instructed to carry you." The man was neither respectful nor rude. He was just doing his job.

Richard snatched the garment from the page and pulled off his nightclothes. With the boy's help, he dressed and put on his shoes, taking as much time as he dared. His guards stood silently before the open door. The king looked around his room. He had nothing to bring with him; everything had been taken. Straightening to his full height, he declared himself ready.

The watergate at the Tower flowed directly into the Thames. Seeing the boat at the bottom of the steps, Richard lost his composure.

"No, this is not the way I was supposed to be treated," he insisted, pulling back.

Unimpressed, his guards took the king by the arms and thrust him into the boat. One of them took up the oars while his companion restrained the prisoner until he slumped onto his seat. Other accomplices shut the gates behind them and they slipped into the river, heading downstream.

"Oh, why was I ever born?" Richard wailed. "No one is to know the fate of this unfortunate king!" His guards let him moan and groan as much as he wanted, for by now they were traveling with the current and the wind threw away his words like so much clatter. After a while the king exhausted himself and sat mutely, watching the shore glide by in the darkness. He couldn't see much, but he knew when they were passing Greenwich. By the time they got to Gravesend, he was too tired to complain anymore.

Over the next couple of weeks, Richard was dragged all over the country until he finally rested at the great Lancastrian stronghold of Pontefract, way to the north. It was King Henry's plan to confound any possible followers, and he succeeded flawlessly. Richard disappeared from sight. With very few exceptions, no one had any idea where he was locked away. And with very few exceptions, Richard was never seen again by his countrymen.

Now parliament could turn its attention to the Counter-Appellants. The whole John Hall incident had proved only a diversion; the issues still needed to be addressed. There was plenty of suppressed anger on both sides, and Richard's favorites knew they were on a knife's edge. Some of the Lords had been victims of Richard's policies; others were heirs of those who had not survived. Some of them had initially supported the king and had been outwitted by him, to their great loss. Some had benefitted at the expense of others. The Lords were only united by their hatred of the Counter-Appellants.

On 29 October, Justice Thirning opened proceedings. "We bring charges against the following confederates: Edward Rutland, Duke of Aumale; John Holland, Duke of Exeter; Tom Holland, Duke of Surrey; John Beaufort, Marquis of Dorset; Thomas Despenser, Earl of Gloucester; and John Montagu, Earl of Salisbury." These were six of the eight infamous Counter-Appellants; the other two, Thomas Mowbray and William LeScrope were already dead. "These charges are threefold: one, that they presented their appeal in the Parliament of 1397-98; two, that they consented to the Duke of Gloucester's murder; and three, that they assented to the confiscation of Duke Henry's inheritance."

Rutland jumped to his feet. "We deny absolutely that we had anything to do with the Duke of Gloucester's death! I did not advise it, assent to it, or agree to it. I knew nothing about it until the king announced it in the hall of Nottingham castle."

Lord Fitzwalter, interrupted. "You cannot hide your misdeeds behind the king's skirts! I say you helped him plan the duke's death!"

John Holland, added his voice to the fray. "We were coerced into doing what the king commanded."

"And I say you lie!" Fitzwalter roared.

"I stand ready to defend myself," Rutland answered scornfully.

"I will prove you guilty with my body," shouted Lord Morley.

"And I challenge you," retorted Holland.

Once again, the hall was in an uproar. Exasperated, Henry stood, ordering the archbishop to pound his staff. "That will be enough!" he shouted. "I will have no more fighting in this parliament!"

Grumbling, the assembly sat back down.

"We will take a one-hour recess. Bring your tempers under control while I confer with the Archbishop of Canterbury." He gestured for Arundel to follow and left the room; they retired to a private chamber.

Sitting at a table, the king removed his coronet and held it in both hands, staring at the elaborate gold metalwork. It was a lighter circlet, worked with acanthus leaves—not the massive jewel-studded crown he wore at his coronation. Arundel could see he wasn't really looking at it.

"This gets heavier and heavier every day," Henry said, finally putting it on the table. "How can I keep peace and satisfy my tempestuous Lords at the same time?"

"They want blood," Arundel said.

"And what if I let them eliminate these dukes and earls? That leaves me even more exposed to the demands of those who supported me in my enterprise. These Counter-Appellants serve as a bulwark between me and them. Besides, I believe they are not irreconcilable."

"I see what you mean. Though they did serve Richard through self-interest, mostly."

"I believe they did. And now it's in their interest to serve me, as long as I show clemency."

The archbishop scratched his neck. "However, the Lords will expect some sort of punishment. If you show too much mercy, they may take that for weakness."

"You are right, of course." Henry twisted a ring on his fourth finger. "We shall strip them of their new ranks, all achieved in 1397, as well as the material rewards they received—all their ill-begotten lands and estates."

"And we will make them understand if they ever raise a finger in Richard's behalf, they will be declared traitors."

"Very well." Henry put the crown back on. "Let's get this over with."

The members were restless but settled back down when the king returned to his high-backed chair. Henry nodded to the archbishop, who stepped forward.

"King Henry has made his decision. He has decreed that the six Counter-Appellants on trial shall revert to their former rank. Henceforth, Edward Rutland, John Holland, and Tom Holland will be stripped of their dukedoms, John Beaufort will lose his marquisate, and Thomas Despenser and John Montagu shall lose their earldoms. All the lands and goods they received in 1397 shall be confiscated and returned to their rightful owners. As security for the future, they are prohibited from distributing livery badges, and if they become an adherent to former King Richard in any way, they do so under pain of treason. The king," continued the archbishop, "does not want to threaten the populace. He intends to make his judgments in righteousness and truth, with mercy and grace."

Henry was satisfied with this sentiment. As he expected, the assembly was not. Leniency was not a quality they wanted in their king at the moment. But he felt reconciliation was the best way to reestablish a form of peace in the kingdom.

Very quickly, he was undeceived. Even before parliament was over, he found a letter in his chamber threatening a rebellion if he permitted the Counter-Appellants to live. And a few short months after that, events were to prove the anonymous penman correct, though not in the manner his threats were intended.

CHAPTER 12

Every time Henry received a letter from Joanna he withdrew into his solar, dismissed his servants, and sat in his window seat. He relished these few moments alone when he could forget about his troubles. This day, he was especially glad there were no witnesses, for the news took him by surprise. His hand shook and he leaned his head against the wall, closing his eyes until his heart slowed down.

Chewing his lower lip, he put the letter in his lap. Oh, how he wished he could sprout wings and fly across the Channel, take her into his arms and never let go. Was it a sin to covet this woman, not even knowing whether she returned his feelings or not? Did he dare hope?

Once again he raised the missive, trying to read between the lines:

> *My dear friend,*
> *I have sad tidings to pass on to you. My husband took to his bed a week ago, complaining of pains in his chest, and he never got up again. He breathed his last this very day, leaving me as regent of Brittany for our little son who is only ten years old. May God take my lord into His keeping and forgive his sins.*

Dead! The Duke of Brittany was dead! No man should rejoice over another's demise, but the duke had led a long and fruitful life. Henry was ashamed of himself for immediately thinking the duchess was no longer out of his reach. Yet it couldn't be helped; the notion came of its own accord.

He scanned the rest of the letter, seeing little that gave away her state of mind.

I shall write again soon once I have made arrangements for his state funeral and ensured the stability of our disaffected nobles. My thoughts go out to you in your time of trial.
Yours affectionately,
Joanna

The date on the letter was 1 November. That was a week ago, and his own troubled reign was only five weeks old. Suddenly he felt the need for a queen who would share his deepest concerns and give him solace, for truly he felt completely alone. What good was the crown when you were surrounded by people you couldn't trust? How much simpler life had been when he was merely Henry Bolingbroke, Earl of Derby. How he missed those days already.

And suddenly, the woman he longed for was released from what must surely have been a difficult marriage, considering the Duke of Brittany was old enough to be her father. Although Henry saw how affectionate they acted toward each other, in his heart he believed that her devotion was purely platonic.

He owed much to the duke, for without the man's generous aid he might not have made it back to England in good time. He was glad that his behavior had been impeccable during his stay there; nothing had been done to betray the sacred bond between host and guest. His feelings and desires were his own. No one could fault what he kept inside his heart.

But now...

She had expressed herself well, back when he spent those innocent hours in her company, playing music together. A connection, she said. Of the spirit. Did her feelings extend beyond mere empathy? He felt that they did, and his own most certainly drove him to distraction. How should he approach her?

There was no way he could wait. Henry sat at his desk and pulled over a blank sheet of parchment. He dipped his quill slowly, trying to decide what to say.

Dearest Joanna,
I received your tidings with sadness. Your duke was the most solicitous partner and I know you miss him terribly. The country will miss him. In time, and with your guidance, your son will most certainly prove himself a worthy successor.

135

Henry chewed the end of the quill. With the formalities out of the way, how was he to continue? Should he wait until some time had passed? After all, she was the grieving widow. Or was she?

I don't know how to say this, but my heart goes out to you in more ways than one. As a friend, I offer my sincerest condolences. As a king, I offer you something more. When the time is right, I hope that you might consider a place by my side as queen of England.

There. It was said. Why pretend otherwise? He was gambling that she felt the same way he did. If not, well... It could be disastrous. For him.

He picked up the parchment, getting ready to tear it in two. Then he stopped. No. It was not in his nature to take the easy way out. If he wasn't a decisive man, he wouldn't be king. He would trust his instincts.

Sealing the letter, he called for a messenger. Best to send this right away, before he changed his mind.

A week before Christmas, the Abbey House at Westminster was host to a suspicious collection of visitors—suspicious, that is, if you were King Henry. In earlier days, they were often seen together, for these were the very men so recently pardoned, to the great discontent of Henry's supporters. While William Colchester waited for his guests to show up, he sipped from his special batch of Bordeaux wine with Bishop Merks. William was abbot of Westminster and Merks had been put under his watch after defending the king at the last parliament.

"I have asked our most important allies to come first," William said. "What we will be proposing is so dangerous we can only trust very few with full disclosure."

Merks shifted uncomfortably. "Are you sure you want me to be here?"

"Of course, my friend. Your bravery in speaking out against the usurper makes you a natural leader."

Shaking his head, Merks looked up as a servant went to answer the door. "Poor Richard. He did not deserve his treatment."

"That's what we intend to redress. Oh, here are the Hollands." John and Tom came in, shaking their cloaks.

"It's starting to sleet," John said. "Maybe it's better that way. Who would want to follow us in this weather?" He handed his cloak to the servant then turned to the bishop. "I am glad to see you are well. I feared the king would turn his vengeance on you."

Merks reached out, touching John's arm. "God is with me," he said simply.

As they helped themselves to the abbot's wine, Rutland came in, followed by Despenser and Salisbury. All of them had recently been freed from incarceration—some in the Tower, some elsewhere—and they were not entirely at ease.

"These are troubling times," said Rutland. "So much has happened behind closed doors. And now we have to worry about disgruntled barons coming after us for anything they can get their hands on." He looked around. "Where is our last Counter-Appellant? Where is John Beaufort?"

"He is in King Henry's camp now," said Holland. "We cannot trust him."

"There is much to discuss," said the abbot, taking a fireplace poker and prodding the logs. A spray of embers flew up the chimney. "As soon as Maudeleyn gets here, we can begin. The rest will be introduced to our plan as we require them." He stood, his face stern. "We cannot risk too many people knowing all the details."

Shortly thereafter, their last conspirator arrived. Tall, elegant, red-haired, and fine-boned, Richard Maudeleyn swept in with a little smile, pulling off his hood. For a moment, everyone looked at him sharply, holding their breath. He bore such an uncanny resemblance to the former king his very presence affected them deeply. Now that Richard was gone they remembered his best qualities and forgot the worst. As they stared at the king's look-alike, his soul seemed to shine through Maudeleyn's eyes.

Then the cleric spoke and the illusion vanished. "I'm sorry to have kept you waiting," he said. "Have I missed anything?"

Blinking, the abbot shook his head. "Not at all. Now, if you will, dinner awaits in the next room."

The table was set and the food laid out. All servants had been dismissed. William went to the door to establish that no one waited outside, then sat down and helped himself. They ate quietly, hesitant to start a discussion that would assuredly lead them into the greatest danger.

Finally, John Holland sat back, pushing his knife into what remained of a chicken leg. "My friends," he said, "you all know why we are here. A great wrong has been done to my brother the king, and it is our task to put things to rights."

The others nodded, though no one answered him.

"We all know that King Henry will be hosting a tournament at Windsor on the Epiphany," he added. "I propose we hide our retainers in carts of harnesses ahead of time in preparation for the joust. When the moment is right, we will give the signal and they will kill the guards and let us in." His co-conspirators appeared to be concentrating on their food, though he knew they were listening. "There *is* a precedent," he insisted. "The same thing was done very successfully back in 1314 when the Castle of Linlithgow was recaptured by the Scots after Bannockburn."

"We can catch the whole royal family there," said Salisbury. "King Henry's reign will be the shortest in English history."

Killing the king was an unpalatable thought, but there was no alternative.

"Good," said John Holland. "There is more. I have two men in my employ who are ready to carry out Richard's escape from Pontefract." The abbot knew about the plan; the rest of the men were totally unprepared. Maudeleyn dropped his knife.

"How did you find out where he was?" asked Despenser.

"Harry Hotspur. He is greatly offended that King Henry betrayed his oath. Very little happens in Yorkshire without Percy's knowledge. Once he learned Richard had been imprisoned at Pontefract, he sent his priest to us with an offer to help." The others murmured their amazement.

"As you probably know," John went on, "the castellan is Robert Waterton, an old retainer of Lancaster. His loyalty is unassailable. Fortunately, our priest has a friend inside who is more obliging. They will drug Waterton's posset the night of 1

January and rescue the king, bringing him to Scotland and safety. With King Richard out of the country, our own enterprise will have a much better chance of success." He took a sip of his wine.

The plan was daring. John could see the hesitation around the table. "We won't expose Richard to any of our violence. Maudeleyn can impersonate him until it's safe to bring him home."

Letting out a sigh, Maudeleyn picked up his knife. "I *would* feel much better if the king was safely out of Lancaster's hands." Reluctantly, the others agreed.

"It's no less dangerous than the rest of our plan," John insisted. "There's no turning back from treason."

"Unless the treason is perpetrated against a traitor," Rutland said.

"Exactly. Remember what we have to gain. Are you with me?" John swiveled around, looking back and forth across the table. Everyone nodded silently.

Satisfied with their reactions, the abbot went to the door of his side chamber and opened it, poking his head through. "Are you ready?" he asked the cleric inside. Hearing an assent, he turned to his guests. "We have prepared covenants for you." The secretary had drawn up six small deeds which were notched in such a way they all fit together to make one large sheet of parchment.

John Holland took out his seal as Earl of Huntingdon. "I swear by my soul to be faithful to my partners even unto death," he read aloud, "and restore King Richard to his kingdom or die in the attempt. I shall be the first to affix my seal." He dripped a circle of wax on each of the six deeds and pressed his signet.

His nephew Tom stepped up. "To this, I do swear," he said and put his seal as Earl of Kent next to John's. Rutland looked at John and hesitated before affixing his own. Salisbury, Despenser, and Maudeleyn swore an oath and followed in turn. The abbot and bishop were not to be part of the fighting and did not put their seal to the deeds. As prelates, their oath to be silent was quite sufficient.

As John passed each copy to his confederates, he said, "Between now and the fourth of January, we shall each gather a force and assemble at Kingston-upon-Thames. May God bless our enterprise and restore King Richard to his rightful place."

The abbot of Westminster made the sign of the cross over their bent heads, trying to ignore the fact that their success meant the death of Henry of Lancaster and his four sons. Not for the first time, he wondered if God had turned his back on this unhappy country.

Richard Plantagenet lay in his bed staring at the ceiling. It was too cold to open the shutters, and night fell so early this time of year he might as well go to sleep. What else was there to do? He could hear the holiday celebrations downstairs and tried not to think back to his own Christmas festivities. Courtiers showed off their elegant robes and glittering damsels danced to the lively music played by French minstrels. Jugglers and mummers and magicians outdid each other with bawdy witticisms, while poets and bards captivated their listeners. He remembered his first Christmas with Anne, before they were even married, when Geoffrey Chaucer entertained them with his newest composition, Troilus and Criseyde. He was so distracted by his bride-to-be he barely listened; he couldn't keep his eyes off her sweet face. *Oh, Anne.*

Richard put his hands over his face, though in near total darkness there was nothing for him to hide from. If Anne had lived, so much would have been different. She may even have kept him from his fatal slide into vengeance which led to his undoing. He remembered what she said, that night before she breathed her last. *"You mustn't lose your faith,"* she said. *"I will be watching over you. Remember, you must be strong. Don't let your enemies find any reason to rebel against you. Be kind..."* Richard sighed. In his grief, he had failed to heed her words. Was she truly watching over him? What would she say to him now?

Was this little prison destined to be his home for the rest of his life? From a kingdom to a tower—how his world had collapsed. He was lucky they gave him more than one chamber, but he had already inspected every corner, counted every footstep. How was he going to survive without losing his mind? How long before he no longer cared? Already he had quit counting the days, though he reckoned he had been there about two months.

At least they allowed him a candle at night. He stared at the flame, watching it flicker as an occasional gust slipped in between the shutters. His candle was his company while he reviewed every mistake he had made—every irresponsible command, every vindictive accusation. Even so, he might have gotten away with it all had he been more careful about Bolingbroke's inheritance. Who would have thought Henry had the initiative to invade with only a handful of followers? Oh yes, Richard could see that his biggest error was taking all his best soldiers to Ireland, leaving England under the feeble care of his uncle the Duke of York. His second biggest error was not returning the moment he had learned about Bolingbroke's invasion. *Curse that Rutland. It was all his fault! I never should have listened to him!*

Even these recriminations weren't enough to keep him awake. He didn't know how long he had been asleep when a click and stealthy footsteps woke him up. Reaching for a dinner knife he had secreted beneath his pillow, Richard stiffened, prepared to strike as soon as his murderers came close enough. What else could they be?

But they weren't quite furtive enough. Assassins didn't make noises. Holding his breath, Richard watched as two men approached his bed and stopped.

"Your majesty?" one of them whispered.

He didn't respond, not certain what to do.

"Wake up, your majesty," the other said softly. "We don't have much time."

Somewhat reassured, Richard sat up. "Who sent you?"

"Your brother, John Holland. We've come to take you away from here."

He didn't need to be told twice. Reaching for a tunic, Richard pulled it over his head. One of the men knelt and helped him on with his shoes.

"Come, sire. We must be as silent as possible."

"What of the constable?"

"His wine was drugged. Fortunately, there was a lot of drinking tonight."

"The most difficult part will be getting you out of the castle," the other said. "Once we are in the cellar, I know a passage to the outside."

Richard had no choice but to trust these strangers. Throwing a cloak over his shoulders, he followed them from the room and down the winding stairs. They stayed as close to the wall as possible.

Pontefract was a large castle and Richard had seen none of it outside of his own rooms. One of his rescuers led the way and the other stayed behind him as they navigated the rough passages mostly used by servants. At the first doorway, they saw a guard sitting on a bench, leaning against the wall. Stopping, the man in front of Richard put a finger to his mouth and they waited. A snort and a snore told them all they needed to know. Carefully, they tiptoed past him. A little further along, they could hear another guard walking and again they paused, hugging the wall. He passed at the end of the corridor without looking to the side. Richard began to tremble though his companions ignored his distress, nudging him forward. They found their way to a storeroom which was deserted, and down another flight of stairs. The man in front of Richard pointed for them to follow through a wine cellar, then he took a sharp left between two huge barrels. He pulled aside a curtain against the wall, exposing a small door. He tried to lift the latch, but it was stuck. The door wouldn't budge.

"Damn!" He jiggled the latch again. "Blasted door hasn't been used in years." He looked around. "We can't afford to wait." Raising his leg, he pushed his foot against the wood next to the lock. The door shivered, sending an echo throughout the room.

"Careful!" the other growled. "You'll raise the whole castle." All three froze, waiting to hear if they had awakened any guards. Nothing yet. "Go on. Try it again."

This time the latch moved and the door creaked open. The first man swept the cobwebs out of the way before ducking and moving into a tunnel. Neither had brought a torch, so they felt their way forward in the dark. Something slithered over Richard's foot. He shuddered.

The last man closed the door. Step by step they continued deeper into the tunnel. Richard thought he had never seen such blackness. He was grateful to hear the shuffling of his companions' feet; at least he knew he wasn't alone. They were going steadily downhill, which was very disconcerting, and there was not enough space to stand up straight. An occasional grunt denoted a stubbed toe or a scraped hand. More than once Richard tripped, only to be supported by his more robust escorts. Soon he lost all track of time and place, and it became an effort to put one foot in front of the other.

On and on they went until finally the front man bumped against an obstruction. He felt around until his hand touched a wooden bolt.

"Here it is," he said, relief flooding his voice. He pulled the bolt to the side and a door creaked open, letting in a blast of cold air. Peeking outside, he waved to the others. "There are the horses, just as we left them."

Richard stepped out and took a deep breath. They were near the bottom of a hill, way below the castle, surrounded by trees and undergrowth. Off to the side stood three horses, saddled and ready to go.

"Fortunately, there is no moon," said one of the men. "We will take lesser-known paths through the forest but we must ride all night. Come, your majesty."

"Where are we going?"

"Scotland. You are not safe in England."

Shrugging, Richard placed his foot into the man's clasped hands and let himself be hoisted onto the horse's back. He was weak from so much inactivity though determined to put as much distance between himself and his pursuers as possible. It seemed that his companions knew their way and they disappeared between the trees.

A few hours' riding was almost more than Richard could tolerate, yet his rescuers insisted he continue a little farther. He was bent over his horse and could barely keep his eyes open. The sun was coming up and they were still in the forest, surrounded by gloom. The only sounds were an occasional bird calling and the footsteps of their mounts.

"There's a stream to our left," said one of the men. "Let's find a place to tie up before the king falls from his horse."

Richard raised his head, objecting to their tone. Yet he found he was too exhausted to speak. Dismounting, the man took his reins and led him deeper into the shadows. Once they located the stream, they searched a bit more until they found a suitable place to rest. His guide laid out a blanket and Richard collapsed onto it, falling immediately asleep.

It was still daylight when he awoke, and he raised himself onto his elbows, observing his companions. They both leaned against a tree and, seeing the king awake, the dark-haired one offered a leather flask. Richard sat up, accepting a drink.

"I am indebted to you both," he said, "and I don't even know your names."

"I am William Blythe," said the dark-haired man, taking back his flask. "And this here's Father John Bennett."

"Well, William Blythe and Father Bennett. I don't know how to thank you."

Blythe laughed. "You'll have plenty of time to think about it. There's no going back for us, you know. Once they discover I'm missing from the castle, my life will be forfeit. What about you, Father?"

Untying a strap from around a bundle, the other looked up. "Since I am a cleric, I am safe from that punishment. However, my master, Sir Harry Percy, has charged me to rescue you from your confinement."

"Hotspur? He sent you?"

The friar nodded. "He feels that a great injustice has been done to you and he sent me to your brother, John Holland. He and your other supporters are planning a rising in your name, and they sent us to take you to safety until it is all over."

"A rising? Who?"

"Let's see. Both Hollands, the Earl of Rutland, Salisbury, Despenser. Your cleric Maudeleyn, as well. That's all I know about."

Pursing his lips, Richard stood. He had to make water and turned his back to them, stepping away. This was all so sudden, he didn't know what to think. First, everyone let him down, and now they were rebelling in his name? How could this be?

When he returned, Blythe offered some bread and cheese. "We don't have much to eat, but as soon as we are safely away we have coin to pay for lodging and food."

Bennett pulled a homespun tunic from his bag, a hood and a wool cloak. "You must dress as a traveler, sire. One of us." He laughed briefly. "For now."

Silently, Richard accepted the garments. He was in no position to object. After all, he was simply Sir Richard Plantagenet now. "Then don't call me sire. Or majesty. Those titles don't belong to me anymore. You are right. I am one of you now."

Reddening, Bennett shook his head. "I didn't mean to offend."

"No, no, you did not offend me. I feel like a great burden has been lifted from my shoulders. Call me Dickon."

"Dickon." The friar looked at Blythe. "That will take some getting used to."

"That's what my Cheshire archers called me. They were the only people who tried to save me, aside from the Welsh."

Nodding, the others packed their bags. It was time to move on.

CHAPTER 13

They were far from Scotland; it was 130 miles to Carlisle, just south of the border. Blythe explained that the best way to avoid pursuit was to stay to the less populated western side of Yorkshire. They could travel along river valleys where there would be plenty of water. Richard agreed to whatever they wanted. He had only traveled to Scotland one time, fifteen years ago, and that was at the head of an army. They had hugged the east coast where they would be easily provisioned. He knew nothing about this part of the country.

Travel was slow. They stayed in villages whenever possible and the occasional farmhouse along the way. Richard had very little to say though he spent a lot of time thinking. When he was imprisoned in Pontefract, his thoughts were mainly of the remorseful kind: what he did wrong, where he miscalculated, how he let his fears overcome his better judgment. But now... He was free. No more parliament, no more tolerating people he hated, no more treason. His biggest concern was being captured again. Still, the farther they traveled the safer they felt. Like his companions, his clothes were worn, his hands were dirty and his horse was a common palfrey. He no longer attracted attention. He could do whatever he wanted. This wasn't such a bad life.

It took three weeks to reach Carlisle. Even so, they skirted the city and continued north. When they reached a port at the end of the Solway Firth, Richard was in for a surprise. His companions kept talking amongst themselves until finally, they turned to him.

"Dickon," said John Bennett, "we've made it safely to Scotland. We think it would be best to take a ship into the Highlands. You will be safer there."

The Highlands. He had heard the Highlanders didn't even respect the king of Scotland, let alone the king of England. "I thought—"

"We can't vouch for your safety, otherwise," Bennett said. "You don't know who your enemies are right now. Or your friends."

Richard couldn't disagree with that. "What about the horses?"

"We'll sell them. We could always use the money."

What else was there to say? His guides soon arranged for them to travel on a merchant ship going north. Passengers were an inconvenience, but they paid well and stayed out of the way. Richard lost track of the days, and when the captain finally told them it was time to disembark, he asked where they were.

"This is the Isle of Islay," the captain said. "If you look there—" he pointed to a castle they were just passing, "that is the fortress belonging to the Lord of the Isles."

Bennett put a hand on Richard's arm. "That is good. He is an influential man, I am told."

Chewing his lip, Richard glanced at his companion. "We may want to avail ourselves of his hospitality." He lowered his voice. "I don't want him to know who I am."

The other nodded. "I understand. I am a poor friar and you two are my companions."

The captain was glad to be rid of them. They climbed down a gangplank and were soon on their way. The castle was about two miles from the port, perched on a craggy hill overlooking a natural bay. It was small and well-fortified. Richard couldn't fathom the Gaelic spoken by the guards. But Father Bennett had made enough trips to Scotland to make himself understood and they were permitted inside the walls. As was usual with great lords, all travelers were welcomed and they found a place to sit at a lower table. Richard was famished and ate heartily, unaware that a lady sitting at the high table was observing him curiously.

A bard stepped up and began a long and sonorous recitation, again in a dialect Richard didn't understand. He found the singsongy voice comforting, and before long he put his head on his arm and drifted off to sleep. This didn't last long; a hand grasped his shoulder and pulled him up. Startled, Richard was about to object when the man ordered him to his feet in a voice that brooked no argument. He looked at the friar who shrugged helplessly.

"I said come with me," the man growled. He was tall and burly and obviously used to being obeyed.

Leaving his companions behind, Richard followed the man to a small chamber off the hall, where he was left alone. There was a table and chairs and a tapestry on the wall, and Richard was deciding whether to sit or not when the door opened. A woman and man entered and Richard stared at them; they seemed somehow familiar.

"Do you see?" she said to the man. "It must be him." She spoke in English with an Irish accent.

"How can that be possible?" her companion said, shaking his head.

"I tell you, it's him. My husband entered the service of King Richard in Ireland. This man." She pointed to Richard, taking a step closer. "Your features are very easy to remember."

This was so unexpected Richard didn't know how to respond. He looked at the man. "I ask your pardon, my lord. I am a stranger here."

"I am Rob MacDonald, Lord of the Isles. My good-sister says you are King Richard, though you don't look like a king."

Bowing his head, Richard thought for a moment. After weeks of traveling and innumerable hardships, he didn't want to get captured and sent back to England. "I am a simple freeman."

"I doubt it not," said Lord Rob. "You must be mistaken, my dear."

"We know King Richard was taken prisoner by the usurper. This could be him."

"Well—"

Richard kept his head down.

"Wait until Alec comes tomorrow. He'll know the king," she urged.

"Very well. Please be our guest for the night. You may sleep with the servants."

Bowing slightly, Richard withdrew. This was already too uncomfortable. He slipped back into the hall and found the others. Bennett was craning his neck looking for him.

"We have to go," Richard said, leaning over him. "I've been recognized."

The friar was shocked. "How can that be?"

"That woman." Richard gestured with his head as she sat down at the table. "Her husband entered my service in Ireland. He'll be here on the morrow."

Bennett finished chewing and swallowed hard. "You want to travel this strange land at night? I don't know where to go. Besides, how are we going to get off this island?"

"I must leave!"

"Wait. Calm down," John said. "Please sit, Dickon." Reluctantly, Richard obliged.

The friar leaned toward his ear. "If you don't want to be recognized, deny everything. Better yet, pretend you are unlearned. Simple-minded. If you try to run away, they might stop you."

Letting out his breath, Richard reached for his cup. "Perhaps you are right. I am so tired. I just want to rest."

"They'll lose interest," Blythe assured him. "Why would they bother with three poor travelers?"

Later, they laid out their cloaks on the rushes in the hall. Richard put his sack under his head and fell asleep immediately. He woke up in the middle of the night and lay awake, listening to the snoring and the snuffling of dogs rooting for scraps. *What am I doing here?* he thought. *More importantly, what do I want?*

Events in England were so far removed from this part of the world, he might as well be on the moon. Did anyone here care who was king? It was terrible not knowing what was happening back home. Had the rebellion succeeded? How were they going to find him? Once he was settled, he would have to send Bennett back.

Another dark thought kept intruding. Did he even want to be king? Look what they did to him. Everyone abandoned him at the first sign of trouble—all but a few, and they were probably declared traitors by now. Nobody looked past their own self-interest. What if it happened all over again? What if they killed him this time? Or locked him up in a dungeon? Was it worth the risk to be king again? He hadn't been happy since Anne died. It was all a sham.

He may be a poor, wandering nobody, but at least he was free.

149

It was early when they came for him. Bennett and Blythe were still sleeping when a guard bent over Richard, shaking him. "Come," he said. "The Lord wants to see you."

Richard rolled over and pushed himself up. "I need to make water."

"Hurry then. I'm coming with you."

If he was thinking of escape, that wasn't going to happen. Annoyed, Richard went outside and made use of the ditch. His guard watched unconcernedly then gestured for him to follow.

Alec MacDonald, younger brother of the Lord of the Isles, was enjoying his breakfast when Richard was led into the room. His eyes opened wide and he turned to his wife.

"See," she said, "it has to be him."

Standing, Alec walked over to Richard to get a closer look. Deciding to maintain his pretense, Richard stared at the floor. The other put a hand under his jaw and raised his head.

"It is uncanny," Alec agreed. "I would swear it is him. What is your name?"

"Dickon." Richard had to restrain his impulse to jerk away.

"What are you doing here, Dickon?"

"My friends and I are just passing through."

"You don't just pass through the Highlands."

Richard shrugged. "We were looking for work."

"I doubt it." Moving Richard's head back and forth, Alec studied him. "What is your real story?"

"I have none. I am a poor freeman."

"You don't speak like a poor freeman. You speak like an educated man."

Richard shook his head. "I was educated by churchmen."

"Hmm. It was only a few months ago that I entered King Richard's service. Not long enough for me to forget your face. I don't know exactly what happened in England. I heard something about a rebellion." He stepped back. "I'm not sure I'm still in your service, sire, but we cannot take responsibility for you."

"I don't know what you are talking about," Richard said. "I am not your sire."

Alec turned to his wife. "We will send him to my sister Agnes. Her husband, Lord Montgomery, is well connected with King Robert. They will know what to do."

Stepping toward the door, Richard looked at the guard who was blocking his way. "I am grateful for your concern, but you are mistaken. I am not the man you think I am."

"If that is the case, Lord Montgomery will release you." He pointed at the guard, then to Richard. "Put him on the next vessel to the mainland and take him to Eglinton Castle. Bring six men with you."

"Wait!" Richard was beginning to panic. "My companions!"

"We will see they are taken care of. Go in peace."

Richard had no idea where he was going, but it seemed resistance would not help him any. He was taken across to the mainland and lodged for the night in Eglinton Castle. Lord Montgomery was on campaign, and it was decided to move Richard to another castle, about eight miles south. By now he was thoroughly alarmed and continued his insistence that he was only a commoner. Surely they would lose interest and let him go.

The hilltop castle was tall and rectangular, built much like a Norman keep. It was surrounded by a stone curtain wall with a gatehouse and four massive round towers. Richard's heart sank when they walked him across the inner bailey to the keep; it seemed too much like a repeat of his Pontefract experience. Much to his surprise, he was shown into a chamber decorated with beautiful wall hangings and a large canopy bed. A page followed and proposed Richard avail himself of a bath—a suggestion he eagerly agreed to. While he waited for the page to heat the water, Richard wandered over to the window which gave a good view of the town spread beneath the castle hill. Beyond that, the landscape was flat and sprinkled with a few trees. There wasn't much else to see.

"Where are we?" he asked the page.

Looking up in surprise, the youth poured some hot water into the bath. "This is Dundonald Castle, belonging to King Robert."

"Oh?" That was encouraging. "Is the king in residence?"

"He is here most of the time. When you are finished soaking, he invites you to sup with him."

"Invites me?"

"Please. Your bath is ready."

After weeks of wandering through the wilderness, this was the epitome of luxury. The page even helped him off with his clothes, while other servants came in with new tunics and laid them on the bed. Forgetting his troubles, Richard allowed himself to be washed and dressed.

By the time he was led to the king's chamber, Richard almost felt like his old self. Almost. The way he was pampered, it would be difficult to maintain his pretense. After all, most of his life every need had been taken care of. The last month spent as a poor wayfarer already seemed drab and far away.

He didn't know what to expect. The king of England had never met the king of Scotland, nor had they even exchanged diplomatic courtesies. The occasional hostilities between their two countries were more of a clash between borders than dominions.

The door opened and Richard was faced with a broken old man, sitting by the fire in an armchair, a cat in his lap and a black dog at his feet. He looked to be about the same age as old John of Gaunt, and his bent posture indicated a familiarity with discomfort.

"Welcome," he said, waving Richard into the room. "Sit with me by the fire while we wait for our dinner." At least his smile was genuine. "You must tell me your story."

The dog stood and sniffed Richard's leg as he sat.

"This is Douglas," the king said, patting the dog's rump. "He was once as fierce as a wolf, but not with me. And what do you call yourself?"

"Dickon." Richard nodded in greeting.

"Dickon. Of course, my cousins of the Isles tell me a different story. They think you are the king of England." He chortled, almost a cough. "Fancy that. But you see, I don't know what Richard II looks like, so I must trust their judgment. We have heard strange stories of rebellion and usurpation." He watched as Richard gripped the arms of his chair. "Perhaps you know more than we do."

"Sire, they are much mistaken. I am a poor freeman."

"Come now, Dickon. I can tell from your speech that you are no freeman."

Richard sighed. He wondered how much trouble he was in.

The door opened and servants came in with food. King Robert rose and beckoned for Richard to follow. He hobbled to the table.

Despite himself, Richard ate with a good appetite while Robert chattered away about the weather and the mild winter they were having. Suddenly the king stopped and pointed his knife at Richard.

"You are to be my guest. I think we should be honest with each other."

Bringing the chalice to his lips, Richard looked over the edge at his companion.

"We are both prisoners here," Robert went on. "Of course you must stay until we learn what is happening in your country. And myself..." He wiped his mouth with a napkin. "My brother, the Duke of Albany, is the governor of Scotland. He is very efficient, very strong. A good ruler. He should have been the firstborn." Shaking his head, Robert cut a piece of meat. "I was never forceful like Albany, nor was I as aggressive as my younger brother whom they call the Wolf of Badenoch—and for good reason. Can you imagine being squeezed between two such temperaments?" He scoffed at himself. "In my youth, after my horse kicked me in the leg and crippled me, I lost all faith in myself. Scotland demands a strong and robust king. I was none of those things. Oh, they trot me out for special occasions, though for the most part I am hidden away here, out of sight." He smiled sadly as Richard's eyes widened. "So yes. If you are King of England, it seems we are both in the same sinking ship."

Coughing to hide his confusion, Richard took another sip of wine.

"I will make you as comfortable as possible," Robert assured him. "You have nothing to fear from me."

Putting his chalice down carefully, Richard made a decision. This sick old man didn't seem like much of a threat. And his candor deserved an appropriate response.

"Well King Robert," he sighed, "you are right. We do have a lot in common."

"There. That's better. Now tell me, what happened to you and how did you get here?"

It was a relief to tell someone his story. Once he started, Richard couldn't stop and they spoke into the night. Or rather, Richard did most of the speaking. The king of Scotland was a good listener, and his questions belied a strong knowledge of English politics.

"And now that I am safely lodged in your castle," Richard said, feeling much more comfortable, "I'm not sure what the future holds. I'm not very well suited for anything but kingship." He glanced sideways, grimacing. "And I'm not very good at that either."

"Or you could just be unlucky," Robert said. "Regardless, now I understand your need for dissimulation. Never fear; I can keep your secret until we decide you don't need it anymore. If your friends succeed at bringing you back—"

"I wished they had asked me first!"

"Ha! The less you know the better. Of course, if they fail..."

"I'm a dead man. Or I would have been if left in prison. I feel like a wraith as it is. Isn't that what you call it?" Suddenly he needed a drink and filled his wine cup again.

"Nonsense. You are young and have much to live for."

"Do I? I've lost everything, even my name."

Robert pursed his lips, considering. "If I were your age..."

"And now I've lost my freedom," Richard said, looking hard at him. "I assume."

"Let's just say you are my dear guest. You may wander the castle at will."

Things could be worse. Richard resolved to be patient. Not that he had much choice. Again.

CHAPTER 14

For once Edward of Rutland was glad his retainers rode behind him, leaving him to his own thoughts. His route led him in either of two directions: the appointed meeting place at Kingston, or his father's manor in Burnham, close to Windsor. It was time to decide. Musing, he watched as a courier rode toward them from the opposite direction. He recognized the man, a confidential servant of John Holland.

"My lord," the messenger said, leaning over with a letter. He didn't even need to dismount.

Taking the dispatch, Rutland dismissed him. "I thank you for your trouble. I will send my own man with a response."

Looking confused, the other nodded and turned back. It was not his place to question an earl.

Waiting until the courier was safely on his way, Rutland opened the letter. *To Edward, Earl of Rutland. We are surprised and distressed that you are not here at the appointed hour. We remind you of your bond and your oath. Whatever the reason, make sure you meet us at Colnbrook in time for our projected enterprise.*

Their concern was well placed. During the last few weeks, Rutland had vacillated in his intentions. He hadn't asked to be part of this rebellion; the others had just assumed he would join them. For many years he was one of them—one of Richard's closest advisors and even a friend, on a good day. As one of the Counter-Appellants, he had shared their disgrace.

But there was more. He kept thinking of that last day in the Tower, when Richard had called him a villain and a traitor and kicked his hat across the floor. Richard nursed his resentments for years; the man may never forgive him, even if rescued. The other conspirators knew nothing of this disturbing moment. The only witnesses were his father and King Henry. Was it worth the risk to rescue a king who might prove his own undoing?

Rutland frowned. Loyalty to the others would only go so far. They wouldn't save him if he was arrested. On the other hand, his father had guaranteed his good behavior. If he betrayed that trust and joined the rebellion he could be disinherited.

He hated to admit it to himself, but his unsavory reputation wasn't entirely unjustified. He didn't necessarily mean to shift loyalties; it's just that situations arose when he had to make unfortunate choices to protect himself. Nonetheless, people didn't trust him. Look at the fiasco during the last Parliament! The floor was littered with gages. If he betrayed the Counter-Appellants this time, his notoriety would cling to him the rest of his life.

On the other hand, if he exposed the conspiracy, the king would be eternally grateful. So what was the difficulty?

Reaching the crossroads, he turned the horse toward his father's manor.

As usual, the Duke of York could be found in his solar sunk deep in a chair with lots of pillows to support his arthritic back. He was dictating a letter to his secretary and raised his cane in welcome as Rutland came in.

"How do you feel today, father?"

"No better nor worse than usual," he grunted. "That will be all for now," he waved to his secretary. "Throw another log on the fire before you leave, would you?"

His secretary obliged while his son helped himself to some wine.

"There's something I need to tell you," Rutland said, sitting down.

"What has happened?"

"A conspiracy, father."

York stiffened in his chair, letting out a grunt of pain. "Against the king?"

"I'm afraid so. They tried to involve me. I went along at first, um, so I could learn what they were planning. Here." He pulled out the deed with all six seals and handed it to his father.

Smoothing his scraggly beard, the duke read the document. "Restore King Richard or die in the attempt?" His mouth fell open. "Whose seals are these? I recognize both Hollands and yours..."

"And Salisbury, Despenser, and Maudeleyn. There are many more involved, of course."

"What madness is this? When is this supposed to happen?"

"The attack will be on the Epiphany. We must get to the king."

"We? What are you planning?"

"They, father. *We* are going to stop them."

Disbelieving, York waved him on.

"They are sending confederates hiding in wagons along with the harnesses and trappings for the tournament," Rutland continued. "At their signal, the men will kill the guards and open the gates to let the rebels in."

"And kill the king?"

"They have many supporters," Rutland said defensively.

"I don't care. Help me up." His son supported his shoulders as York pushed himself out of the chair with his cane. Straightening, the duke pursed his lips. "Why did you wait so long?"

Rutland hesitated. "King Richard—"

"King Richard my ass. You don't give a fig for King Richard. You couldn't decide who to support. What? Did you conclude that this venture will fail?"

For once, Rutland was stung. "I'm trying to do the right thing."

"For a change. You have a lot of explaining to do. I see why you need my help. Come, we can't afford to tarry."

In the shortest time possible, York, Rutland, and a small escort were thundering to Windsor. They gained immediate entry to the king, who was privately dining with his four sons.

"What is this, uncle?" Henry said, lifting his hand in greeting. "I am always happy to see you, but I thought it would be tomorrow."

The duke knelt before the king, kissing his hand. "We bring grave news, sire."

"Get up, get up. What has happened?"

York gestured for his son to move forward. Rutland knelt beside him.

"This is most unusual," Henry said. "Get up, both of you."

Standing quickly, Rutland gave the deed to the king. Henry scanned it and looked up with a frown. "My Counter-Appellants? They seek to restore King Richard to the throne? How?"

"In all the confusion surrounding the tournament, they plan to kill your guards and yourself—your family."

Henry paled. "Then their accomplices could be in the castle already!"

"Yes. That's why I am here."

There was no time to think—or ask the same questions York did. Henry was a man of action; talk would come later. "Come. We must leave this place at once."

Henry's sons were already moving. Hal, the oldest at fourteen, was helping Humphrey with his shoes. At ten years old, Humphrey was surprisingly mature and he did not think to cry. Thomas was collecting their weapons and John, only one year older than Humphrey, followed his brother, trying to help. Thomas gave him his dagger. "Put this in your belt," he said.

"We must get to London and raise an army," the king said to York.

"Sire, this might take us right through the gathering-ground of the rebels," Rutland objected.

Henry looked at him hard. "You can distract them if need be," he said. "We will be disguised. It will be just us."

On the king's orders, six horses were prepared for his journey. It was late afternoon by now and not much daylight was left. Startling the guards, the king and his little party flew out through the gates and rode at top speed. It was over twenty miles to Westminster and he was determined to make it that night.

"Let us ride to the north of Colnbrook," Rutland said to the king. "We will miss most of the rebel army. The leaders plan to launch their assault from there."

Just four miles east of Windsor, the village of Colnbrook sat on the main London to Bath road. It was used as a resting-place for travelers, and on this night it was to play host to a growing band of determined assassins. Henry wisely decided to follow Rutland's lead. They left the road and picked their way across muddy fields strewn with stubble from last season's crops. At the edge of the fields, gloomy forests provided enough cover for them to slip under the hanging branches when they spotted strangers at a distance.

"How long do we have to put up with this?" Henry asked. "At this speed we'll never make it to Westminster."

"Not much farther. Are you all right, Humphrey?" Rutland leaned over, adjusting the boy's cloak. "There, up ahead. We'll take that game trail back to the road."

By then, they were in deep twilight. The riders found the road and kicked their mounts into a canter. Unfortunately, they left their detour too soon, for up ahead a large band of riders came toward them ready to cut them off.

"I'll handle this," Rutland said. He moved ahead of the others.

"Who goes there?" shouted a gruff voice.

"I am the Earl of Rutland. Who are you?"

"I am in the service of John Holland. We are to meet him at Colnbrook."

"Well, go then."

"But you are heading in the wrong direction, my lord." The man sounded suspicious.

"That is none of your business. What is your name?"

The other hesitated. "Rupert Smith, my lord."

"Well, Rupert Smith, continue on your way. Tell your master I will join him anon. Let us pass."

Shrugging, the man shouted to the others. "Stand aside. Let the Earl of Rutland pass."

Kicking their mounts forward, the six wasted no time. They had many more miles to go, and they didn't slow down for the next group of soldiers, who stepped aside without trying to stop them. Halfway to London, Rutland cursed as another small group approached.

"Will this never end?" he muttered to himself. Fortunately, on closer observation, he recognized the mayor and four aldermen.

As they came nearer, the mayor heaved a great sigh of relief. "I feared for your safety, sire. I have tidings that a rebel army six thousand strong have gathered against your majesty."

Henry glanced at Rutland. "I thank you, Lord Mayor. You have confirmed what I already learned."

The newcomers turned their horses so they could accompany the king. "I have proclaimed that all those willing to serve your majesty and the city of London should repair to the council-house and enroll their names. Give me one day and I will have an army."

"That is very well done. The day after tomorrow, then, we will march west toward Windsor and confront the traitors."

It was midnight before they reached Westminster Palace. The boys were ushered to bed and the others were assigned rooms for the night. Before he was ready to retire, Henry pulled York and Rutland aside.

"Cousin, I need you to tell me why you waited until the last possible moment to warn me," he said to Rutland.

"Sire," the other demurred then paused, intimidated by Henry's stare. "I was torn between my loyalty to you and my loyalty to Richard."

"He recognized his error late," York interrupted, "but his good intentions came clear in time."

"You were nearly the death of me." Henry's voice was flat.

"I assure you, sire," York interrupted again, "he will make this up to you."

"Peace, uncle." Henry held up his hand. "I understand about torn loyalties. Cousin, there are many who advised me to punish you. However, I also recognize your past service to the crown. I give you one more chance to redeem yourself. Go and ride to Colnbrook. Do your best to discourage them. Tell them I am approaching with a large army—and I will be. If they don't disperse, encourage them to march away from London. I intend to catch up with them before they can do more mischief." He paused, gripping Rutland's wrist. "Do I have your word of honor that you will do as I say?"

Rutland swallowed. "I swear."

Henry stared at him, almost daring him to look away. "Good," he said finally, letting go. Without another word, Rutland bowed and backed away. He didn't want Henry to change his mind.

When the leaders of the conspiracy showed up at Colnbrook hoping to find Rutland, they were alarmed to see he was still missing. Many of the recruits had already camped around the village; others enjoyed the hospitality of alehouses clustered along High Street. Rupert Smith elbowed his way through a crowd that had gathered in the road.

"My lord," he called. John Holland turned, recognizing his voice.

"There you are, Rupert. When did you get here?"

"Just after sunset, my lord. We passed the Earl of Rutland on the road."

"You passed him? Was he moving slowly?"

"No. He was going the other way. Toward London. He told me to tell you he would join you anon."

Alarmed, Holland turned toward his companions. "That was hours ago. Why would he be headed toward London?"

The others were at a loss.

"Was he alone?" John asked Rupert.

"Nay, he had a few others with him. By then I couldn't make out who they were."

"Something's not right." Holland pulled his horse's rein, nudging closer to his nephew. "I think we should move without him."

"You mean tonight?"

"Before it's too late." He looked at the others. "What do you think?"

After a short discussion, they all agreed. Sending a messenger ahead to Windsor, they arranged for four hundred of their armed followers to accompany them. The contingent reached the castle in the middle of the night. Shooting a flaming arrow into the air, they gathered before the castle gates, preparing to surge inside as soon as their confederates gave them entry. Hearing a shout behind the walls and a clash of arms, the rebels pulled their swords and waited. As planned, the gates flew open and they pushed their way through.

Something was not quite right. There were many fewer defenders than expected, and after a pitiful struggle they threw their weapons to the ground.

John Holland turned to Salisbury. "Secure these men and we will find the king." Gesturing to his nephew and a score of other followers, Holland ran inside the building. Frightened servants backed against the wall; no one of import stood out to block their way. They ran upstairs to the royal apartments, only to stop short before an open door. The obvious signs of an interrupted dinner greeted their horrified eyes.

"They have flown!" Holland slammed his fist against the door. Whirling around, he saw a handful of servants huddled together, watching. "When?"

"Sometime around mid-day," one of them said.

Pursing his lips in anger, he pointed down the hallway. "Search the other rooms," he growled. "We need to be certain they are all gone."

It wasn't long before the insurgents were satisfied their prey had fled. By then, John Holland had recovered his composure. "All is not lost," he said to the other leaders. "We can still make this rebellion work." Selecting his most reliable retainers, he told them, "Go. Far and wide. Tell the people we have Windsor Castle under our control. Hie thee to Wantage, Farangdon, and Cirencester; they are awaiting our tidings. Tell them that Henry flies before us, and King Richard has escaped from prison. Raise more fighters for our cause!"

Messengers rode to the neighboring towns, spreading the news. Meanwhile, after leaving a garrison at Windsor, the rebels rode back to Colnbrook to gather the rest of their army. They decided to rest a few hours before starting their march toward London.

Throughout the day on the fifth of January, King Henry waited for his forces to collect while he sent messages to all the ports, forbidding any ships to leave the country. Then he sent letters to the sheriffs, ordering them to arrest the traitors.

Left alone for a moment, he opened his bible and pulled out a letter that had obviously been well-thumbed. He unfolded the paper and read it again, finding great comfort in the words.

My Dearest Henry,
I read your letter with great joy, for I dared not hope that you felt the same way I did. I rejoice that your venture has turned out so triumphantly. I am eager to hear of your achievements—which may our Lord make as good as your noble heart can desire, and as good as I could wish for

you. I pray you, my most dear and honoured lord and cousin, that you would tell me often of the certainty of it, for the great comfort and gladness of my heart. It is my dearest wish to join you as soon as I may. For now, I must ensure that my son is firmly seated in his inheritance, for he is yet some years from his majority. And I must obtain a dispensation from one—preferably both popes—so there will be no obstacles to our union. Rest assured that my heart is devoted to you and our future happiness.
Yours in love,
Joanna

Kissing the letter, Henry refolded it and slipped it back into the Bible. He knew Joanna had many challenges ahead before she could leave the country. As granddaughter of the old King John of France through her mother, and of course as Duchess of Brittany, she would have been expected to show allegiance to her French kin. In all likelihood, they wouldn't favor an English union. She would doubtlessly be an unpopular choice with Henry's own subjects for the same reason. But he didn't care. He had been alone for too many years, and now that he had found a kindred spirit he would move heaven and earth to have her.

A knock on the door interrupted his reverie and a guard stepped through. "Sir Robert Waterton has asked to see you, your majesty."

Surprised, Henry waved him in. The man wasn't expected; Waterton should have been at Pontefract guarding Richard. Robert quickly knelt before him with his head bowed, and the king dismissed the guard.

"Something has happened," said Henry. It was more of a statement than a question.

Swallowing, the knight had to suppress a sob. "I am most distraught. I have terrible news."

"Richard."

"He has escaped."

His eyes widening, Henry gripped the arms of his chair. It was a moment before he realized he had quit breathing. "How?"

"On the night of the 1 January, someone drugged my wine. Mine, and my household guards." He dared to look up. "It was one of my yeomen. He has disappeared, along with Richard. We didn't discover the treachery until the next morning. We searched for miles without finding any sign of them."

Torn between rage and despair, Henry wanted to strike the constable. With Richard at the head of the rebellion, his chances of survival were narrower than before. However, the pain on Robert's face changed his anger to pity. This man had served him faithfully for as long as he could remember; there wasn't a disloyal bone in his body.

"I have failed you, sire," Robert said. "I submit myself to your justice."

Henry frowned. "Punishing you won't help matters. How many know?"

"Only my garrison at Pontefract."

"Then they must be sworn to secrecy, on pain of death."

Henry's voice came out sharper than he intended, but Robert nodded, barely able to hide his relief. "I have already done so," he assured the king.

"No one is to know. I cannot take the risk. Carry on as before, as though he is still in your charge. Return at once and wait until you hear from me."

Nothing loath, Waterton left as quickly as he could. Henry stared at the closing door.

That Richard's escape was coordinated with the rebellion was beyond doubt. Damn that Rutland! He must have known about it. Already Henry was envisioning the reproaches that were bound to come from all the people who had advised against his policy of clemency. Of course, that would be later. If he survived.

By midday, Henry marched out of London with twenty thousand men and paused at Hounslow Heath—halfway to Colnbrook—to wait for reinforcements. It was difficult for him to stay in one place; it was easier to keep moving until he discovered how many ranged against him. On the other hand, the last thing he needed was to stumble into an ambush. Coming to a decision, he summoned the Earl of Somerset and his faithful Sir Thomas Erpingham.

"Take four thousand archers between you and two hundred lances. You will be my advance guard. Do what you can to hold them off until I arrive with reinforcements."

164

Biting his lip, Henry watched as the soldiers mounted and rode out to find the renegades. He learned toward the Earl of Warwick, who sat astride his horse.

"I wonder what's keeping the citizens of London," he said.

Warwick pulled himself up pretentiously. "Dear sire," he said, "if you would have followed our counsel concerning King Richard, there would have been no occasion for this day."

Henry had little patience for Warwick. Like most of the barons, he had lost all respect for the earl after his pathetic self-abasement during the 1397 Parliament. "What reason did I have to put the king to death?" he said testily. "He had done nothing amiss. Besides, I did not have the right." He stroked his beard. "But by St. George, I promise you, if I encounter him with them now, either he or I shall die."

Warwick had turned away at that moment, when a trumpet announced someone's arrival. He swung back in confusion. "What was that you said?"

Catching himself, Henry cleared his throat. "I assure you, if this rising is truly in favor of Richard, he will be the first to die." He looked around, suddenly aware that others were listening. "Who just arrived?"

"I believe it's the constable of Barnard's Castle bearing the banner of London. He has a considerable force."

The army cheered and Henry allowed himself a smile, calling for wine. He took a long draught then handed the cup to Warwick, saying, "Drink and don't be afraid. We shall have a glorious day."

The young Earl of Arundel came up soon thereafter and Henry greeted him. "Dear cousin, we are glad to see you." He pointed to the road ahead. "Now we can advance. Let it be known that no person should be so bold as to pass my horse. I wish to be the first to come to blows!" He held up his sword to the clamoring troops and led the way westward across the heath.

By dawn, the rebels were ready to march on London. As they lined up the banners and trumpeters in front of the army, Rutland came riding in. Although his co-conspirators were relieved to see him, they couldn't keep the annoyance from their voices.

"What happened to you? We expected you two days ago," said John Holland.

Dismounting, Rutland adjusted his saddle. "I had no excuse to get away from my father," he said easily. "I didn't want to raise suspicions. And it was just as well that I stayed. The king has raised such a large force we would not be able to stand against him."

His statement was met with trepidation. "With all our thousands of followers?" said Salisbury, gesturing to their waiting army.

"When I left, he had already gathered twenty thousand men and was waiting for more."

Holland turned to Salisbury. "This changes everything."

"We've gone too far to turn back now," said Despenser.

"But we dare not confront the king head-on." John Holland scratched his head. "Not until we have more support."

"I think we should move west," Rutland urged. "With Wales and possibly Cheshire supporting us, we will be strong enough to take a stand."

They didn't need much convincing. Everyone knew how fast King Henry could move.

"We can cross the Thames at Maidenhead," Tom Holland said.

And so it was decided. Maidenhead was ten miles west of Colnbrook. John Holland would lead the army with Maudeleyn at its head, proclaiming King Richard had returned. Tom Holland, his nephew, would protect their rear. There was no time to waste and the day was just beginning.

There were two bridges at Maidenhead and the rebels passed over the river in good order. They were nearly across when Rutland spotted Henry's advance guard. This was his moment. Plunging his spurs into his horse's flank, he dashed toward the advancing force, shouting "They all flee!"

Tom Holland and Salisbury stared at Rutland's back, momentarily confounded. "My God," Tom cried, shaking himself out of his hesitation. "He has betrayed us! Salisbury, take the rest of the men and join my uncle. I will defend the bridge."

"May the Lord protect you," Salisbury said, putting a hand on his arm before riding off. Meanwhile, Tom shouted for his mounted infantry to line up in front of the bridge and for the archers to hide in the woods nearby. Both sides were fairly matched in numbers, and Henry's guard approached cautiously. Then, with a blast of trumpets, they charged.

As the royalists rode forward, the archers plied them with arrows, slowing them down. Their own archers responded, though with little effect. The mounted men clashed into the rebel defenders, and many horses went down. Their riders leaped from their saddles, prepared to fight on foot. It wasn't long before they were all mixed together—knights and rebels—and yet Somerset's men couldn't make any progress toward the bridge. The entrance was narrow and not everyone could engage at the same time. Fighting was fiercest at the center, and fallen men had to be dragged away to make room for the next combatants.

For three hours Tom managed to hold the bridge until King Henry caught up with his troops. For a while it looked like the reinforcements would push their way through, but the rebels found strength in desperation. Tom stood fast until nightfall, when finally the exhausted men could fight no longer. There was no moon and it was impossible to distinguish friend from enemy. Like it or not, King Henry would have to wait until daylight.

While keeping up a convincing front at the bridgehead, Tom Holland ordered his army to slip away. "Go west to Cirencester," he ordered. "I will meet you there." He guarded the end of the bridge until the royal army had settled for the night, and at his signal they quietly abandoned their post. Nobody followed them.

CHAPTER 15

Tom Holland, Earl of Kent and his men traveled hard and caught a few hours' sleep before continuing west to Sonning, just north of Reading. Queen Isabella was confined there in the Bishop's Palace. They were dusty and sweaty when they arrived, but she received them joyously since she knew they were King Richard's adherents.

The earl dismounted and knelt before the queen, kissing her hand. She was ten years old by now, but her training and position gave the impression of a girl in her teens. Isabella still wore her hair long and unbound, a rich, tawny brown that accented the creamy blush of her cheeks.

"What tidings do you bring?" she asked breathlessly.

Standing, he made a grand gesture with his arm. "All the country rises in rebellion against the usurper!" he cried, then took two strides toward one of her servants. He grabbed King Henry's badge on the man's tunic and tore it off. Excited, she turned to another page and did the same, throwing the badge on the ground and stamping on it.

Turning the boy to the Tom Holland, she put a hand on his shoulder. "This is young Thomas Mowbray, the son and heir of the Duke of Norfolk," she said. "He has been serving me since his father's exile."

Holland knelt on one knee, bringing himself to eye level with the boy. "I pledge to avenge your father's outlawry," he said. "He was treated shamefully. Henry Bolingbroke has much to answer for."

The youth was quite overwhelmed by the attention. He was thrilled that someone shared his antipathy toward King Henry and he bowed in return.

All the other servants tore off their own badges, while Isabella called for ale and even went so far as to hug Tom. Accepting a mug, he raised it to her then downed its contents in one draught; his companions were quick to empty their cups as well.

"And now, your highness, we must go, for our task is not yet accomplished. Be of good cheer, for before long you will be able to welcome your beloved king in person."

Shedding tears of happiness, Isabella followed the men to the door and watched as they mounted their tired horses and waved farewell. Once again, she was doomed to wait—as if waiting for Richard's return from Ireland wasn't bad enough.

Cirencester, a large market town in Gloucestershire, stood about seventy miles west of Colnbrook and thirty miles to the east of the Severn. This is where they had all agreed to meet. By evening the next day, their army was encamped in the fields surrounding the town and the lords all decided to lodge at the inn. They had much to discuss since their plans had gone awry and they needed to formulate their next course of action. Thirty other knights stayed with them to provide additional security.

John Holland, the Earl of Huntingdon took charge of the meeting. He greeted his nephew Tom and slapped him on the back, congratulating him on his formidable defense at Maidenhead. Sir Thomas Blount, the ex-bishop of Carlisle was already there, having come from a different direction. Lord Despenser was present with the Earl of Salisbury and Maudeleyn.

"The people are with us," John insisted. "We need only stay our course."

The others grumbled their agreement, though without much enthusiasm.

"We can't stop now! King Richard is on his way to Scotland. He depends on us!"

"Are you certain?" interrupted Despenser.

"As certain as I can be. I have heard nothing to the contrary."

"I hope so," muttered Maudeleyn. "I don't know how long I can sustain this deception."

"As long as is necessary!" John was beginning to feel his temper rise when one of his squires came up and whispered in his ear. He pulled back in surprise then turned to the others. "An archer wearing King Henry's badge lodges in this inn." He turned to his nephew. "Tom, get the constable and bring him here. Stay, the rest of you. I will go speak to him."

Already on edge, John Holland was not feeling particularly gracious when he climbed the stairs and pounded on the door. Not waiting for an answer, he burst into the room, finding the man with his legs stretched out before a fire.

"I am the Earl of Huntingdon. Whence come you?"

Sitting up cautiously, the man put down his mug. "My lord, I come from the parts of Wales whither I was sent by King Henry."

"Why did the king send you to Wales?"

"With all due respect, that is my business."

"And I say it is my business," retorted Holland. "I think you are spying on us. Traitorous rascal! You shall be quickly drawn and hung in spite of your master!" He lunged forward and grabbed the archer by the arm, dragging him from his chair. "You will come with me!"

The archer tried to pull away but John Holland was a brawler from way back and he knew all the moves. Boxing his captive's ear, he tripped him and dragged him out the door, hollering for help. They were halfway down the stairs when Tom came in with the constable.

"Arrest this man," John bellowed. "I want him drawn and hung this very evening!"

Quickly taking in the situation, the constable nodded. "I will do so, my lord." Reaching out, he took the archer by the arm and led him from the inn. Happy to be rid of this distraction, the two Hollands went back to their fellow conspirators.

The constable wasn't to be taken in so easily. "Come to my house," he said to the archer. "You must tell me what this is all about."

The archer was given food and wine, and he assured the constable he knew nothing about why he was assaulted. "He called me a traitorous rascal! He obviously confused me with someone else."

Shaking his head, the other came to a decision. "I wondered why they had brought such a large army. I thought they were up to no good, and now that they have accused you of being a spy, I am sure of it. I shall summon all available fighting men and confront them."

The townsfolk were already alarmed and responded quickly. Before dark, the constable had assembled fifty archers and two score yeomen armed with clubs, scythes, spears, and axes. They all gathered in the street before the inn, and the constable had a trumpeter send up a blast before he pounded on the door.

John Holland came out onto the step, which was only wide enough for two men, while the others gathered behind him in the doorway.

"My lord," bellowed the leader, "I arrest you on the part of King Henry, and command that none of you depart from this house without my permission."

Undeterred, John strode forward and slapped him with the back of his hand. "Rascal! How dare you try to arrest us? You shall be hung tomorrow as soon as it is light. Villain! Here is King Richard who is our sovereign king." He pointed at Maudeleyn, who took one step forward.

For a moment the constable lost a little of his bravado, but he soon recovered. "That cannot be the king," he said, "in company with scoundrels like yourself."

"Who are you to speak so proudly?" Holland slapped the other side of his face. "I insist you beg the king's pardon."

This was too much for the citizens of Cirencester. Two men rushed forward and pushed him aside, then Maudeleyn came down the steps and tried to strike the closest attacker. John Holland went into a frenzy, kicking and punching while the other rebel leaders flew out the door and jumped into the fray. The townsmen were armed and half a dozen charged the defenders, swinging clubs and shoving them backward. By now there was quite a scuffle, when the constable shouted, "I command you in the name of King Henry to seize these lords. They are all enemies of the king!"

Alarmed, the rebels backed up against the wall. They had no weapons and obviously their rank no longer defended them. Maudeleyn retreated into the room, followed by Despenser. The others were still trying to fend off their attackers when the archers released a slew of arrows, turning the fight into a slaughter. Tom Holland fell back against his uncle, a shaft sticking out of his neck. Blood spurted over the ground. Shouting, John grabbed him around the shoulders and dragged him through the door while Salisbury tried to cover for them. He snatched a spear from an overconfident fighter and turned it on him, thrusting it into the man's leg. He pulled the shaft out and knocked away a spade aimed at his head, but he wasn't quick enough to dodge a scythe that came from behind, slicing right through his neck. His head flew several feet before landing in the street, face down.

The door slammed, shutting out the shrieking mob as the lords gasped for breath, staring at each other. Tom was already dead, and John wrapped his arms around him, groaning his dismay. The other knights crowded into the room.

"Listen," said Thomas Blount, pushing through the crowded chamber. "You only have a moment. They want the leaders. My lords, go now. Use windows in the rear of the building before they surround the inn. Get away while you can." He took Despenser by the arm and shoved him toward the back of the room. He pushed Maudeleyn after him then pulled Holland to his feet. "Go. Now. We will keep fighting them so you can get away. Create a disturbance to draw these people from the inn, or we are all lost. Go. Bring help."

Seeing the sense in his words, the three leaders took his advice and climbed out the rear windows, taking a last look before slipping away. They dashed down an alleyway then stopped at the end, peeking around the corner of a building. Two men headed toward the inn; aside from them, the road was empty.

"There, another alley," said John, pointing to the side. "Stay close." The three darted down the passage, then another, sensing they were nearing the edge of town. Hugging the outside wall of a blacksmith shop, John leaned over and glanced into the window; no one was there.

"The smith must be attacking the inn," he said bitterly. "The fire is still burning in the forge. Let us take advantage of it. That should draw them away."

The other two agreed. Slipping into the shop, he took a shovelful of coals and dashed them against the wall, dropping some hay onto the glowing embers. A little flame caught easily, and they added more hay. Then they carried coals to the house next door, throwing them against the wall and adding more combustibles. Soon black smoke rose from the new fire and red flames darted up the wall. Again and again, they spread the fires until they were convinced they had done enough damage. The three of them took to the street, heading out of town toward the safety of the waiting army.

Meanwhile, the rebel knights put up a good defense. Archers outside the inn kept up a flurry of arrows every time they saw movement. During this distraction, several yeomen strove to force the doors both front and back. Four of them even found their way inside though they only succeeded in getting themselves killed.

In the confusion, the three rebel leaders easily escaped from town; they were disappointed to see their fire did not have the desired response. In fact, it had the opposite effect. Their army had faded away! Clinging to the edge of the forest, they skirted the empty and trampled fields until Holland caught sight of his steward waiting with a dozen horses. He waved, rushing forward.

"Dear God, what has happened?" he gasped, his chest heaving.

"My lord, seeing the fires, the men shouted that King Henry had come. They ran, the cowards! Although to tell you true, they were deserting ever since we got here."

Grasping his horse's saddle with both hands, John laid his forehead against the leather. The others watched in concern while his chest heaved and sobs wracked his frame. Finally, he lifted his head, tears running down his face. "We are finished. There is no helping our cause. We have no choice but to flee." He put a hand on his steward's shoulder. "Hugh, my nephew was killed. He was too young to die."

The steward crossed himself. "It gets worse and worse. God rest his soul."

Despenser sighed. "He may be the lucky one. Our prospects don't look good."

After staring at Despenser for a moment, John nodded. "You could be right. I think we should split up." Having made up his mind, he mounted his horse and raised a hand in farewell. "It's in God's hands, now. I'm for Essex. Are you ready, Hugh?"

His steward nodded, pulling three horses aside and mounting one of them. "We'll bring two spare horses."

Despenser took the reins of another. "I'll find safety in Wales."

Maudeleyn gasped, not expecting to be abandoned. "What should I do?"

"Hide that face of yours. Try going north. You'll be safer on your own." Turning his horse, John rode away without a backward look.

The knights left behind in Cirencester had no idea they had been abandoned. They valiantly fought throughout the night. By morning they were so exhausted there was no alternative but to surrender. Thomas Blount shouted from an upstairs window that they would throw down their weapons and come out. The townspeople, just as spent as they were, quickly agreed.

After some discussion, they decided to tie the prisoners together and take them to the king. Each yeoman rode a knight's horse and they led their captives on foot all the way to Oxford. They picked up the head of Salisbury and mounted it on a pole, carrying it side-by-side with the freshly decapitated head of Tom Holland.

King Henry was staying in the abbey of the Carmelites, just outside of town. He was surprised and relieved to see the unexpected procession.

"Sire, the brave men of Cirencester halted the advance of your traitors," the constable announced. "Three of the leaders got away, but their army disbanded."

The king looked up at the grisly heads. "Tom Holland and Salisbury," he said to himself, "who would have seen me dead." He turned to Erpingham. "Take these knights. We will give them a fair trial," he said. Then he approached the citizens of Cirencester, who fell to their knees.

"My loyal countrymen," he said. "You have performed such a good service I am in your debt. I shall not forget what you have done for me. Stay awhile and refresh yourselves."

Wined and dined and promised to be relieved of future taxes, the men of Cirencester went home content, riding their appropriated horses.

The next day King Henry made a proclamation. "Send sheriffs far and wide to search out and arrest Sir John Holland, Earl of Huntingdon, Lord Thomas Despenser, and Richard Maudeleyn. Bring these men to justice, whatever it takes." This time there was to be no forgiveness.

King Henry waited a week for more rebels to be brought to Oxford. At the end of that time, a trial was held. The knights from

Cirencester were joined by ninety others apprehended in the vicinity. Henry presided over the court of justice, questioning each of them in turn.

One of the captives looked familiar and the king beckoned him forward. "Remove that man's bonnet," Henry ordered. The guard obeyed and the prisoner looked up, shamefaced.

"John Ferrour!" exclaimed the king. "I didn't expect to find you in this wretched company."

Swallowing, the man hesitated. At least the king recognized him. "I beg your forgiveness," he said finally. "They threatened my life if I didn't join the rebellion. I had no choice, though they didn't get good service from me."

Henry fought back a smile; he needed a moment of levity. There was no way he could possibly condemn this man. "I remember, John Ferrour, that you saved my life during the Peasants' Revolt. If you hadn't disguised me in the Tower of London, I would surely have been murdered. I am happy to repay this debt." He flicked his hand. "You are free to go, but don't let this happen again."

Bowing, John snatched up his bonnet. "Sire, you can rely on it." Bowing again, he backed away and lost himself in the crowd.

John Ferrour had made a good point. Many of these men were simple villeins, coerced into joining the uprising. By the time the day was finished, all but twenty-seven of the prisoners were acquitted. The last were condemned as traitors. However, Henry knew that subjecting them all to the fullest punishment wouldn't sit well with the populace. He needed to retain their good-will, while making sure they were suitably discouraged from fomenting trouble.

"I condemn the ringleaders to a traitor's death," he said, raising his voice. "As for the rest, the sight of so many people butchered in such a manner would be terrible, and the sound of it most odious. Therefore the rest of the prisoners shall be decapited."

Four of the knights, including Thomas Blount, suffered the full penalty of drawing, hanging, beheading, and quartering. Brave to the last, Blount submitted to his punishment with stoicism. As the executioner slit open his gut and removed his intestines—tying his bowels "with a piece of whipcord that the breath of the heart might not escape"—he asked Blount if he would drink. "No, thank God," the man replied. "You have taken away wherein to put it."

Along with the other three, his body was cut into quarters and parboiled. The pieces were carried to London in sacks hanging from poles across the shoulders of men. They would later be salted and sent for display all across England. Tom Holland and Salisbury's heads accompanied these trophies, presented to the cheering Londoners as a gift from the king.

Oblivious to the sacrifices made by the knights he left behind, John Holland, Earl of Huntingdon and Hugh, his steward, traveled east to Essex. It took several days, and they were encouraged by the lack of pursuit; they suspected that most of the attention would be given to the midlands. By the time they reached the coast, a storm was brewing. They sold their horses and purchased a small boat with the intent of crossing over to the continent. Taking a chance they launched it, to no avail. The wind picked up and blew them back to the shore. Rain turned to sleet and before long they were soaked through. It was impossible and they gave up for the day, finding shelter in a small coastal town.

Unbeknownst to the travelers, the king's proclamation had reached Essex. Strangers were not uncommon in any town with a port, but this evening they were scrutinized with more than usual interest. After all, a man could always use a reward. When John and Hugh turned up at the local public house, they immediately felt uncomfortable. Ordering two mugs of ale, Holland inquired about a room for the night. The innkeeper looked him up and down.

"I've never seen you in Sandgate before. What is your business here?"

Annoyed at the question, John threw a coin on the counter and started to walk away. "My business is my own," he said over his shoulder. Then he thought better of it; hostility would just make them even more suspicious. "But if you must know," he added, "We're on our way to Dover, on the king's matter."

"I see," the other said. "Well, I have one room left. You can pay for it now."

John settled up with the innkeeper and encouraged Hugh to go upstairs right away. "We don't need any trouble," he said. "Let's get out of sight."

They traded off keeping watch throughout the night; luckily, they were not disturbed. By morning the skies were clearing and the rain had stopped so they tried again; Holland wanted to get as far away from Sandgate as possible. Under the watchful eyes of local dock laborers they launched their craft, trying to act innocuous. Unfortunately, their luck was no better than before; they couldn't make any headway across the Channel. The current kept pushing them back to shore. So they took down their little sail and found themselves rowing along the coast, around the point of Kent and into the Thames estuary. Once again they battled the wind; their craft was driven into the marshes on the north bank. There they found an old mill and spent the night, hungry but dry. Frustrated, in the morning they tried again with the same results.

"I am sorry, Hugh," Holland said as they bowed their heads against the wind. "This weather will be the death of us. I see no other choice but to throw ourselves on the mercy of my old friend John Prittlewell, who lives near Wakering, just northeast of here."

Exhausted, his companion was ready to agree to anything. They pulled their boat ashore. There was no foliage to cover it so they left it on the sand and trudged across the marsh looking for a road. Eventually, with the help of a suspicious farmer, they found their way to Barrow Hall. Sopping wet and bedraggled, Holland knocked at Prittlewell's door. A servant answered, recognizing him and trying to hide his astonishment.

"Is your master at home?" Holland asked, then looked over the man's head. "Ah, there you are, John. Can you help a friend in need?"

Recovering himself, the servant opened the door wide and looked out to see if they had horses.

"We are on foot and in need of shelter," Holland said, pulling off his dripping cloak. He smiled weakly at Prittlewell, who had cautiously approached. "With your blessing, I will tell you what has happened, if you would be so kind as to offer us some mulled wine."

"Of course, of course, my lord. You are always welcome."

The two newcomers gratefully followed their host into a chamber with a large fireplace. They bent over the welcome flames, trying to warm up. Before long, they were seated at a table as the servants brought in food and wine. Holland did his best to explain their situation without giving away too much of his own guilt. Their host listened without comment.

Holland was beginning to relax, thinking they had escaped pursuit. Alas, he was not to be so fortunate. Unbeknownst to him, while they were preparing their boat at Sandgate, one of the curious observers had gone for the sheriff, who knew Holland by sight. Anxious to earn a reward, a group of locals launched a pair of skiffs, hoping to catch up with the fugitives. Experienced seamen, they knew Holland would not be able to cross the Channel, so they stayed closer inland, finally spotting his boat at a distance. They tried to catch up but lost track of him in the estuary. However, there were few enough settlements near the marshes that it was worth continuing the search. Eventually, someone spotted the abandoned boat, and with renewed vigor they made toward the nearest village. A local farmer volunteered that he had encountered a pair of strangers who asked directions to Barrow Hall. The rest was simple. As the fugitives finished their meal, their pursuers surrounded the house.

Holland was helping himself to a second serving when someone pounded on the door. "John Prittlewell," a gruff voice shouted, "let us in."

John stood uncertainly, looking from Holland to the door. He was a timid man and regretted bringing potential trouble into the house. The last thing he needed was to be arrested harboring an outlaw.

The sheriff was not a patient man. "We know you harbor the traitor John Holland," he yelled. "Turn him over to us and we will refrain from holding you to account."

Prittlewell wrung his hands. "I'm a poor man," he said.

For once, Holland took pity. He pointed to Hugh. "It's me they want. John, could you at least find a hiding place for my steward?" Hugh started to object but Holland stopped him. "Don't be a fool, man. Get out if you can."

Prittlewell turned to his servant. "Send him to the cellar. He can hide behind the barrels." The pounding became more insistent and Hugh grunted his thanks before following the servant.

"I've been enough trouble to you," Holland said. "Come. I will give myself up." He threw on his cloak and strode to the door, jerking it open. The movement was so sudden the sheriff was startled. He took a step back then lunged forward, grasping his prisoner by the cloak.

Holland's guess was correct. The posse was so excited to capture him they neglected to search for any companions. They took him roughly by the arms and bound his hands, pushing him before them.

"Where are you taking me?"

"We'll get some horses in Wakering. You are going to Pleshy. The Countess of Hereford has offered a rich reward for your head." The sheriff laughed, enjoying the joke.

Holland shivered. There was no one who hated him more. She was the mother in-law of the Duke of Gloucester—the dead Duke of Gloucester. Her daughter, Gloucester's wife, had died of grief after their only son Humphrey expired, just after King Richard's capture. The countess was also the sister of the dead Earl of Arundel, executed by order of King Richard to satisfy his vengeance.

As they rode to Pleshy—the former residence of the Duke of Gloucester—more and more people joined the march. John Holland had made many enemies over the years, and his day of judgment was an event not to miss. By the time they reached the fortress, many thousands had gathered.

The Countess was waiting for him alongside the young Earl of Arundel who eyed Holland with such hate John knew he was doomed. He tried to put on a good face, though he lost his composure when his captor pulled him from the horse and forced him to his knees. Arundel towered over him.

"Sir, what say you?" the young man growled. "Do you not repent that you counseled the king to put my father to death? Rascal! I remember all the times you forced me to blacken your boots when I was your hostage. You treated me like a slave! But now I will be avenged for this and for the spite that you and your lord and master have shown me."

He grabbed Holland by the upper arm and yanked him to the very spot where the Duke of Gloucester had been arrested by Richard two years before. There was already a short bench set up to be used as a block.

Panic-stricken, John struggled against his captor. "For God's sake, have pity on me, for I never did you any harm! For God's sake have mercy!"

"Wretch! You deserve no mercy," Arundel sneered, pushing him down again. He turned to the crowd. "I have been told by the king," he shouted, "to bring him the prisoner, dead or alive. By the rood, I will have my vengeance!"

Mobs are an unpredictable force, and Arundel was surprised to see they grumbled uncomfortably instead of cheering him on. Holland was aware enough to notice that they took pity on him. "Ah, if I had only gone to Rome to serve the Pope," he cried, aiming his plaints at the sympathetic crowd, "by Saint Mary I should not have been in this plight. Alas! I stayed to serve the king and now it's too late. I beg of God to pardon my sins!"

By now, the crowd was objecting to his treatment and begged the Countess to be merciful. But she would have none of it. "Curse be ye all, you villeins!" she shrieked. "Have you not enough courage amongst you to put a man to death?" She singled out one of her esquires and pointed to the man. "Come forth, William, and do your duty."

Passing through the silent crowd, the man came up with his axe and knelt before John. "My lord, forgive me your death. I'm commanded to deliver you."

Raising his hands, still tied at the wrists, Holland was at his most eloquent. Witnesses remembered how his sapphire blue eyes filled with tears, making them glisten. "My friend, are you the man who will deliver me from this world?"

"Yes," the other said, "yes, by my Lady's orders."

"Wait, my dear friend. Why would you take away from me the life that God has given me? I never wronged you. And I can see there are seven thousand or more who have no wish to do me any harm. For God's sake, consider. And come, kiss me. I forgive you."

Shedding tears, the man kissed Holland on the forehead then got up, trudging back to the Countess. He fell to his knees, crying,

"Madam, I cannot do it. I can't put such a nobleman to death for all the gold in the world."

Furious, the Countess pointed a shaking finger. "You shall do what I have commanded, or I will have *your* head taken off!"

Self-preservation overrode his pity. William gripped his axe, returning to Holland. "My lord, I ask your pardon. Forgive me your death." He untied John's hands so he could hang onto the block.

It was the end and John knew it. "Is there no help for this? Then I pray to God and to all the saints in Paradise, that they will have mercy on my soul. I beseech you, for God's sake, to deliver me easily from this world." Holding back his sobs, Holland put his head on the block.

Unfortunately for him, William was no executioner. Hands trembling, he swung his axe and missed the neck altogether. He struck such a heavy blow to the shoulder that he knocked Holland to the ground.

Pushing himself up, John howled in frustration. "My God, man, what are you doing? I said deliver me easily!"

William had lost what little nerve he possessed. Pushing John back down, he swung his axe again and hit his victim on the same shoulder. The next blow hit him on the back, then the head. Each strike elicited a yowl of "God have mercy!" from the earl. Finally, on the ninth try, William hit the neck but still did not complete the stroke. One of the men in the crowd pushed him out of the way and severed Holland's head with a large knife. Sobbing, William dropped his axe and fell to his knees next to the dead earl.

Arundel stepped forward and picked up the head by its hair. "Justice has been done," he cried. "The king awaits the Earl of Huntingdon."

He strode through the silent crowd, kicking Holland's body as he passed. Later, the headless corpse was recovered by the local priests and buried in Pleshy's collegiate church, founded by the Duke of Gloucester three years before his death. Neither one of them would have been pleased with that arrangement.

Matters did not go any better for Thomas Despenser, who sought safety in his own castle at Cardiff. By the time he reached the fortress, he learned that King Henry was already seeking his capture, willing or unwilling. Wales would not provide him with safety, and Despenser resolved to go to the continent. Putting his affairs in order as best as he could, he collected his jewels and took a boat into the Severn. Unfortunately, once they were in the middle of the river, the captain had other ideas.

"I am sorry, my lord. I cannot take you to France."

"Why? I will pay you well," said Despenser, shocked at the man's change of attitude.

"I am not prepared for such a journey. I will take you to Bristol where you can find a merchant ship."

"This is not a matter of choice. I command you to take me across the Channel."

"My lord, I will take you nowhere but Bristol."

Drawing his sword, Despenser brandished it at the captain. "And I say you will do as I command!"

The captain stepped back a pace when suddenly the hatch flew open and armed men poured out of the hold, rushing the surprised lord. Before Despenser knew it, he was trying to fend off twenty sailors, who soon overwhelmed him and threw him to the deck.

"Traitors," he roared. "Who is your master?"

"We serve the king of England," the captain said scornfully. "Helmsman, take us to Bristol."

When they reached the port, Despenser was unceremoniously hauled off the ship, bound and gagged, and presented to the Mayor of Bristol. Soldiers held back the screaming mob while the prisoner was taken to the castle. He was thrown into the same cell that held the unfortunate LeScrope, Bushy, and Green, not six months before. For a day and a half, Despenser listened to the clamor of the irate citizenry until finally his guards came and unlocked his door.

"Where are we going?" the prisoner asked.

"You must come with us." A big, burly man took him by the arm and prodded him out of the cell. Once outside the castle, the shouting turned into cheering. As he stumbled through the crowd, Despenser's legs nearly failed when hands grabbed at him to tear his clothes from his body. More soldiers came forth and surrounded the prisoner as they led him to the market-cross.

Stopping, his captors moved aside and he finally understood why he had been taken from the castle. A space had been cleared for his execution. In front of the makeshift block stood the Earl of Rutland, a grimace of distaste on his face.

"The king wanted to speak with you before your death," Rutland said. He gestured to the crowd. "The people of Bristol won't allow it. I'm sorry I can't do any better than this."

"You bastard," Despenser spat. "I hope you rot in hell."

Rutland shrugged as the prisoner was shoved to his knees. The crowd roared.

Thomas Despenser was the lucky one; his head was decapitated with one stroke.

CHAPTER 16

Richard Maudeleyn had never felt so alone in his life as he did those miserable days while he made his way on foot across the countryside. His story was short and uneventful. After three weeks of wandering, he was discovered by a shepherd and brought to London, where he was imprisoned in the Tower. He had good company: William Colchester, the Abbot of Westminster, Roger Walden, former Archbishop of Canterbury, Thomas Merks, Bishop of Carlisle, and a fellow priest and knight, all of whom were scheduled to appear at the king's court of justice on 4 February.

King Henry had been welcomed back into London like a conquering hero. The heads of John and Tom Holland led the procession atop the tallest poles, bouncing and grimacing at the crowd. These trophies were followed by trumpeters announcing the king who rode a glorious white stallion alongside his son, the Prince of Wales. Henry graciously acknowledged the cheering of his adoring countrymen, while Hal was content to nod now and then, respecting the accolades directed at his father. After them, pipers, clarioners, cornemusers, and flouters improvised while a troupe of minstrels gamboled in front of the Earl of Rutland. His squire carried the head of Thomas Despenser mounted on another lance, followed by a great company of men-at-arms and archers. All headed to the Tower of London.

Once there, Henry was quick to disappear. His day was not over. All along he had anxiously awaited new tidings concerning the missing Richard Plantagenet. Nothing was forthcoming. As of yet, he hadn't told anyone about Richard's escape. But too much time had passed; he was going to have to accept the fact that capture was unlikely.

There was one man Henry trusted with the truth: he summoned Archbishop Arundel to join him in his solar. Thomas would know what to do.

Closeted alone together, the archbishop began by placing a small pile of papers on the table between them. "There is much to be done," he said in a businesslike manner, picking up a letter from the top of the stack. Henry put his hand over the papers.

"Not now," he said. "There's a matter of utmost importance I must discuss with you."

"Oh?" Arundel was miffed that Henry was keeping something from him. "What is this about?"

"Richard Plantagenet."

"Oh? I thought he was safely ensconced at Pontefract."

Henry looked pained. "He was. He escaped on the eve of the rebellion."

Paling, the archbishop leaned back in his chair. "How can this have happened?"

"Waterton brought the tidings himself just as we were gathering forces to meet the rebels. One of his yeomen was suborned. The constable and his men were drugged, apparently while celebrating the holiday."

"Why didn't you tell me?"

Frowning, Henry wished the archbishop was a little less self-important. "We had much more immediate things to worry about. The damage was done. He was long gone by the time I knew about it."

"Who else knows?"

"No one. Only Waterton and the garrison at Pontefract."

"And of course he has no idea where Richard went?"

"Of course not." Henry picked up a quill, smoothing its feathers. "Undoubtedly, he's out of the country."

"Well, if he was in France we should have heard of it by now," said Arundel. "So we can assume he is in Scotland unless we learn otherwise."

Despite himself, Henry was reassured by Arundel's calm voice. The archbishop could be depended on to see things logically.

"So we have to anticipate what he's going to do," Arundel mused, tapping his fingers on the table. "After this disaster of a rebellion, he's lost what little support he had. The Scots bear no particular love for our erstwhile monarch." He reached for the wine and Henry pushed the pitcher toward him. "There's a possibility our good King Richard may not want to come back." He glanced sideways at Henry. "What if we were to declare him dead?"

"Dead?" The king didn't know how to take this.

"That's what I was trying to tell you." He picked up the paper again. "This came from France. The ambassador, Pierre Blanchet has brought a new set of instructions from King Charles. The French court has heard that Richard is dead, and they want to proceed with negotiations for the return of Queen Isabella."

"How can this be?"

Arundel shrugged. "Spies, rumors. After all, it's been three months since he was taken away. I have learned that rumors abound in London already. Now, this is from the Council." He picked up a second piece of paper. "In response to the hearsay, they feel some sort of action needs to be taken. Here is what they write: 'If Richard is alive, as is supposed, then strict measures should be taken to keep him in security according to the judgment of parliament. But if he is dead, his body should be shown openly to the people, so that they might have certain knowledge of his death.'" He raised his eyes. "There's no reason to delay. Even the Council is prepared."

"I don't like this." Henry got up and paced the room. "People are going to say I murdered him."

"Not necessarily. Who is to say he didn't die of natural causes?"

"Everyone. The timing is terrible."

"Would you prefer that people say you let him escape?"

"Oh." It felt like someone punched him in the stomach. "Can't we just let it be? He's out of sight."

"You've *let it be* long enough already. You can't keep this a secret forever."

"I know, I know." He sat heavily. "I dread the repercussions."

Arundel waved away his objection. "We'll never have a better opportunity than now. I understand they captured Maudeleyn."

"Yes." Henry looked hard at the archbishop.

"Well?" Arundel was trying hard to show patience.

"So Maudeleyn is to get a royal funeral." Henry grimaced, not liking the whole concept.

"From a distance, no one will be able to tell the difference. Instead of a funeral effigy, we'll encase his body in lead and keep his face uncovered for all to see. Once Maudeleyn is executed, we'll send his body to Pontefract so they can start the funeral train and bring the former king back, showing him to the people along the way. We'll give Richard his due."

"And what if he comes back?"

It was Arundel's turn to grimace. "We'll have to make sure he doesn't."

That was totally unsatisfactory and both of them knew it. "No one is to know," said Henry in a low voice. "Not even the prince."

The other nodded. "Except for those who will make it happen. Erpingham?"

Henry rubbed his cheek with his hand. "I trust him with my life. Yes, he'll know what to do."

On the Wednesday after Candlemas, following a show trial that lasted most of the day, Maudeleyn was drawn on a cart with his fellow priest and the knight to Tyburn for execution. The other prisoners—the senior ecclesiastics—ranked too high for the scaffold. But these three were not so fortunate. By the time the party reached Cheapside, it was too dark to see and the mayor ordered forty-four torches and four lanterns to be brought, and so they could continue to the gibbet.

It was all very efficient. The three prisoners were quickly led up the steps to the scaffold. The mayor asked their names; Maudeleyn was the only one who answered. "God in heaven," he gasped, "shall I be quartered?"

"There's no time for that," the mayor answered. "But you will be beheaded."

Maudeleyn was as relieved as a man could be in his situation. "O Lord God, have mercy on me," he cried, raising his hands, still tied at the wrists. "And blessed be God that I was ever born, for I die this night in the service of my sovereign, the noble King Richard."

Allowing the condemned man his prayer, Mayor Fraunceys stepped back down to the ground. He gestured for the executioner to continue. As he watched, someone tugged at his sleeve and he looked around, surprised to see Thomas Erpingham.

"Sir Thomas! What brings you here?"

The knight pointed at to the prisoners. "That man. Maudeleyn. King Henry commands you to recover his body and his head and bring it to the Tower."

"The Tower? What an unusual request."

"These are unusual times," Erpingham said as the axe fell and Maudeleyn's head rolled in the straw. "Take care of this personally, Lord Mayor. No one need know about this."

Shrugging, the mayor agreed. "As you wish."

"Thank you. The king will see to it you are amply rewarded for you silence." Taking one last look at the gallows, Erpingham turned and lost himself in the crowd.

There are times one must never question one's betters. Mayor Fraunceys knew this was one of those times.

Hal was surprised that his father requested he come along to Eltham Palace, but he kept his feelings to himself. They were accompanied by the usual small army of retainers. The king rarely went anywhere without his harbingers to requisition lodging, his purveyors who rode ahead and commandeered supplies, his knights, esquires, clerks, and household servants. Although one of Henry's complaints about Richard's court was the excessive personnel, in reality, he didn't reduce their numbers one bit.

Hal looked to his side where his brother Thomas rode stiff and straight in his saddle, conscious of his new status as Lord High Steward of England. Whether they were ready or not, Henry's sons were to be put into positions of responsibility. Thomas glanced back at Hal and raised his chin, expressing his resentment at his older brother's honors.

His envy gave Hal no satisfaction. Although he was beginning to accept the greatness thrust upon him, he still felt like he was in borrowed clothes. None of his titles felt earned; perhaps if he could prove himself worthy he would come to embrace his destiny. After all, the burden of blame was on his father—not him. Bolingbroke usurped the crown; he would inherit it.

Once they reached the palace, Henry brought Hal and Thomas into his library. This was his favorite place, for he loved his manuscripts and books. He rarely invited anyone into this private space, and the boys were duly impressed. Gesturing for his sons to sit, Henry walked over to a two-tiered desk that also served as a bookcase. He ran his finger down the embossed binding of his favorite volume. It was apparent he was gathering his thoughts, and the boys watched him curiously.

Finally, he turned. "There's something I must tell you, and this is very difficult for me. Word has reached me that Richard Plantagenet has passed away."

Thomas looked at Hal, for he knew how close his brother was to the former king. For his part, Hal was having trouble accepting the words.

"Passed away?" Hal said. "You mean died?"

Henry looked pained. He had agonized over telling Hal the truth. This was more than a state secret; if Hal knew Richard had escaped, there was no telling what he would do. It wouldn't be surprising if he decided to go out and search for the king, regardless of the scandal—especially if he found him. The boy's loyalty to Richard was as astonishing as it was inconvenient. That was the one thing Henry had never considered in all his plans. Hal had been a hostage; where did this affection come from? What did Richard do to deserve it?

His mouth suddenly dry, Henry wished he had some wine. "I'm told that after Richard learned about the rebellion and the death of his supporters, he stopped eating." He paused, waiting for Hal's reaction. So far there was none. "My constable sent in a priest to convince Richard that starving himself to death was a mortal sin. After that, he tried to eat, but he had gone so far his throat constricted and he couldn't swallow. He died shortly thereafter."

Hal looked down at his hands; he was clasping them too tightly. When he raised his head, his face was drawn.

"I'm supposed to believe this?" he said.

Henry held his breath. If his own son didn't accept this story, how was he going to convince his detractors?

"You know King Richard," Thomas said scornfully. "He was always one for immoderate behavior."

"How do *you* know?" Hal shot back. "You know nothing about him."

"I know he was vindictive, selfish, and spiteful."

"That's a lie!" Hal lunged, grabbing Thomas by the tunic. Alarmed, his brother tried to push him away, but Hal pulled him out of the chair and fell on top of him, pinning him to the floor.

Henry was appalled. "Stop it! Both of you!" Hal was about to punch his brother in the face when Henry grasped his arm and yanked him away. "How dare you fight in my presence!"

Breathing heavily, Hal broke loose from his grasp. He glared at his father. "You starved him to death!"

Shaking his head, Henry stretched out a hand. His son turned away. "No, Hal. I swear it was none of my doing."

Still on the floor, Thomas wiped his mouth. "You're a disgrace!"

"Stop it, Thomas," Henry growled. "Don't make things worse." He took a step toward Hal. "Sit down, son."

Hal was about to refuse, but his common sense reasserted itself. Sullenly, he walked over to a chair and dropped onto it. Thomas got off the floor and went to the other side of the room.

"Listen to me," Henry said. "Do you really think I would have ordered Richard killed so soon after the rebellion? I'm not a fool. We still have many enemies, and this is one disturbance I didn't need, on top of everything else."

Breathing heavily, Hal stared at the floor.

"I was as shocked as you to hear about this," Henry added. "You must believe me. There were many times I was urged by others to execute him, and I always refused. Why would I resort to such a terrible crime?"

The logic in this argument wasn't lost on Hal. He didn't want to believe his father was capable of such an act. It was too terrible to contemplate. Slowly he nodded and Henry let out his breath.

"I am sorry, father."

"It's all right. I'm afraid you won't be the only one to accuse me of his death."

"We must prepare a proper funeral, to reassure the people."

"I've already given the orders. He will be brought back to London in slow stages from...Pontefract."

Pontefract. Hal hadn't been told where King Richard was kept. It was just one more indignity he had been forced to swallow. "He died, all alone. Abandoned. Poor man," he mumbled.

Henry heard him but decided it was better to pretend not to. Besides, he needed a drink.

On 6 March, the funeral car, draped in black cloth, started its slow procession from Pontefract castle. Four banners decorated the canopy—two with the arms of Saint George, and two with those of St. Edward. As instructed, the body was encased in lead, leaving only the face exposed from the brow to the throat. As it progressed south the conveyance stopped at major towns along the way so services could be held in the churches and the people could view the king's remains. Reaching St. Albans, the community held a solemn requiem for his soul, and the following morning the abbot celebrated mass. Next stop would be London.

This was the most prominent part of Henry's demonstration, and he was ready with all the trappings—or at least, the symbols he was willing to allow his defeated rival. Richard was not to be given his full regalia, though he did have a crown suspended over his head. Four black horses pulled the carriage led by two men in black. Four similarly dressed knights walked by its side. No one else was allowed to get close to the hearse. King Henry took his place behind the carriage and carried the funeral pall. After him walked his four sons; Hal's face was particularly pale and he spoke to no one.

They processed through Cheapside and paused for two hours, permitting the populace to walk past and observe the late king's features. Moving on, three hundred men accompanied the cortege to St. Paul's, all dressed in black and carrying torches.

King Richard's body was brought into the cathedral and placed on a bier. On Saturday, a requiem mass was held attended by King Henry, and on Sunday a second mass was celebrated where the nobility was invited. Once again Henry was present.

After the funeral services were over, the coffin was placed back into the hearse and, lacking the three hundred attendants, immediately sent off to King's Langley. Richard may have spent a fortune on his tomb in Westminster Abbey, but Henry had other ideas; he had no interest in setting up a shrine to the usurped king. He stood before the cathedral with his sons and watched the carriage start its twenty-seven mile journey to the church of the Black Friars. His job was done. He had no need to attend the funeral.

The sad procession traveled without stopping, and it didn't reach its destination until the middle of the night. A handful of friars brought the body into the church and laid him on the altar, lighting candles to keep him company in the darkness. The following morning, the last offices were performed by the Bishop of Lichfield and the Abbots of Waltham and St. Albans. Aside from the friars, no other witnesses were present—no nobles, no local citizens, no mourners. Even the accustomed funeral dinner was eschewed, much to the annoyance of the abbots, who had come a long way without recompense.

Robert of Scotland stood at the doorway of Richard's solar, looking sadly at the king who sat quietly next to the fire, a blanket wrapped around his shoulders. Holding an open book in his lap, Richard seemed content to stare at the flames.

From the first, the two of them had found comfort in each other's presence. Robert truly believed Richard was who he claimed to be, and he enjoyed the king's quiet confidences. Their conversations were largely academic—a pleasure for Robert, who found few of his own family who valued higher learning. Unfortunately, Richard tended to lapse into depression, and there was little the Scot could say that would help.

Robert coughed as he came into the room, sitting opposite the other. Richard looked up at him, showing slight curiosity.

"My friend, I have some tidings," Robert said. "We have had a messenger from England." He hesitated, waiting for a response. None came. "Prepare yourself," he went on. "There has been a rebellion against Henry of Lancaster."

192

Richard's eyes widened, though he couldn't help but notice the grim look on Robert's face. "Your tidings are not good," he said with a sigh.

"No. The rebel leaders were killed by the rabble. Shameful."

Richard's hands drew into fists. "Who were killed?"

"The Earl of Huntingdon, the Earl of Kent, Lord Despenser, the Earl of Salisbury. That's all I know about."

"The Earl of Rutland?"

"I believe he was for the king."

Richard stared at him, tears running down his face. "They were my only friends." He looked at the fire again. "Dear God, why couldn't they have waited until Henry showed his true colors?"

Robert didn't know what to say. He knew what it felt like to lose supporters. But he had never reached such depths of misery. He took a deep breath; might as well get it over with. "Prepare thyself, sire. There is more."

Not taking his eyes from the fire, Richard wiped his face. "What could be worse?"

The king came forward and knelt beside him, putting a hand on his arm. "They held your funeral."

Disbelieving, Richard turned his head.

"It was said you starved to death. Some think the king ordered that food be withheld after the failed rebellion. The body was brought from Pontefract Castle to London in a carriage, encased in lead. Only the face was exposed for everyone to see. It was all very proper, with a funeral procession and obsequies at St. Paul's Cathedral. How could this be?"

Richard pursed his lips. "Maudeleyn. My half-brother and my secretary. He looked so much like me people were often fooled. Poor man must have played a part in the rebellion and paid for it with his life. Poor, sweet man." More tears this time, and he didn't bother wiping them away. "Then it's irrefutable. King Richard is no more." He grunted briefly, a humorless sound. "At least Maudeleyn can share eternity with my queen at Westminster Abbey."

Robert said nothing, and Richard saw that something was amiss. "What else?"

"The body was taken to King's Langley and laid to rest there."

"King's Langley? I wasn't even given my own tomb?"

The other didn't bother to state the obvious; Richard wasn't going to Westminster Abbey in either case. Already Richard seemed to be drifting off.

"Can I get you anything?"

Shaking his head, Richard put a hand over his mouth.

"I'll leave you alone," said the King of Scotland, anxious to get away. This was just too painful to share.

CHAPTER 17

A year passed thus, while Richard Plantagenet fell deeper and deeper into depression. He rarely spoke unless necessary and showed little interest in the outside world. Once in a while he would rally and play a game of chess with King Robert, or listen to the music from a traveling minstrel. For the most part, however, he was content to sit with the cat on his lap or nod off in his chair after staring out the window.

Much happened in England while Richard was occupied with his own misfortunes. His successor, Henry IV, had briefly invaded Scotland within months of taking the crown in an attempt to assert his new regality. Desperately short of funds, he failed to make any impression on the Scots. Henry withdrew, having gained nothing but empty promises that they would consider his claim of overlordship. King Robert was able to divert Richard with stories of his enemy's mortification. That helped ease the pain.

Scotland wasn't Henry's only reversal. On his way back to London the king learned of a Welsh rising led by one Owain Glyndwr, who visited fire and destruction on his recalcitrant neighbor Reginald Grey of Ruthin. Turning immediately to the west, Henry led his army into Wales, chasing the elusive enemy deep into the mountains. Again, he failed to engage. Lack of funds and terrible weather forced them to turn back.

Throughout all this, the English exchequer was desperately short of money. In his anxiousness to protect his fledgling government, Henry had removed most of Richard's officers and appointed Lancastrian retainers, from top to bottom. He knew all too well that most of them were unqualified, but loyalty was more important than experience. Predictably, it didn't take long for their fumbling efforts to rebound, and revenues dropped to a trickle. Tax collectors were assaulted and even murdered. Authority was weak and bands of ruffians attacked travelers on the roads; riots broke out with little provocation.

Henry was soon to learn that his aborted Welsh campaign was only the beginning of his troubles with Glyndwr. Repeated raids into the Marcher territories unsettled his border barons, who were quick to complain. During the January Parliament of 1401, the Commons insisted on enforcing the most repressive anti-Welsh legislation since Edward I. No Welshman was henceforth permitted to acquire property or burgess status in English towns—within their own country. They were forced to help support English garrisons in their own castles. No full-blooded Englishman could be convicted in Wales except when sentenced by English justices. Gatherings of Welshmen were forbidden unless permitted by their lord. Minstrels and bards could not accept payment, for fear they were spreading sedition. Henry tried to discourage these prejudicial laws, but his hands were tied. If he refused to cooperate, they wouldn't grant him any funds.

None of these laws would have been enacted in Richard's reign. The Welsh were in no mood to acquiesce.

Spring came late to Scotland, and Richard was happy to loiter in the garden and listen to the birds, even though he had to pull his cloak tighter to stay warm. Over the castle walls in the distance he could see the mountains shrouded in mist. This land was so different from anything he had ever known before. He marveled at its wild aspect while wondering if he could ever feel comfortable here. Not that it mattered; anywhere was better than that dreadful cell at Pontefract Castle where he wondered daily when the assassin would make his appearance.

He turned at the sound of footsteps, watching the young guard approach. He was never really alone, but again it didn't matter. One day was the same as the next and he had no desire to escape. If it made King Robert happy to keep a guard on him, who was he to complain? They fed him well and left him alone. That's all he wanted.

He had already lost interest when the guard cleared his throat. "Dickon," he said, using the name Richard preferred, "a man is here to see you. He says he is your valet de chambre and has traveled hundreds of miles to find you."

"Oh?" Mildly curious, Richard looked at him again. "Does he have a name?"

"He says his name is William Serle."

"Serle?" That got his attention. "Here? How did he find me?"

"I don't know. Do you want to see him?"

Richard shrugged. "I suppose it could do no harm." Looking at the entrance to the garden he spotted William, still in his traveling clothes and clutching a sack. Richard beckoned the newcomer over as the guard walked away.

Glancing briefly at the man as he passed, Serle strode up to Richard and fell to his knee. "It is you. I almost gave up hope."

"Get up, get up. There is no need for that."

Blinking in confusion, Serle found a seat across from Richard, disconcerted at his informal reception. He wasn't sure what to expect from his master, but indifference was not among the possibilities. Surely Richard was glad to see him? After all, he had served the king faithfully for decades. He had even performed the unsavory task of putting an end to the Duke of Gloucester—without complaining. He fled into exile after the Epiphany Rising and had lost everything. All for this ghost of a man who sat before him.

Staring for a little while, Richard finally spoke up. "How did you find me?"

"I heard two men helped you escape from prison and have been spreading rumors for months, to anyone who would listen. I finally found one of them, a friar who serves Sir Harry Percy. He told me they took you to the Isles before you were separated. Once I learned about this royal castle, I thought it would be a good place for you to take refuge."

"It is a good place."

"Sire..." Serle hesitated.

"Don't call me sire. I am Dickon here."

"Dickon?"

"Only the king knows who I am. Everyone else thinks I am a dullard."

William was at a loss. He had come all this way to find a king. He didn't recognize this person. "I came here to help you."

"Help me? How can you help me?"

"Don't you want to regain your throne?"

"Why would I want that? It brought me nothing but misery." His eyes flashed for a moment. "I heard about the rebellion. There's no one left to support me."

Pursing his lips, Serle thought of a different approach. "Already the people complain about King Henry. He has broken his promises. Robberies and murders have destroyed the peace. Royal purveyors steal from the merchants; there is no money in the exchequer. The crops failed and famine stalks the land. King Henry said he would rule better than you and he has brought our country nothing but misery. Your people are worse off than before..."

"This is no more than they deserve."

"There are many who feel you were treated badly."

Richard frowned. "Where were they when I needed them?"

"Disorganized. Still in Ireland."

Waving his dismissal, Richard turned away. "It matters not. It's over. King Richard is dead. His body lies at King's Langley."

Lowering his head, Serle couldn't hide his dismay. All of his fortunes hung on this feeble king. He must bring him back to reason.

"Sire," he said. "I have kept this for you." Opening his sack, he dug into its contents until he felt what he was looking for. Pulling his hand out, he smiled when Richard gasped. "Yes, your signet ring. I took it when you left Carmarthen."

For a moment Richard reached for it, then dropped his hand. "Keep it still," he said softly. "It's no good to me."

This couldn't be happening! Closing his hand around the signet, Serle stood. "Why don't I send some letters in your name? Once people learn you are still alive, there will be such a swell of support you won't be able to resist." And, he could only hope, Richard will snap out of this senseless behavior.

A sad smile crossed the king's face. "Do what you want," he said softly. "It won't make any difference."

Taking that for a yes, Serle gave him one last nod and backed away, noticing that Richard didn't even bother looking at him. In his heart, he believed it was only a matter of time before the king shook off his lethargy. And when that time came, he would be on hand, once again, to accept Richard's gratitude for a task bravely accomplished.

There was one thing that would have interested Richard, had he known about it. The French were furious at Henry and even threatened to invade the country until they heard Richard was dead. No, they would not recognize the usurper. And Charles wanted his daughter back—at least, he did until the stress brought about another bout of madness. His illness served to delay her recall, and Henry took advantage of the respite to see if she would marry one of his sons. There was a question of 200,000 francs dowry paid to Richard after his wedding, and the French wanted it back, along with her jewels. Needless to say, the dowry was spent long ago.

Isabella of Valois was probably the only person in England who did not know about Richard's funeral. She was fourteen now and kept in close confinement at Havering-atte-Bower, where she was taken after the failed rebellion. Her prison was an old royal palace to the northeast of London, modest but comfortable. She knew Richard's life was in danger and was worried sick about him. Alas, no matter how much she cried and demanded to visit her husband, she was politely refused. So she was relieved when the Prince of Wales was announced, for of all King Henry's children he was closest to her in age and they had gotten along well before he went to Ireland. Before her life fell apart.

Hal came in by himself and knelt before her—a gesture of respect sorely lacking these many months. He had grown much taller since she last saw him, and his shoulders had filled out from training. Unsurprisingly, his stiff posture had not relaxed, nor had his eyes softened; they were guarded as usual.

Blinking back tears, she held out her hands. "You are a welcome sight, my lord. Thank you for visiting me."

Slowly he stood and together they walked over to a window seat. Tucking a lock of hair behind her ear, she smiled self-consciously. It had been so long since she had a visitor, she was not dressed like a princess. Hal didn't seem to care.

"Do you have everything you need?" he said, trying to find a good place to start a conversation.

Isabella nodded. She knew that's not why he was here. "I had hoped to see my husband," she said softly. She knew this was none of his doing, but she had to make her feelings known to somebody.

At least Hal had the grace to look embarrassed. "I loved King Richard like a father," he said earnestly, trying to take her hand. "He was very good to me."

"Loved?" Her eyes narrowed. "You love him no longer?"

He sighed. There was no easy way to say this. "My lady, there is something I must tell you."

She pulled her hand away, panic spreading over her face. "What has happened to him?"

As he struggled to find the words, Isabella broke into tears. "He's dead, isn't he?" She covered her face with her hands. "My servants spread some rumors but I didn't believe them." Her breath came in sobs. "My poor Richard. How could you do this to him?"

Stricken, Hal fell to his knees. "I swear to you, I am overcome with anguish. I didn't even know where he was kept."

Lowering her hands, she looked at him doubtfully. "Do you expect me to believe that?"

Hal shook his head. "I am not privy to my father's decisions."

"How can that be?"

He hesitated, biting his lip. "It seems my father trusts no one, except for the archbishop. And perhaps his inner circle. We are not close."

She was not convinced. However, there was no point in arguing. "How did Richard die?" Her voice was so soft he barely heard her.

"It is said that after the rebellion, he stopped eating. This went on for almost two weeks when they sent a confessor to reason with him. Relenting, he tried to eat but by then he was unable to swallow. Sadly, he expired shortly thereafter."

"Dear God, he starved to death?"

"That is what I am told." This sounded weak, even to him. What could he do? Richard's death was shrouded in mystery.

"Do you believe this?" Isabella's voice was harsh.

"Of course I do." Hal tried to sound sincere.

"I expect to attend his funeral," she said firmly. Once again, he hesitated and she couldn't restrain her tears. "You wouldn't stop me, would you?"

Hal had to fight back his rage at his father. He was furious to discover Isabella hadn't been told about the funeral and insisted he be the one to break the tidings to her. Now he regretted it.

"It's too late, Isabella. The king thought it best for you not to attend."

"Not to attend?" Her voice rose to a shriek.

Hal stood, stepping back. "He sent me to tell you. He thought it would be best for you to hear from my lips."

Did she even heed him? Turning away, she threw herself onto the cushion, crying uncontrollably. Looking around the room, Hal went over to a sideboard and poured a cup of water. He knelt by her side, holding it out.

"Here, drink this."

Hiccoughing, she sat obediently, accepting the water.

"I promise you, I will do my best to see you are well taken care of," he said.

She stopped drinking. "What does it matter? I've lost everything I care about."

Defeated, Hal got up to leave.

"Wait."

He stopped, his back to her.

"When?"

He was hoping she wouldn't ask. Turning, Hal wiped his hands on his sides. "The funeral was 12 March."

"That was months ago!"

He waited for her to start wailing again and she surprised him by her restraint. "I see how it is," she said sadly. "Once again I am a pawn in your game. I am not supposed to have feelings. I must do what I am told for I have no choice."

She was breaking his heart. "My dear friend, you are not the only one."

Henry's response gave her pause. She cocked her head, considering him for a moment. "I am sorry we are enemies," she said. "In another world we might have been friends. Please, Hal. Help me go home."

Not trusting himself to speak, he nodded and turned to leave. His father may have wanted him to court Isabella, but he could see there was a huge gulf between them that would never be crossed. How could she ever forgive the family that ruined her life? Like it or not, King Henry's sins were his own. He may despise the usurpation, but he couldn't deny his destiny. Perhaps when he was king he could undo some of the wrongs his father had committed.

Hal hesitated before leaving, thinking to reassure her. With a heavy heart, he knew he couldn't make any promises. As he closed the door softly, he took the memory of her sobbing with him.

Eventually, King Henry had to give in to the repeated demands for Isabella's return. The biggest difficulty was the dowry. After much back-and-forth, it was decided the money would be deducted from the outstanding balance of King John's ransom, still unpaid after thirty-six years. Her jewels, at least, could be collected and returned—at least, those she brought with her. Any gifts she received after her marriage would have to stay in England.

So the somber princess, dressed in her widow's weeds, was brought to London and temporarily lodged in the Tower. Although the king tried to extend every courtesy, she shrank from him, pouting and agitated. Finally, to everyone's relief, a safe-conduct was issued for up to five hundred persons. The cost was tremendous: a third of the king's annual household's fees to cover the expenses for wages, lodging, supplies, carpets, tents, and other apparatus. King Henry could ill afford this show of wealth, but he had an image to sustain. The Cinque Ports were obliged to provide three barges and two balingers, and orders were sent to other ports to keep armed vessels in readiness in case of trouble. Isabella was escorted through London, still dressed in black. The citizens grumbled as the royal party passed through; they attributed the troubles of the last few years to her arrival as King Richard's unwelcome queen. Many grumbled that she would probably stir up future problems as her family sought revenge.

Another month was to pass while Isabella waited at Dover for the last of the negotiations to wrap up. Finally, accompanied by Worcester, her ladies of honor, her chamberlain, confessor, and secretary plus the party of escorts, they crossed the Channel without incident.

Reaching Leulinghen, the very spot she first met her husband, Isabella was returned to her countrymen with a big show of formality. Blinking back tears, the Earl of Worcester took her by the arm and presented her to the Count of St. Pol. He stated he would be willing to fight, *à outrance*, anyone who asserted that she was not "just as she had been received". Fortunately, his concern wasn't necessary; the princess-royal was joyfully embraced and Worcester accepted letters of quittance. Unbeknownst to the English, the dukes of Burgundy and Bourbon hid behind a nearby hill with five hundred men, just in case there was trouble. Fortunately, nothing happened. Neither side had any reason to start a diplomatic incident, and Isabella graciously bid adieu to her English ladies and even divided her remaining jewels between them.

Prince Hal could not attend Isabella's departure, for his presence was urgently required in Wales. On Good Friday while the garrison of Conwy was attending mass in town, a confederate of Gwilym and Rhys Tudor entered the castle disguised as a carpenter. It was an easy task for him to overcome the two guards left on site and open the gate for the insurgents. They moved right in and raised the drawbridge against the English. The impregnable fortress was taken without a blow!

Hotspur was not present that day when Conwy was taken. Nonetheless, this was on his watch. Returning posthaste from Beaumaris Castle, he summoned Hal from London and set about laying siege. Conwy was too strong to be overwhelmed by direct assault; there was no other choice. After four weeks with 120 men-at-arms, 300 archers, and many fruitless assaults, Hotspur turned to negotiation. He allowed the Tudor brothers their freedom with thirty-five other rebels in exchange for nine guilty accomplices, who were summarily beheaded—after being treacherously seized in their beds and turned over to the English.

To pay for this debacle, Hotspur personally had to advance £200 from his own pocket—a considerable sum when a laborer earned 2 pounds a year. This was on top of all the money previously owed him for the maintenance of his troops. Through the month of May he wrote increasingly urgent letters to the king's council, complaining his soldiers were suffering from lack of payment. He even went so far as to negotiate with Glyndwr in person in an attempt to end the rebellion.

Harry Percy and Owain Glyndwr were not total strangers. Both of them served in King Richard's army in 1385 during the Scottish invasion; both had engaged at tournaments over the years—for Owain, too, was a celebrated jouster. They secretly corresponded in May and arranged to meet at a place of Owain's choosing.

Always ready for adventure, Hotspur agreed to wait for two Welsh knights who would bring him to a small dwelling in the forest—alone. His trust was not misplaced; Owain truly wanted a royal pardon, and he petitioned for a three-month's truce. Hotspur went back satisfied that he had performed a good deed. He duly sent the request to the king's council, but their response was far from satisfactory. "It is neither honorable nor befitting the king's majesty to forgive such a malefactor his offense," they wrote. "We would have preferred you had destroyed this rebel rather than permit him to cause further violence to the kingdom."

No money was forthcoming—just this insulting letter. Enough was enough. Harry's response was immediate. "It is not in keeping with my rank," he wrote, "to rely on deception and murder rather than truth and honesty. As for the funds which we so desperately need, if remedy is not forthcoming, I will be forced to resign my post, for I can no longer bear the expense. If any town, castle, or March under my rule is overrun for lack of subsistence, the blame must be cast upon those who refuse payment to my troops."

Hotspur waited two weeks for a response, but his was a lost cause. His mind made up, he met with Prince Hal at Flint Castle and took him aside. They climbed to the top of the tower to look over the estuary. This was the same spot where Richard had stood, watching the approach of Bolingbroke and bemoaning his fate. Had he known this, Hal would have deemed it the most appropriate place to receive the bad news which was obviously brewing.

At least Hotspur didn't procrastinate. He leaned on the parapet, turning to the other. "Hal, you know I have been writing to the council for months, demanding payment for our troops. I've had the same problem with my garrisons in Northumberland. I'm at my wit's end—and I'm at the end of my resources. I can't do it any longer." He looked down at the lad, fighting his guilt. "I'm relinquishing my command in Wales. They need me back in the North."

Hal looked at him, his mouth quivering. He wanted responsibility though not this much!

"I'm sorry, lad," sighed Harry. "This is none of your fault. Still, I suspect your father will give *you* more aid than me. Surely he won't leave you without support. You'll be safe here, meanwhile."

"What am I to do?" Hal finally asked.

"You've proven yourself very resourceful," the other said. "You are fully capable of leading a detachment of soldiers, if need be. Trust your instincts, Hal. You have the makings of a great commander."

The prince didn't feel particularly confident. During this last year, when they did ride out on sorties, he had always acted as second in command after Hotspur. Everyone knew his position was honorary. Who was going to obey him?

As if reading Hal's mind, Harry took him by both shoulders. "Remember who you are," he urged. "Your rank is everything. Use what I've taught you, treat your men honorably, and they will follow you."

And then he was gone. Hal stayed on the parapet and watched him ride away with a score of retainers. That was so like Harry to dash off without another thought. For only a year, Hal had been serving under his tutelage. Hotspur had been made Constable of Chester, Flint, Conwy, and Caernarfon castles—in addition to his other duties as Warden of the East Marches and Justice of North Wales. He was indefatigable. Nothing slowed him down. You couldn't help but admire the man.

Hal felt a familiar ache in his heart. After all, he was only fourteen. Hotspur was two years older than the king, and once again he had a father figure to advise him. Hal hated to admit it, but he needed someone to look up to. And yet, he couldn't warm up to his own father. Why? He knew his father loved him—or at least he thought so. They never seemed to understand each other. Was it because his father was never there for him? He spent most of his youth under the tutelage of governesses. When he was eight his mother died, and his grandmother took in the children. No great household gave him knightly training, like so many other noble sons. It wasn't until he became King Richard's hostage that he was made a squire—by the king himself. It was more than an honor; Richard treated him like family. He thrived under the attention. And suddenly it was over.

Hotspur was just the man to make up the difference. It had been so easy to take instruction from this legendary knight. He was everything Hal wanted to be. And now, in too short of a time, he was gone, too. Another advisor lost. First, Richard, now Harry.

He was on his own, this time. He had better get used to it.

It was the end of June. It didn't take long for the Welsh to rise again and attack town after town, burning and pillaging. Prince Hal summoned knights, esquires, and archers from nearby shires who owed the king service. He was secretly surprised and gratified that his orders were accepted without demur. Nonetheless, he was relieved when King Henry joined him with more troops at the end of September. It was a lot to take on.

They advanced into the heart of Wales, leaving destruction and famine in their wake. Again, as in times past, Owain Glyndwr and his men melted into the mountains, refusing to engage with the invading army. Winter came on and the English withdrew, having accomplished little. Hal moved to Beaumarais and the island of Anglesey—formerly granted to Hotspur—and the Earl of Worcester was assigned as his advisor. That was all right with Hal; the earl was just as accomplished as Harry, and Hal still had a lot to learn.

CHAPTER 18

Henry was in his study when the squire, Antoine Riczi was announced. The Breton was the regular messenger used to deliver letters between Henry and Joanna and he was always welcomed with good cheer. Henry even stood to greet him, he was so glad for a letter. Today, he was even more encouraged to see the expression on Antoine's face; the squire was radiant.

"You bring me good tidings," Henry exclaimed, holding out his arms. "How goes it with your fair duchess?"

"Ah, she is better by the day, as you will see in her message," the other said, bowing and holding out a letter.

Henry pulled it from Antoine's hand and went over to the window, gesturing for the squire to help himself to some wine. Kissing the paper, he gently worked the seal loose.

My dearest Henry, Antoine will give you all the details, but I am delighted to tell you I have received a dispensation from Pope Benedict to marry anyone I please within the fourth degree of consanguinity. If it is your desire, Antoine is willing to stand as my proxy so that we may be married at the soonest.

His mouth open in wonder, Henry whirled around. Antoine raised his cup as a toast. Changing his expression to a wide grin, the king let out a shout of glee. "You are the angel of happiness!" he exclaimed. "Tell me all about it."

"Well," said Antoine, taking a seat across from the king, "it wasn't easy, as you might suppose. I believe you know she had her young son raised to the throne of Brittany as duke..." He paused as Henry nodded. "She still has told no one about her intentions to wed yourself. She feels that once the marriage is accomplished, she will smooth the path for the royal family's acceptance."

Henry took a deep breath and nodded. "Your mistress is as wise as she is beautiful," he said wistfully. "And brave. I wish she were here today."

"Her heart is here. You can be certain of that."

The king went to his desk, picking up a quill. "We shall have the ceremony right here, at Eltham Palace. I shall summon the Archbishop of Canterbury, my Beaufort brothers, the Earl of Worcester, and my other great officers." He went to work, personally writing the invitations while the squire watched him with satisfaction, sipping his wine.

Within a week, all the witnesses had arrived and a private ceremony was held, just as the king desired. Antoine Riczi was dressed in an elegant houppelande of dark blue velvet lined with white satin, made just for the occasion; he even outshone the king. But Henry didn't care; he was honoring his bride. Placing the ring on Antoine's little finger, he said, "I, Henry King of England, take you, Joanna of Navarre, to be my lawfully wedded wife. With this ring I plight my troth."

Antoine's response was memorized. "I, Antoine Riczi, in the name of my worshipful lady, dame Joanna, the daughter of Charles lately king of Navarre, duchess of Bretagne, and countess of Richmond, take you, Henry of Lancaster, king of England and lord of Ireland, to my husband, and thereto I, Antoine, in the spirit of my said lady, plight you my troth."

It was all done very quickly. Henry turned to his witnesses, expecting to be congratulated. The archbishop, who was removing his stole, nodded pragmatically. Henry Beaufort briefly grasped the king's hand before turning to his brother. Some of the others were helping themselves to food. Worcester came forward with a chalice of wine and a big smile on his face; he could always be relied upon to make the diplomatic gesture.

Waiting his turn, at least Erpingham seemed genuinely happy with Henry's prospects. They turned together and looked at the room.

"Their enthusiasm is a bit subdued," Henry said dryly. "I guess this is what I have to look forward to."

Erpingham shrugged. "They have to get used to the idea of another French queen."

"Breton," Henry reminded him. He hesitated. "All right, French. She *is* the granddaughter of old King John. Perhaps she will help bring our countries together."

"We can only hope. As long as you are happy."

"Thank you, my friend. You're the only one who met her. She'll win the others over in time."

Riczi was sent home with a Lancaster collar of SS links studded with jewels, as well as Henry's ardent wishes for Joanna's quick removal to England. Alas, he was going to have to wait nine months before he saw his bride.

By spring of 1402, rumors of Richard's survival and impending return were so rampant King Henry sent commissions to all his sheriffs to suppress alehouse gossip. Mysterious letters professing to be from Richard were received by many who had been his supporters in the old days. Bearing the king's seal, these letters never ceased to cause consternation.

Wandering Dominican and Franciscan friars were particularly caught up in the movement, and because they were welcomed wherever they went, their rumors went with them. At first, a couple of friars were caught and hanged to discourage sedition, but this proved to be no deterrent. It was rumored the friars were collecting money to send to Glyndwr to aid in his rebellion. This was too much, and the king decided to interfere. Eleven friars were arrested at Leicester, and one of them, the warden of the convent, was a master of theology named Roger Frisby. They were brought to London and Henry resolved to interview them before their trial.

The friars were a ragged bunch, wearing undyed brown and grey tunics, some barefoot, others with a rope around their waist. They were prodded into the judge's chamber where the king sat in a high-backed chair, observing them with a frown. Frisby stepped forward.

"Why do you persist in spreading this vile story that Richard Plantagenet lives and plans to take arms against my person?" the king demanded.

"King Richard's return was prophesied by St. Bridlington himself."

"Bridlington's so-called prophecies have already been proven false. Do you say, then, that Richard is alive?"

Frisby drew himself up. "I do not say that he is alive, but I say that *if* he is, he is the rightful king of England."

Henry's frown deepened, though this wasn't enough to deter him. He had always enjoyed a good debate, even if it was too close for comfort. "You know King Richard abdicated."

"And you know he was not at liberty. Thus, his abdication was unlawful. This makes you a usurper."

Henry stood. "I did not usurp the crown. I was properly elected."

Knowing he was already damned, Frisby was determined to have his say. "That election means nothing if the rightful incumbent is alive," he said scornfully. "And if he is dead, then you killed him, and if you killed him you lose any title or right you have to the kingdom."

"That is a lie! Begone!" His face livid, Henry pointed out the door.

The unfortunate friars were taken to Westminster in chains, charged with sedition then urged to plead guilty. All refused and claimed their right to a public trial; they knew the people were with them. And their faith wasn't misplaced. First, a jury from London refused to convict them so they were brought to Holbourn. Here, too, the authorities met with the same resistance. So a third trial was held at Islington and finally the court got the result they wanted. The friars were hung at Tyburn and their heads struck off, their bodies flung into a ditch. Only later did their fellow friars dare to recover the corpses. While they performed this sad duty, many of the jury members approached them and asked their pardon. They had feared for their lives and condemned the friars under compulsion.

Within a month, Henry declared an amnesty against the preachers. Popular unrest could no longer be denied, and the last thing he wanted was a downward spiral of repression, resistance, and defiance. He had risen to the throne in a surge of popularity, and it was beginning to look like he had already used up much of his subjects' goodwill. He did not want to be thought of as a tyrant. There must be a better way to convey legitimacy.

Jean Creton was surprised when King Charles received a letter from Scotland. After he had returned from England after King Richard's capture, he had resumed his old position as the king's *valet de chambre*. Naturally, he was one of the first to hear anything of importance. Today was especially interesting. The look on the king's face was so unusual he feared another episode was coming on. But no, Charles's mouth was opening and closing in surprise and he held out the letter to Jean.

"Can this be possible?" the king said.

Taking the missive, Jean glanced at it quickly then perused it again, his face a mirror of the king's.

"Escaped from Pontefract? A guest of King Robert in Scotland? I pray to God this is true!" He handed the letter back to Charles who pointed at the corner.

"It's the king's seal. I recognize it!"

As others in the room crowded around the French king, Creton began striding back and forth. "He reached out to us, your majesty. He needs help! Let me write to him at once!"

Everyone was talking and the king nodded to Jean, who wasted no time collecting a quill and ink. He sat down and poured out his heart in a letter to King Richard, who he had admired greatly.

"*My heart melts to hear you are alive,*" he started. "*Your image has been ever before my eyes, and night and day I think of you.*" He wrote many pages and ended with urging Richard to send a token that he is yet alive, or at least some evidence of his wishes. "*Do not hold back in anger because your misfortunes are not yet avenged. Come to France, where you will find faithful friends ready to die for your cause and your young wife who is waiting for your embrace.*" Wiping away a tear, Jean was taken with another thought. "*I would that I could come across the Channel in person, to see you once again.*"

Creton sent the letter immediately, but still, he wasn't content. He had to do something more. King Charles agreed with him; he must go in person and determine whether King Richard was still alive. Only then could poor Isabella know if she was free to marry again.

It took a long time for Jean Creton to reach the other side of Scotland. When he was finally shown into the refugee's chamber, he was shocked to see the change in the man's countenance. Long ago he had pushed the unhappy episode at Flint Castle from his mind. He preferred to remember King Richard as the proud, handsome monarch fully in charge of any situation, confident of his own regality. What he saw here was a stooped-over shell of a man sipping from a bowl of soup, barely cognizant of his surroundings. Only when the figure raised his head and looked at him did Jean recognize the flicker in Richard's eyes, quickly squelched.

Unsure of himself, Creton slipped across the room and fell to his knees. "Your majesty," he murmured. "I have come from France to see you."

Cocking his head, Richard didn't quite know what to do. This Frenchman had accompanied him during his last month of freedom; he had witnessed everything. Despite himself, Richard felt a tear course down his cheek. He stretched out a hand and put it on Jean's head. "Sit, my friend," he said, "there is no majesty here."

A little abashed, Jean pulled up a stool. "Did you get my letter?"

Putting his bowl on a side table, Richard moved his hand to a little pile of papers next to it. He pulled out the letter from underneath a crystal stone. "I read it many times," he said. "I am so grateful for your comfort. It is good to know I haven't been forgotten."

"Never!" Jean caught himself and lowered his voice. "Sire, you must come back with me. Come to France. We can restore your health and challenge the usurper." Having hoped to encourage the king, Jean's heart sank at Richard's lack of response. In fact, the king wasn't even looking at him. "Sire?"

After a long hesitation, Richard picked up his bowl again. "There's no sire here. Haven't you heard? King Richard is dead. His body rests at King's Langley. Long live the king." Those last words came out expressionless.

"You can't let it be! There are those in England who call out for your return." Jean waited for an answer but none came. "Then why did you send us a letter?"

"A letter?" Richard raised his eyes to the ceiling in thought. "Oh, that must have been William Serle. He has possession of my signet."

Jean pursed his lips, considering the implications. "You did not send the letter?"

"No. He took it upon himself."

"Then he seeks to raise a rebellion in your name. All is not lost!"

Richard brought his glance back to Jean; there was only sadness in his eyes. "You are mistaken, Jean. All was lost years ago. Why would I ever want to throw myself back into that lion's den?"

This was totally unexpected. It never occurred to Jean that Richard wouldn't want his crown again. "I don't understand."

"You don't? It's a miracle I'm not dead. I was saved from terrible imprisonment, or worse. I have no power. No money. Aside from yourself and the mad King Charles, I have no supporters. What few I had in England got themselves killed in my name. Why would I want to go back to that? Ever?"

Jean was at a loss. This wasn't the man who jealously guarded his sovereignty.

"What about Isabella?" he finally asked.

"Isabella?" For a moment, Richard's face softened. "That sweet child. Give her the opportunity to have a real life, Jean. What could I possibly offer her?"

"She grieves for you, sire."

"There is no sire here, I tell you!" The little burst of temper didn't last. "Jean, she is so young. She'll recover. Let her mourn the passing of her handsome king. He lives no more."

"But surely we can help you."

Putting down his bowl for the last time, Richard took hold of Jean's hand. "Listen to me, my friend. I am a broken man. I have no future, nor do I want one. I want to be left alone. I couldn't rule a kingdom, nor do I want to. The king of Scotland feeds me well. All my needs are taken care of. Let me be and forget about any grand plans of restoring me. I won't have it."

"But—"

"King Richard is dead. I am not the man you seek. Please, Jean. Promise me you'll tell your master I am an impostor. Please do this for me."

It was Jean's turn to weep. "I cannot bear it."

"Promise me, I beg you. I must have your promise."

There was no denying it. Richard was in earnest. Lowering his head, Jean said, "I promise."

"Ah, good. Come, walk with me in the garden. I could use some air."

They spent the rest of the day in idle conversation. Robert joined them, and Jean could see real affection between the two kings. Robert treated Richard like an equal—not a prisoner. But the following morning Jean was undeceived. As he prepared to leave, the King of Scotland visited him in his chamber.

"Richard told me why you came," Robert said, sitting on the bed. "He is very fond of you."

Nodding in acknowledgment, Jean tried one more time. "My master desires to help him. He's Richard's father in-law, you know."

"Yes, I do. Richard speaks very highly of him." He coughed. "You must understand, Jean. King Richard is my guest, now. He is safe here."

"Sire, I can see you are very good to him. But he wastes away in exile. His people need him."

"Do they?" Robert narrowed his eyes. "Does England need a king who has no will to rule? You need look no farther than your own country. When your sovereign is ill, God preserve him, his brothers throw the kingdom into chaos with their bickering. England needs a strong king. As does Scotland." His eyes took on a faraway look. "Which I know all too well."

He handed Jean a golden chalice studded with jewels. "Give this to King Charles with my esteem. Tell him that Richard is in good hands. It's very possible the English will contend that my guest is an impostor; after all, they staged a very expensive funeral. This is the way Richard wants it. Regardless, we will continue to provide him asylum for as long as he lives."

Defeated, Jean bid Richard farewell. His heart ached for this broken-down king. However, he could see there was no choice but to accept the failure of his mission. As Jean took his leave, Richard said, one last time, "Promise me."

"Oui. I promise." And he watched as the other turned away, leaning down to pet the dog before looking out the window. He didn't acknowledge his visitor any further.

Jean returned to France a sadder, more thoughtful man. When King Charles asked him if he saw Richard, his response was, "I did see a man who resembled him, but this is not the king I had known in 1399. Here, your majesty. This is a gift from the Scottish king."

"How disappointing." Charles accepted the chalice and rotated it, admiring the jewels. "Where did Richard's seal come from?"

"Apparently it was stolen by someone who was trying to stir up trouble."

"Oh, there is plenty of that going on over there. Henry of Lancaster will never have a quiet moment, I promise you."

Jean bowed and started to back from the room. However, the king wasn't finished. "There's no impediment now, to Isabella's marriage to the Duke of Orleans' son," he said, "though the poor girl is still overcome with grief."

Pausing at the door, Jean wondered for a moment whether Richard would change his mind. "She'll need time, I think, before she weds again. She's still young."

"Indeed, indeed. We shall see."

CHAPTER 19

Henry was at Westminster when the messenger arrived. He had been in the middle of reviewing the exchequer's receipts and welcomed any interruption that would take him away from this unpleasant task. Henry's dear friend John Norbury had been acting as Lord High Treasurer of England since the coronation, but it was plain to everyone the poor man was not up to the task. The coffers were empty and the kingdom was terribly in debt.

Putting his quill down, Henry gave the messenger his full attention. However, the man's face gave him reason to dread what was coming.

"Sire, I have just come from the Duke of York. He is gravely ill and has sent for you. It is feared he may die."

Caught by surprise, Henry looked at Norbury, his lips quivering. "He is my last surviving uncle. I must go to him."

The other put a hand on his arm. "Of course you must. Where is he now?"

"King's Langley. He was born there, and I suppose he will die there, too." He sighed. "Rutland is in Guyenne, so I'm sure he would expect me to be there for his father."

"Then we should leave tomorrow. I'll come with you. Let me tell the servants."

Deep in thought, Henry watched as Norbury left the room. Without his uncle's support, he may never have prevailed in his return from exile—or at least, not without a considerable amount of fighting. After the coronation, York had taken a leading role as one of the senior peers in his government. There was no doubt Henry had disappointed the man; he shuddered when remembering the oath sworn at Berkeley. Another damned oath. To give his uncle credit, once he changed his course York never reproached Henry for usurping Richard. Was that because he recognized the inevitability of the situation? Henry hoped so, though he never had the courage to ask. Some things were better left alone.

The next day, the king left with a small retinue for King's Langley. The old palace had been a favorite residence of King Edward II and Edward III, and a Dominican Priory adjoined it. Henry hadn't been there for years.

When they arrived, Norbury was surprised to see that Henry's first stop was the Priory. He was strangely quiet so John contented himself with offering his silent companionship. They opened the door and stepped inside, grateful that the late afternoon sun was still strong enough to light their way. Stained-glass windows threw beautiful designs on the floor as they slowly walked down the center aisle. Dust sparkled in the sun beams.

Henry was obviously looking for something. He pointed at one of the stone tombs, beautifully carved with angels blowing horns. "That is the grave of Piers Gaveston. Remember him? He was the favorite of Edward II and caused untold problems until he was killed by my ancestor Thomas Lancaster. He was excommunicated at the time, and the king had to get papal dispensation before he could have him buried in a sacred place."

He kept moving. Obviously, Piers was not the one he was looking for. Approaching the altar, he stopped. In a little alcove to the left, two alabaster tombs with the Plantagenet coat of arms sat, surrounded by lit candles.

"Richard," he said simply. He did not kneel, or cross himself. "This tomb is for Richard. I just had to see it."

Ah, Norbury thought. *Richard plagues him yet.*

"And the other one is his older brother Edward, who died as a child. Now they can keep each other company." Turning away, Henry said wearily, "Let's go." They went out of the church and were greeted by York's servants.

"How is my uncle?"

"He has been waiting for you," the chamberlain said.

Built of timber and stone, the palace was well over 125 years old. The ceilings were low and aside from the great hall the rooms were mostly small and comfortable. In a chamber draped with tapestries and warmed by a fire, even on this late summer evening, the duke was propped up in bed. His eyes were closed and his chest labored, wheezing with every breath. He looked much older than his sixty-one years, but Henry knew he had been tormented by arthritis in his spine for a very long time. The chamberlain bent over the sick man.

"He's here, your grace."

York's eyes fluttered open and he reached out his arms. "My dear boy. Come closer. My old eyes don't see as well as they used to."

Henry approached the bed and knelt. "I was so distraught to learn you are not well."

"It's my heart, you know," said the duke. "Don't mourn me. I am ready to go to my maker." He took Henry's hand. "I wanted to see you one more time. Your father would be so proud."

Kissing his hand, Henry held it to his forehead. "You have been like a father. I don't know what I would have done without you."

York smiled weakly. "Did you see his tomb?"

"Richard? Yes."

"It gives me comfort, to know he is here. Soon I will lay near him, in the sarcophagus he had built for himself. When he no longer needed it—after the queen died—he gave the tomb to my dear wife and now I will use it, too, when I join her." He stopped, gasping for breath. "Take care of my son," he said. "He has done many things he must atone for." He coughed. "That is between him and God, but I foresee that he has difficult times ahead. He will need your help." Closing his eyes, the duke lay back again. "The same goes for you, nephew," he whispered. "We are all held accountable in the end."

Henry put York's hand back on his chest. He had his answer. His uncle had forgiven him.

Edmund Langley, the first Duke of York, died in his sleep that night. In his will, he made provisions for Rutland and his daughter Constance. His second son, Richard of Conisburgh—who was twelve years younger than Rutland—was left out of the will altogether. As Henry had once overheard, the duke suspected Richard was illegitimate, begat by his first wife Isabella of Castile and John Holland, half-brother to King Richard II. Well, as far as Henry was concerned, if York rejected him, the boy was on his own.

Once the funeral was over, other difficulties came hard on its heels. Owain Glyndwr waxed bolder and bolder, and in late summer he launched a devastating attack on a lordship owned by the Mortimers. Wealthy Marcher Lords in their own right, the Mortimers commanded great loyalty among the local population. The Welsh assault was an insult that couldn't be ignored, and the men from Hereford and neighboring districts gathered under the leadership of Sir Edmund Mortimer.

Edmund was the uncle of the young Earl of March—the eight year-old boy left behind after his father was killed in Ireland. Ever since that terrible day, Edmund had served as the acting head of the family. King Henry had taken his nephew as hostage, since the boy was considered by many to be the true heir to the throne. There was nothing Mortimer could do anything about that, but he was a pragmatic man. His nephew was now being raised alongside the royal princes. As long as the boy was safe, Edmund saw little advantage in making trouble. Nonetheless, he had heard rumors lately claiming he was a secret messenger between Owain and the Earl of Northumberland. Since Harry Hotspur was his brother in-law, he assumed this was the source of the gossip. Nonetheless, Edmund had enough problems without this stain on his reputation. A new campaign would be the perfect opportunity to clear his name.

The Welsh had attacked the castle in Knighton overlooking the river Teme. Although fortified with stout timber walls, the castle was destroyed alongside much of the town. This handiwork delayed the aggressors long enough for Mortimer to catch up with them. By now he had accumulated two thousand men and a large contingent of Welsh archers.

Edmund Mortimer was in his mid-twenties, handsome, robust, and a natural leader. He sat astride his horse next to Walter Devereux, Thomas Clanvow, and Robert Whitney—all leading English magnates who had gained extensive experience fighting in the Marches.

"There," he pointed. "The Lugg valley. We'll follow the river toward Pilleth. They will surely head that way and we can cut them off. There's an old church of St. Mary's with a holy well."

"Yes," agreed Devereux. "I remember. The church is on the slope of Bryn Glas. It has a far view of the countryside."

They moved forward, unaware that the Welsh commander, Rhys Gethin, was served by an extensive spy network. He already knew that the English approached. When Mortimer's force came within sight of Bryn Glas, they were shocked to see a large army spread out over the top of the hill.

"Bastards!" grumbled Edmund. "How did they get here so fast?"

"We outnumber them two-to-one," Whitney said. "And they don't seem all that well-armed. It's unusual for them to accept a battle."

"There's no time to turn back. Forward!" Mortimer shouted as his men closed into a loose formation behind their shields. They charged toward the hill, only to find themselves beset with a storm of arrows. Gethin had deployed a vanguard of archers in the valley at the base of the hill—just out of sight. Once their first flight of arrows had been loosed, the Welsh archers climbed toward the summit, firing as they withdrew. Their attack maddened the English, who followed them uphill, trying to catch them. But they were heavily armored and soon began to tire.

Once the Welsh determined their enemy was slowing, they decided to attack and charged down the slope, shrieking like demons of hell. "Archers!" cried Mortimer. "Stop them!" The other commanders took up his shout.

Something was wrong. The archers were turning their weapons against his own men! They were joining the Welsh and attacking the middle of his force, wreaking havoc with the startled fighters. "Traitors!" the men shrieked as they fell without striking a blow. Then the attackers were among them. Armed with spears, rocks, swords, and long knives, the Welsh fought like madmen. In just a few minutes the distraught English turned and fled, exposing their backs to pitiless blades. Many were trampled underfoot. Most didn't get away.

Stunned, Edmund fought on until he was thrown to the ground. The Welsh knew who he was and were under orders to capture him. Struggling, he finally threw his sword down and raised his arms, surrendering. Thomas Clanvow did the same, and they were quickly trussed up and taken away. The other English leaders were not so lucky and left their bones on the battlefield; it was said that over 1100 men were lost. Just to finish the job, the Welsh destroyed the tower connected to St. Mary's.

King Henry couldn't ignore the insult. Orders were sent far and wide to gather an army and meet him at Lichfield. At the same time, disquieting news had reached him that 12,000 Scots had crossed the border and were ravaging the West Marches. Well, the Percies would just have to deal with the Scots. It was time to smash the Welsh once and for all.

In an ambitious plan, Henry decided to invade the country from three directions simultaneously. One army was to collect at Hereford under the command of the Earls of Arundel, Stafford, and Warwick. A second force was to start from Chester under Prince Hal's banner, and King Henry would attack from Shrewsbury. They were all provisioned for fifteen days; this was to be a savage and rapid campaign.

While waiting for his army to gather, he settled down to review the usual batch of petitions and missives. The letter on top caught his attention immediately; it was from the Duke of Orleans. He pried open the wax seal, expecting to enjoy a friendly chat. What he saw instead almost caused him to drop the letter. Blinking, he started it again:

> *I, Louis, by the grace of God, son and brother to kings of France, duke of Orleans, write in the desire which I have to gain renown. I expect you to feel the same, since idleness is the bane of lords of high birth who do not employ themselves in arms. I can think of no better way to seek renown than by proposing for you to meet me at an appointed place, each accompanied by one hundred knights and esquires, there to combat together until one of the parties shall surrender...*

What nonsense was this? Henry couldn't believe it. While he was preparing for war, this idle duke presumes to challenge him? Considering their past friendship, this unexpected letter was unforgivable; it had no instigation on his part! Without waiting for his temper to settle, he wrote a stinging response:

We write to inform you that we have seen your letter containing a request to perform a deed of arms. This has caused us no small surprise, for the following reasons. First, on account of the truce agreed on, and sworn to, between our cousin king Richard, our predecessor, whom God pardon! and your lord and brother. Secondly, on account of the alliance that was made between us in Paris. Since you have thought proper, without any cause, to act contrary to this treaty, we have annulled the letter of alliance received from you and henceforward we throw aside all love and affection toward you. For it seems to us that no honorable knight, or any person whatever, ought to demand combat from him with whom a treaty of friendship exists. In reply to your letter, we add that considering the very high rank in which it has pleased God to place us, we are not bound to answer any such demands unless made by persons of equal rank with ourselves.

He couldn't stop there and continued in the same vein for another two pages, ending with a covert threat that he may at some time in the future visit his possessions on Louis' side of the sea. At that point, Henry would bring as many persons as he desires and Louis could confront him then. Meanwhile, in the future Louis should be more cautious in his letters.

Satisfied that his honor had been restored, Henry sent off the letter and turned back to matters at hand. He had a rebellion to suppress.

Unfortunately, no one counted on the September weather. No sooner had Henry and his force of thirty thousand left the borders of Shropshire, they rode into the teeth of a ferocious sleet storm. Heads down, gritting their teeth in disgust, they doggedly trudged into the gloomy forests, hoping to find relief from the freezing rain. There was no dry wood to be found for fires, no way to stay warm. And still, the king led them on, plundering where they could and searching in vain for the enemy.

On the fourth night, Henry was so exhausted he fell onto his pallet without even removing his armor. As he lay in his pavilion listening to the wind blast against the canvas sides, the dripping water spread along the edges of the roof and turned into a stream, splattering against the ground. Weighed down by the surges of rain collecting on the roof, the pavilion began to sway with the gusts. All of a sudden, one of the sides gave way with a big tear, pulling the stakes out of the ground. The tent poles listed dangerously then, with another blast of wind, the pavilion fell on top of him, smothering the king with several pounds of fabric and wood and water.

"Help me!" Henry shouted, his voice coming out as more of a gurgle. He feared for a moment that no one had heard him. One of the poles lay across his chest and his arms, and he writhed around, unable to budge under the weight. "Help! Help!" He moved his head back and forth to keep the water from running into his mouth. Finally, he heard someone shout and men ran forward, grasped the soaked canvas and pulled it off of him. It was such a tangle they couldn't figure out where the opening was. "I can't breathe," Henry gasped, until a lucky flap slid off his face and exposed him to the deluge. He choked as the others grasped the poles and heaved them away, along with the bulk of the material. They grabbed him by the shoulders and hauled him to his feet. He hung onto one of the men to keep from falling.

"Your armor saved you, sire," gasped Erpingham, whose strong arms held the king upright. "Dear God, Glyndwr must be a sorcerer, calling up such a tempest."

Grateful for his friend's support, Henry gasped for breath while he regained his balance. "Always there for me, Thomas. Is your tent any dryer?"

"Come. I have some blankets I hid under a deerskin. You're shaking."

Indeed he was. Henry knew how close he had come to disaster. He let his friend grasp him by the elbow and lead him forward. They could recover his things in the morning.

A weak and unpromising sunrise exposed the worst of the wreckage. Henry's pavilion wasn't the only casualty, though the size of the structure made it the most vulnerable. Men were picking up the pieces of broken-down shelters, wringing out their clothes and pouring water from shoes. They sluggishly tied packs onto the backs of horses that hung their heads dejectedly. A couple of Henry's captains approached him cautiously.

"Sire, this is getting us nowhere," one of them said. "At this rate, our men will start deserting in a week."

Henry sighed, tightening his belt. "I can't just turn around and slink away. What kind of message would that send?"

Nobody had an answer. The king had to be seen as strong and merciless. Otherwise, the Welsh would wreak even more havoc.

"We go on," Henry assured them. He could see none were encouraged at the prospect. "The weather has to break sooner or later."

But no, it was Henry's misfortune that the rain continued without letup. One day merged into the next and men started dying—the ones who didn't desert. For twenty days they chased the elusive Welsh into the mountains until finally, Henry called a halt. For the third time, the king invaded Wales and came home empty-handed.

When he arrived in Westminster, bedraggled and frustrated, he was greeted with news so far removed from what he had experienced, he didn't know whether to be joyous or jealous. The Percies had won an overwhelming victory against the Scots. His overweening subjects had proven themselves once again.

The roster of prisoners from Homildon Hill was incredible. Over a thousand Scottish barons, knights, and esquires gave themselves up. The earls of Moray, Angus, and Orkney were among the prisoners as well as thirty French knights. Most important of all, the Earl of Douglas—who lost an eye—and Murdoch, son of the Duke of Albany, were in Percy's hands.

Dunbar, the Scottish Earl of March who had recently changed his allegiance to the English, had been largely responsible for the victory. Experienced and level-headed, he had managed to restrain Hotspur, who wanted to plunge into the fighting with his knights. But no, this was an archery battle. Let the Scots learn the lessons so thoroughly demonstrated at Crecy and Poitiers. Very little hand-to-hand combat was necessary, much to the disappointment of the hotheaded chivalry.

As soon as Henry heard, orders were sent out to the victors that the prisoners were not to be ransomed. Bring them to London where they would be kept in honorable captivity. It was the king's right; England would be safer that way. A captive Scot was an idle Scot. With no one to lead them, there would be no incursions over the border. Along with these orders came a promise that when it came time for the ransoms to be paid, the captors would receive their just dues. Alas, very few men believed the king. Most thought he intended to keep the ransom money himself to fill the royal coffers desperately short of funds. Henry's promises were worth as much as the unpaid tallies from royal purveyors.

The Percies were at the top of the list. As Henry brandished the king's letter, he and Harry glared at each other. "I will not go," insisted Hotspur for the third time. "How dare the king ignore the rules of chivalry and demand the prisoners for himself. It's just not done!"

"Son, don't be foolish. If you ignore the king's demands, you will bring his wrath down on our heads."

"You and I both know we are too far away to fear his wrath!" Spitting the last word, Harry turned away, gesturing his refusal. Then he spun around again. "After all we've done for him. What has gotten into his head? Ungrateful bastard." Having exhausted his anger for the moment, Harry sat down at the table with a grunt.

Percy knew his son's mercurial disposition all too well. Now was a good time to cozen him. "Look at it this way. Once we give him our cooperation, we can extract some concessions."

"Not likely, as I see it. He is trying to impose his will on us. You wait and see; he thinks we are too powerful and seeks to bring us down."

"No, no. This isn't just aimed at us. Come now. I already promised to deliver my prisoners."

Harry shook his head. "Giving in will weaken our cause. You know he wants the Earl of Douglas. It's the only way he can wash away the shame of that humiliating Welsh campaign. And there's something else," he added, leaning forward and pointing his finger. "I have my suspicions that the king has no intention of ransoming Mortimer. I may need the Douglas ransom to pay for his release."

Percy snorted. "That's nothing but speculation."

"The way he trounced on the Earl of March's claim to the throne? He has no regard for the Mortimers, and you know it."

"That's another matter altogether."

"It is and it isn't. It just proves the king won't keep his promises."

A troubled silence fell between them. But Hotspur wasn't finished. "You know Douglas surrendered to me personally, and by the laws of chivalry only I can ransom him. I refuse to betray his trust. Besides, the poor man hasn't recovered from his wounds. It would be agony for him to travel in his state."

"I'll grant you that," sighed Percy, sitting across from him. "Perhaps once I turn Murdoch over, that would appease the king."

"It's going to have to. I will not go."

This time, Hotspur refused to give in and Percy left him behind. He presented himself at Westminster Hall for the 1402 Parliament, bringing his most prominent prisoners: Murdoch, Earl of Fife and son of the Scottish governor, Lord Montgomery, Sir William Graham, Sir Adam Forster, and three French knights. Announcing himself with a fanfare, Percy presented the hostages who knelt just inside the door, then again in the middle of the hall, and a third time in front of the enthroned Henry. They remained kneeling while the king stood, sweeping his eyes across their heads and settling on Percy. He was not smiling. Henry restrained himself, making assurances they had nothing to fear; they were taken fighting like brave soldiers and he would respect the laws of chivalry. Then he invited them to join him at dinner in the Painted Chamber.

It wasn't until later that the king summoned the earl to his council chamber. He confronted Percy in front of a much smaller batch of witnesses, blaming the father for the disobedience of the son. Dispensing with any formalities, Henry went right to the point.

"Why is Harry not here? Where is Archibald Douglas?"

Of course, Percy was expecting a confrontation but his own frustration simmered close to the surface. He didn't know whether he was angrier at the king or his son. At the moment, it didn't matter.

"Sire, you can see they did not come."

"Yes, I can see. I want to know why."

"You'll have to ask my son. He will answer for himself."

"I'm asking you! Douglas has been the instigator of all our border troubles. I want him under lock and key." Henry caught himself clenching his fists.

"He is, I assure you. Harry takes personal responsibility for him."

"I demanded that he bring Douglas to London. He has no license to flout my commands."

Percy was nearing the end of his patience. "Sire, you forget. We are committed to our guardianship, but we have emptied our coffers in your service. The ransom money will help relieve our debt."

"I have paid you £60,000. What more do you want?"

That was too much. Stamping his foot on the ground, Percy let slip his restraint. "That is not true and you know it," he shouted. "You still owe us £20,000 in cash and bad tallies. And you wonder why Harry is upset."

It was Henry's turn to snap. "Haven't you been paying attention? Look what I've had to deal with!" He threw up his hands. "Two rebellions, back and forth from Scotland to Wales, piracy interfering with trade, expenses of the Calais garrison, the defense of Guyenne, protecting the southern coast against the French. My God, no wonder there is no money in the exchequer. I have paid you as much as I can and there is no more!"

Clearly, Percy was not concerned about Henry's problems. His voice lowered to a growl. "When you entered the kingdom you promised to rule according to your council. By now you have received large sums from the country, and yet you say you have nothing. God grant you better counsel!"

Henry was momentarily taken aback. He couldn't admit it, but all his life he had let someone else worry about finances. Money was always there to draw on when he needed it. The day he took the crown he was the wealthiest man in England. How did it disappear so quickly? He knew a large percentage of his expenses went to annuities—and these annuities had been granted without consulting his council. He *had* to; how else was he going to hold on to his supporters? At the same time, he needed to continue paying annuities to Richard's retainers and for the same reason.

He was about to say something when Percy bowed and backed from the room. Neither of them trusted himself to pursue an argument that would just end up with more bitterness, and Henry let him go. Besides, his real quarrel was with Hotspur.

Once Henry Percy returned to Northumberland, he vented some of his anger on his recalcitrant son. "As soon as I walked in the door, he wanted to know where you were. And where was Douglas."

"What an ungrateful wretch," Harry spat. "It wasn't enough that we won the most significant battle in fifty years. He has to cheat us out of our just desserts."

"I agree with you, son. But it wasn't right that I had to take all the abuse. Things went from bad to worse. I had to leave before I said something I would live to regret."

Harry grunted, looking at the ground. "All right. I see that I must face him, myself. But by God, Douglas stays here!"

In his usual fashion, once Hotspur made up his mind he acted upon it right away. Taking a small retinue, he rode to London.

When Harry was introduced into the king's chamber, he was greeted in much the same manner as his father was. Turning in his chair, Henry said, "Did you bring Archibald Douglas with you?"

Briefly kneeling, Hotspur shook his head. "He cannot travel," he said.

"I wasn't asking about his health," the king retorted. "I commanded you to bring him."

"Sire, as a knight I must observe common decency. He cannot travel."

"That is not the reason. You continue to defy me!"

Pursing his lips, Harry was quickly losing his temper. "You defy the laws of chivalry! It is not your right to demand our prisoners!"

"As your king it is certainly my right! They are firebrands and their retention is good for the country."

"Breaking faith with the Scots will only outrage them further."

"That is not what is at question here."

"That's because you don't understand their customs. They only surrender to the man who has defeated them. No one else!

Besides, since you will not reimburse what we are owed, how else am I going to pay my soldiers? I may need the money for Mortimer's ransom seeing that you refuse to pay it."

"I will not have good English gold leaving the country to aid our enemies!"

That was too much for Harry. "Shall a man expose himself to danger for your sake, and you refuse to help him in his captivity? Why is it you beggared the exchequer to ransom that dog Reginald Grey, who started this rebellion in the first place?"

Henry was not about to justify his defense of his Marcher baron. "I'll tell you why I won't ransom Mortimer. He is a traitor! Why else did he allow Glyndwr to capture him so easily? And you! You are a traitor, too! I heard you had Glyndwr in your hands and didn't capture him."

"We were negotiating under a flag of truce! Of course I didn't capture him!"

"And where did your negotiations go?"

"Four times my father and I came to a settlement with the Welsh. And four times you rejected the conditions. Your stubbornness forces them into rebellion."

"I think you negotiated for yourself!" Overcome by resentment and disappointment, Henry struck Hotspur on the cheek. As the other gasped in shock, Henry drew his dagger and Harry slapped his hand onto his own hip, forgetting that he had relinquished his blade at the door.

His face a deep red, Hotspur retreated a step. "Not here, but in the field!" he exclaimed, then turned his back on the king and stormed out the door, slamming it behind him.

CHAPTER 20

Hotspur did not return to Northumberland right away. Sending his retinue home, he headed west for Shrewsbury, where his uncle Worcester currently resided as Lieutenant of South Wales. Worcester would know where he could find Owain Glyndwr; his knowledge would surely be more recent. After Harry had left Cheshire in such a huff his sources of information had dropped off.

When Hotspur reached Shrewsbury he was relieved that Prince Hal was on another one of his destructive raids; in his mood he didn't want to talk to the boy. Instead, he had himself quietly announced to the Earl of Worcester who was busy procuring supplies for the stronghold. Worcester's face lit up when he was announced; the affection between the two was more like father to son than uncle to nephew.

"It is so good to see you." Giving a welcoming hug, Worcester put Harry at arm's length. "You look sound and hale. But I wasn't expecting you anytime soon. Is something amiss?"

Hotspur grunted. "You can well imagine. Do you have wine?"

"Over there, on the sideboard. What happened?"

Harry helped himself and poured some for his uncle. "It's the king again. We had a terrible argument."

"Money?"

"More than that. He demanded our hostages from Homildon Hill. I refused. He called me a traitor and struck me on the face!" His temper rose just thinking about it.

"I see. Our Henry is cracking under the pressure."

"I suppose. You know, he refuses to ransom Mortimer."

Worcester was raising his own cup and stopped. "I was afraid of that."

Harry pursed his lips. "I suppose you know my father and I have been negotiating with Glyndwr."

"Yeess." That came out slowly.

"We were attempting to end his rebellion before it got out of hand. As you know, the Welsh have valid grievances. Owain has made some overtures to us that are beginning to look more appealing, considering how King Henry is behaving. If the king is turning against our family, we need to protect ourselves."

Letting out his breath through pursed lips, Worcester leaned forward. "Be careful, Harry. Don't make any hasty moves."

"I need to speak to Owain, myself. I thought you might be able to help me find him."

Worcester got up and went to the door, making sure no one was listening outside. He sat again and leaned toward Harry. "My man-servant, Kevin Morys, has a sister in the Welsh camp. He can take you there."

"Ah." Harry leaned back. "I hope we can find Mortimer, too."

"I think you will. I understand Glyndwr is treating him like one of the family."

"Oh?" Hotspur raised an eyebrow. "That is indeed news."

"Can you spend the night? I would prepare a letter to your father as long as you are here."

"Gladly." Enjoying the wine, Harry realized just how exhausted he was. A long night's sleep would hold him in good stead.

The next morning, Kevin was already saddling the horses when Hotspur came outside. "You are lucky today," the man said. "Last I heard, Owain Glyndwr was somewhere in Ystlyg, in Powys. It should be about twenty miles west of here."

"I'm glad to be under your guidance, Kevin. Lead the way."

Worcester's servant showed little hesitation, though the roads were rough and muddy, and travel slow. As they entered deep into rebel territory, Harry noted scouts in the trees watching them. He realized he was more fortunate than he thought; Kevin was a known entity. By himself, he might not have made it thus far.

As the sun went down, they reached their destination. Kevin was greeted by guards as they passed, and they entered a clearing with a rustic farmstead. A handful of soldiers crowded around a fire, roasting a pair of rabbits; the aroma was terribly distracting. Dismounting, Harry glanced at them hungrily before he saw a cabin door open. In the corner of his eye he saw Edmund Mortimer duck under the lintel, straightening to his full height.

"Edmund!" Hotspur shouted, slipping from his horse. He dashed across to his brother in-law, throwing his arms around him. They hugged enthusiastically before Edmund pulled away and turned Hotspur toward his companion, who had come out the door after him.

"Harry, you know the Prince of Wales."

Embarrassed for a moment, the other bowed. "Forgive my rudeness, sire," Harry said. "I was so excited to see Edmund I forgot everything else."

Owain laughed—a hearty, cordial sound. He was a handsome man, tall and elegant. Descended from two princely dynasties, he carried himself like a natural successor. Educated, accomplished, and wealthy, he had responded to his country's need for a leader and proved himself by example. One of the first to experience English discrimination after King Richard's downfall, Owain inspired the Welsh to join together and resist a common enemy.

"Well come, Sir Harry Percy." He held out a hand.

Clasping it with both his own, Harry gave him one of his most engaging smiles. "I have come a long way to speak with you," he said. "I am so pleased to see you've taken such good care of Edmund."

"More than that," Mortimer said, gesturing to the door. A beautiful girl stepped forth and he put an arm around her. "Meet Catrin, Owain's oldest daughter and soon to be my wife."

"Oh ho!" Hotspur was dazzled by the new host of possibilities. "You haven't been languishing at all, while I've been worried sick about you."

"My Lord Owain has extended his most gracious hospitality."

"Come," said the prince. "You must be hungry. We have much to discuss."

Following them inside, Harry was glad of the shelter, despite its meager appearance. There were no windows and the room was only lit by a fire in the middle of the floor. They all sat on piles of hay.

"I apologize for the modest accommodations," said Owain, "but as you can see we are in the process of reducing the English estates hereabout."

Hotspur cleared his throat. "Fortunately, Wales is no longer in my care. It might interest you to know I have just come from King Henry. He hasn't recovered yet from the humiliation your weather inflicted upon him. They say you are a sorcerer and can control the elements."

Owain laughed briefly. "I would that I could. I'd save the worst for warfare and spare us the rest of the time." He leaned forward. "And what did the king have to say?" His brown eyes glistened in the firelight.

"He said I was a traitor for not arresting you when I had the chance." Harry looked over at Mortimer. "He won't ransom you."

"I'm not surprised," said Edmund, hugging Catrin closer. "It no longer matters. I am going to declare for the Prince of Wales."

Hotspur didn't know whether to be pleased or appalled. The former emotion won. "This changes everything," he said simply.

"You know that I have been in communication with your father," Owain said to Harry. "We have much in common. Your father wants to rule the North. I want to rule my own poor country. And Mortimer," he nodded at Edmund, "represents the true king of England. Lancaster stands in our way—nay, he seeks to destroy us. I suspect the Percies, too, are in his sights."

Swallowing, Harry nodded. "I can offer you more," he said. "The rumors about King Richard are true."

The others sat up straight, staring at him.

"Did you receive a letter with the king's seal?" he pursued.

Owain hesitated for a moment. "Yes, it came to my manor at Glyndyfrdwy before it was destroyed by that hellhound, Henry of Monmouth." His face clouded over. "I didn't know what to think of it."

"It was partly my doing. Richard's survival, that is. The king escaped from his prison at Pontefract Castle."

Everyone was still staring.

"I was dismayed that Lancaster stole the crown rather than give it to your nephew." He spoke apologetically, putting a hand on Edmund's arm. "We helped Henry get his patrimony back, but he went all the way and we couldn't stop him. It is my greatest regret. And he treated King Richard most atrociously, throwing him into prison like that."

He turned to Owain. "Richard's allies knew how I felt; I didn't even attend the banquet after the coronation. However, when they sent me a messenger, I dared not commit myself to their conspiracy. It all felt too risky. It was too soon. However, I knew King Richard would surely be killed if they failed. So I sent my confessor to them instead, to help the king escape if they could arrange it. And they did, with the aid of a yeoman inside Pontefract Castle. The two of them brought Richard to Scotland. Unfortunately, they lost track of him. He was recognized and taken away from them." Harry frowned. "It was not well done, but yes the king lives. I believe those letters are from him."

The room was silent while the others considered his shocking revelation. Owain let out his breath in a whistle. "That does indeed change everything. King Richard was a good lord to me, and to the Welsh."

Harry leaned forward. "I, too, received a letter with the king's seal. Now we know how to find him. When I get back to Northumberland, I will send my friar and tell Richard to be ready."

"Ready? Are you saying what I think you're saying?"

"Henry has broken every promise he made. And now that he has called me traitor and struck me with his own hand, he has severed every bond between us. The whole country suffers under his rule. He does not deserve to be king."

Owain scratched his fingers through his beard. He glanced at Edmund then back at Hotspur. "Are you ready to risk all? I am behind you, but think on this."

Harry sighed. "I must consult my father. He has a wiser head than mine."

"He is sensible and prudent," said Owain. "We have time, and much to consider. Between the Percies, myself, and Mortimer, if we plan our moves properly we can succeed. At the very least, we should start by contracting a pact of mutual loyalty. If King Richard lives, I am his man."

"And I," said Mortimer.

"And I, as well," said Hotspur. "Otherwise, we fight for the Earl of March, the true heir to the throne. With God on our side, we cannot fail."

It was with great difficulty that Joanna of Navarre disentangled herself from Brittany. First, she had to go to France and persuade King Charles that marriage to the king of England was a good thing. France hadn't even recognized Henry as king yet, and she put herself forward as a goodwill negotiator between their two countries. Joanna was a wise and experienced mediator; it was well-known that she alone had been able to smooth the irascible temper of her late husband. Then she had to send diplomats to Pope Boniface with the same argument; the Roman pope couldn't afford to antagonize the English king, so he also gave his blessing.

The worst undertaking was still ahead. At first, Joanna wanted to bring all her children to England. But as her son was already declared duke of Brittany, this would be impossible. At this point, Philip, Duke of Burgundy and Joanna's uncle, decided to take matters into his own hands. He showed up at Nantes on his best behavior and showered Joanna, her children—even her servants—with gold and jewels. Then he explained, delicately and firmly, that the boys needed to be brought up under his guardianship. In the end, she saw she had no choice and bid the children to get ready to follow the duke. Fortunately, they saw it as a great adventure.

Once she said farewell to her boys, she wasted no time departing for the coast in the company of her two young daughters, their nurses, and a large train of Breton and Navarrese attendants. She would meet up with her escort at Camaret, near Brest in Brittany.

Initially the English ships had trouble getting to the Continent. It was the middle of January—not the most auspicious time to be crossing the Channel. Bounced around in their galleys for eleven days, they had seen the coast of Brittany but were blown back to Portsmouth by a gale. Before crossing again they had to apply to the treasurer of England for more funds, as the crew had grown mutinous.

Once Joanna's escort made it to Camaret, the English celebrated by imbibing an exorbitant amount of wine—at Henry's expense. The duchess arrived in the midst of their festivities. The Earl of Worcester greeted her after she had changed out of her traveling clothes, doing his best to make her feel welcome. Balding, stocky, but physically fit, Percy was the epitome of grace and courtesy. He bowed over her hand and glanced up with a twinkle in his eye, appreciative of Joanna's good looks.

"I am Thomas Percy Earl of Worcester and the king's chamberlain. Let me introduce you to John Beaufort, the Earl of Somerset and the king's half-brother. And this is Henry Beaufort, Bishop of Lincoln and the king's other half-brother. It's easy to tell them apart," he laughed. John was lean and red-headed; Henry had brown hair, well-delineated by a tonsure. Besides, the size of his belly betrayed his enjoyment of good living.

"I'll be in fine company, I can see," responded Joanna. "You can fill me in on the details of the king's younger days."

The bishop smiled. "Our father John of Gaunt was the most charming man you could ever meet—when he was so inclined. Our dear brother takes after him. Wouldn't you say?" He turned toward John.

"Absolutely. Henry takes after him in loyalty, as well. You will see how the people love him."

"As do his brothers, I see."

This was the beginning of a friendly conversation that grew less formal as they waited for the rest of Joanna's baggage train. Soon, they were all talking like old friends; the duchess had that kind of effect on people. Joanna learned that Worcester was a career politician in the service of his third king; he had already long served as soldier and admiral. She gathered that Somerset was a military commander and the eldest of four children born of Gaunt's illicit relationship with Katherine Swynford. After Gaunt married his mistress their children were legitimized by Richard II. Henry Beaufort was next in line and demonstrated a lively intellect; it seemed he had great aspirations that went beyond his current bishopric.

Finally, Joanna's belongings arrived. It took thirty-six carts to carry all her possessions; luckily, three ships had been sent to accommodate her and her train. The king's flagship was commanded by the young Earl of Arundel, who took great pleasure in showing Joanna to her quarters. Her bed had been fitted with Imperial cloth of gold, embroidered with royal arms. The curtains were made of crimson satin.

"How thoughtful of Henry," she said, turning to her daughters. "You can sleep here, with me."

FitzAlan turned and instructed the seamen to bring her most personal baggage into the cabin. The rest would be stowed in the hold. "The king wanted to make sure you were comfortable," he said. "Now we have to see what the weather will bring."

At first, everything looked promising. They embarked with a favorable wind and Joanna stood on the deck next to Worcester while they watched the coastline recede.

"I will miss my country," she said quietly. "They say it rains a lot in England."

The other chuckled. "You'll see why everything is so green. The rainbows are stunning—unlike any I've seen anywhere else."

"That's an interesting thing to mention."

"Since we can't help the rain, we might as well appreciate the beauty it brings." He looked up, noticing that some dark clouds headed their way. "Unfortunately, at sea it's another matter. I would recommend you go below. I think our pleasant day is at an end."

It didn't take long for his prediction to come true. The unpredictable January weather soon caught up with them. Their ships tossed for five days before they were able to finally disembark at Falmouth. This left them almost all the way at the end of Cornwall instead of Southampton, their original destination. Joanna swore she would travel overland rather than get on a ship ever again.

Their agreed-upon plan was for the queen's party to travel north from Southampton to Winchester, and poor Henry was beside himself with anxiety. He had received messages about the storms in the Channel, and there was no way of knowing whether they had been driven back to the Continent, west to Cornwall, or God forbid, lost. He had stopped at Farnham on his way to Southampton when a bedraggled messenger found him—sent ahead by Joanna's slower-moving cavalcade.

"Sire, the duchess has safely landed at Falmouth with all your ships intact," he said, bowing. "She sends you greetings and tells you she intends to come the rest of the way by road."

"Falmouth! Thank God," said Henry, hastening to give the man a bag of coins. "No wonder it took so long. You have made me a happy man."

Now he was even more anxious than ever—with anticipation. It was almost three hundred miles to Falmouth, and the messenger probably wouldn't have traveled more than thirty miles a day on these winter roads. The queen's entourage would likely move at least twice as slowly. So if he hurried perhaps he could meet her halfway. There was no time to lose.

Taking Erpingham and a score of knights with him, Henry left at dawn. By the time he had stopped for the night at Clarendon, they had traveled fifty miles.

"At this rate, you'll be a fright when you meet her," Erpingham mused.

"I'll be worn out, that's for certes." Henry said, pulling off his cloak.

The other grinned. "Playing the bone-tired gallant knight while she is shaking from cold in the pouring rain. What a sight that will be!"

"It certainly would. I suspect, though, my Joanna will prevail against the weather. Perhaps the sun will grant her a reprieve."

They sent a man ahead to Exeter to warn of their coming. Over the next few days they traveled another eighty miles. Henry could barely control his anxiousness. He hoped to meet the queen there, or at least precede her. Messengers were sent ahead to discover her progress and report back so he could pace himself.

The timing was perfect and so was the weather. As Henry had hoped, the clouds parted and the sun peeked out through the mist as he entered the town through the east gate. At the same time, he could hear the crowds cheering as Queen Joanna and her party approached from the west gate. Restraining his enthusiasm, Henry nodded to the town folk lining the street as his cavalcade passed down the muddy lane between thatched cob houses. Then he stopped, watching. Like a vision she came closer, riding between Henry Beaufort and Worcester.

On impulse, the king leaped from his horse, giving his reins to Erpingham and hastening to meet the approaching company. Bowing from the waist, he swept off his turban-shaped hat and flourished it before him, glancing up with a grin. His brown hair blew in the breeze, enhancing his image as a ruddy and vigorous knight.

"Welcome, Queen Joanna!" he exclaimed. Reaching up and taking his wife by the waist, he pulled her from the saddle and drew her close, kissing her in front of the cheering crowd. Then he kissed her again.

Putting her arms around his neck, Joanna laid her head next to his. "I've been wanting you to do that for a long time," she said warmly before letting go and turning to her companions. "I have been well taken care of and I love your country already," she said loudly.

Slipping her arm through his, the king escorted her through the gatehouse at the Bishop's Palace. The Great Courtyard was surrounded by stables and lodgings, and both parties quickly dispersed as the weary travelers went inside, seeking comfort and sustenance. The bishop was away at the moment but his chancellor greeted the king and brought him to the great hall, accompanied by his closest attendants. The Queen was escorted to her chambers so she could freshen up after her long journey.

Hiding his impatience, Henry talked idly to the chancellor while he waited. Fortunately, it didn't take long. Joanna came through the great double doors, and stood still, searching for him. She wore a dark red sideless surcoat embroidered with peacocks with a pure white underdress. The collar of SS links was proudly seated along the edge of her bodice, and she wore a cloak pinned to the shoulders with gold clasps. Her hair was wrapped and covered with a veil, affixed with a circlet of gold and pearls. Henry felt a thrill running through his veins and he took a step forward, holding out his hand.

Joanna broke into a smile and she paused a moment, admiring her handsome prince before she strode forward, forgetting her dignity. The king held out his other hand and she placed hers inside of his, marveling at his deep brown eyes and the way they crinkled at the corners. For a moment neither spoke a word, then Henry knelt before her as the witnesses clapped in appreciation.

"A proper entrance," he said simply. "You are divine."

Fighting back tears, Joanna forgot about all her trials, all the sacrifices, and felt a warmth flow from his hands into hers. She marveled at how the long months faded to nothing.

Standing, Henry held onto her right hand and led her to a pair of thrones on the dais. The slowly gathering crowd parted before them. Sitting, he waved for the minstrels to play; his guests relaxed and started talking amongst themselves.

The royal pair were left alone as they leaned toward each other, forgetting about the rest of the world. "I thought this day would never get here," he said softly. "How I longed for you."

"There were so many obstacles to overcome."

"You left everything behind." He kissed her hand. "A lesser woman wouldn't have been able to do it."

"A lesser man wouldn't have appreciated me."

"You are a godsend and I will never cease to adore you."

She sighed. "I hope your countrymen will agree."

With a wry smile, he looked out at the gaily dressed courtiers. "It won't be easy. They still complain about foreigners. But once they see how fair you are, how can they resist your charms?" His eyes sparkled. "I would see more of those charms."

Since they were already married by proxy, there was no impediment to their sharing a bed. After staying an appropriate amount of time, they decided to disappear. The king's guests bowed as the couple passed through them on their way to the private apartments, pausing along the way to exchange courtesies. The bishop's chamber had already been prepared and a lively fire welcomed them. A tray with two chalices of wine accompanied a gilded box of comfits. Joanna's ladies curtsied when they entered the room, and the queen dismissed them with kind words. When the door closed, she turned to the king, a slight blush enhancing her cheeks.

"Henry." It was her turn to stretch out her arms and he gathered her up, kissing her face, her neck, her lips. "Oh, you don't know how long I wanted to hold you," she murmured between kisses.

He pulled off her veil and unpinned her hair, kissing the strands as they fell about her shoulders. Sweeping her up, he carried her to the bed, laying his bride down gently and running a finger along her cheek. "Let me look at you. I can't believe you're finally here."

Her lips trembled a bit, though she tried to stop it. "I had to leave my boys," she said. "My poor boys. The Duke of Burgundy took them away to Paris and the little ones didn't even realize they would not be seeing me again. They could scarcely manage their horses as they followed one after the other. He even took my baby." She released a deep, ragged breath.

"I'll make it up to you, I promise," Henry said, kissing her again. "You are so beautiful."

Their nuptial night was as satisfying as the two of them could have wished. As they were both the same age and had both been married before, there was no shyness, nor reluctance. Theirs was truly a love match in their late prime of life, and they had worked very hard to bring it about.

Even Henry's worst critics couldn't begrudge him a few hours of happiness. For now, let the stresses and aggravations stay outside the door. After years of loneliness, Henry finally had a partner he could trust.

The wedding ceremony was held a few days later at Winchester Cathedral, presided over by the king's half-brother, Henry Beaufort. Much of the aristocracy was present, and a great feast was held thanks to Bishop William of Wykeham who lent the king two years' worth of taxes to cover expenses. Two weeks later the newlyweds rode to London by way of Blackheath, where they were met by the mayor, aldermen, and sheriffs accompanied by six minstrels specially hired for the occasion. There was much ceremony and celebration as the royal party crossed London Bridge and headed to the Tower, where Joanna rested for the night. The following day she processed through Cheapside to Westminster Abbey, where she was crowned with all ceremony by both the Archbishop of Canterbury and the Archbishop of York.

Moving the celebrations to the palace, the guests were regaled with another lavish feast. Venison, roast cygnets, woodcock, rabbits, quails, and bitterns were served along with cream of almonds, custards, fritters, and pears in syrup. Delicate subtleties made of sugar and paste, decorated with crowns and eagles enhanced the palate between courses of partridges and plover. Courtly pageants entertained the guests and even a tournament, where the young Earl of Warwick rode as queen's champion against all comers.

CHAPTER 21

After the coronation festivities, Henry took his bride to Eltham Palace, in Greenwich. This had been a favorite royal residence all the way back to Edward II, and many improvements had been made over the years. They rode through a huge enclosed park and crossed a stone bridge over a wide square moat, through a fortified gateway and into an inner court surrounded by service buildings.

"King Richard added those gardens," Henry said, pointing to a wall covered with ivy. "He also built the new royal lodgings. Wait until you see this."

Joanna could see that Henry loved this place. She put an arm through his and extended her other hand, trying to catch a few snowflakes drifting down from lowering clouds. A fine dusting covered the ground. "It is beautiful," she breathed, admiring the carved wooden doors that brought them into the great hall. Two rows of servants flanked the entrance, bowing as they passed.

"Over here," said Henry, directing her to an adjacent hall. Carved whimsical animal heads grinned at them from exposed beams in the high ceiling. "This is the dancing chamber. We've made great use of this over the years. And here are the royal apartments." They continued their tour as the servants unloaded the wagons. "I intend to build new timber-framed lodgings for the both of us. For now, this will serve." He led her through an elaborately decorated bedroom and swung open the door at the other end. Joanna gasped in pleasure. It was a bath room, with tiled floors and glazed windows. "My predecessor certainly appreciated his comforts," Henry said. "Hot and cold running water, too. And over here, my favorite room."

Though Joanna would have liked a few more minutes to appreciate the bath and its accoutrements, her husband's enthusiasm was infectious. Next to the bed, another door opened to a library, complete with shelves and tables and a large stone fireplace. "This is where I do most of my work," Henry said. "That other door leads to my chamberlain's office. By tomorrow he will have a pile of petitions for me to consider." He took her hand. "I would have you by my side, for I know you are the wisest of councilors." She lowered her head modestly, pleased by the compliment.

"But for tonight, let us take our leisure. We've had little enough time to rest!"

Back in the great hall, Henry's courtiers were feeling festive. Minstrels played lively tunes and partners lined up to dance, bowing to each other and showing off their beautiful robes. Joanna and Henry walked arm-in-arm through the crowd, accepting congratulations.

Another gift-giving presentation was prepared for the new queen. This was to be a comparatively intimate gathering. The only person of importance missing was Prince Hal. He had been obliged to return to Wales after the coronation. Henry wasn't sure how he felt about his son's absence; Hal and Joanna were still comparative strangers. Did the lad prefer it this way?

King and queen sat side-by-side on the dais with her two daughters. Sir Thomas Erpingham approached, having been granted first place as Henry's boon companion. Kneeling, he raised up a gold and enameled hanaper and gave it to the queen. Letting out an aahh, she took the chalice by the wide stem and removed the lid, smiling at the knight. "The king can carry me back to my bedchamber after I fill this with wine," she laughed. "This is magnificent."

"Only the best for the most magnificent of queens," the knight responded, bowing.

Henry nodded, smiling at his wife.

Next after Erpingham, Prince Thomas approached, kneeling before the royal couple. Henry beamed at him, proud that his son accepted his stepmother so easily. It was no difficulty for the lad; she had shown favor to him from the very first, way back in Brittany.

Thomas held out a little velvet box which she accepted with a grave nod of her head. Opening it, she caught her breath, pulling out a sparkling necklace with an emerald pendant.

"To match your eyes," Thomas said. Joanna was charmed, and leaned forward, kissing him on the forehead. She took his hand as he stood. "Here are your two sisters, Marie and Margaret," Joanna said, gesturing to her daughters. Both girls were under ten years of age, so Thomas had little interest in them. But he nodded pleasantly before stepping behind them.

The next two princes, John and Humphrey, came forward, side-by-side. As Henry suspected, they were thrilled to have a new mother. Blanche had died when John was five and Humphrey four, so they barely remembered her and were still young enough to need nurturing. Joanna was more than happy to oblige; she had raised nine children and was still missing her boys.

Giving them a special smile, Joanna leaned forward, stretching out her arms. They both came up the steps and bowed.

"We commissioned this for you," Humphrey said shyly, looking at his brother. John held out a package wrapped in silk.

Joanna glanced at Henry before unwrapping the present. His face glowed with happiness, just like a doting father. She knew from her first husband's duties that a ruler never had enough time to give his children the attention they needed. Things will be different now. Smiling, untying the string, she made a little gasp of pleasure. A pair of gold tablets glistened in the candlelight, intricately carved with the figure of the Virgin Mary.

"Oh, these are so beautiful," she murmured, her eyes filling with tears. "I can hang them from my belt. My dear boys, I will cherish them always."

Henry leaned over, admiring their gift. "You kept it a secret all this time!" he exclaimed.

"We wanted you to feel welcome, my lady," John said, glowing with pride.

"Call me mother, if you like," she said, kissing him on the forehead. She kissed Humphrey next and gave them both a hug. Then she looked up as a little girl followed the princes, dressed in a lovely imitation of her own gown. Joanna looked at Henry.

"This is Philippa, my youngest," the king said, dropping to his knees. His daughter gave a perfect curtsey then stood, running into her father's arms. Henry picked her up, standing. "She couldn't wait to meet you."

He put his daughter back on her feet and Joanna's girls came forward, admiring her dress. The queen knelt and put her arms around Humphrey and John. "I feel very welcome indeed," she said, admiring her new family. "Very welcome indeed."

As predicted, Henry was back to work the following day, and he arranged his library so that Joanna could sit at a desk next to his. She had brought her own officers in her train because of her extensive dowry lands in Brittany. So between the two of them, the royal couple presented a most diligent aspect to Henry's busy household. It pleased them both to work together, for they discovered they had similar points of view.

They soon decided to take their meals in the library as well, and Henry found this to be a good time to speak privately.

"I have been troubled about my relationship with the Percies," he confided to her, just a few days after they settled in. "I owe them so much. Unfortunately, they believe I owe them more than I am able to give."

She raised an eyebrow, silently willing him to go on.

"You see, our most consistent problems come from Scotland. Over the last several generations, the Percies have proved themselves the ablest defenders of our borders. As a result, they have assumed powers that encroach on royal sovereignty. My—" he cleared his throat—"my predecessor tried to moderate their control by appointing outsiders to the wardenship. Men from outside the north, that is. Unfortunately, this proved to be a disaster; they didn't understand the customs. That is a mistake I won't repeat." He cut a piece of meat and placed it on her trencher. "After my coronation, I needed the Percies more than ever. Naturally, I rewarded them and probably gave them too many commissions. I don't know. I didn't have much choice." He shrugged. "Harry is the justiciary of north Wales, Chester, and Warden of the East Marches of Scotland. Not to mention governor of Berwick and Roxburgh. Among others." He sighed.

She wasn't familiar with all these places but knew better than to interrupt. "Do you trust them?" she asked finally.

He grunted. "I must. Though I can see they are unhappy. I made a mistake insisting they hand over their hostages after Homildon Hill."

"I remember you wrote me about that. Perhaps you can make amends."

"Amends..." Quickly glancing at Joanna, his eyes took on a faraway look. "Amends. You know, there is a possibility. Rather than making an issue about the Douglas ransom, what if I granted them his whole bloody earldom? That would keep them busy!"

"It would be a way for you to relent gracefully."

"At the same time, they would reassert England's old territorial claims south of the River Tweed. A win for both of us. Joanna, you are ingenious!"

She laughed. "It was none of my doing, but I'll take the praise anyway."

"The best part is that it will cost me nothing." He held up his knife. "I think this will work."

Over the course of the month, Henry had many opportunities to appreciate Joanna's good sense and calm perspective—especially when he opened the next letter from Louis of Orleans. The farther down the letter he read, the angrier his expression. Finally, he could no longer restrain himself.

"Listen to this," he said. *"At the time I made said alliance I never conceived it possible you could have done against your king what it is well known you have done."*

Deflecting the obvious insult, she asked, "What alliance?"

Henry looked up from the paper. "Oh, before I left Paris we signed an oath to support each other's friends, oppose each other's enemies, uphold each other's honor, and come to each other's help in times of war or unrest. He supported my return to England, but now he pretends he knew nothing about it." Frowning, he went back to the letter. "Here he says, *from the moment I was informed of the acts you committed against your liege lord, I assumed you knew you could no longer rely on my support—for you must have known I could not have any desire to preserve your friendship."* He put the paper down. "Janus-faced bastard."

She was about to say something when he picked up the letter again. "There's more: *With regard to your high situation, I do not think the divine virtues have placed you there. God may have dissembled with you, and have set you on a throne like many other princes whose reign has ended in confusion. And, in consideration of my own honour, I do not wish to be compared with you."*

Putting his hand over his eyes, Henry sighed. "I fear he may be right." He read a little further. "And here: *How could you suffer my dear niece the queen of England to return so desolate after the death of her lord, despoiled of her dower by your rigour and cruelty?* And then he challenges me to single combat."

With tears in his eyes, he looked to Joanna for consolation. "From where I started, I never wanted this. How could things have gone so badly?"

Joanna came over and rubbed his shoulders. "Look how successful he is, overwhelming you with a confusion of words. That's just how they attacked the Duke of Brittany, throwing him into a frenzy. We learned, over the years, to address their reproaches one at a time, pointing out their malice and restating the facts as they should be seen. Approach him calmly and rationally, without rancor, then make the letters public for all to see, along with your responses. That, my dear, should end the argument." And so it did, for the moment. Henry's response was so lengthy, so verbose he undoubtedly exhausted the duke in reading it. It took considerably longer for Henry to convince himself.

After giving the Percy situation much thought, Henry decided that offering the Douglas earldom should gain him lots of goodwill and cost the exchequer nothing. All they had to do was conquer it. Much to his satisfaction, his proposal was gladly accepted by the Percies, who wasted no time preparing their forces. Just over a month later, Hotspur made his first foray into Scotland. He attacked the Tower of Cocklaw in Teviotdale, deep into Douglas territory, thinking this would be an easy target. The English even brought siege equipment and set about the tedious business of surrounding the stout little castle. What he didn't count on was the dogged defense of the besieged Scots, who refused to come out and face him on the field. After repeatedly assailing the fortification he soon concluded that their efforts were fruitless. The example of Conwy was still fresh in Harry's mind.

After reading about Hotspur's setbacks and evaluating his own reserves, Henry Percy concluded that their resources were insufficient. They didn't have the means necessary to recover the Scottish territory—especially considering the king was still in arrears for their other expenses. He sent repeated letters to Westminster and even went so far as to say that great dishonor would fall on him and his son if money was not forthcoming. King Henry's response was terse. The exchequer was hampered by demands from the Welsh rebellion. The earl was on his own.

Percy was not pleased with his refusal; had the king played him for a fool?

Matters did not improve in Scotland. After a few weeks of pointless attacks, Hotspur called a parley with James Gladstone, the tower's captain. They agreed upon a six-week truce, provided the Scots leave the siege equipment undisturbed. If Scotland's governor, the Duke of Albany didn't relieve the castle by 1 August, they would surrender to the English.

Six weeks! A lot could happen in that stretch of time. Harry returned to Newcastle where his father was waiting for him, and during the long ride back he had time to nurse his grievances. King Henry may have backed down from his position concerning the prisoners at Homildon Hill, but it was too little, too late. He had already shown his true intentions. Did he not call Hotspur a traitor? He was still refusing to pay them what he owed, and in the meantime Westmorland was receiving cash for his services. Henry was showering Neville with favors and responsibilities. The situation was painfully obvious; Westmorland stood to replace Percy as the power in the North. Unless he and his father did something about it.

Yes, a plan was forming in his mind. If they did this right, they could dislodge Henry from his usurped throne and still achieve their aims in Scotland. Why wait?

Henry Percy was hunting when Harry clattered into the courtyard. "Where did he go?" Hotspur called, and when he learned of his father's destination, he leaped from his horse and saddled a new mount himself. Spurring his steed, he took off after the hunting party, followed by a handful of exhausted retainers. Although it looked like rain, there was still a long afternoon ahead of them and he didn't want to wait.

It didn't take long to find his father. They had already taken down one stag and Percy was in a good mood. He turned, surprised to see Harry galloping toward him.

"What-ho!" he called. "I wasn't expecting you so soon. Were you successful?"

Hotspur pulled his reins, leaning back in the saddle. "That damnable castle was well defended. I didn't want to waste my time so we arranged a truce." He dismounted, pulling a water skin from his saddle. He tipped his head back, taking a long drink. "We have more important things to do."

"Oh? What's more important than claiming our new lands?"

"Listen." He took his father by the arm and pulled him aside. "I've given this a lot of thought. We have six weeks available. It's time we reestablished our influence. This is the perfect opportunity for us to make our vision a reality."

"What vision?" Percy stopped, his eyes widening. "Are you talking about Glyndwr's pact of mutual loyalty?"

"I knew you'd understand. What better time to plan a strike against the king? I've already sent my friar to Richard in Scotland. We should hear from him soon. We know Owain has begun his conquest of South Wales; he can draw off the English while I gather forces in the West Midlands. You can raise an army in the North so Henry won't know where to turn—"

"Whoa, whoa. You are way ahead of me."

Harry let out his breath in an impatient huff. "Henry of Lancaster is destroying this country. Let us put an end to him."

"And put Richard back on the throne? Is that what you are saying?" Percy gestured his dismissal. "After all that has happened? He's not likely to be very grateful."

"If we put him back on the throne, how could he not? If he comes, that is. Aside from those letters, what effort has Richard made? None that I can see." Harry shrugged. "If not Richard, then Mortimer. *Mortimer*, on the other hand—"

"Will need our guidance." Percy was warming up to the idea. "We can be back on top again."

Giving his son a nudge, the earl led him back to the hunting party. "Go on without me," he told them. "Harry and I have duties to attend to." Mounting, the pair rode back to the castle, for indeed they had much to plan and very little time; they had to be ready to resume the attack at Cocklaw by 1 August. If all went well, they could have the North of England under their rule—and southern Scotland, too.

By early July, Hotspur was in Chester. He had already sent a messenger to his uncle, the Earl of Worcester, and another to Owain Glyndwr. He and his father decided it would be unwise to leave the Scottish Marches unguarded during this critical time; besides, Percy might be the one who would carry on with the Scottish campaign. Nor would it serve Hotspur to attract attention by marching south with his northern forces. Instead, he would travel with his usual retinue. As justice of Cheshire, he would be seen as performing his normal duties. Better for Harry to raise an army of Cheshiremen still loyal to Richard. It didn't hurt his cause that they hadn't forgotten the pillaging of Henry's troops four years before. Additionally, the Welsh from the border territories would supplement his army, for they too were Richard's partisans—and his own, now that he had allied with Owain Glyndwr.

In a surprising turnabout, Hotspur approached his prisoner Archibald Douglas with a proposition. He would release the hostages if they would agree to go on campaign with him. By now Harry and Douglas had discovered mutual interests and an understanding had grown between them. The Scot gladly accepted his proposal.

The first part of Hotspur's plan would be to capture Shrewsbury. This was Prince Hal's headquarters and maintained the only royal force not drawn away by the Welsh. If he could capture Prince Hal in the process, so much the better; the lad could be used as a hostage. Meanwhile, Earl Percy would begin recruiting in the North so he could offer a simultaneous challenge to the king—or be ready to join Hotspur if needed. At the end of June, King Henry had written to Percy that he would not be coming north to aid him at Cocklaw. That fit into their plans perfectly; London was so far away that once Henry learned about the rebellion, it would be too late for him to react.

Harry was confident of his plan. In the first week of July, at Chester he made a proclamation: King Richard was still alive and marching to overthrow Henry of Lancaster. All who would join Richard's army are to meet at Sandiway, twelve miles east of Chester, by the third week of July. Recruits came pouring in, brandishing their longbows of yew and their great axes, ready to fight for the restoration of their beloved king. Many wore the badge of the white hart.

The Earl of Worcester was surprised to see his own servant who had been sent to Northumberland with a message to his brother. He was not expected for another week.

"What news, Kevin?"

The other quickly doffed a cup of ale then wiped his mouth. "It's Hotspur, my lord. He's on his way to Chester to raise an army."

"Chester?" Worcester sat down, dumbfounded. "Why, in God's name? I thought he was besieging Cocklaw Castle."

"They declared a truce. Percy sent me here as soon as they made their decision. They are going to declare for King Richard."

"Declare? For Richard?" Worcester couldn't believe his ears.

"They've decided to move forward with their plans. Your brother is going to remain in Northumberland to guard against the Scots. Owain Glyndwr is raiding in southwest Wales to draw English forces away from the Marches. King Henry is safely in London. Once Hotspur has collected a force of Cheshiremen, he will march directly to Shrewsbury—and hopefully capture the prince who will be used as a hostage."

"He's heading here? What does he want me to do? Seize the prince for him? Hardly likely, considering half the garrison serves as his bodyguard."

"Nothing so dangerous," Kevin said. "But he does hope you will join him. With your retinue."

Worcester rolled his eyes. He was well informed about the recent agreement patched together between Henry Percy, Owain Glyndwr, and Edmund Mortimer, uncle of the eight year-old Earl of March. Up until now, he had hoped this was just another of his brother's schemes. Toppling Henry from the throne would certainly increase Percy influence, no matter whom they raised in his place. It all seemed so precarious!

"Why is Harry mustering in Chester?"

"Well..." Kevin hesitated. "He left his own troops in Northumberland; it would have raised too many questions if he brought them south. There are plenty of Cheshiremen who despise Lancaster. Harry intends to proclaim that King Richard is alive and that he will be coming to recover his throne—"

"And all Richard's loyal supporters will flock to his banner. Oh, Harry, Harry. What have you done?" He put his face in his hands. "I must think."

Kevin pulled a letter from his pouch. "He sent this for you."

His hand shaking, Worcester took the letter. He knew what was at stake here; there was no other word for it but treason. He also knew he could refuse his nephew nothing.

"*Dear uncle,*" the letter said, "*you have always told me to trust my instincts. And now, my instincts are shouting that this is our moment. Please join me in declaring our resolution. I know you command the hearts of many men. I hope they will accompany you.*"

Worcester looked up; his servant was studying him. "Has he told you when?"

"He has ordered his recruits to gather by mid-July. Since he is Justice of Chester, no one is bound to question his presence there. He hopes to keep his movements a secret from the king."

"Not likely. Our best hope is that Henry will be far enough away he can't respond in time. Myself, on the other hand..." He sighed, lighting a candle and holding the corner of the parchment over its flame. "I'll have to wait until the last minute before joining him. I can't give away my intentions too soon or we lose the element of surprise. I think most of my retainers will accompany me. And many of the prince's disaffected Cheshire soldiers."

He stood, putting a hand on Kevin's shoulder. "I release you from my service, if you so desire. No man should be forced into treason."

The other shook his head. "I bear no love for the prince, nor the king. I am with you, my lord."

"I am grateful to have you."

253

And he was. Kevin was the one who spread the word among his soldiers, swearing them to secrecy and preparing them to leave on the seventeenth. Until then, Worcester acted like nothing was amiss, continuing to perform his everyday duties as sub-lieutenant to Prince Hal. He didn't dislike the boy, though he couldn't exactly say he liked him, either. Young Hal was efficient, resolute, but guarded. He never wasted any words, either in jest or friendship. He didn't seem particularly fond of his father either, and that reticence seemed shared by the king. It wouldn't be all that difficult for Worcester to renounce him—aside from his breach of loyalty, that is.

During all this activity Harry Percy's friar John Bennett came back from Scotland—alone. He was tired and bedraggled, having ridden as fast as he could to Chester. Known to all Harry's guards, he was immediately brought into the command tent and given something to eat and drink while they searched for their captain. Finally, Harry rushed in, throwing the tent flap aside. He stopped short, taking in the lone friar sitting at the table.

Appreciating the man's obvious exhaustion, Hotspur restrained his impatience. "Bennett," he said evenly, "you have done me a great service. I hope you found Richard."

Shoving a piece of bread into his mouth, the other looked up with bloodshot eyes. "Aye. I found him, my lord. He was in bad shape. Bad shape. The king was not himself. He recognized me but showed no interest in returning to England. None whatsoever." Bennett swallowed, reaching for his ale. "He told me King Richard was dead and buried. No amount of reasoning would shake him from his despair. I talked until I was blue in the face, to no avail. It's hopeless, my lord. He is dead to us, and we're better off for it."

Pacing back and forth, Harry smacked his fist into his hand. Finally, he stopped. "Do you think he'll change his mind?"

"No. He is not the man you remember. Imprisonment has broken him."

"Damnation. I told everyone he was going to meet us."

Bennett took a deep breath. "You must tell them the king is dead. Tell them the Mammet in Scotland is an impostor. Either way, it's unlikely the Scots would ever let him go. He's too valuable as a pawn. He's aware of that and doesn't seem to care."

Hotspur was not the kind of man to fret over something he couldn't control. Resuming his pacing, he muttered to himself until finally he sat down across from the friar. "Perhaps it's for the best," he said. "We fight for Mortimer, now."

CHAPTER 22

At the last minute, King Henry decided he would go north to after all. Since he wasn't able to send the money so insistently demanded, at least he could support the Percies in person. As it turned out, on the very day Hotspur arrived at Chester he rode in to Northamptonshire. He sent a letter to his council in London. "*Send Prince Hal £1000 as soon as possible*," he wrote, "*while I continue north to give aid and comfort to our very dear and faithful cousins the earl of Northumberland and his son. I will assist them at the battle they have honorably pursued for us against our enemies the Scots*".

Blissfully ignorant, the king continued north for three days, reaching Nottingham where a messenger was waiting for him. He shook the rain from his cloak and called for some ale, which he downed in one draft while reaching for the letter. "Where are you from?"

"Macclesfield, sire, in Cheshire. The sheriff sent this letter. I went to Derby first and was told you were heading this way."

"Get yourself something to eat while I read this," he said. "Whatever it is, I'm probably going to have to send some response."

The messenger bowed and backed from the room while Henry opened the missive, sitting comfortably on a wide bench. But the words brought him to his feet.

"What is this?" he exclaimed, bringing Erpingham into the room at a run. The knight stopped short at his expression. Shock, hurt, and disbelief fought each other on the king's face.

"What happened?"

Henry dropped his arm holding the letter. He glanced at Erpingham, his eyes unfocused. He took another look at the missive and handed it over.

The other read it quickly and groaned.

"How could this have happened?" Henry moaned, putting his hand over his face. "Has Harry lost his senses? Raising an army? He calls me Henry of Lancaster and proclaims that King Richard is still alive?" Moving his fingers to his lips, Henry considered the implications, staring at his friend. "Could it be?" They had not mentioned Richard's escape after that terrible day, when he sent Erpingham to recover Maudeleyn from the executioner.

The other shook his head. "I don't believe it. He's taking advantage of all the rumors."

"Dear God, I hope so." He sat down heavily. "If the son is rebelling, the father must be too. Thomas, I don't understand. They were my greatest supporters. I've given them the wardenship, castles, titles—everything I could. We had our disagreements, certainly. But not enough to cause...this."

The Scottish earl of Dunbar came into the room, drawn by Henry's exclamation. Erpingham handed him the letter.

"Those faithless traitors," he said disparagingly. Ever since he had gone over to the English, his rivalry with the house of Percy knew no bounds—especially after they received their new grants in Scotland. Their disputed lands bordered on his own territory—that is, if he could ever get it back. "I told you Hotspur couldn't be trusted."

"I know, I know," said Henry. Although he appreciated Dunbar's advice and experience, he distrusted the man's lack of loyalty. The Scottish Earl of March had abandoned his country because of a personal insult; he could just as easily go back if he felt unappreciated. Henry put a hand on his arm. "It seems you are right. Though up until now, Harry showed no signs of faithlessness."

He sighed, then dredged up his usual decisiveness. Now was no time for self-pity. "Erpingham, we need to send a letter to my son in Shrewsbury right away. Put out a call to the sheriffs and magnates. Summon as many as we can reach on short notice. The council needs to raise loans to pay for my troops. Send scouts to spy on Hotspur's movements. Tomorrow, we go west to Derby."

Up to that point, the king didn't have many soldiers with him so he was able to move with his usual speed. He rode on to Burton-upon-Trent then to Lichfield. There he was forced to delay for two days while supporters caught up with him. After that, his growing army marched to St. Thomas's priory near Stafford. He thought to wait for further reinforcements, but Dunbar urged him to move swiftly before Hotspur's own forces grew too large.

The town of Shrewsbury was built inside a large loop in the Severn, so that it was surrounded by the river on three sides. The fourth side was a narrow strip of land facing north into England, protected by the city wall with a powerful barbican and a large castle. Only two other gates in the wall accessed bridges that crossed the river—one to Wales, and the other east to England.

Prince Hal was indeed in residence, waiting for the royal exchequer to respond before he could plan his next offensive into Wales. However, all thoughts of Glyndwr flew from his mind when his breakfast was interrupted by one of his men-at-arms.

The man dashed into his chamber without knocking. "My Lord," he gasped, "the Earl of Worcester is gone!"

Hal stood, dropping his knife. "When?"

"He left sometime during the night, taking his retinue with him!"

"Where did he go?" Hal wasn't really expecting an answer, but his surprise was so complete he couldn't get his thoughts in order.

"There's evidence they took the bridge to Wales."

"No. It can't be." Wiping his mouth on his sleeve, Hal came around the table. "Come with me. There must be an explanation."

As they passed through the great hall toward the barbican, the castle was in an uproar. Soldiers ran back and forth, people were shouting, dogs were barking. The prince climbed the tower stairs to the roof, finding his captain looking north.

"Do you see anything?" Hal asked. The man shook his head. "How many men are missing?"

"It appears that over a quarter of our forces have left."

"Dear God. What is happening?" He crossed his arms, deep in thought. "Close all the gates if you haven't done so already. We need to send scouts to the north and east. And to Wales." He put his hand over his eyes. "How could Worcester have turned traitor?"

258

In another time and another place, Worcester would have asked himself the same question. In reality, there was no choice. If he fought against the rebels and his nephew was killed—no matter by whom—he would hold himself responsible. He couldn't fight against Harry Hotspur on the battlefield. It was beyond all reason. At least he could console himself that he commanded the loyalties of so many men; eight knights, forty-eight men-at-arms, and 212 archers rode with him.

It gave Worcester no satisfaction to leave his old life behind. Nonetheless, he couldn't help but notice that his fortunes had been waning for some time. King Henry had recently removed him from Steward of the Royal Household and gave the post to one of Westmorland's retainers. He was sent west instead and appointed Lieutenant of Wales and tutor of the prince. However, not six months later the king gave the lieutenancy to the sixteen year-old Hal and demoted him to second in command. That gave little hope for further advancement.

On the other hand, now he was committed to a cause he had never seriously supported. All for the sake of his headstrong nephew.

But the look on Hotspur's face was worth all the risk when he caught up with him, halfway to Chester. His brown eyes sparkling, Harry threw out his arms and caught his uncle in a bear hug, nearly crushing the breath from his lungs.

"I knew you wouldn't fail me," he exclaimed, glancing over Worcester's shoulder at the new troops. "And look who you have brought. Welcome, one and all!" Letting go of his uncle, he plunged into the throng, patting men on the back, shaking hands, even calling some by name. "Greetings, friends. Come, we are setting up for the night. There is plenty of food and lots of ale."

Once the newcomers were settled, Harry brought Worcester into his pavilion, pouring two goblets of wine. Suddenly his face fell and he was serious. "I had to tell the men today that King Richard is dead." He passed the wine to his uncle.

"Did you really believe he was alive?"

"I thought so. It was my man who helped him escape. Unfortunately, things didn't work out as planned. I'm convinced now that King Richard is a lost cause." He shrugged. "I told my men we were fighting for the Earl of March. Not everyone reacted graciously."

Worcester smiled wryly at the understatement. "That was a big risk you took, promising Richard's participation. Did anyone try to leave?"

Hotspur looked up at the roof. "Some. I had to threaten a few of them. In the end, I encouraged them to avenge Richard Plantagenet. It's a worthy cause."

This was a side of his nephew Worcester never saw before. He had never been guilty of duplicity. Or did his zeal overwhelm his good sense? "Why did you do it, Harry? Why this rebellion?"

About to plunge into his practiced rant, Hotspur stopped himself with a sigh. "It didn't have to be this way," he said sadly. "Lancaster broke his oath to us. Many times. He was never supposed to be king. Remember what he said at Doncaster?"

Worcester shook his head. He was in Ireland at the time. With King Richard.

Catching himself, Harry grunted. "Sorry, of course you weren't there. When I asked him if he would take the crown for himself, he said, 'No, that is not my intention. I intend to bring the king under control with good and strong leadership.' That's what he said. 'If anyone more worthy of the crown could be found, I will willingly withdraw.' Of course, I thought he meant the Earl of March. My nephew. He lied. He took us for fools, and look what happened."

Like a tiger he started pacing back and forth. "We argued with him not to take the crown. To no avail. I didn't know how to stop him. My father didn't know how to stop him. We tried. We reasoned with him. But his mind was set and we could only watch helplessly as events moved forward. He was obstinate. The best we could do was gather what benefits we could for the family."

And there were many, thought Worcester. He wasn't sure if Harry was fooling himself. Yet he could see that today his nephew was filled with remorse.

"I have to set England to rights," Hotspur continued, mostly to himself. Suddenly he stopped and turned. His mind had just changed direction. "One of my men intercepted a letter from the king. It was sent from Burton-on-Trent, dated the sixteenth."

"Burton!" Worcester stiffened. "I thought he was in London!"

"Aye. We thought so too. Apparently he changed his mind."

"But that changes everything! He's close enough to challenge us."

"Well then, we'll have to face him."

Worcester frowned. "We may lose."

Hotspur was undeterred. "Once we have the prince in our power, the king will negotiate."

The other was about to respond when the tent flap opened and the Earl of Douglas entered. It was hard to say who was more surprised: Douglas or Worcester.

Harry whirled around. "Ah, come in, come in. I was just telling my uncle King Henry is not where we thought he was. He wrote me a letter from the Midlands. We may have to race him to Shrewsbury."

Worcester blinked. Since when had his nephew befriended his hostage and brought the man into his confidence?

Seeing his face, Hotspur was amused. "I promised him his freedom if he fights for me. He is a formidable warrior."

"That I know!" Worcester recovered himself quickly. "You are an asset to our cause," he said. To himself, he added, *and he doesn't have to worry about being called a traitor*. But that was an unworthy thought and he chided himself. Douglas could get killed, just like the rest of them. Warfare was a tricky thing.

Two days later, Prince Hal knew what he was facing; he also had a good idea why Worcester had left him. Under the Percy banner, Hotspur's army was spread out along the landward side of town. A herald had come forth, demanding entry; of course he had been refused. Hal immediately raised his own standard atop the castle tower and ordered extra soldiers to man the walls. Shrewsbury was the ideal defensive bulwark and he wasn't afraid of being stormed by any rebel army, no matter how threatening. His scouts had reported that the king was on his way, so he need only sit tight and wait.

261

Why did Hotspur turn traitor? He had absolutely no idea and his lack of knowledge bothered him. It was only a year ago they had been friends; he still thought of Harry as his mentor. What had happened?

But Hal was not one to waste a lot of time fretting over something he couldn't control. If Hotspur wanted to fight him, so be it. The Epiphany Rising had shown him how fickle men's loyalty could prove. This was just more of the same. The worst part of this waiting game was watching the smoke billow up from the houses and shops of the unfortunate suburbs. The Cheshire men were undoubtedly amusing themselves with an orgy of looting and plundering. At least the residents had time to find shelter within the town walls. That was the best he could do for them.

Hal wouldn't move from the heights of the tower, and he was one of the first to see the banners of the approaching army. It was the king, coming from the east! Before long the road was filled with colorful surcoats and banners. Soon, the blasts of trumpets could be heard from afar, announcing the triumphant arrival of Shrewsbury's deliverer.

Hotspur heard them, too. Abandoning his siege, he drew his army a few miles northwest to the hamlet of Berwick, where they spent the night.

As the rebels withdrew, Hal led a small retinue over the east-facing bridge and galloped to meet his father. Still astride their stallions, father and son embraced before the army, relief on both their faces.

"I'm so glad you are all right," Henry gasped. He had surprised even himself at the extent of his worrying.

"I don't think Hotspur expected you," Hal said. "You must have flown here once again. Already he is withdrawing, having failed to gain access to Shrewsbury."

"The Earl of Dunbar persuaded me not to wait any longer for reinforcements," Henry said, gesturing to a short, stocky knight by his side. "As usual, he was right."

Dunbar nodded at Hal. "Where is he headed?" he asked.

Hal turned on his horse. "I believe he is moving upriver a bit. I doubt whether he is going far."

"He's on the other side of the Severn," the king mused. "We must cross over."

"The river makes a loop just northeast of us." Hal pointed. "There's a ford at Uffington. You can camp near Haughmond Abbey, just beyond. That will give you a broad view of the area."

Agreeing, Henry gave orders for his forces to move toward the river. He paused when Hal put a hand on his arm.

"The Earl of Worcester went over to him," the prince said.

Another shock. Henry jerked his reins and his horse sidestepped. "How can that be?"

"I wondered the same thing. I had no idea he was discontented. He took a quarter of my men and disappeared overnight."

The king groaned. "Dear God. It keeps getting worse. Worcester has done so much for us. I sent him to get my queen." Those last words came out slowly. "I trusted him with her life."

Hal frowned. "I would swear his reversal is recent."

"I can't believe they are firm in this venture. I must try to negotiate with them."

Negotiating was very much on Worcester's mind, as well. Their plan to besiege the city and capture the prince was shattered. Before they were even settled for the evening, reports came in that King Henry was crossing the River Severn, and his army was much larger than theirs. He had to go out and have a look.

Uncle and nephew stood on the top of a hill gazing east. "Think about it," said Worcester. "Your element of surprise is gone. There's still time to reconsider. The king doesn't want to fight you. He will offer good terms."

Hotspur put an arm around his shoulders. "Back down? I'm not made to do that. My father would never forgive me."

"You mean, you would never forgive yourself. From what our scouts are telling us, we are outnumbered two-to-one. There's no shame in negotiating."

"Perish the thought. We fight."

"With archers on both sides? It's never happened before on English soil. You know it will be a blood-bath."

Hotspur sighed. "We must stand up for what is right."

"Are you so convinced Henry should not reign?"

"There's no question in my mind. Uncle, if you don't have the stomach for this fight, I won't object to your leaving. You must follow your own conscience."

That hurt. Almost embarrassed, Worcester brushed away a tear. "You know I can't turn my back on you."

Harry turned one of his devastating smiles on his uncle. "I know. I will give you this. If Henry tries to negotiate, I will send you as my spokesman."

That was the most Worcester could wish for. At least there was an outside possibility they could fix things in the morning. All that night, they wrote and rewrote the complaints against Bolingbroke that brought the country to the brink of rebellion until Worcester could be satisfied he approved his nephew's decision.

On Saturday, the Eve of St. Mary Magdalene, both armies had moved to within sight of each other, just a couple miles east of Shrewsbury. There was farmland between them, giving a long view. Even from a distance the king could see that Hotspur had the high ground, and the long slope was obstructed by hedges and small ponds. The rebels were in a good position.

As the Percies were breakfasting, the Abbot of Shrewsbury was introduced. Harry offered him a spot at their table but the abbot shook his head, clutching a staff.

"I come from King Henry," he said. "He sends me to tell you he does not wish to fight. He asks of you what are your grievances? Perhaps he can remedy them. The king would offer terms if you will disperse your men."

Worcester was a seasoned negotiator and knew better than react. Harry was much more impulsive and a smug smile crossed his face. "Terms, you say? After I disperse my men? Would I not be a fool?"

Taken aback, the abbot lowered his head to think. Then he tried again. "Forgive me if I misspoke myself. The king is anxious to work out an agreement."

Hotspur nodded. "Yes, we have prepared a list of grievances. I have it here." He gestured to Worcester who was holding the scroll. "Here is our manifesto. We charge King Henry with seizing the throne illegally, demanding excessive taxes, disregarding the law, and breaking his oaths." He was about to say more but thought better of it; this was enough for the opening salvo.

The abbot cleared his throat. "These charges are many and momentous. Yet I know the king does not want to do battle with such an honorable opponent." He bowed. "My lord, will you send someone you can trust to accompany me so that he may present your case privately to the king?"

Harry looked at his uncle. "I have already chosen a spokesman," he said quietly. The Earl of Worcester will represent me."

Seeing Hotspur's resolve, Worcester forgot any residual objections he might have harbored. Harry was committed, and he must be too. He stood. "Very well. Let us go to the king."

He and the abbot mounted their horses, and as they rode out of the camp Worcester could see that the royal army was already making their dispositions. Henry was drawing up his forces in three divisions at the foot of the slope. It looked pretty straightforward, except for the numbers.

The king was waiting for them. As Worcester followed the abbot into the royal pavilion, he had to suppress a momentary hesitation. Henry's face was so distressed—so reproachful—he almost lost his newfound resolve. He had served the king well, and was certain his sudden betrayal was as shocking as it was unexpected.

But Henry had learned how to act like a politician these last few years, and he spoke no words of reproach. He was seated on a portable throne, dressed in full armor with his helmet sitting on the ground beside him. A servant poured a goblet of wine and offered it to Worcester.

"Sir Harry Percy has sent the Earl of Worcester to speak for him," the abbot said, stepping aside.

Henry cocked his head, ready to listen. Once again, the earl marveled at how kingly he looked, his handsome face framed by a closely-trimmed beard, his dark brown eyes full of intelligence. He may not have been direct heir to the throne, but he was every bit the Plantagenet prince. It was such a pity he hadn't remained simply the Duke of Lancaster; he might have been happier in the long run. Except for the bile of King Richard, who would have hunted him down and butchered him, given the opportunity. Oh, why did politics have to be so calamitous?

Deciding not to kneel in supplication, Worcester nodded briefly. "Sire, we feel the time has come to declare the people's growing disaffection with your rule. I present to you Harry Percy's manifesto, which clearly expresses his grievances." He handed the document to a waiting knight who carried it to the king.

Henry received the parchment but did not open it. "I would rather hear it in your words."

Worcester was prepared. "Very well. We feel you need to consider the consequences of your actions. First, you had sworn at Doncaster that you would not claim the kingdom—only your inheritance and lands—and that Richard would still reign under the guidance of a council. And yet you imprisoned the king, took his crown, and starved him to death." His eyes flashed, partly because he remembered his own role in Richard's downfall. "He didn't deserve to die."

Pursing his lips, Henry hesitated. "That was none of my doing," he said finally.

How could any man with a conscience believe that bald-faced lie? Worcester had to take a deep breath before going on. "Secondly, you had promised not to exact taxes except with the advice of the three estates, and only in great emergencies. And yet, you have done just the reverse several times in these last three years."

Henry shrugged. "This was with the approval of parliament."

"That's exactly our concern. You packed parliament with your own knights and liegemen so they would do your bidding. You appointed your own retainers as sheriffs and justices."

"As you know, I need people I can depend on in positions of responsibility."

Was this a pointed reference to his own demotions? Worcester felt his resolve hardening. "And fourthly, you refused to ransom Edmund Mortimer from the Welsh, driving him into rebellion. At the same time, you confine the young Earl of March and deny his rightful succession to the throne." He straightened, raising his voice. "Hence, we, as the true protectors of the Commonwealth, defy you and your party as destroyers of the very

266

country you swore to safeguard. We have sent riders far and wide with copies of our manifesto so everyone will know why we must fight."

Henry gripped the arms of his throne, though this was his only display of anger. "Sit, my lord," he said, gesturing for his knight to bring a chair. "Let us discuss this." He waited while the other sat reluctantly then leaned forward. "Please understand. I do not want to fight. You are all my subjects, and I grieve for anyone who would lose his life for such a misunderstanding. This can all be avoided if we just come to an accord."

Stalling for time, Worcester put his goblet on the ground. "Much has been done that cannot be undone—"

"All the more reason to refrain from bloodshed! We must look forward, not backward. What can I do that will appease Harry Percy?"

Was this an opening? Worcester resolved to take it. "Sire, I will return to camp and confer with my nephew."

"Please do, and tell him I extend my arm in peace."

CHAPTER 23

Leaving the king's pavilion, a sober and pensive Worcester looked over the battle preparations before he mounted his horse. It was a short ride back to his own encampment, but it gave him enough time to get his argument straight in his head. He knew the day's resolution depended on his negotiating skills—with both Henry and Harry. How to bring these two together?

One look at Harry's face and his uncle's heart sank. Clearly anxious to get things started, Hotspur jumped up from sharpening his dagger. Taking two long strides forward and looking out of the tent to see if anyone accompanied his uncle, he said impatiently, "Well? Has our king come to his senses?"

Worcester sighed deeply. "He is troubled, Harry. He wants to know how he can appease you."

Hotspur flung his dagger to the ground; the point sunk deep into the dirt. "We've been through this already."

"Wait. Consider our position. Henry told me that he extends his arm in peace. Does this sound like a man who wants a battle?"

"Whether he wants it or not, he's got one. He must understand there are heirs to the throne with a better claim than his."

"Harry, whether we like it or not, he won the throne by conquest—or at least, by popular support. Either way, he's not likely to give it up."

"Then we will take it from him. It's that simple."

Worcester sat on a stool. "It's not that simple at all. How many will lose their lives because of your stubborn resistance?"

Taken aback by the truth of this statement, Hotspur spun away from him. Encouraged, the other pressed on. "These men fight for you because they admire you. Do they deserve such recompense?"

Thomas saw immediately he went too far. Harry turned back in anger.

"They know what they are fighting for. The man is a usurper. There is no other way to make it right."

"Please, Harry. Give me something to go back to Henry with. You are wrong; there are other ways to remedy the ills that plague our country. What about your pact of mutual loyalty?"

"With Owain?"

"And your father. This fight involves all of you."

"Hmm." Harry pursed his lips. "Perhaps my aims are too narrow." Bending, he retrieved his dagger and sat on the ground, wiping it on his leg. "Perhaps we should start by insisting that the English retract some of their oppressive laws against the Welsh, as my father and I recommended several times." He looked sideways at his uncle. "Of course, Henry will probably accuse me of collusion." He laughed shortly. "On the other hand, if we were plotting against him, Owain would be here today, wouldn't he? That's a good response."

Worcester shrugged. "All right. What else?"

"Well, I believe this would be a good time to negotiate the return of Richmondshire, which was taken from us in favor of Westmorland. Neville has encroached on our governance of Northumberland. It is a policy that needs to be reversed."

Nodding, Worcester stood. "Very well. I'll see what I can do. This will be a good way to gauge Henry's commitment."

And so began a series of negotiations that went back and forth for many hours. Henry spoke with sympathy, but he refused to budge on any demands threatening his regality. Finally, as they approached the hour of vespers, they had run out of arguments. The disputes had gone full circle; Hotspur remained adamant that Henry must step down and resign the crown. This, the king absolutely refused to consider.

At the last, King Henry stood, putting his helmet under his arm. "There is nothing more I can offer. I'll say this once again: put yourselves in my hands and trust to my favor."

Sadly, Worcester shook his head. "We cannot trust you," he said.

"Then let the bloodshed be on your head, not mine!" the king exclaimed, turning his back on the earl. "In the name of God, take the banners forward!"

Bowing briefly, Worcester strode to his horse and mounted, taking one last look at the royal pavilion. Already, trumpets blared and men were running to their assigned places. The time for negotiation was past; slaughter lay ahead.

By the time he reached the rebel encampment, Worcester saw they had already assembled in three battalions across the ridge. He was so disheartened he didn't know how he would be able to face a battle. And there was his nephew, vibrant and sprightly, giving orders and waving his arms as though preparing for a tournament. Even Worcester's love for Harry wasn't enough to raise his spirits.

As he dismounted, Hotspur came up and took his horse's reins. "You tried, uncle. I know you did your best. We were just too far apart." Although his words were solicitous, his eyes gleamed with excitement. Harry wasn't looking for reconciliation. He wanted to fight.

It was two hours before dusk. Harry Percy's army was deployed along an east-west ridge overlooking a long, sloping hill. The ground was covered with a tangle of peas whose long stems would hinder a cavalry attack. Ditches along the edge of the field offered additional obstacles. It was hoped these difficulties would offset the disadvantage of numbers—for the king's army was immense, well over ten thousand men. It was divided into three divisions. Henry's banner stood to the right; the left was commanded by the Prince of Wales; and the center was led by the Earl of Stafford, cousin by marriage to the king. Already the vanguard was moving forward.

"Ready your arrows," shouted the archers' captains, well aware that Stafford's force also included several well-trained English bowmen. Hotspur's Cheshire archers were famous for their skill and ferocity, yet on Henry's side many bowmen were veterans of the French wars. But there were two big differences; Hotspur's archers were equipped with shields, and their downhill trajectory would give more impetus to their shafts. Undeterred, the royal soldiers moved up the slope toward the rebels.

Once the advancing army was within bowshot, the order to release was given and thousands of arrows began their deadly descent, turning the sky black. The lethal whoosh of projectiles filled the air before the relentless shafts plunged into their targets, slicing through leather jerkins, shattering bones and penetrating limbs. Screaming with agony, men crumpled to the ground, falling like wheat before the scythe. And still, they trudged forward until the rebels were in their range. Halting, the royal archers responded with their own devastating firepower. Both sides maintained a remorseless storm as long as they could. The slope was covered with a nightmare of thrashing men—some pierced with multiple arrows, others desperately trying to crawl away from the upheaval.

But arrows run out quickly and the barrage didn't last more than ten minutes. Miraculously, some of the vanguard made it through to Hotspur's defensive line. Ready for them, the archers drew their blades. Terrible hand-to-hand fighting ensued. The Earl of Douglas pushed his mount toward Stafford's banner, smiting right and left at whoever stood in his way. Seeing the Scot coming directly at him, Stafford shouted his war cry and grasped his sword with both hands. He swung it at the rider in an attempt to unhorse him. But Douglas had the advantage in both skill and height. He blocked Stafford's blow before following through, bashing him in the head so forcibly the earl fell to the ground. Two of the Cheshiremen leaped onto the prone man, piercing him through the gaps in his armor; a dagger through the eye slit finished him off.

Stafford's death communicated itself immediately through the ranks; the overwrought royalists broke into a rout and retreated down the hill. Some of the rebels followed, intent upon slaughter, though most of the archers took advantage of the momentary break to retrieve arrows from the battlefield.

Hotspur took in the carnage and quickly decided they needed to attack at once. "After the king!" he shouted to his uncle. Pointing his sword in the air, he cried, "Esperance Percy!" He urged his mount forward and his cavalry joined in the assault.

Douglas and Worcester were right behind him, followed by men-at-arms on foot. All headed for King Henry's banner.

The two armies clashed with a roar of shouting men, screaming horses, wood against steel. Plunging into the midst of the royal troops, the rebels cleared a path before them as the royal banner swayed and dipped in the crush. But it stayed up, and Douglas sighted the king's livery, spurring his horse forward. He struck the king's sword aside and smashed him in the shoulder, knocking him onto the ground. Leaping from his mount, Douglas held the point of his blade to his opponent's neck. "Surrender!" he bellowed. The other attempted to roll away from him and strike his sword aside; Douglas was faster and drove the point home. He reached down and yanked off the helm, only to discover that his victim was not King Henry at all.

"A decoy!" gasped Worcester, still astride his horse.

Cursing, Douglas remounted and pointed at the royal standard. "There's another one in the king's livery. How many Henrys do we have to kill?"

The fighting was fiercest around the royal banner, while on the other flank Prince Hal saw his opportunity to put pressure on Hotspur's rear. Raising his visor, Hal called out an order, when a deflected arrow knocked him in the face and pushed him back into the saddle. Crying out in shock, his nearest knights crowded around him, gathering the prince into their arms and lowering him to the ground. The arrow had lodged in his cheek, next to the nose.

"Get it out!" groaned Hal. "Someone, help me."

No one wanted the responsibility, but finally one of Hal's favorite knights stepped forward. He knelt on the ground, trying to ignore the battle raging to his right. He pulled off his gauntlet, then his glove. "Here, bite this." He eased the glove between the prince's teeth then grasped the arrow, trying to wiggle it gently. It didn't move. He stopped, breathing heavily. "I think it's stuck in the bone," he said.

Hal grunted loudly and his friend took that as a command to go on.

"All right. Brace yourself." He gripped the wooden shaft and twisted it slightly, rocking it a little then giving a tug. With a sucking sound the arrow came out—without the head.

Groaning, Hal dropped the glove from his mouth. "Help me up," he gasped.

Astonished, two of the knights held an arm and pushed against the steel backplate, wrestling Hal to his feet. The prince gritted his teeth and closed his visor, reaching for his saddle and remounting with a little help. Someone handed up his sword. "I'm all right. We attack. Now."

Who was going to argue? Hal was driven by sheer strength of will and his followers couldn't help but rebound, totally inspired. They galloped up the slope, scattering the disorganized resistance, and dove into the rebel flank, forcing the foot soldiers to turn and defend themselves.

While the prince wreaked havoc on the leaderless rearguard, Hotspur and his cohort fought like men possessed, while the king's defenders redoubled their efforts. Unbeknownst to the rebels, the Earl of Dunbar had persuaded a reluctant King Henry to withdraw to the rear of the army. Henry had already killed more than thirty men and he was nearing the end of his strength.

All Percy saw was a standard-bearer dressed in the king's livery, and he drove toward the man, followed by his thirty knights. Once again Douglas got there first, delivering the death blow and tearing off the man's helm. This time Hotspur recognized him. "Walter Blount!" he shouted derisively. "Another of King Henry's sacrifices!"

"Damn," shouted Douglas, "have I not slain two king Henries with mine own hand? 'Tis an evil hour for us that a third yet lives to be our victor."

Not everyone saw that the stricken king was a counterfeit, and cries of "Henry Percy king!" echoed across the battle. From the edge of the field, King Henry heard the shouts. Enraged, he put his helm back on and plunged into the fighting. Dunbar followed. The crush was so thick they couldn't make much progress. The fighting had intensified, for the king's standard had fallen and the men were crazed with fear and delirium.

Daylight had faded and the moon was full, but slowly an eerie shadow began to move across its face, casting a ghostly light over the battlefield. Most of the warriors fought on while the moon underwent a total eclipse; they were too occupied with killing to notice. Glancing up, others saw the eclipse as an omen, and men on the edges of the battle began to slip away. Prince Hal had nearly surrounded the rebel force and they redoubled their efforts to break free.

Percy and his knights were completely isolated from the rest of their army; the fighting was still fiercest around the fallen standard. Hotspur pulled his mount into a rear, knowing the stallion's sharpened horse shoes would connect with the knight charging him. With a screech the other horse fell back, only to be replaced by a dozen men on foot, jabbing at him with spears, maddening his own mount. There was no room when the animal tried to step back and it stumbled, striving to regain balance. Hotspur bent over its neck, but just at that moment one of his knights went down, pinned under his own horse. The stallion shrieked, flailing its hooves, and the shock pushed the fighting men into Harry, who desperately struck at first one side then the other. He felt his arm weakening as he shouted, "To me! À Percy!" He could see men trying to force their way through the crush, but it was too late. Sheer force of numbers told against him and he was dragged from his mount, still brandishing his sword. Harry Hotspur went down under a flurry of blows, never to rise again.

Worcester and Douglas were separated from Harry at the end, and though they fought on doggedly, they heard the cries of "Henry Percy Dead!" This time the true king pushed his way through, and the royal troops were already chasing fleeing rebels who scrambled for cover in the failing light. Forgetting everything else, Worcester flung himself from his mount and frantically stumbled across corpses and groaning wounded, searching for his nephew. No one could say where he was, and he almost despaired, sorting through heaps of bodies all jumbled together. Finally, he saw a group of men gathered around a fallen knight and he knew...

The onlookers stepped aside as Worcester threw himself to his knees next to Harry Hotspur, broken and gashed, his visor opened and his eyes staring.

"Oh, my poor boy. What have they done to you?" All the frustrations of the last day, all the regrets, came out in a howl of agony. Men stepped away from him in dismay and respect. Tearing off his helm and gathering up the body of his nephew,

Worcester clutched Harry to his chest, sobbing into his shoulder. All this was for nothing! Wasted lives and shattered hopes.

Leaning over and gently placing Hotspur on the ground, Worcester looked up to see the king standing before him, tears running down his face. "He was my friend, once," Henry said before turning to his companions. "Take the Earl of Worcester. He is your prisoner."

The earl did not resist as two knights grasped him by the arms. But he forced them to stop for a moment. "Respect his body," he said. The king nodded briefly before his captors jerked him away.

Meanwhile, the rout continued though it wasn't at all clear who had gained the field. Friends and enemies alike collapsed in exhausted, bloody heaps; if it weren't for the death of Harry Percy the royalists might have considered themselves in deep trouble.

While the broken body of Hotspur was respectfully carried away, the Earl of Worcester was tied to his horse and taken to Shrewsbury Castle to await his fate. King Henry sent knights to find his son, and an incoherent and nearly unconscious Hal was brought back to him on a makeshift litter. The prince had stayed in his saddle all the way to the end, leading his steadfast men in an astonishing flanking movement that fatally hampered the rebel army. Once the battle was over, the prince had collapsed.

Removing his gloves, the king bent over his son, gently turning his head to look at the terrible wound. "He fought like this?" he said in wonder. "Dear God, what a paragon he is." He stood, turning. "Alfred! Harold! Where are my surgeons? We need to get him under cover!"

The king's physicians came running, directing the litter-bearers to bring their charge into the royal pavilion. They didn't dare move him any farther during the night.

King Henry's wounds were superficial but he was treated next. A camp bed was set up next to Hal, and the king spent the night at his son's side, refusing to leave him alone. He lay awake listening to the groans and screams from those less fortunate than he, left to survive or die under the waning moon.

Turning on his side, Henry concentrated on Hal's breathing. His son was sleeping soundly—or maybe he was unconscious. He couldn't tell.

"I don't know whether you can hear me or not," he said softly. "I wanted you to know how proud of you I am. You have proven yourself a worthy heir to the throne. I couldn't have wished for anything better." Oddly, Henry felt easier talking to Hal like this rather than to his disapproving face. Would they ever find a way to say what they really felt? "I know you've been unhappy with me. This is not how you wanted things to turn out. I would have done it all differently, if I only could. Dear God, how the crown weighs heavily on my head. But if I had done nothing, our great dynasty would have withered away and your inheritance would have been dispersed. I hope you come to understand that one day." He lay back and closed his eyes. "I hope you learn to forgive me."

The next morning, Henry's surgeons went to work on the prince. In reality, they didn't know what to do. The arrowhead was deep inside the skull. They tried salves, charms, praying, and more potions. They may have temporarily kept the wound from infecting, but their efforts were ineffectual and they knew it.

The king spent most of the day surveying the battlefield. Aside from the Earl of Stafford, nine other knights were killed and thousands of yeomen. The farther from the center of the conflict, the more the bodies faced away, cut down in their flight. Limbs were hacked to pieces; guts spilled across the ground; bloody faces bit the dirt. The stench of feces and urine permeated the still air. Some of the wounded had been turned over and dispatched, stripped of their armor and possessions.

The corpses covered an area of more than three miles. Already the survivors were digging a huge mass grave, for in this heat it was advisable to get as many bodies underground as possible. Crossing himself, Henry turned to the Bishop of Shrewsbury.

"I will endow a church on this very spot," he said, "to pray for the souls of the dead." He turned around again, surveying the field. "This battle should never have happened. These are my countrymen; I grieve that they gave their lives for such an unworthy cause. But I give thanks to God for my victory." He bent over and picked up a banner with the arms sewn onto it belonging to one of his dead knights. "Such a waste. I must see to my son."

Making a roundabout way back to his pavilion, he called for the physicians who both scrambled up to him, falling to their knees.

"Sire," Alfred bowed his head, "we have done all we can. The prince lives yet. I'm sorry to say we cannot remove the arrowhead. We feel there's only one surgeon who can help you: John Bradmore."

Henry gave them a stern look, but he was aware that punishing these men wouldn't help matters. "Bradmore," he said, letting out a breath. "He's in prison for counterfeiting coins."

"His surgical skills are way beyond ours. And you know he's also the most proficient metal worker in our trade. All of us have purchased surgical instruments from him."

The other physician nodded in agreement. "If anyone can save the prince, he can."

Once again, Henry made his decision quickly. "All right. If anything changes, you will find me in Shrewsbury. I will have Bradmore released."

He shouted for one of his knights who stood nearby. "I need you to ride to London at once," he said as the man approached. "You must arrange for the surgeon John Bradmore to be released by my orders. He's at the Tower. Accompany him to Kenilworth Castle where these men will be taking my son."

Turning back to the physicians, he gestured for them to rise. "Take the prince to Kenilworth by easy stages. That brings you closer to London. It will save some time. Make sure the blacksmith has everything ready for him."

Bowing, the others consented, relieved to pass on the responsibility. They froze when Henry paused just before mounting.

"Don't let him die," he said. The threat was unmistakable.

CHAPTER 24

It was sixty miles to Kenilworth. The physicians were faced with a daunting task. Preparing a litter to be carried between two horses—front and back—they fashioned a tent around it to protect their patient from the sun. They wrapped Hal's head the best they could to protect the wound after applying a salve. The prince lapsed in and out of consciousness, but so far he was not feverish. Accompanied by a score of Hal's closest companions, the sad party traveled as quickly as they dared. Knowing they moved much slower than the king's messenger, they hoped Bradmore might be waiting for them.

He wasn't.

Hal was put into a dark room and cool cloths were laid on his forehead to offset the July heat. The physicians applied more ointments to his wound and prayed continuously. Finally, the long-awaited surgeon made his appearance and took in the situation with one glance. He put down his traveling sack and knelt at the prince's bedside. Tall and thin with a long, hooked nose, Bradmore commanded respect with his piercing black eyes. He recognized both of the royal surgeons.

"When did you get here?"

"Two days ago. He has mostly been unconscious."

"Then at least I don't have to restrain him. Is he feverish?"

"No, thank God."

"I'm glad you are here. There is no time to waste. We'll need more light."

Jumping to obey him, the physicians opened the shutters while Bradmore unpacked his bag onto a table. "We must dilate the wound while at the same time we must keep it from infecting. You have done well," he said, glancing up. He knew the others would be more cooperative if he praised them. "Can you tell how deep it is?"

"We think the arrowhead lodged itself at the base of the skull."

"Possibly six inches deep, front to back. All right. Let us begin."

He leaned over Hal, gingerly touching the skin around the angry hole. Grimacing, the lad opened his eyes, clearly knowing where he was. The surgeon smiled grimly.

"I am glad you're awake. My name is John Bradmore. Your father sent me to care for you."

Hal tried to speak, swallowed, tried again. "I've heard of you." The words came out as a squeak.

"Good. Don't try to talk. It's a miracle the arrow struck where it did. A little to the left or a different angle and we might not be here today. Now listen carefully. I'm going to have to enlarge the wound so I can extract the arrowhead. This will take a couple of days. Do not fear; I will get it out."

Relieved to be in good hands, Hal relaxed. Meanwhile, Bradmore went back to his table. He started with a probe which he called a tent, made from a pith—the center pulp of a shoot from an elder branch. This he cut a little shorter than six inches in length and wrapped it tightly with a clean linen cloth, dipping it in rose honey. Holding it up, he said, "I am going to insert this tent into the wound. You see, the honey will contract the tissue and keep it from sticking to the cloth, while at the same time it will slow down the healing. We don't want the wound to close up any more than it already is."

The others held their breath while Bradmore carefully worked the tent as far into the hole as he dared. Then he stood up, stretching his back. "We will let it sit for the length of two turns of the hourglass. Then I shall insert a fresh one. Meanwhile, show me the blacksmith's forge."

Bradmore had to come up with something totally untested. He would have to build an instrument that would not only probe deep into the wound, but grasp the arrowhead with enough strength to dislodge it from the bone. How was he going to do that?

When the time came to prepare a new tent for insertion into the wound, Bradmore instructed the other surgeons. This procedure would have to continue day and night, and he would need help; once he started concentrating on forging his instrument, he couldn't go back and forth. Gesturing for the others to approach, Bradmore gently pulled his tent from the wound and inserted the replacement, smeared in honey. Prince Hal gritted his teeth but bravely refrained from moving; all could see he was in great pain. "You're doing well," Bradmore said. "I'm greatly encouraged."

He turned to Alfred. "At the beginning, we won't have much improvement. You will see that by tomorrow, we'll be able to make our tent longer and longer, then wider and wider until we reach the arrowhead."

Once he was satisfied the other surgeons could manage the technique, Bradmore instructed the resident blacksmith to ready the forge. He had brought enough raw materials from his own workshop to get started. Thin bars of iron would suffice to create the most delicate tools, and with the blacksmith's help he stoked a fire hot enough to render his rods malleable.

The plan was to forge a tapered and concave tong, small enough to fit inside the arrowhead. Then he would insert a long screw to go inside the tong so that when he turned it, the ends of the tong would expand until it filled the cavity. This way the instrument would hold the arrowhead from the inside and he could pull it out. He had never made anything remotely like this, but once he conceived it he was certain he could build it.

Meanwhile, successively larger tents expanded the deep wound. Hal was awake much of the time, and his friends kept him company while pretending his condition was not alarming. Everyone knew better. Appreciating their uneasiness, Bradmore kept up a cheerful chatter and even succeeded in getting Hal to eat now and then.

"We're almost there," he said finally, inserting his longest tent yet. "I believe we have finally opened up a path to this vexatious arrowhead. Tomorrow we will extract it." He nodded encouragingly while Hal's friends exclaimed their relief. Then he bent over the prince. "I will mix a soporific for you. You don't want to be awake during this, and I don't want you to move."

Grunting, Hal agreed. "I think you're right. Wake me up when it's over."

Bradmore's soporific was in the form of a sponge soaked in a formula composed of opium, black nightshade juice, henbane, mandrake, climbing ivy, hemlock, and lettuce. He told the prince to inhale it deeply, and as expected the patient fell into a deep sleep. "I have used this many times with great success," he told the witnesses. "I would spare the prince as much pain as possible."

Instructing Harold to boil some water, Bradmore turned to his work. Having dipped the tongs in wine and wiped them clean, he removed the last tent from the wound. Ignoring everything else in the room, Bradmore scrutinized the hole and carefully lowered the tongs into it, making sure not to touch the inside of the wound. Holding his breath, he pushed the instrument slowly into the cavity of the arrowhead until he sensed it had touched the bottom. Good. He took a deep breath and slowly turned the screw, knowing that the end of his tongs would gradually widen until it completely filled the arrowhead, pressing against the sides.

He could feel it; the connection was firm. Once done, it was time to break the point free of the bone. The resistance was daunting. But Bradmore was a patient man and he knew the value of dogged persistence. There was limited space for him to work and he had to gently rock the tongs back and forth, back and forth. At first, nothing happened. Biting his lip, Bradmore concentrated on the tip of the tong. Finally, with a little jolt he felt it come loose.

But that was only the beginning; he had to withdraw the arrowhead without damaging the tissue on the way out. More concentration. Slowly, gently, he pulled on his tongs until finally, the tip came out of the wound.

The men around him gasped in amazement. "Thank God!" they said, crossing themselves and congratulating the surgeon as he held up the instrument in triumph.

There was no time to waste. "Alfred, I need the boiling water. Harold, more white wine."

The wine was easily found and Bradmore filled his *squirtillo* with it. He held the syringe up to the witnesses then squirted the wine into the wound, cleansing it. Meanwhile, he took some of the boiling water and mixed it with breadcrumbs which he then strained through a cloth. Then he took some barley flour and honey and mixed it with the breadcrumb water, boiling it again until it formed a paste. The last ingredient was turpentine resin, which, when combined with the paste created an ointment he used for a dip with a new set of tents. He started with the longest probe, tightly wrapped with linen.

"We need to wake the prince," he said to Alfred. "Mix a concoction of vinegar and fennel roots and soak four small sponges." This formula was well known to the other surgeons, so they were able to quickly oblige. The sponges were inserted into the nostrils and ears of the patient until he stirred. Withdrawing the sponges, Bradmore bent over his patient.

"It is over," he said softly. "The arrowhead has been removed."

Sighing, Hal closed his eyes and opened them again. "I'm alive!"

"You are the bravest patient I ever tended. You must be braver yet. It will take some time for your wound to heal. Don't worry; I'll be with you." He stood while Hal's friends gathered around the bed, talking quietly to him. Relief was etched on their faces; not only was Hal the heir, he was very popular with his intimates. Bradmore knew that their concern would aid the healing process.

For the next three weeks, Bradmore set about the task of closing the wound. Using his new ointment, every second day he shortened the tents so that the hole would heal from the bottom upwards. Twice a day he applied an ointment to Hal's neck which he called *Unguentum neruale*, then covered it with a hot plaster to ward off the possible spasms that would indicate tetanus. That was Bradmore's greatest fear; the relationship between wounds and muscle spasms was well known since ancient times and it would likely be fatal. Fortunately, the treatments worked and after twenty days, when he considered the wound perfectly cleansed, he applied a new unguent to regenerate the flesh.

Once Hal was out of danger, he began the long process of convalescence. No one needed to tell him that the right side of his face was terribly scarred. He was alive. That's all that mattered.

CHAPTER 25

Saddened by the devastation wrought over the bloody battlefield, King Henry gave Hotspur's body to Lord Furnival, Harry's nephew, to be buried at Whitchurch. He then moved on to Shrewsbury Castle, from where he immediately sent a message to Westmorland. The earl was directed to suppress the army of traitors led by the Earl of Northumberland, wherever he might be. If Percy was captured, Westmorland was to bring him alive to the king.

The next order of business was to convene a court to try the ringleaders for treason. Henry called a council of his closest advisors, and while they gathered Erpingham pulled him aside.

"I've just come from town. People are declaring that Harry Hotspur is still alive."

"Alive!" Henry's cry drew the attention of everyone in the room. He slapped his palm against the table. "Not again. I will not have it! This is like Richard all over again. I will not be plagued with an army of counterfeit Hotspurs. Thomas, have them bring his body back from Whitchurch and display him here, in Shrewsbury, for all to see." He felt a surge of anger well up. "Damn him. If Harry Percy had gotten his way, it would be *my* body displayed before the people. After three days, send his head to York and dismember his body. Let him be treated like the traitor he was."

Nodding, Erpingham went off to obey the king's order. Sobered by this unfortunate necessity, Henry took a seat at the table. He looked long and hard at his followers. "We are here to pass judgment on The Earl of Worcester, Sir Richard Venables, and Sir Richard Vernon." He took a deep sigh. "The Earl of Worcester has served the crown long and dutifully, all the way back to the Black Prince. As you know, he is a Knight of the Garter. I am reluctant to put so noble a lord to death."

283

"Noble! He led this rebellion!" someone shouted. Others joined in the uproar.

"My lords, my lords," bellowed John Norbury, who sat at Henry's side. "This is not a cock fight!"

Henry stood. "Enough blood has been shed."

"He is a traitor!" the council members shouted. Many shook their fists. Erpingham came back and stood at Henry's other side. He and Norbury were the only two who remained silent. The objections were relentless.

Thwarted, Henry sat back down. "All right," he said, and the shouting diminished. "The three ringleaders shall be executed. But we have seen enough gore. They shall be decapitated only. Let their heads be taken to London Bridge."

The others were mollified. In this, at least, the king had his way.

The executions took place the following day. As Henry watched from the top of the battlements, the earl and the two knights were taken from their prison and drawn to the scaffold on a wagon. Nearby, propped up against the pillory between two millstones, the corpse of Harry Hotspur faced the procession with sightless eyes. Henry fancied he could see Worcester bid farewell to his nephew as he passed, but the tears came too fast and blurred his vision.

As soon as the executions were over, King Henry left the city, bound for the North. He sent messengers to Kenilworth with instructions to keep him informed about Hal's progress. But he, himself, had to keep moving. There was still one Percy who needed to be dealt with before it was too late—the Percy who had helped him to his throne.

END OF BOOK THREE

AUTHOR'S NOTE

June 21, 1403, was a terrible day for England, but it served to secure Henry's grasp of the throne. Although he would face other revolts in the future, never again would he come so close to losing what he had worked so hard to retain.

Harry Hotspur's head was sent to York where it was stuck on a pike over one of the gates. His corpse was rubbed in salt and quartered; the parts were sent to hang above the gates of London, Bristol, Newcastle, and Chester. Just to make sure everyone understood that Hotspur was dead and gone, Henry sent proclamations of his death all over the kingdom and followed up with warnings against speaking ill of the king's government. Eventually, Henry agreed to permit the head and quarters to be collected and sent to Hotspur's widow, Elizabeth Mortimer. Where he was ultimately buried remains a mystery.

Worcester's head was sent to London Bridge, where it sat until 18 December. After that, it was taken down and reunited with his body, to be buried at the abbey church of St. Peter at Shrewsbury.

The Earl of Douglas was seriously wounded in the groin and lost a testicle. He was captured again, this time by Sir James Harrington.

John Bradmore, who had miraculously saved Prince Hal's life, was pardoned and given an annuity. He later wrote a book about his surgery called the *Philomena,* which included the arrow removal. Five years after the battle the king awarded him the post of "Searcher of the Port of London". He died in 1412.

Henry Percy, Hotspur's father was absent from the Battle of Shrewsbury. Whether by accident or on purpose, his motives and movements are debated by historians to this day. Ditto for Owain Glyndwr. The background to this rebellion was brilliantly discussed by Peter McNiven, whose article *THE SCOTTISH POLICY OF THE PERCIES AND THE STRATEGY OF THE*

REBELLION OF 1403 is referenced in my bibliography. I am inclined to follow his theory that neither Hotspur's father nor Glyndwr were looked for at Shrewsbury. If the king had stayed in London like they expected, Hotspur's forces would have been more than enough to accomplish the first part of their multi-layered rebellion. King Henry's surprise decision to travel north at the last minute just happened to put him within striking distance of Shrewsbury. And his characteristic speed and decisiveness took Hotspur by surprise.

Princess Isabella, who was shamefully returned to her father without her dowry, continued to mourn King Richard. Five years later she was affianced to Louis of Orlean's son Charles, whom she married in 1406. Charles was only eleven years old to her sixteen. It was said that she wept bitterly the day her hand was pledged to her future husband. Sympathetic courtiers assumed she cried to lose the title of queen of England. But those closest to the princess suspected that her heart still belonged to King Richard and always would. Allegedly the young couple was happy together, but poor Isabella died in childbirth only three years later.

And now to the question of King Richard's survival. I was astounded to learn about this when reading the preface of CHRONICQUE DE LA TRAISON ET MORT; it's also in the text (yes, it's translated). The author gives us a very convincing argument about Richard's survival, supported by the Appendix of Tytler's HISTORY OF SCOTLAND (Vol. 3), entitled "Historical Remarks on the Death of Richard II". Tytler started out by being skeptical on the subject but soon changed his mind: "In investigating this obscure part of our history, it was lately my fortune to discover some very interesting evidence, which induced me to believe that there was much more truth in these reports than I was as first disposed to admit. This led to an examination of the whole proofs relative to Richard's disappearance and alleged death in England, and the result was, a strong conviction that the king actually did make his escape from Pontefract castle... I am well aware that this is a startling proposition, too broadly in the face of long-established opinion to be admitted upon any evidence inferior almost to demonstration."

I must admit, I found Tytler's evidence most convincing, even though he didn't go beyond admitting this was a hypothesis.

What pushed me over the edge was Henry's remark to the Earl of Warwick just before they went after the rebels of the Epiphany rising: "But by St. George, I promise you, if I encounter him with them now, either he or I shall die." It's difficult to interpret this any other way than his knowledge of Richard's escape. The more I wrote about it, the more convinced I was that Richard's escape was truly feasible.

Taking a broad look at King Henry's reign and the difficulties he experienced trying to legitimize his usurpation, in the end it almost doesn't matter whether Richard survived or not (well, it mattered to Richard). Reports concerning his escape to Scotland and potential return harassed Henry throughout his reign. Those rumors took on a life of their own, resurfacing every time someone wanted to cause trouble. I think Paul Strohm said it best in his *Reburying Richard: Ceremony and Symbolic Relegitimation:* "In the years after 1402, the certainty that Richard was alive and well in Scotland seemed less tenacious than the desire that it be so." It gave the disgruntled country a focus, a sense that Richard represented better days.

Letters from Scotland bearing the king's seal didn't help matters; William Serle was later to pay dearly for his efforts. The most serious threat came from Hotspur, when he used Richard as a means to gather an army from Cheshire. Even though at the last minute he admitted Richard wasn't coming, the damage was done. After Shrewsbury, cries for Richard's return substantially diminished, and they evolved into an oath to fight for Richard if he was alive, or for Mortimer if the king was dead. The last time this tired-out declaration was used was during the Southampton Plot in 1415 on the eve of Henry V's expedition to France.

There is no doubt that *someone* was being taken care of in Scotland, first by King Robert III and afterward, his brother the Duke of Albany. This mysterious person, often called the Mammet (or puppet), was supported at great expense all the way up until his death in 1419, where he was buried at Blackfriars in Stirling. Whether this person was in his right mind or not remains part of the mystery. But it's certainly possible that if he was Richard Plantagenet, he may have fallen into such a state of depression that politically, he was dead anyway. I would imagine he might have felt some satisfaction in knowing that his ghost would certainly haunt Henry until the end.

As for Henry Bolingbroke, one wonders how often he looked back wistfully at those heady days following his landing at Ravenspur—when he was the darling of England and could do no wrong. It must have disheartening to learn that having the kingship was much less rewarding than striving for it.

BIBLIOGRPHY

Armitage-Smith, Sydney, JOHN OF GAUNT, Endeavor Press Ltd, 2015

Barron, Caroline, THE TYRANNY OF RICHARD II, Historical Research Vol. XLI, no. 103, May 1968

BATTLEFIELDS OF BRITAIN: BattlefieldsOfBritain.co.uk, authored by James Lancaster.

Bennett, Michael, RICHARD II AND THE REVOLUTION OF 1399, Sutton Publishing, 1999

Biggs, Douglas, THREE ARMIES IN BRITAIN: THE IRISH CAMPAIGN OF RICHARD II AND THE USURPATION OF HENRY IV, 1397-99, Brill, Leiden, The Netherlands, 2006

Boardman, A.W., HOTSPUR: HENRY PERCY MEDIEVAL REBEL, Sutton Publishing, UK, 2003

Creton, *Metrical History*: See Society of Antiquaries

Davies, R.R., THE REVOLT OF OWAIN GLYN DWR, Oxford University Press, 1995

Fletcher, C.D., NARRATIVE AND POLITICAL STRATEGIES AT THE DEPOSITION OF RICHARD II, Journal of Medieval History 30 (2004) 323-341

Giancarlo, Matthew, MURDER, LIES, AND STORYTELLING: THE MANIPULATION OF JUSTICE(S) IN THE PARLIAMENTS OF 1397 AND 1399, Speculum, Vol. 77, No. 1 (Jan. 2002) pp.76-112

Given-Wilson, Chris, CHRONICLES OF THE REVOLUTION 1397-1400 (The Reign of Richard II), Manchester University Press, 1993

Given-Wilson, Chris, HENRY IV, Yale University Press, London, 2017

Jones, Terry, WHO MURDERED CHAUCER? A Medieval Mystery, Thomas Dunne Books, New York, 2003

Lomas, Richard, THE FALL OF THE HOUSE OF PERCY 1368-1408, John Donald, Edinburgh 2007

McFarlane, K.B., LANCASTRIAN KINGS AND LOLLARD KNIGHTS, Oxford at the Clarendon Press, 1972

McHardy, A.K., THE REIGN OF RICHARD II From Minority to Tyranny, 1377-97, Manchester University Press, 2012

McNiven, Peter, THE SCOTTISH POLICY OF THE PERCIES AND THE STRATEGY OF THE REBELLION OF 1403, John Rylands University Library, Manchester, 1980

Mortimer, Ian, THE FEARS OF HENRY IV; The Life of England's Self-Made King, Vintage Books, London, 2008

Saul, Nigel, RICHARD II, Yale University Press, London 1997

Sherborne, James, WAR, POLITICS AND CULTURE IN FOURTEENTH-CENTURY ENGLAND, The Hambledon Press, 1994

Society of Antiquaries of London, ARCHAEOLOGICA, OR MISCELLANEOUS TRACTS RELATING TO ANTIQUITY Vol. 20 (containing Creton's French metrical History), Reproduced by Forgotten Books, 2018

Strickland, Agnes, LIVES OF THE QUEENS OF ENGLAND From the Norman Conquest, Blanchard & Lea, Philadelphia, 1852

Strohm, Paul, ENGLAND'S EMPTY THRONE: Usurpation and the Language of Legitimation 1399-1422, Yale University Press, 1998

Tytler, Patrick Fraser, HISTORY OF SCOTLAND, William Tate, Edinburgh, 1829

Usk, Adam of, CHRONICON ADAE DE USK, A.D. 1377-1421, Reprinted by Forgotten Books, 2017

Wilkinson, B., THE DEPOSITION OF RICHARD II AND THE ACCESSION OF HENRY IV,
The English Historical Review, Vol. 54, No. 214 (Apr., 1939), pp. 215-239

Williams, Benjamin, CHRONICQUE DE LA TRAISON ET MORT DE RICHART DEUX ROY DENGLETERRE, S & J Bentley, London, 1846 (Reproduced by Forgotten Books, 2018)

Wylie, James Hamilton, HISTORY OF ENGLAND UNDER HENRY IV (In 4 volumes), Longmans, Green & Co., London, 1884

CPSIA information can be obtained
at www.ICGtesting.com
Printed in the USA
LVHW050843290521
688876LV00024B/907

9 781734 797428